SILENTS!

H. P. OLIVER

MYSTERIES IN HISTORY

HPO Productions
Mysteries In History
8698 Elk Grove Boulevard
Suite 3-271
Elk Grove, California 95624

Printed in the United States of America

ISBN-10: 0615580866

ISBN-13: 978-0-615-58086-9

DEDICATION

In memory of the actors, writers, technicians, craftspeople, and moguls who came to Hollywood a century ago and made the pictures move.

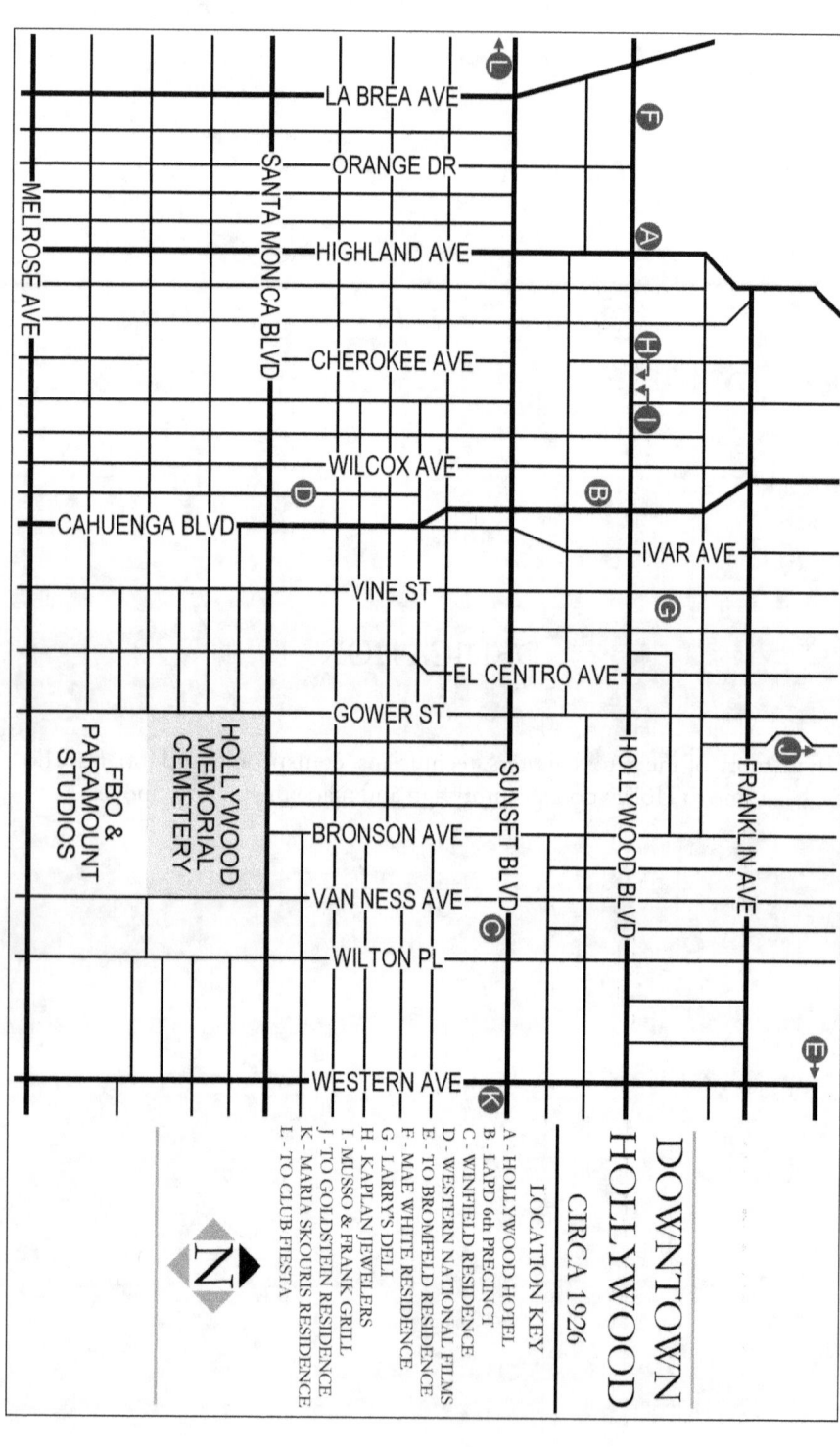

DOWNTOWN HOLLYWOOD
CIRCA 1926

LOCATION KEY

A - HOLLYWOOD HOTEL
B - LAPD 6th PRECINCT
C - WINFIELD RESIDENCE
D - WESTERN NATIONAL FILMS
E - TO BROMFIELD RESIDENCE
F - MAE WHITE RESIDENCE
G - LARRY'S DELI
H - KAPLAN JEWELERS
I - MUSSO & FRANK GRILL
J - TO GOLDSTEIN RESIDENCE
K - MARIA SKOURIS RESIDENCE
L - TO CLUB FIESTA

SILENTS!

ONE

Sunday - September 5, 1926

"Rock of Ages" floated lightly down the first floor corridor of the Hollywood Hotel's west wing. It was Sunday morning, and Hattie Mae couldn't go to church because she had to work, so she praised the Lord in her own way, but she praised Him softly out of consideration for the "Do Not Disturb" placards hanging from the doors she passed with her wooden cart full of fresh linens and towels.

Actually Sundays were Hattie Mae's favorite of the six days she worked each week. For one thing, her shift ended at noon on Sundays. For another, this was the day Miss Lillian always left a "little something" in her room to thank Hattie Mae for such good maid service.

Most of the hotel's long-term guests left a little change for their room maids, but in Miss Lillian's case, the tip was usually three crinkly new one dollar bills. It seemed like an awful lot of money to Hattie Mae, whose weekly pay was only nineteen dollars. Still, Miss Lillian Lawrence could afford to be generous because she was a famous actress in the movies. She was also, Hattie Mae thought, a very fine lady.

When Hattie Mae reached the end of the corridor, she knocked quietly on Miss Lillian's door. It was still too early for most guests to be out of their rooms, but Miss Lillian was always up with the sun, not like some lazy folks who laid around in their beds 'til noon, often making Hattie Mae late for Sunday dinner because she couldn't leave until all the rooms along her corridor were made up.

After knocking twice, Hattie Mae tried Miss Lillian's door. It opened, so after selecting the softest towels from the stacks on her cart, she walked in. With the curtains drawn the room was dark, but Hattie Mae didn't stop to switch on the overheard light because her arms were full of towels.

The maid's eyes were on the chest of drawers to her right where Miss Lillian always left her tip, so she didn't see the handbag on the floor just inside the door. Hattie Mae tripped over the bag and fell headlong to the floor, landing inches from the dead body of Lillian Lawrence. In the dim light Hattie Mae stared into a pale face with a gaping mouth and a trickle of blood from a small red dot above one vacant green eye.

Hattie Mae screamed at the top of her lungs and kept on screaming. Her screams woke several guests, including Mister Rodney Mason in the room across the hall. Mister Mason called the front desk to complain about the racket. Hattie Mae was still screaming a few minutes later when the hotel's assistant manager, Dennis Plant, arrived in the corridor outside Lillian Lawrence's room and looked through the open door.

In spite of his youth and lack of experience at hotel management, Mister Plant handled the situation quite well. After overcoming the initial shock of seeing a half-naked dead woman on the floor next to an hysterical maid, he got Hattie Mae on her feet and out into the hall where she promptly fainted, thus putting an end to the screaming.

Plant then returned to the room, closed the door, and switched on the light to take a closer look at Miss Lawrence. Deciding she was definitely dead, he picked up the room phone. When the hotel operator answered, he instructed her to call the police and tell them there was a dead woman in room 187. The assistant manager further instructed the operator to say absolutely nothing at all about the matter to anyone else.

Returning to the hall, Plant found that the commotion made by Hattie Mae had attracted a small crowd of guests. One woman was kneeling over the unconscious maid, trying to revive her. Plant closed and locked the door to room 187 with his master key, frustrating those who were trying to see what all the fuss was about. Then the assistant manager apologized profusely to his guests for the inconvenience they had suffered and urged them to return to their rooms because everything was now under control. He promised there would be no further disturbances disrupting their stay at the Hollywood Hotel.

The assistant manager then turned his attention to Hattie Mae. The woman guest had successfully revived her, but the maid's eyes were wide with shock and tears were streaming down her face. Fearful that the screaming might commence again, Plant escorted Hattie Mae to his office behind the front desk.

- - -

Since Sunday mornings were quiet, the early shift at the Los Angeles Police Department's Sixth Division Station on Cahuenga between Hollywood and Selma consisted of only four men. Two patrol officers were out on assigned beats, another officer manned the complaint desk at the stationhouse, and a fourth officer with at least the rank of sergeant served as watch commander.

The man in charge on September fifth was Detective Sergeant C. K. Mackie. The sergeant was a big man, hefty and standing an inch or two over six feet. The gray in his hair and carefully trimmed mustache set against ruddy Scottish features gave him an air of experience and competence that was well substantiated by an exemplary record with the department. Only the twinkle in his pale gray eyes hinted that there might be a sense of humor behind Mackie's business-like appearance and demeanor.

With twenty years of service, Sergeant Mackie had more than enough seniority to avoid Sunday duty, but frequently took it for two reasons. First, it was a good time to catch up with the paperwork that accumulated on his desk during the week. Second, working Sunday shifts excused him from going to church with his wife Helen.

It wasn't that C. K., as Sergeant Mackie was known by his friends in the department, didn't take his faith seriously. He took it very seriously. Mackie just couldn't tolerate sitting through an entire service on those hard pews in that stuffy church. However, the sergeant made it a point to compensate for this by being particularly devout on those occasions when Helen put her foot down and insisted that he accompany her to church.

Patrol Officer Paul Otis, with six months of service in the department, was manning the complaint desk when a Hollywood Hotel telephone operator named Elaine Parsons rang through to report the discovery of a dead woman in room 187. Otis painstakingly recorded the pertinent information on a "Complaint Received by Telephone" form and assured the caller that her report would be dealt with promptly. Otis then hurried down the hall to the Detective's Room where he found Sergeant Mackie industriously filing a thick stack of various and sundry bulletins from his overflowing IN tray.

Barely concealing his excitement at actually having something of importance to report, the young patrolman snapped to attention and said, "Sergeant Mackie, sir, we have just received a report that a dead body has been found at the Hollywood Hotel!"

Mackie calmly closed his filing cabinet drawer and asked, "Have we now?"

"Yes, sir! Here is the information, sir."

The sergeant took the telephone complaint form and settling back in his chair, said, "Relax, son. Let's see what this is all about."

Patrolman Otis snapped into an at ease posture while Mackie carefully read the report. Finally, he said, "I guess I'd best take a run over there and look into this."

Otis eagerly asked, "Do you wish me to call in some of the off-duty officers, sir?"

Mackie smiled at Otis' enthusiasm and answered, "No, son, let's not spoil anybody's day off just yet. I'll take a look first and let you know if we need to call in the cavalry."

The sergeant casually returned the patrolman's snappy salute, and then donned his uniform jacket and cap. Outside, he climbed into the Dodge Brothers roadster the department provided for his official use and stepped on the starter. The engine sprang to life immediately because Mackie insisted it be maintained to do so.

Then the detective sergeant was off up Cahuenga Avenue to Hollywood Boulevard, where he waited for the newly installed traffic signal to show green in his direction before turning left. Mackie would have been well within his authority to turn on the roadster's raucous siren and run the signal, but the dead woman wasn't going anywhere, so he saw no reason to raise a ruckus.

C. K. knew the Hollywood Hotel well. His father and uncle both worked on the place as carpenters when the original lobby and first forty rooms were built in ought-three. Back then Hollywood Boulevard was called Prospect Avenue and the area around the new hotel was mostly empty land. In the twenty-three years since, both the hotel and its neighborhood had grown to the point where there wasn't a vacant lot within a mile of the place.

The Hollywood Hotel was originally built to accommodate the influx of tourists beginning after the turn of the century. Then, when the motion picture people came to town, the hotel became their favorite gathering place. This was in part due to the fact that the Hollywood had been the only really fashionable hotel in town until the Christie, Plaza, and Knickerbocker hotels went up during the past few years.

To Mackie's mind the design of the Hollywood Hotel characterized one of the biggest differences between crowded east coast cities and sprawling Los Angeles. The big hotels he saw on visits to the east were built vertically because it was the only direction available. The Hollywood, however, spread out to fill the empty space around it, just as the city of Los Angeles was spreading out to fill the empty land to the north, east, and south.

The original hotel structure was more or less Moorish in style and consisted of north, east, south, and west wings forming a box around the central courtyard. The four two-story wings were connected at three corners, leaving an opening to the northwest. The south and east wings met at a three-story, octagonal tower with a steeply peaked, overhanging roof. The hotel's main entrance was originally through this tower which faced the intersection of Highland and Prospect Avenues. A covered veranda fronted this entire corner of the building.

As the hotel expanded, the south-facing wing was extended to fill the entire block of Prospect between Highland and Hillcrest. At the center of this expansion was an elaborate, four-story section topped with twin turrets and domed towers. The main entrance was moved to this grand new focal point of the hotel which was reached via a semi-circular driveway beginning and ending on Prospect Avenue. One approached the elegant new lobby via broad steps leading from the curved drive and through a four-column portico.

When viewed in its entirety, the front of the hotel left an impression of many windows, most decorated with small balconies and awnings beneath a jumble of adjacent, but dissimilar roof lines ranging from curves to peaks. At first this architecture seemed rather chaotic, but since the palms and evergreens planted along Prospect—now Hollywood Boulevard—had matured, one viewed the hotel in smaller sections which were individually quite pleasing to the eye.

Some of the Hollywood Hotel's popularity was due to the fame of its dining room. The elegant Dining Room of the Stars actually had golden stars painted on the ceiling in recognition of the motion picture celebrities who frequented the place. Mackie had only eaten in the swanky dining room once, but he'd been there often on official business.

Back before the Volstead Act outlawed alcohol in 1920, hotel visitors occasionally over-imbibed and got out of hand creating situations requiring his services. Now the only difference was that folks brought their gin with them instead of ordering it from the waiters. At least that was how the hotel explained any intoxication encountered on its property.

C. K. parked his Dodge along the circular driveway and walked into the lobby where he was immediately greeted by a Mister Dennis Plant, who identified himself as the hotel's assistant manager. Plant escorted Mackie to room 187 and unlocked the door for him.

The detective sergeant stood just inside the doorway for some time, carefully recording the scene in his mind. The room, he estimated, measured about sixteen feet east to west and ten or eleven feet north to south. The hall door was in the west wall. The head of the bed was to his left, against the same wall, with a nightstand on either side of it.

An open door in the south wall to his immediate right led into a small bathroom. A chest of drawers stood against the wall just beyond the bathroom door. An overstuffed armchair was positioned in the southeast corner of the room, and a dressing table sat between two windows in the east wall. C. K. guessed a closet was probably concealed behind another door at the east end of the north wall. He noted the position of the body next to the bed, the general condition of the room, and other details, like a faint odor of cigar smoke lingering behind the strong stench of death that was beginning to permeate the room.

Detective Sergeant Mackie learned the hard way that first impressions of a crime scene were important because valuable information was frequently lost once other police officers, the coroner's men, and reporters began trampling

5

all over the place. He even knew of instances where crucial evidence was deliberately removed from murder scenes, sometimes while high-ranking department personnel conveniently looked the other way. The most flagrant example of this in his personal experience was the William Desmond Taylor murder.

Upon arriving at Taylor's bungalow to begin his investigation, C. K. found people from the Famous Players-Lasky Studio, where Taylor was a well-known movie director, busily carrying out boxes brimming with everything from bootleg whiskey to personal correspondence. Carefully stepping around Taylor's body on the living room floor, they were methodically stripping the place of anything that might even hint at a scandal involving either Taylor or the studio. And they were doing all of this right under the nose of a highly placed captain of detectives. When Mackie demanded to know what the hell was going on, the captain ordered him to go somewhere and have a smoke until instructed to do otherwise. This time, however, Mackie was first to arrive at the scene of the crime, and he was making sure he had a clear picture of the hotel room before anyone could mess it up.

Finally, Mackie knelt next to the body. The blonde was very young and had been quite pretty before someone shot a bullet into her right temple. She lay partially on her left side facing the door with her feet toward the bed. The victim was apparently about to retire for the night when killed because the bed covers were turned back she was wearing a filmy pale blue nightgown.

Mackie stood again and moved around the room taking care not to disturb any of the objects scattered about the floor. These included a broken lamp beside the nightstand closest to the door, a toppled wooden chair next to the dressing table, several cosmetic items near the chair, a handbag just inside the hall door, and half a dozen folded towels between the handbag and the body. Stepping around the bed, Mackie found one more item on the floor—the apparent source of the faint cigar odor he'd detected earlier.

The butt was less than two inches long, but nearly an inch in thickness. It had a few bite marks on the tip and showed signs of having been crushed out before it was thrown to the floor. A vivid scarlet and gold band around the butt exclaimed that the cigar was an El Pantera imported from Havana, Cuba. A glass ashtray atop the chest of drawers contained some ash from the cigar and appeared to be where the butt had been snuffed. Unless she had some unusual smoking habits, someone else had been in the dead blonde's room since it was last cleaned.

Sergeant Mackie turned to Plant, who was still standing in the doorway, and asked, "How often are these rooms cleaned?"

The assistant manager answered the question with an air of pride, "Every single day."

Gesturing to the dead woman on the floor, Mackie said, "Any idea who she was?"

"Of course," Plant answered. "Her name is Lillian Lawrence. She's a . . . or she was a famous motion picture actress."

Plant's tone expressed surprise that Mackie did not recognize the dead woman. The sergeant made no comment, but again congratulated himself on being the first to arrive at the scene. The deaths of motion picture celebrities became messy cases, and he was in a position to keep this one under control.

Mackie asked, "Who found the body?"

Plant said, "The housekeeping maid for this wing found her when she came in to make up the room."

"How long ago was that?"

Looking at a silver pocket watch from his vest pocket, the assistant manager thought for a moment and then answered, "About half an hour ago, a little past eight. The front desk received complaints about a woman screaming, so I came right over here."

Mackie said, "I see. And this is how you found the room?"

"Yes. As near as I can tell, the maid entered the room with an armload of fresh towels, saw Miss Lawrence there, and started screaming. She was on her hands and knees next to the body—about where those towels are—in a state of complete hysteria when I got here."

Mackie nodded and asked, "Has anyone else been in the room since then?"

"No, just me. I didn't touch anything, though. I took Hattie Mae, the maid, out into the hall and came back in to see if anything could be done for Miss Lawrence. She was obviously . . . ah . . . deceased, so I used the room phone over there to instruct our hotel switchboard operator to call the police. Then I locked the room and left."

The sergeant nodded again and said, "Tell me, Mister Plant, was the room door locked or unlocked when you got here?"

"It was unlocked and slightly ajar. I assume the maid unlocked it when she came in to do the room."

As he listened to Plant's descriptions of the morning's events, Mackie walked over to the east wall and checked the windows. The drapes were drawn, and pushing them aside, he found both windows to be closed and latched. He said, "Okay, Mister Plant, if you will kindly lock the door again and direct me to a telephone, I need to make some calls."

"You can use the room phone right there, if you want."

Mackie shook his head. "I prefer to use a direct line. There's less chance of anyone listening in that way."

Plant looked shocked and said, "Oh no, Sergeant! Our operators are instructed never to listen in on our guests' conversations."

Mackie smiled pleasantly and said, "Just the same, Mister Plant, I would prefer a direct line."

"As you wish, Sergeant. The closest one would be in the lobby."

On their way to the lobby, Mackie asked, "How many people know about this so far?"

Plant thought about the question for a brief moment, and then said, "Only the housekeeping maid who found Miss Lawrence, the switchboard operator who called you, and myself. A few west wing guests came out into the hall to find out what the commotion was about, but I don't think any of them saw anything."

"Good. Let's keep it that way as long as possible."

The assistant manager nodded and said, "Absolutely, Sergeant. I've already instructed the telephone operator not to tell anyone, and the maid is still too upset to say anything. I assure you that the hotel wants no more fuss made over this tragedy than necessary."

"Being as how the woman is a celebrity, there's bound to be a ruckus once the newspapers catch wind of this. That can't be helped, but the longer we can keep it quiet, the more time we have to go over the crime scene before evidence is disturbed."

Plant led Mackie to an ornate desk across the lobby from the registration counter. On the desk there were a small wooden sign that said "Concierge" and a telephone. C. K. used the phone to make two short calls.

The first was to the stationhouse. When Patrolman Otis answered, Mackie told him to call the department's Criminal Investigation Laboratory and tell them to get a technician out to the hotel as soon as they could. He also instructed Otis to send one of the two officers on patrol over to the hotel. No, it didn't matter which, just whoever happened to call in first. The sergeant's final instruction was for Otis to call the coroner's office and have them come out to pick up the body.

Mackie's second call was to a rooming house down on Sunset near Western. He told the woman who answered that he wished to speak with Detective Lieutenant Winfield. The woman asked him to please hold on the line while she went to get Mister Winfield.

TWO

The first things most people noticed about Detective Lieutenant Robert Winfield were his blonde hair and fair complexion. In fact, his hair coloring was so light that when he tried to grow a mustache, the result was virtually invisible from more than a few feet away. This was disappointing to Winfield because without benefit of mustache or beard his soft features and blue eyes made him look more like sixteen than twenty-six. That, he felt, was a definite disadvantage to someone in a position that required an air of authority.

The lieutenant's size, however, tended to make up for his youthful appearance. He stood a full six feet in height and weighed in at nearly 180 pounds. That had been Winfield's weight after four years of boxing at the University of California in Berkeley, and it was still his weight today. He spent at least an hour in strenuous exercise every morning to make sure it stayed that way.

By eight a.m. on Sunday, the fifth of September, Winfield had already completed his morning exercises and bathing. Now he was sitting on the front porch of his rooming house reading the Hollywood Daily Citizen and enjoying the warm, early morning sunshine. Warm, sunny mornings were a rare occurrence where Winfield grew up in San Francisco. He liked the comfortable climate in southern California and decided that it made up for some of the other things Los Angeles seemed to lack.

The decision to accept a position with the Los Angeles Police Department wasn't an easy one. After nearly four years as a patrol officer in San Francisco, he knew it was time to move up, but there was no immediate likelihood of an opening in the S.F.P.D. Detective Division. For this reason and other personal considerations, he applied for positions elsewhere.

Winfield's degree in penology from Berkeley and his practical experience with the department in San Francisco earned him two offers. The first to arrive was a position as Detective Sergeant in the city of Madison, Wisconsin. In spite of his reluctance to leave the west coast, he was about to accept the job when an offer from the City of Los Angeles turned up in his mailbox.

The Los Angeles opening was at the rank of Detective Lieutenant and paid a far sight more than the job in Wisconsin, but the L.A.P.D. was struggling with serious internal problems. Stories about crooked cops in Los Angeles were a regular topic of conversations in police squad rooms throughout the country. While Winfield knew better than to believe all he heard through the grapevine, the fact that L.A. seemed to have a new chief of police every few months leant some degree of credence to the stories of bribery and police violence.

Los Angeles Mayor, George Cryer, had just appointed his fourth police chief, a former L.A. vice cop named James Davis. Word was the new chief was a spit and polish kind of guy whose no nonsense tactics had earned him the name "Two Gun Davis." Rumor also had it that Davis was a strong-arm cop who believed that if it took a little head bashing to keep citizens in line, then so be it.

Winfield had some misgivings about working in a department with such a poor reputation and for a chief whose philosophy was completely contrary to his own belief that good police work came about through the application of brains, not billy clubs. Still, the L.A.P.D. offer was generous and the need to change the circumstances of his life in San Francisco grew stronger every day, so he accepted the position, reporting for duty on the first of May, 1926.

As Detective Lieutenant Winfield, his first duty posting was to the Sixth Division out in the rural community of Hollywood. Hollywood, he learned, was incorporated as a city for a short time, but the citizens had voted for annexation to Los Angeles many years ago. Winfield's superior, Captain Albert Royce, explained that Hollywood was a good place to learn the ropes because, as he put it, "not much real crime happens out there in the sticks."

At first, that reasoning didn't make much sense to the new lieutenant. It seemed he would learn more quickly if he were in the thick of things rather than on the outskirts. Then Winfield met Detective Sergeant C. K. Mackie and soon came to realize that his posting to the Sixth was for the express purpose of learning how to be a good detective from the veteran sergeant, in spite of the fact that C. K. was technically his subordinate.

Winfield figured this out after asking some questions and learning that Mackie was one of the most decorated officers in the department. The thirty-nine year old sergeant was a former beat cop who worked his way up through the ranks on the strength of merit. C. K. had a reputation for being an honest, thorough man who could be as tough as the situation warranted, but preferred a more relaxed approach to dealing with citizens than most cops. The only question left unanswered was why Mackie had not been promoted to the opening Winfield filled.

Their first few days together had been an uneasy period for the young lieutenant. He expected the sergeant to harbor some resentment toward him as an upstart college kid and perhaps because Mackie had been passed over for the lieutenant's job. However, when C. K. displayed no such feelings, the two men quickly formed a unique partnership.

Winfield made it clear he respected the sergeant's experience and that he was anxious to learn all he could from him. Mackie apparently appreciated this attitude and, without the Lieutenant knowledge, informed all hands at the Sixth that, in spite of his inexperience, Winfield was in charge and anyone failing to show the proper respect would answer to the sergeant. Winfield's uneasiness at being the rookie soon evaporated, and he found he was slipping into his new role with relative ease.

Getting used to his new hometown was another matter. The differences between San Francisco and the little community of Hollywood went far deeper than their obvious differences in size and population. An article in the Sunday Hollywood Citizen Winfield was reading underscored one of those differences. The story was about the renovation of the Hollywood Bowl.

The Bowl opened, the article reported, seven years ago as a crude outdoor amphitheater in a small valley known as Daisy Dell at the northern end of Highland Boulevard. Wooden benches and a platform stage had since been built, but symphony performances, theatrical events, and the annual Easter sunrise services held there became so popular that an entirely new, larger Bowl was now under construction. In San Francisco such an undertaking would have been met with resistance from the city's old money families for the simple reason that an amphitheater would benefit the common folks of the city and thus was an unnecessary expense. In Hollywood, however, nearly everyone eagerly embraced such projects with almost childlike enthusiasm.

A rendering of the new stage designed by popular architect Frank Lloyd Wright accompanied the article and showed a tall triangular shaped shell behind a large oval stage. When completed, the stage would be nearly 140 feet wide by 90 feet deep with dressing rooms and storage beneath it. The expanded seating area would accommodate an audience of 17,000, and an automobile parking area was planned for the space behind the shell. Winfield was just reading about how contractors moved 36,000 yards of dirt to enlarge the natural valley in which the Bowl was situated when he heard the rooming house phone ring.

Something, perhaps a cop's sixth sense, told the lieutenant the call was for him. He was so sure of this that by the time Missus Haney, his elderly landlady, stuck her head out the screen door to tell him he was wanted on the telephone, Winfield was already on his feet. The telephone was located on a small round table just inside the entry. He picked up the handset and said, "Winfield speaking."

Even though tinny through the receiver, he immediately recognized C. K.'s normally rich baritone voice saying, "Sorry to be botherin' ya on your day off, Bobby, but we've got a bit of trouble on our hands this morning."

"I wasn't doing anything important, C. K. What's afoot?"

"Seems a pretty little blonde motion picture actress has gotten herself killed here at the Hollywood Hotel. We got the call about an hour ago, and I came out to look into it. She's lying on the floor of her room with a bullet in her brain."

Winfield felt a familiar twinge of anticipation spread from the bottom of his stomach as he asked, "Who is she?"

"Name's Lillian Lawrence. Ever hear of her?"

"Sure. And you'd know her, too, if you'd stop being such a cheapskate and take Helen to the movie shows once in a while."

C. K. grunted and said, "Otis is calling the crime lab people and the coroner. I've told the hotel's assistant manager to keep things quiet, but word's bound to get out before long, so I suggest we go over the girl's room as thoroughly as we can before we've got a crowd on our hands."

"I'm on my way, C. K."

"It's room 187. I'll wait for you there."

Lieutenant Winfield quickly added a necktie, vest, and coat to the white shirt and trousers he was wearing and climbed into his official department vehicle—a year-old Dodge Brothers Business Sedan, painted black like Mackie's roadster. It took three tries to get the four cylinder engine running smoothly, and Winfield made himself yet another mental note to ask C. K. how he got his machine to start and run so much better than anyone else's.

At twenty minutes past nine Winfield turned into the hotel's circular drive. He immediately spotted C. K.'s Dodge and then noticed one of the Model T Fords driven by patrol officers parked near it. Even though department vehicles carried no markings, Winfield knew that Hollywood residents recognized police automobiles when they saw them, and it occurred to him that having three department automobiles parked in front of the hotel was going to attract unwanted attention.

He drove around the block and parked on Highland. Then, after asking directions at the front desk, Lieutenant Winfield went to room 187 where he encountered Patrol Officer Allen Olmstead standing guard outside the door. He returned Olmstead's informal salute and entered the room.

Inside, Sergeant Mackie looked around the door of the closet he was inspecting and said, "Welcome to your first homicide, Bobby."

Technically this wasn't Winfield's first homicide. He had participated in several murder investigations in San Francisco, but he didn't feel that point required clarification at the moment. Instead, he simply nodded and C. K. returned to his exploration of the closet, leaving the lieutenant to familiarize himself with the crime scene.

Looking around room 187 of the Hollywood Hotel, Winfield was surprised at its austerity in comparison to finer San Francisco hotels. The pale green paint on the walls was certainly no match for the elegant wall coverings found in the rooms of the venerable Saint Francis on Union Square, and the stark furnishings were a far cry from the luxurious appointments of the Fairmont, atop Nob Hill.

The only parts of room 187's décor that even hinted at luxury were three framed oil paintings of reasonably good quality. Even these, however, had been hung, one to a wall, with no apparent thought as to whether or not the painting's shape, coloring, or subject fit its location.

Winfield grimaced at what passed for luxury in these parts and knelt on a cheap imitation Oriental rug to examine the victim. She hadn't been much more than a child, really—maybe nineteen or twenty at the most. Still, she was apparently old enough to be planning marriage, he observed, because there was a small diamond engagement ring on the third finger of her left hand.

Lillian Lawrence had been of average height—five-four or five-five—with a slim build. He guessed she couldn't have been much over 115 pounds. Her medium-length blonde hair was done in a popular style—combed back with a part down the left side and curled at the neck. Its light color contrasted with the deep suntan that colored the girl's fine skin beneath the pallor of death. Her eyes were still open and he found their green coloring a little surprising. In the black and white motion pictures you could tell she was blonde, so he expected her to have the blue eyes typical of most blonde-haired people, including him.

Winfield also noted she was small-boned with long, slender arms and legs. In death, Lillian Lawrence seemed slimmer and more delicate than he remembered her on the motion picture screen, but there could be several reasons for that, including that motion picture cameras tended to make people look larger and heavier that they really were, or so he'd heard.

With C. K. now leaning in the closet doorway watching him, Winfield looked closely at the bullet hole in Lillian Lawrence's right temple. Winfield noted, "Looks like a small caliber bullet from the size of the entry wound."

C. K. said, "That was my impression. And she must have died instantly because there's almost no bleeding. Notice anything else interesting?"

"Well, from the position of the wound, I'd guess the bullet went straight into her brain. Since there's no exit wound, it must have hit bone. Being a small caliber, bone would stop it."

C. K. smiled and said, "All true, but look closer."

Winfield leaned close to the girl's right temple and saw what Mackie was getting at. The skin immediately around the bullet hole was peppered with tiny black specks—traces of gun powder and powder burns that were only found around a gunshot wound when the weapon was fired at extremely close range.

The lieutenant rocked back on his heels and said, "Looks like the gun barrel must have been right up close to her head when the shot was fired."

"That would be my guess."

Winfield stood up and looked at the position of the body, wondering how the lower half of the girl's nightgown had gotten bunched up, leaving her naked from the waist down. He voiced the obvious question, "Think she was raped?"

C. K. shook his head. "No, I don't. For one thing, I don't see any of the physical signs that usually go with a rape. And for another, take a look at the bed there behind her."

The sergeant pointed to an area of the turned-down bedclothes above the victim's feet and said, "See how the sheets are wrinkled? How it's kind of pulled toward the edge of the bed?"

Winfield nodded and Mackie continued, "It looks like she was sitting on the edge of the bed when she was shot and the nightgown got bunched up under her as she slid off to the floor."

Winfield said, "That makes sense, but it would mean the killer had to be standing right up against the nightstand, and even at that, he'd have to be left-handed."

The lieutenant stepped over the body and assumed the pose he was describing, using his left forefinger to simulate the gun. Mackie said, "Feels awkward as hell, doesn't it?"

"Yes, it does. You know, from the body position and the powder burns, it looks more like she shot herself, but there's no gun."

"And no suicide note. As a rule, people don't kill themselves without leaving a final message of some kind, either for a loved one or a friend or just for the world in general."

Winfield thought for a moment and then asked, "Any chance somebody got in here and removed some of the evidence, like a suicide note and the gun?"

"Anything is possible at this point. Plant, the assistant manager, said the maid who found the body and he were the only ones who've been in the room, and he locked it after that, but judging by her advanced state of rigor mortis, she probably died sometime last night, and that leaves plenty of opportunity for just about anything to happen. It's pretty clear that somebody else was here, though."

"Why?"

Mackie gestured at the things strewn about the floor and said, "Unless we had an earthquake I didn't notice, somebody knocked all this stuff on the floor."

"How do we know Miss Lawrence didn't do that herself? Maybe she wasn't very tidy."

C. K. pulled one of the chest drawers open and said, "But I think she was. Look in here. Undies are all carefully folded and stacked, everything neat as a pin. Same thing in the closet. The mess on the floor doesn't fit with that. And then there's the cigar."

Startled, Winfield looked at Mackie and said, "What cigar?"

"The one over here on the floor. And when I first came in, the room stunk of cigar smoke."

Winfield moved around the bed and leaned over to look at the butt and its brightly colored band. He said, "Havana. Looks expensive."

Mackie shrugged and said, "But even the cigar is kind of strange."

"How so?"

Look on the chest of drawers behind you. There's an ash tray with ashes in it, and the cigar looks like it was crushed out in there before it was thrown on the floor. A careless person, or someone in a hurry, might throw a cigar on the floor, but not after taking the time to crush it out first."

Winfield looked at the ash tray and said, "I see what you mean. It would take more effort to turn around and throw the butt on the floor than to just leave it in the ash tray. And all this stuff on the floor seems a little strange, too."

Mackie added, "Yes, it appears to me as though someone simply wiped an arm across the top of the chest and the dressing table, clearing everything onto the floor."

"And since nothing has been disturbed in the drawers and closet, our mystery person wasn't searching for anything or robbing the place; he was just making a mess. The question is why?"

Mackie said, "He might have been trying to make it look as though there was a struggle in here or that the room had been burglarized."

"Or," Winfield added, "It might have been done in a fit of anger. Either way, whoever did this was left-handed, just like our killer. See how all the stuff on the floor is to the right of the dressing table and the chest?"

Winfield demonstrated by moving his arm in a left to right sweeping motion above the top of the dressing table, showing how that would result in everything falling to the right. Mackie nodded and said, "That would be the most natural movement, but he didn't wipe everything to the floor. The ash tray is still on the chest and he missed some stationary and a pen on the dressing table."

Shrugging at this, Winfield turned his attention to the items on the floor beside the dressing table. There was a silver hand mirror and a matching hair brush, two or three expensive-looking perfumes and assorted make-up items—lip rouge and the like. Then he examined the things that looked like they came from the top of the chest of drawers. They included a copy of Sinclair Lewis' novel, Babbitt, and a black leather handbag. He asked, "Have you checked the handbag yet?"

"Yes. Besides the usual female necessities, there was a key to this room and twenty-seven dollars and change in a wallet. Oh, and a California driver's license in the name of Lillian Lee. The description on it fits our victim."

Winfield nodded and said, "Must have been her real name. I guess movie actors always change their names. I don't know why she did it, though. There's nothing wrong with the name Lee."

"Doesn't have enough syllables. Movie star last names mostly have two syllables, like Gloria Swan-son, Mae Mur-ray, Douglas Fair-banks, . . ."

"Well, I'll be! You do know something about movie actors, after all."

"Oh yes, indeed," C. K. said disparagingly. "I've hauled most of them home at one time or another to sober up. They don't seem nearly so glamorous when they're puking all over the inside of your automobile."

Winfield smiled and turned his attention to the third item on the floor next to the chest—a thick sheaf of paper which had been hole-punched in the upper left corner and bound with a ring fastener. The cover sheet said, "THE BIG SISTER by Archibald Wheatly." The following sheets contained what he guessed were stage directions for a motion picture. Most of the pages had lines crossed out or added, and there were notes scribbled in the margins.

He looked up at Mackie and said, "This must be the script, or whatever you call it, for a movie she was working on."

Mackie nodded and Winfield asked, "What about these towels? They look fresh."

"Apparently the maid was bringing them into the room when she discovered the body. Plant found her on her hands and knees next to the body, so it's probably safe to say she dropped them."

"Anything in the closet or the bathroom?"

"Nothing in the bathroom besides tooth powder, a toothbrush, and the like. The closet has a three-piece set of good quality luggage on the floor, all empty, and a lot of expensive-looking clothes hanging on the pole. There's also a jewelry box on the shelf in there, but the stuff in it is costume jewelry—expensive, but no real diamonds or anything like that."

Winfield wandered over to the closet and looked through the girl's clothes. He said, "From the amount of stuff in here, it appears she was planning on staying for a while. There must be at least a dozen pairs of fancy shoes, all neatly stored away in their boxes."

After rummaging a little further, Winfield closed the closet door and said, "The lady definitely had expensive tastes. That fur jacket in there must have cost plenty."

"Yes, I noticed that. If robbery had been the motive, they'd have at least taken the fur and maybe some of the more expensive costume jewelry. I think it's fairly safe to say that Miss Lawrence was killed for some personal reason."

"And," Winfield added, "I'd say there's a good possibility she knew her killer, maybe very well."

With a twinkle in his eye, Mackie said, "And what makes you think that, Mister Detective Lieutenant?"

"For one thing, there's no sign of forced entry, so she must have let the guy in. And since she let him in without putting on a robe over her nightgown, it would seem they must have had a close relationship."

"Unless," Mackie added with a grin, "Our killer is a woman."

"Sure, a woman who smokes big fat Havana cigars."

"Okay, I'll give you that point."

Winfield was looking into the wastebasket and said, "What's all this stuff?"

Mackie looked over the lieutenant's shoulder and said, "Some wrapping paper, a little string, and a receipt from the Sun Drug Company at Hollywood and Cahuenga. It's dated September fourth, yesterday, and it shows that Miss Lawrence purchased three items totaling four dollars and twenty-one cents."

Winfield picked up the receipt. "She bought a pair of Holeproof Hose, some lip rouge and a bottle of witch hazel."

He dropped the receipt back into the waste basket and said, "I wonder if they really are."

Mackie looked at him and said, "If what really is what?"

"If the stockings are really hole-proof."

C. K. grinned and said, "Bobby, my boy, someday, if you ever take a bride, you will learn many things, one of them being that there is absolutely no such thing as a hole-proof stocking. If stockings never wore out, the companies that make them would soon be out of business."

Winfield grinned back at Mackie, saying, "Thank you, Sergeant, for those words of wisdom."

Mackie was saying, "Think nothing of it, Laddie," when the room door opened and Patrol Officer Olmstead announced that the coroner's men had arrived.

Winfield said, "Send them in."

The two coroner's deputies—a short, bald one and a tall, husky one—were wearing suits and might have passed for clerks except for their heavy boots. The boots, Winfield guessed, were probably necessary because the coroner's customers weren't always as cooperative as Miss Lawrence in regard to the places where they happened to die.

Mackie knew the short one, who appeared to be in charge, and greeted him. "Hello, Eddie. Sorry to louse up your Sunday this way."

Eddie replied, "Hi, Sarge. Hey you got a looker this time. Nice legs, too!"

Winfield didn't care for Eddie's lack of respect and he definitely didn't like the way both men were eyeing the naked lower half of Lillian Lawrence's body. He put a stop to it by saying in an icy tone, "Sorry, men, but you'll have to wait until our Criminal Investigation Laboratory people show up before you can move her. We need pictures of the body. In the meantime, I would prefer it if you waited out in the hall with Officer Olmstead."

The tall one, who was apparently along for his brawn, turned toward the door, but the short one glared at Winfield and said, "Who the hell is this stuffed shirt, Sarge?"

Before Mackie could answer, Winfield stepped forward and towering over the short man said, "This stuffed shirt is Detective Lieutenant Winfield, Los Angeles P.D., badge number four-one-three. Now get your butt out in that hall before I throw you out!"

The short guy took a reflex step backward and said, "Jeezus! No need to get all hot under the collar, Lieutenant. We're goin'."

At the door he stopped, and deliberately avoiding Winfield's stare, asked, "Any idea how long we gotta wait, Sarge?"

Mackie, who was doing his best to keep a straight face, said, "We called the lab the same time we called you, so they should be here any minute."

"Okay. I just hope they hurry. We got better things to do than cool our heels out in this hall."

When the door closed behind him, Mackie let loose the grin he'd been stifling and said, "Bobby, my boy, I've got to hand it to you. You sure know how to make new friends."

Still irritated by the little man's attitude, Winfield said, "Didn't you see how those perverts were looking at the body. Makes me sick just thinking about it."

"True, Eddie has his faults, but he also knows his business. I just hope he isn't on duty some cold, rainy night when we've got ourselves a corpse up on the Cahuenga Pass. After the reception you gave him, Eddie might just leave us stuck up there all night before he got around to picking up the body."

Apparently ignoring Mackie's words of wisdom, Winfield said, "Let's go interview some people. Unless you can think of anything we've missed here."

Taking one last look around the room, Mackie said, "I think we're done here."

On the way out, Winfield told Olmstead, "We're going to talk to whatever witnesses we can round up. Don't let the guys from the coroner get impatient and take off with the body before our laboratory people get here."

"And when the lab guys get here," Mackie added, "Tell them we want fingerprints, photographs of everything, and all the loose stuff in the room tagged and boxed. Tell them this is liable to turn into a headline case and we don't want to be caught with our britches down around our ankles again. Got it?"

"Yes, sir," Olmstead said, "Photographs, fingerprints, and the loose stuff tagged and boxed. I'll see they get the message, sir."

THREE

Anticipating questions the police might ask, Dennis Plant had instructed a desk clerk to bring Lillian Lawrence's guest folio to his office. Now he studied the top of three or four pages summarizing the charges and payments on account made by the guest in room 187.

When Plant found the entry that answered Detective Sergeant Mackie's question, he said, "Miss Lawrence checked into the hotel on August fourteenth. That was about three weeks ago."

Mackie added this fact to the entries in his notebook under the heading:

Lillian Lawrence Death
Dennis Plant Interview – 9/5/26 @ 9:55 a.m.

Most of the previous notes on this page concerned Hattie Mae's discovery of the body and steps taken by the assistant manager prior to Mackie's arrival at the hotel. Thus far these were the only entries describing how Miss Lawrence's body had been found because the maid was still in such a state of shock that she was unable to answer questions coherently. After making sure of Hattie Mae Brown's home address so they could talk to her later, Winfield had given permission for the housekeeping matron to drive her home.

Now Mackie and Winfield were sitting in the assistant manager's office learning whatever Plant could tell them about the circumstances of Lillian Lawrence's death. Mackie finished his notation about the victim's date of arrival at the Hollywood Hotel and asked, "Do you know how long Miss Lawrence planned to stay?"

"No. The length of stay entry simply says, 'Indefinite.' That's not uncommon, though. Movie people often check in for long periods while they are working on a film. They seldom know how long the shooting will take."

Winfield asked, "Is that why Miss Lawrence was here? Was she making a motion picture?"

Plant shook his head and said, "I really don't know. That was my assumption, but I can't say for sure. She was one of our quieter guests. I seldom saw her, and I don't recall actually speaking with her more than once or twice."

Gesturing toward the guest folio on Plant's desk, Mackie asked, "Did she give you a permanent address when she checked in?"

The assistant manager looked down at the top page of the folio again. "Let me see. That should be . . . here it is, 'care of Western National Studios, 6320 Santa Monica Boulevard.'"

While Mackie wrote this down, Winfield asked, "A minute ago you described Miss Lawrence as one of your quieter guests. By that do you mean she kept to herself?"

"I meant that we very seldom saw her. She left early on weekdays, usually about six in the morning. And she never spent much time in the public areas of the hotel when she was here. That was probably because she didn't want to be bothered by people who recognized her. Some actors are like that, and others are disappointed if people don't pester them."

Surprised, Winfield said, "You say she left the hotel every day at six?"

Plant smiled and said, "You must be new to Hollywood, Lieutenant. When they are working, actors have to be at their studio by the crack of dawn. That's because it takes a couple of hours to put on their costumes and makeup. So to get in a full day of filming, they have to get there early."

"I see. What about yesterday? Did Miss Lawrence leave at six yesterday morning?"

"I can't say for sure, but I doubt it. Yesterday was Saturday. Studios don't usually film on weekends anymore. They used to and sometimes they still do it if they're behind schedule. As a rule, though, they shut down on Saturday and Sunday."

Winfield nodded and said, "So she probably had the day off. Do you have any idea what she did yesterday? Where she might have gone? Who she might have seen? Anything like that?"

"I can't tell you much about that because my shift begins at two a.m. and ends at ten. But I did see Miss Lawrence twice yesterday. The first time she was having breakfast in the dining room. I remember being surprised to see her there. As I said, we didn't often see her around the hotel."

Mackie chimed in, "What time was that? I mean, when you saw her eating breakfast?"

Plant frowned in concentration for a moment, and then said, "It must have been after eight—maybe eight-thirty. I take my lunch break between seven and eight, and it was after that."

Mackie made a note in his book and asked, "And when did you see her the second time yesterday?"

"It was a few minutes after ten. Miss Lawrence walked out through the lobby just as I was going home."

Winfield asked, "Do you have any idea where she was going? Could you tell by the way she was dressed or anything?"

Plant shook his head. "I have no idea. She was walking, though. She went east on Hollywood Boulevard."

Still writing, Mackie asked, "Who here at the hotel might be able to tell us more about Miss Lawrence's activities yesterday?"

You should talk to Mister Harrison, our manager. He gets here at the end of my shift and usually stays until about six. Then our night manager comes on until two in the morning when I get here again."

Glancing at his wristwatch, Winfield said, "Then Mister Harrison should be getting here pretty soon?"

"Not today. I'm working an extra shift because Mister Harrison is out of town for the day. He won't be back at the hotel again until tomorrow morning at ten."

Mackie asked, "What's the night manager's name, and where can we find him?"

Pulling a typed list from his top desk drawer, Plant said, "His name is Richard Boyd, and he lives in an apartment building . . . yes, here it is. The Casa de Paz Apartments, 1822 North Ivar, number six."

Noting this information in his book, Mackie said, "Do you think he'd be there now?"

"I imagine so, but he's probably asleep. It would be better if you could wait until later."

Nodding, Mackie responded, "We'll wait as late as we can, Mister Plant, but the longer it takes us to get on the killer's trail, the longer he has to get away."

Winfield was still thinking about Lillian Lawrence walking up Hollywood Boulevard Saturday morning and asked, "Did Miss Lawrence own an automobile?"

"Yes. She has . . . or had, one of those new Pontiac cars, a two-door coupe'. It should be out in the parking area behind the hotel."

Mackie looked up from his notebook and said, "A Pontiac? That's not the sort of machine well-to-do movie people usually drive, is it?"

The assistant manager smiled and said, "Quite true, Sergeant. You are much more likely to find them in a Lincoln or a Duesenberg. Or maybe a Cadillac. But somehow that car of hers suited Miss Lawrence. It's sort of olive green with a black landau top—not at all stylish or flamboyant, but Miss Lawrence wasn't the flashy type. In fact, I sometimes wondered how she ever became an actress because she seemed so quiet—almost shy—in comparison to most of the film people we see here."

Taking off on a new line of questions, Mackie said, "Did Miss Lawrence have any regular or frequent visitors here at the hotel that you know of?"

Plant thought for a moment and said, "Only two that I recall. Miss Mae White visited her quite often. They seemed to be good friends. Her only other regular visitor was a gentleman. I don't know his name, but I saw him sitting in the lobby every so often, usually on weekends. Miss Lawrence would meet him there, and from the way they greeted each other, he might have been her beau." Then he added quickly, "But I don't know that for a fact. It just struck me that way."

Winfield raised his eyebrows at the mention of Mae White. Miss White was one of the most famous actresses in the movies. He remembered hearing one of the young women who live at Miss Haney's say that Mae White's last picture, Fame and Fortune, was more popular than Mary Pickford's most recent film, Sparrows.

He'd not seen Fame and Fortune yet, but he recalled being quite impressed with Miss White and her performances in other films. Then Winfield wondered if C. K. knew Mae White—if she was one of those who'd gotten sick in his Dodge roadster while being escorted home to sober up. This thought was jarred from his mind at the sound of Mackie's voice asking Plant if he could describe the young man who called on Miss Lawrence.

The assistant manager said, "He's probably about my age, not more than twenty-six or twenty-seven. I would say he is of medium height and weight. His hair is light brown and he looks like the outdoor sort. You know, rugged features, deep suntan, like that."

"What sort of clothes does he wear?"

"Oh, he is always dressed nicely, but I got the impression he was uncomfortable in a tight collar and necktie. You know how men who wear business clothes all the time look at home in them? Well, this fellow doesn't look that way."

Mackie was writing quickly to get all of the man's description down in his notebook. Winfield took up the slack by asking, "And Miss Lawrence had no other visitors that you recall?"

Plant shook his head. Then Winfield asked, "Do you mind if we take a look at Miss Lawrence's hotel account?"

The assistant manager handed the folio to Winfield who glanced at each page briefly before passing them on to Mackie. Aside from her weekly room rent, Lillian Lawrence had incurred very few charges since her arrival at the hotel. There were two purchases in the gift shop and only three or four meals in the dining room. The last entry was one of these. It confirmed Plant's recollection of seeing Miss Lawrence at breakfast the previous morning because it recorded a charge of one dollar and thirty-five cents, signed for at twenty minutes past eight a.m. on September fourth.

After looking at the last page, Mackie returned the folio to the assistant manager's desk and said, "Mister Plant, do you happen to know if anyone in the rooms near Miss Lawrence's reported a loud noise, like a gunshot, last night?"

"Not on my shift. Richard didn't mention anything like that, either, when I got here this morning. He did say he got some complaints about a loud party in the west wing and that he had to go and quiet things down over there a couple of times, but I don't know anything further. That's another question you will have to ask him."

Mackie nodded, and turning to Winfield, he said, "Unless you have more questions for Mister Plant, I expect we should go see if any of Miss Lawrence's neighbors saw or heard anything last night."

Winfield nodded in agreement and picked up the list of guests in rooms near 187 the assistant manager prepared for them. As the detectives stood to leave, Plant said, "Gentlemen, I have a question or two for you."

Winfield said, "Go ahead."

Plant cleared his throat and said, "As you can imagine, the hotel would like to avoid as much notoriety in this tragic matter as possible. You have asked me not to speak with anyone about Miss Lawrence's death, but I have an obligation to discuss the matter with our manager, Mister Harrison, as soon as he gets back in town tonight."

Mackie put the assistant manager at ease, saying, "Go right ahead and do that. I asked you not to talk about Miss Lawrence's death because we need time to look for evidence and speak with witnesses before the newspaper reporters and photographers show up and turn the crime scene into a three-ring circus."

Plant turned pale at the sergeant's mention of what might be expected from the press and said, anxiously, "Is there any way that sort of thing can be avoided?"

Mackie looked doubtful. "So far we've been lucky. Our people should be taking their pictures and going over the room right now. And the coroner's deputies are already here to pick up the body. As soon as we've had a chance to talk to those folks," he gestured toward the list of guests in Winfield's hand, "We will report to department headquarters and someone there, probably Captain Royce of the Homicide Division, will contact the newspapers and make an announcement. Unless someone spills the beans, things should be quiet until then."

Winfield added, "After that, however, you can expect members of the press to show up in droves. Of course, there won't be much for them to see because things will be pretty well cleaned up here. With no body or blood stains or any of the other lurid scenes newspapers like to photograph, the reporters aren't likely to stick around long. Besides, we want you to keep room 187 locked for a few days until we're sure we have no further need of it for the investigation. You can tell any reporters who ask to see the room that you are under police orders not to let anyone in."

Plant said, "I understand. I'll make sure our day and night shift people get the message as well."

Winfield thanked the assistant manager for his cooperation and followed Sergeant Mackie out of the office. Passing through the lobby, both officers were relieved to find things still quiet and apparently normal. C. K. smiled to himself, pleased that an investigation involving a film celebrity was being handled properly for a change.

Number 187 was the last room on the ground floor at the south end of the hotel's west wing. It happened that all of the second floor accommodations in the area above Lillian Lawrence's room were vacant the previous night. On the first floor, only three of the rooms near 187 were occupied, the closest being 186, directly across the hall.

As they approached Officer Olmstead, still on guard outside Lillian Lawrence's room, a momentary burst of brilliant light illuminated the crack beneath the door behind him. This puzzled Winfield for a second until he realized the source was a photo flashbulb. Apparently the fellows from the Criminal Investigation Laboratory had arrived and were doing their job.

This was confirmed by Olmstead who informed Mackie and Winfield that the lab people showed up half an hour earlier and were probably just about done. Mackie said that would no doubt please Eddie and his partner who were still waiting impatiently at the opposite end of the hall with their stretcher leaning against the wall.

Winfield knocked on the door to room 186, and after waiting a moment during which there was no reply, he knocked again. This time an angry voiced answered, "Go away! You can clean up the damned room later!"

Winfield and Mackie looked at each other and the sergeant said loudly, "It's the police, Mister Mason. Please open up."

There was more grumbling from behind the door, but a moment later it was opened by a bleary-eyed and very angry Mister Rodney Mason. He took a quick look at each of the officers and said, "What the hell is going on now?"

"Sorry to bother you, Mister Mason, but my name is Winfield and this is Detective Sergeant Mackie. We're with the Los Angeles Police Department, and we need to ask you some questions."

"Sure, why not," Mason said, shrugging his shoulders in defeat. "I'm never going to get any sleep in this damned place anyway. Come on in."

Mason told the officers to find a seat while he put on a dark maroon robe over his white night shirt and flopped wearily on the edge of the bed. Mackie retrieved the notebook from his breast pocket, and opening it to the first empty page, he began the interview. "Your name is Rodney Mason and you're from Rochester, New York. Is that correct?"

"Yes," Mason said, "What's this all about?"

Without looking up from his notebook, Mackie asked, "What do you do for a living, Mister Mason?"

"I'm a salesman. I sell motion picture film and processing chemicals. Now what's going on?"

Winfield answered Mason's question indirectly, saying, "There was a little trouble across the hall earlier this morning. We understand you called the front desk to complain."

Being reminded of the incident raised Mason's ire again. Angrily, he barked, "You bet I did! That crazy colored maid over there was screaming her fool head off! Woke me right out of the first sound sleep I'd had all night!"

Pencil poised, Mackie asked, "About what time was this, Mister Mason?"

"It was exactly four minutes after eight. I know because I looked at my watch while I was calling the front desk."

"And what happened next?"

"A guy who said he was the assistant manager showed up. The door over there was open a little bit, and there was this laundry cart parked outside it. Anyway, this guy goes in and closes the door behind him. A minute later he comes back out with this colored maid who's doing all the screaming.

"So he gets her out there into the hall and she faints dead away. The guy doesn't know what to do with her, so he plunks her down on the floor and goes back into the room again.

"By this time there were several of us out in the hall, and we're all wondering what the hell's going on. Some woman from one of the rooms down the hall starts trying to wake up this colored gal. She's just coming around again when the assistant manager guy walks out of the room and apologizes to everyone for the ruckus. Then he locks the door and gets this maid up on her feet and they take off."

"And," Mackie said, "that was the end of it? You didn't see or hear anything else after that?"

"No. I finally got back to sleep again, and you guys showed up."

Acknowledging Mason's irritation with a solemn nod, Winfield asked, "What about last night? Did you see or hear anything unusual?"

"There were a couple of loud parties down the hall, but that probably isn't unusual for this dump."

"What time were these parties?"

"Well, one of them was already going strong when I got here a little after seven last night. I sat up all night Friday on the train from San Francisco because there weren't any compartments or berths available. Then I spent all day yesterday trying to clean up a mess at the Deluxe film lab over at Fox. When I got here all I wanted to do was sleep, but those people were raising the damned roof down there!

"So I call the front desk and complain. Things finally quieted down around eight, then they started up all over again at two a.m. And then there's all this commotion this morning. I tell you, I'm gonna go nuts if I don't get some sleep!"

Winfield smiled and said, "We'll be out of your hair in a minute, Mister Mason. Just a few more questions. Do you know which rooms the parties were in last night?"

"I think it was the same room both times. I don't know the room number, but it was across the hall and down a ways—maybe two or three doors down."

Mackie asked, "Have you seen anything of the woman who was staying in the room across the hall? A young blonde woman. Pretty."

"Nope. The only ones I've seen go in or out of that room were the hotel guy and that colored maid. Why? Did this blonde gal skip out on her bill or something? Is that what this fuss is all about?"

"No," Winfield answered, "Unfortunately, the young woman is dead. That's why we're asking all these questions."

"Oh, yeah? Well, I never saw her, but I can tell you how she probably died."

Winfield looked startled. "Oh?"

"In this place? Ten will get you twenty she died of exhaustion from lack of sleep!"

Mackie grinned, stood, and said, "Thanks for your help, Mister Mason. We'll be on our way now. Sleep well."

"Sure."

Out in the hall, Winfield said, "Well, now we know where the loud parties were and maybe why Mister Mason didn't hear a gunshot. We might even be able to narrow down the possible time of the shooting because it must have happened while one of the parties was going on."

"Maybe. Keep in mind, Bobby, that the wound was made by a small caliber bullet like a point-two-two. Small hand guns don't make all that much noise, so it's possible Mason and the other guests wouldn't have noticed it even if there hadn't been any party noise, especially if they were asleep."

Winfield nodded. He knew he'd just violated a basic rule of investigation by drawing a conclusion that fit some of the facts while ignoring others. It was a common error made by rookies who were anxious to break a case. The lieutenant knew better and gave himself a mental kick in the pants as a reminder to be more careful.

The next guest on their list was an Edward Cooper in room 185, the room next to the victim's. Cooper said he worked for Mister Carl Laemmle as an accountant and that he was out here from New York to review accounting procedures at Mister Laemmle's Universal Studios. He'd been at the hotel since last Wednesday, but hadn't seen anything of Miss Lawrence during that time.

As far as the previous night was concerned, Mister Cooper had been at a party out in Beverly Hills until around midnight. The man did not remember hearing any unusual sounds after he got back except that someone was having an extremely noisy party. He confirmed Rodney Mason's belief that the party had been around two and said that he, also, called the front desk to demand something be done about it. The party, Mister Cooper said, was next door in room 183.

Room 183, according to Plant's notation, was actually a suite, and it was registered to a Mister and Missus Herbert Ackerman. Mackie knocked on the door and it was answered almost immediately by a thin, middle-aged woman who became extremely nervous when Mackie identified himself and Winfield as police officers. As she hesitantly invited them in, a man's voice from the second room of the suite said gruffly, "Who's at the door, Betty?"

"They're police officers, Herb. They want to ask us some questions."

At that, an overweight, red-faced man came into the room saying, "All this fuss about a lousy little party! I can tell you this will be the last time this hotel gets any of my business."

Before Winfield or Mackie could get a word in, Missus Ackerman said, "Herbert, I knew we shouldn't have had all those people here. I knew it and I told you so. Now we're in . . . ."

"Shut up, Betty! I don't want to hear anymore of your damned whining." Then he turned to Winfield and said, "I'll have you know I'm an attorney, and if you think you can bully me around, you'd better just think again. I know a lot of people . . . ."

Mackie finally interrupted, saying, "Hold your horses, Mister Ackerman. Our business doesn't have anything to do with your party last night."

Missus Ackerman immediately looked relieved, but Herbert looked puzzled. He said, "What do you want then?"

Winfield said, "We're investigating an incident early this morning in room 187."

Betty Ackerman said, "Oh, that woman who died!"

Frowning, Winfield asked, "How do you know a woman died in that room, Missus Ackerman?"

"That poor colored woman was trying to tell me about it. She was awfully upset, though. I could only understand half of what she was trying to say."

"Then you must be the woman who revived Miss Brown after she fainted out in the hall. Is that right?"

"Yes. Is that her name? Miss Brown?"

"Yes. Hattie Mae Brown."

"That poor woman. She was terrified half out of her mind. How is she getting along now?"

Showing just a little impatience, Mackie said, "She's much better now. Someone took her home to rest. How long have you been here at the hotel, Mister Ackerman?"

"Since Friday night. We came down for an alumni gathering and the football game yesterday."

Winfield recalled reading about something like Ackerman was describing in the Citizen this morning and said, "Was that at the University of Southern California, Mister Ackerman?"

"Yes, USC. I took my law degree there, and we came down for the festivities. I practice in Fresno now, but I like to stay in touch with my old classmates."

"I see,' said Mackie, "And you arrived Friday night. Since then have either of you seen anything of the woman who was staying in room 187. She was an attractive young blonde woman."

Herbert shook his head, but Betty Ackerman said, "Oh, my. Is she one who died?"

"Yes. Have you seen her?"

Betty Ackerman said, "Yes. It was last night after dinner. With all of Herbert's friends in here, the room was getting terribly stuffy, so I stepped out for a breath of air. That young woman was just going into her room as I passed in the hall."

Paying closer attention now, Mackie asked, "Was the woman alone or was someone with her?"

"Oh, the girl was by herself, but she seemed very distraught. She was having trouble getting her key in the door, and I noticed there were tears on her cheek. Gracious, I can't believe that pretty youngster is dead."

While Mackie wrote in his notebook, Winfield asked, "Missus Ackerman, can you be more specific about the time you saw her? It's quite important."

"Oh my, I'm not sure. I'm afraid I was a little tipsy . . . ."

Herbert Ackerman interrupted her, clearing his throat and saying, "Ah, gentlemen, we have a train to catch. I have an important trial starting in the morning, so we don't want to miss our trip home."

Winfield stifled a smile at Ackerman's nervousness over his wife's near admission that illegal booze was being served at their party. He said, "I understand, Mister Ackerman, but it is very important that we pin down the time the woman got to her room. Was it before or after the hotel night manager asked you to quiet down the first time?"

Betty Ackerman said quickly, "Oh, it was before. I know that because afterwards we went to . . . we all went somewhere else so we wouldn't disturb anyone further."

Mackie asked, "How was the woman dressed when you saw her?"

"I remember that very well. She had on the loveliest blue evening dress with sequins around the neck here," she moved her hands to show Mackie the location of the sequins, "And she was wearing black evening slippers with a matching handbag—the kind with the long thin strap so you can put it over your shoulder or you can fold up the strap and carry it in your hand. You know the kind I mean? They're all the rage now."

Winfield pictured the purse with a long thin strap and twenty-seven dollars inside on the floor of Lillian Lawrence's room. He hadn't known that handbags like it were all the rage now. He asked, "Do either of you remember hearing any unusual noises last night? Like an automobile backfiring or someone arguing?"

Neither of the Ackermans had heard anything out of the ordinary until Hattie Mae Brown awakened them with her screaming. Then, after making sure he had the Ackerman's address and telephone number in Fresno in case more questions were necessary, Mackie thanked them both and stepped through the doorway after Winfield. Out in the hall, they heard Herbert Ackerman loudly scolding his wife for talking to damned much, as usual. Winfield grinned and C. K. shook his head in amusement.

Seeing Winfield and Mackie come out of the Ackermans' room, Officer Olmstead walked briskly over to them and said to Mackie, "Sir, it looks like things are pretty well wrapped up here. The lab men have left and the coroner's deputies took the body away a few minutes ago. Shall I stay here or return to my regular patrol?"

Raising a questioning eyebrow, Mackie looked at Winfield. The lieutenant said, "I think it's safe for Officer Olmstead to leave now. As long as the room is locked and we have a key, it should be alright. We'll just remind Mister Plant not to let anyone in for the time being."

C. K. nodded in agreement and said to Olmstead, "Okay, son, you can go about your normal duties. But remember, mum's the word about this for now."

Olmstead snapped off a salute that was mostly for Mackie, but included Winfield, and said, "Yes, sir."

Mackie locked the door to room 187 with the key they'd found in the victim's handbag and offered the key to Winfield, who said, "You hang onto it for now, C. K."

"Alright. What's next?"

Looking at his watch, the lieutenant answered, "It's a little past ten-thirty. I suppose we best call Captain Royce and tell him what's going on. Is there a public telephone around here?"

"In the lobby," C. K. gestured, "After you, Laddie."

FOUR

Captain Albert Royce, in charge of the Los Angeles Police Department's Homicide Division, held unswervingly to what he called his fundamental tenets of leadership. The first of these stated that officers under his command were expected to rely on their own initiative in handling investigations. Captain Royce was particularly steadfast in this belief on weekends, especially Sundays.

It was, therefore, with no small amount of irritation that the captain left his breakfast table to accept the telephone call his wife had answered from Lieutenant Robert Winfield. The dressing down Royce was prepared to give his new man quickly vanished from his thoughts, however, when he heard the details of the homicide Winfield and Mackie were investigating.

Another of Royce's policies required all investigations involving persons of public notoriety to be conducted under his direct supervision. While there were those in his command who felt this policy was inconsistent with the captain's first tenet of leadership, that discrepancy apparently escaped Royce's notice, and thus far, no one had stepped forward to question him on the subject. Most of those who had noticed the inconsistency were pretty sure this rule had more to do with the attention such cases received from the press than with effective police procedure.

Captain Royce listened carefully to Winfield's description of the case, making notes on a pad by the telephone. He then instructed Winfield and Mackie to continue according to the plan the lieutenant had outlined and to have a preliminary report on his desk by eight the next morning. In addition, he wanted daily updates on their progress. They were to call him immediately upon the discovery of any significant lead.

Most importantly, Royce told Winfield, they were to find the killer as quickly as possible. An immediate arrest, the captain said, was absolutely necessary in cases of notoriety.

Winfield asked if Captain Royce planned to release any information to the newspapers, and Royce answered that he would handle that aspect of the case personally, making it clear that the lieutenant was to refer all inquiries from reporters directly to the captain's office.

Winfield replaced the telephone handset in its cradle on the concierge desk and looked at Mackie. C. K. grinned and said, "I presume we have our marching orders."

The lieutenant shook his head in amazement at the conversation he'd just had with Royce and said, "The captain expects an immediate arrest and I don't think he much cares who we arrest, so long as we arrest somebody."

Still grinning, C. K. nodded. "Then I guess we'd best go out and find somebody to arrest."

Leaving the Hollywood Hotel lobby, the detectives headed for the sergeant's Dodge, discussing their next move as they walked. They agreed there were three immediate choices: interviewing the hotel's night manager, talking to Mae White, or contacting someone at the studio Lillian Lawrence had given as her permanent address. Western National would have to be notified of Miss Lawrence's death sooner or later, but Mackie's experience with the William Desmond Taylor case told him later was better. The same, he felt, might be true of interviewing Mae White. This process of elimination narrowed their choices to one. Their next step would be interviewing Richard Boyd, the hotel's night man.

Before turning east on Hollywood Boulevard, they drove through the hotel's automobile parking area and located Lillian Lawrence's olive green Pontiac coupe'. The driver's door was unlocked, and a quick search of the car's interior and trunk revealed nothing more interesting than a month-old issue of Hollywood Magazine.

Driving through Hollywood's business district, nearly deserted on a Sunday morning, Winfield thought about C. K.'s insistence that they put off contacting Lillian Lawrence's studio and talking to Mae White until they had interviewed Richard Boyd. The sergeant obviously had a reason for this and Winfield was curious. He said, "C. K., why didn't you want to talk to someone at Western National right away?"

Mackie glanced over at Winfield and said, "I was wondering when you might get around to asking about that. It's a caution learned from experience, Bobby. Let me give you a little education about how things are done in the motion picture business.

"The American people will soak up every gory detail the newspapers print about what goes on in this town, but they won't pay money to see movie shows made by the same people they just read about. You remember that Fatty Arbuckle thing back in '21? It happened in San Francisco."

"Sure. It was before I joined the department up there, but I read about it in the newspapers. Arbuckle was charged with killing an actress during an orgy at the Saint Francis Hotel. Later, I got to know Griff Kennedy, one of the detectives on the case."

"Right. And do you remember how the trial came out?"

"They acquitted him, didn't they?"

"They not only acquitted Arbuckle, the jury gave him an apology. They said he'd been done a grave injustice. But in the end, none of that mattered where his film career was concerned. Paramount, which was part of Famous Players-Lasky then cancelled Arbuckle's contract, and nobody else in town would touch the guy with a ten-foot pole.

"Then, the next year, William Desmond Taylor was killed. I told you about the shenanigans Famous Players-Lasky pulled that time, destroying and removing evidence. But even that didn't help in the long run. There were two well-known actresses involved in that case, and despite the fact that neither of them was ever charged with Taylor's murder, the scandal destroyed both of their careers, Mary Miles Minter because she was underage and slept with Taylor, and Mable Normand because the newspapers found out during the investigation that she had a drug habit.

"So studios are scared to death of scandals. They'll do everything in their power to protect the public images of their actors, and in this town, they've got a lot of power. You can safely bet your last dollar that as soon as Western National finds out one of their most popular actresses has been murdered, they'll be out beating the bushes to cover up any scandal or even any hint of impropriety associated with Miss Lawrence. That means the more investigating we get done before they find out she's dead, the better our chances of finding the killer."

Winfield nodded and tried to imagine what sort of scandal could possibly be associated with Lillian Lawrence. In her films she always portrayed innocent young heroines, and even though he knew that movies had nothing to do with real life, he just couldn't picture the pretty young girl who was by now laying on a slab at the county morgue involved in anything improper.

A block-and-a-half after Mackie turned north onto Ivar, Winfield spotted number 1822 and the sergeant pulled his Dodge to the curb. The Casa de Paz Apartments were on the west side of the street just south of Franklin Boulevard. It was a two-story structure designed in the popular Spanish mission style. Below its red tile roof most of the building's windows were decorated with cloth awnings and ornate window boxes. The exotically landscaped grounds and an elaborate arched entrance made Winfield wonder how a hotel night man managed to afford such first-class accommodations.

Winfield lowered his initial appraisal of the Casa de Paz, however, when the officers found neither a doorman nor buzzers to announce their arrival. They simply opened the massive, wood and wrought iron front door, crossed the tiled lobby, and climbed the stairs to apartment six.

Because of Dennis Plant's warning that the night manager would probably be sleeping at this hour, Mackie was prepared to apologize for waking the man, but when Boyd—fully dressed and awake—opened the door almost immediately, C. K. knew the apology was unnecessary. Instead, the sergeant simply introduced himself and Winfield.

Years earlier, Mackie had discovered that sometimes a lot could be learned by observing how people reacted to unexpectedly finding a police officer at their door. Richard Boyd, a thin young man with thick wire-rimmed glasses, reacted in a way Mackie had found typical of citizens who had done absolutely nothing to warrant the attention of the police. To these people cops on their threshold meant bad news, perhaps even the death of a loved one.

Boyd's concerned expression was amplified by his thick lenses that made his eyes look twice as large as they really were. The magnified eyes darted back and forth between Mack and Winfield as he apprehensively said, "Yes? What can I do for you?"

Winfield answered the question. "Mister Boyd, there was some trouble at the Hollywood Hotel last night. We would like to ask you a few questions about the incident."

Mackie watched the man relax a little, but just a little. Boyd said, "What kind of trouble? What happened?"

Winfield said, "May we come in Mister Boyd?"

"Oh, sure," he said, holding the door open for them. "Come in, please."

Richard Boyd's small apartment was neat as a pin, exactly as Mackie guessed it would be. The inexpensive coffee table that stood between an equally inexpensive couch and overstuffed chair held only one object, an absolutely spotless glass ashtray. The kitchen sink and drain board Mackie could see through an open door held not a single dirty dish or pan. The place reminded C. K. of the expression his sainted mother often repeated, "A place for everything and everything in its place."

Boyd gestured toward the couch and said, "Please sit down and be comfortable."

As Winfield and Mackie settled into the soft couch, Boyd sat stiffly on the edge of the overstuffed chair and waited for whatever was coming. Mackie felt sorry for the fellow. He was obviously the nervous type to begin with, and not knowing why the police were at his door was driving him crazy. Mackie ended the suspense by saying, "A young woman was murdered in room 187 last night."

Boyd's already wide eyes opened even wider. With astonishment in his voice, he said, "Miss Lawrence?"

Winfield said, "Yes, the victim was Lillian Lawrence. We . . . ."

"Oh, my goodness! Who could possibly want to kill Miss Lawrence?"

Mackie said, "All we know at this point is that Miss Lawrence was shot sometime last night. One of the maids," he consulted his notes and continued, "a Miss Brown, found her early this morning."

"That's dreadful!"

Winfield began the questioning by asking, "Did you happen to see Miss Lawrence around the hotel at all last night?"

Boyd said quickly, "Yes, as a matter of fact, I did."

"Please tell us about that. I mean, when and where you saw her."

With the effort of concentration clearly visible on his face, Richard Boyd thought for a few seconds and then said, "I went into the dining room to see Maurice about a complaint Mister Harrison received concerning one of the waiters, and that's when I noticed Miss Lawrence. It surprised me to see her in the dining room. She almost never ate there."

Winfield asked, "Can you tell us what time that was?"

"It couldn't have been much after six-thirty. I go on duty at six and talking to Maurice was the first item on my list of things to do after a brief meeting with Mister Harrison and checking our occupancy rate with the night clerk. Yes, I'm sure it was just shortly after six-thirty."

Mackie interrupted Winfield's questioning long enough to ask, "Who is Maurice? Somebody who works in the dining room?"

"Yes. I'm sorry. I should have explained that. Maurice DeVoe is our maitre d'hotel."

The sergeant noted this in his book and Winfield asked his next question. "Was Miss Lawrence dining with anyone or was she alone?"

"She was dining with a gentleman. He looked familiar to me. I know I've seen him at the hotel before, probably at some of our banquets, but I don't know who he is. I'm sure Maurice would know him, though. Maurice knows everyone who's anyone in this town."

"Can you describe the man?"

"Certainly. I would place his age around fifty. He is rather short and ah .. . rotund. Oh, and quite bald. He was dressed very well. I think his suit was custom tailored."

"Did you see Miss Lawrence again after that?"

No, but I did pass her room several times later in the evening. We had some difficulty with a loud party in room 183. That's only two doors down from 187."

"Tell us what you can about that incident."

"Well, the front desk received a noise complaint from the guest in 186. That was around eight o' clock. The clerk passed it on to me and I went to check on it.

"I found that the guests in 183 were holding a rather large party in their suite. I suspect there may have even been some drinking going on. At any rate, I knocked on the door and asked them to quiet down. They said they would and I went back to my office.

"After that everything was quiet until a little before two a.m. when the party got loud again. This time we received two complaint calls. I returned immediately to room 183 and told them they would have to break up the party or I would be left with no choice but to call the police. I waited out in the hall until the party guests began to leave a few minutes later. Then I returned to the lobby and found that Dennis Plant had arrived to begin his shift."

Mackie read through his notes and said, "So, Mister Boyd, there was a good deal of noise near Miss Lawrence's room around eight o'clock and again just before two. Is that correct?"

"Yes. Of course, I have no idea how long the racket went on before guests called to complain, but I can't imagine it was too awfully long, especially at two a.m."

Winfield said, "Just one or two more questions, Mister Boyd. Before, you said Miss Lawrence seldom ate in the hotel dining room. Can you tell us anything else about her habits at the hotel?"

"I'm afraid I can't be of much help there. I almost never saw her on my shift."

"Was that because she stayed in her room most of the time or because she was gone from the hotel a lot in the evening?"

"I don't believe Miss Lawrence was much of a night person. The few times I did see her, it was always early and she was usually going in the direction of her room."

"What about visitors? Did anyone ever come to see her?"

Concentration showed on Boyd's face again as he thought about Winfield's question. Finally, he said, "Besides the gentleman I saw her with last night, I can only think of two others. One of them was a woman—a film actress. I think her name is Mae White. I'm embarrassed that I don't know these people better. I just don't often go to movie shows."

"That's quite alright, Mister Boyd. The sergeant here doesn't think much of films, either. Who else have you seen with Miss Lawrence?"

"Another gentleman—a younger man, about my age. He struck me as being rather handsome, but I don't think he is an actor. At least, he doesn't behave like one.

"I only remember seeing him with Miss Lawrence two or three times. My impression was that they had been out together, perhaps to supper, and he was escorting her back to her hotel. He never went any farther than the lobby, though. We try to keep an eye on things like that, even in Hollywood. But he always said goodnight to Miss Lawrence in the lobby."

Mackie looked up from his notebook again and asked, "Did they seem to be good friends. I mean, would you go so far as to say they might have been romantically involved?"

"Oh, I wouldn't know about that! The few times I saw them together he seemed to be a perfect gentleman, and even though I don't know Miss Lawrence very well, I always thought her to be a well-mannered lady—perhaps even a trifle shy. That, I believe, is an unusual quality among film actors."

Mackie smiled and said, "You can say that again! By the way, can you tell us where Mister ah . . . DeVoe lives? We'd like very much to talk with him."

"Gosh, I'm afraid I don't know. I think I remember hearing that he lives out in the San Fernando Valley somewhere. His address would be on file at the hotel, though. Would you like me to call Dennis and get it for you?"

Mackie said, "Yes. We would appreciate that very much. And his telephone number, if he has one."

The telephone in Boyd's apartment sat on a small shelf near the kitchen table. Boyd removed a pencil and notepad from a drawer and sat at the table to call Dennis Plant. After a brief conversation, Boyd carefully tore off the top sheet of the notepad. Then he returned the pad and pencil to their drawer and came back into the living room. He said, "Maurice lives in Sepulveda at 10314 Parthenia."

Mackie asked, "Does he have a telephone?"

"Yes," Boyd said as he handed the page from his notepad to Mackie. "I've written it down here."

"Do you mind if I use your telephone? I'll ask the operator to call back with the long distance charges so we can reimburse you for the call."

"Oh, of course. The telephone is right there in the kitchen. You can sit at the table if you like."

As Mackie placed the call to Sepulveda, Winfield said, "Mister Boyd, do you have a telephone directory for Hollywood?"

"Yes. I'll get it for you."

Winfield found no listing for Mae White, but was jotting down the address and telephone number of Western National Studios when Mackie came back and said, "There was no answer at Mister DeVoe's home. I'll try again later, but in case I miss him, what time does he start work at the hotel?"

Boyd said, "Let me think. This is Sunday, so Maurice will be getting ready to open the dining room for supper at five. He should be there by four this afternoon at the latest."

With no further questions to ask, Winfield and Mackie cautioned Richard Boyd to say no more than necessary to reporters about Lillian Lawrence's death and thanked him for his cooperation. Minutes later, they climbed into Mackie's Dodge. C. K. sat behind the wheel thinking for a minute and then said, "I don't guess we can put it off any longer. I guess it's time to go find Bromfeld."

Winfield asked, "Who the heck is Broomfield?"

C. K. said, "It's pronounced BRUM-FELD, and he is the man behind the movies at Western National."

Winfield glanced over at Mackie and said, "You know, C. K., for a fellow who never goes to the picture shows, you sure know a lot about them."

"It's part of the job, Bobby. Over the years I've spent a lot of time in this town. I live here, I grew up here, and I walked a beat here. And now that I'm working out of Homicide Division, whenever somebody gets killed out here, Royce calls good old Sergeant Mackie. So for me, knowing who's who in Hollywood is just like a carpenter knowing which tool to use when he needs to hammer a nail or cut a board."

"I don't suppose you happen to have Mister Bromfeld's address stored away in your toolbox?"

"Nope, I'm afraid not. If I had to guess, I would say he probably lives out toward Los Feliz somewhere, but we don't have to guess. I'm sure there will be a guard on duty at the studio who can put us in touch with Mister L. A. Bromfeld."

"We could go back to Boyd's and look Bromfeld up in the telephone directory. It might save some time."

Mackie shook his head. "Bromfeld won't be listed. People like Bromfeld guard their privacy."

Winfield nodded and said, "I guess they do. I tried to look up Mae White's number, but no luck. You have any idea where she lives?"

C. K. kicked the starter, and as the Dodge's engine turned over, he said, "Afraid I can't answer that one, either."

"Then I gather Miss White isn't one of those you've escorted home to sober up."

Mackie completed a U-turn to head south on Ivar, and with a sidelong glance at Winfield, he said, "No, Laddie, I've never had that pleasure."

At Hollywood Boulevard Mackie turned right, and a block later, he turned left onto Cahuenga. They passed the stationhouse and continued on to Santa Monica Boulevard where Mackie made another right turn. In the middle of the block between Cahuenga and Cole, the sergeant pulled up outside a pair of massive iron gates in a long, high wall that ran down the right side of the street. Above the gates a large arched sign informed Winfield they had arrived at Western National Films.

Mackie honked his horn twice, and while they waited for someone to appear, Winfield studied the huge posters attached to the wall on either side of the gate. In large blue letters against a yellow background, the poster on the left said, "See the Fabulous MAE WHITE in Fame and Fortune." A color rendering set in an outlined oval below the headline showed Miss White down to her suggestively bare shoulders. With her head turned slightly to one side, the dark-haired beauty stared seductively at passersby, a vamp's pout on her Cupid bow lips.

To the right of the gate, another poster proclaimed, "Coming Soon! LILLIAN LAWRENCE in The Big Sister" in large white letters set against a red background. The color drawing below this headline was set in an elaborate rectangular frame. It showed Miss Lawrence with her blonde hair bobbed, mischievously beaming up at an older, gray-haired man who frowned disapprovingly back at her. Winfield wondered if enough of the film had already been made so it could be finished without its leading lady.

C. K. had just honked again when a large man in a dark blue guard's uniform limped into view on the other side of the gate. He yelled, "Keep your shirt on, I'm coming!"

Mackie jumped down from his seat and approached the gate. Following the sergeant, Winfield heard C. K. say, "Hello, Jake, you old war horse! How have you been?"

The guard's face, deeply line and fringed with white hair beneath his cap, peered nearsightedly through the gate. Then he recognized Mackie and said, "Well, as I live and breathe! C. K.! Where the devil did you come from?"

As the two men shook hands enthusiastically through the iron bars, Winfield wondered if there was anybody in Hollywood C. K. didn't know. Then Mackie said, "Jake, I want you to meet Detective Lieutenant Bobby Winfield."

Jake stuck a large paw through the gate to shake with Winfield, and Mackie continued his introduction. "Bobby, this is Jake Blore, about the most ornery cop who ever wore a department shield."

Blore laughed heartily and retorted, "Don't you believe it, son. I couldn't never hold a candle to your partner here when it came to orneriness."

Then in a more serious tone, C. K. asked, "How you holdin' up, Jake?"

"Oh, I can't complain. They treat me alright around here, but it ain't the same as bein' on the force."

"Yeah, I know how it is, but the department's changing, too. Things are a far cry from the way they were in the old days. I think you got out at the right time."

Jake snorted and said, "As if I had any say about leavin'. C. K., you know as well as me that I could still do my job, even with this slug in my hip. They didn't have no right pensionin' me out the way they done. Royce saw a chance to get rid of another straight cop, that's all. I'm surprised he ain't found a way to toss you to the curb by now."

Looking Blore square in the eye, C. K. gestured his head toward Winfield and changed the subject, saying, "Jake, I need a favor."

"Sure, C. K., you name it."

"We need to find Bromfeld. You got his home address?"

Jake's eyes narrowed a little and he said, "Yeah, I got it, but whatcha need to see Bromfeld about?"

C. K. glanced around to be sure nobody was within earshot and said, "Somebody put a bullet in Lillian Lawrence's brain last night. We need to notify Bromfeld and ask him some questions."

Blore's thick gray eyebrows rose in surprise and he said, "Well, I guess you do! Any suspects yet?"

"At his point everybody's a suspect." Then Mackie grinned and added, "Come to think of it, where the hell were you last night?"

Blore laughed and said, "Hell, I was out all night dancin' at the Plaza. Had me a blonde on each arm!"

Still grinning, C. K. said, "I just bet you were. Probably didn't get in 'till dawn, either."

The guard pulled a notebook similar to Mackie's out of the breast pocket of his uniform jacket and found his boss's address. He said, "Bromfeld lives at 23 De Mille Drive. You know where that is, up off Los Feliz?"

"Sure. Right near Chaplin's old place."

"That's it. Well, I'd better get to makin' my rounds. This damned place is a maze. Fella could get lost for weeks back there if he didn't know his way around. Hey, it was great seein' you again, C. K. Why don't you come 'round over to my place some night. Bring the lieutenant here with you and we'll tell him about how it was in the good old days."

C. K. shook Blore's hand through the iron bars again and said, "Count on it, Jake. Now you take good care of yourself."

FIVE

Los Feliz Boulevard began in East Hollywood and ran northeast along the edge of the Hollywood Hills eventually crossing the Los Angeles River into Glendale. Before reaching the river, though, Los Feliz skirted the southern boundary of three thousand hilly, wilderness acres known as Griffith Park.

A scattering of substantial-looking homes and an occasional citrus orchard faced the park on the south side of Los Feliz. At widespread intervals between the homes and orchards, a few narrow, tree-lined residential streets gradually wound their way southward from Los Feliz to Franklin Boulevard. One of these was identified by a small street sign that said, "De Mille Drive."

Noticing the sign as Mackie swung the Dodge onto De Mille, Winfield was reminded of a question that occurred to him when Jake Blore had gave them Bromfeld's address. He turned to C. K. and asked, "This street wasn't named for Cecil B. De Mille, the film director, was it?"

"The very same one. In fact, that's the top of his house you see sticking up through the trees over there."

Winfield whistled his appreciation of the De Mille home. Even though he could see little more than the two-story mansion's red tile roof, there was no doubt about its size. The place was huge. He said, "Makes you wonder if we aren't in the wrong business, doesn't it?"

Mackie shook his head. "No, Bobby, not even for a minute."

"Well, I don't remember seeing a street named 'Mackie' around town."

"And the good Lord willin', you never will, either. But if flashy is what you like, you're in the right neighborhood. That little shanty there next to De Mille's place used to belong to Charlie Chaplin."

Winfield looked through the trees at another mansion, a little smaller and less ostentatious than its neighbor, but still nothing to sneeze at. It was, he estimated, roughly equal in size and amenities to the home in which he'd grown up. The Winfield family home was located in an area of San Francisco now known as Sea Cliff. It was an environment not unlike this conclave except it overlooked the wide mouth of San Francisco Bay and the Marin

Headlands beyond. Another difference, he suspected, was that the money here seemed to be new wealth, whereas the Winfield's station in life was among the old money families in the City.

Even though Lieutenant Winfield left all that behind when he set out to seek his own way in the world, Mackie's attitude toward the wealthy still left him feeling a little uneasy. It brought to mind the snobbery he'd experienced after word that the rookie was a "blue blood" spread around the department in San Francisco. When they got to know him a little, the disdain of his fellow officers became something more like good-natured kidding, but even this acceptance merely bridged the gap between them, not filled it.

Now Winfield hoped he was just being overly sensitive and that C. K.'s disregard for the rich didn't include him, especially since he wasn't rich. The lieutenant and his family's fortune hadn't been on speaking terms for some time, which suited him just fine.

C. K. interrupted these thoughts when he said, "I guess this must be what we're looking for," and turned left between two stone gateposts onto a long, curving drive that eventually ended at a garage building Winfield estimated would easily accommodate four large automobiles. Before reaching the garage, Mackie pulled up next to a broad concrete stairway which ascended twenty feet of hillside to the Bromfeld mansion.

The house, somewhat smaller than the De Mille home, consisted of a long, narrow two-story center section onto which a pair of additional two-story wings had been attached to form a shallow Y. The concrete steps led Mackie and Winfield into the open end of the Y. They passed through an enormous and ornate pillared entryway and stopped before a pair of massive hand-carved oak doors. Winfield glanced at his wristwatch as C. K. reached up and banged one of the two lion-headed brass door knockers.

It was, the lieutenant noted, exactly thirty-five minutes past the hour of noon when a gray-haired man dressed in what Winfield recognized as butler's livery answered their knock. The butler glanced at Mackie's uniform, then gazed haughtily at Winfield and simply said, "Yes?"

The butler's lofty manner wilted somewhat at the authoritative tone in Winfield's voice which clearly indicated he was quite used to dealing with servants. "I am Detective Lieutenant Robert Winfield of the Los Angeles Police Department. Detective Sergeant Mackie and I will see Mister Bromfeld."

"Mister Bromfeld is enjoying his lunch at the moment. Perhaps it would be more appropriate for you to make an appointment through his office to speak with him tomorrow."

With that, the butler began to swing the heavy door shut, but he stopped when Winfield said nonchalantly, "By then Mister Bromfeld will have read about the subject of our business in the newspapers and you will be looking for a new position."

The manservant studied Winfield's impassive expression for a long moment while he reevaluated the situation. Deciding on the side of discretion, he swung the door open wide and stepped back saying, "Kindly step into the foyer. I will ask Mister Bromfeld if he will see you."

While they stood waiting on the marble floor of an octagonal entry area in which most of the walls were decorated with tall guilt-framed mirrors, C. K. arched an eyebrow at Winfield and said, "You seem quite adept at handling the hired help. I'm impressed."

Glancing at their reflection in one of the mirrors, Winfield smiled and said, "Butlers are just stuffed-shirt jackasses. After you give them a good lick with a stiff board to get their attention, they usually behave themselves."

With an amused tone in his voice, C. K. said, "I see."

After a few minutes, the butler returned saying, "Mister Bromfeld requests that you join him on the terrace. Please walk this way."

They followed him into a pretentious room Winfield decided must be Bromfeld's idea of a library and then through a pair of French doors opening out onto a covered patio overlooking the De Mille mansion across the road. A short, fat bald man in his fifties sat opposite a slender woman of about the same age at a circular glass-topped table near the view side of the terrace.

The man stood as Winfield and Mackie approached the table. He was wearing, Winfield observed, a rather garish green satin smoking jacket over gray slacks. The woman, in a loose-fitting white silk blouse and gray skirt, remained seated. The butler busied himself with removing empty plates and other luncheon debris.

The first thing C. K. noticed was that Bromfeld fit Dick Boyd's description of Lillian Lawrence's Saturday night dinner companion perfectly. This dawned on Winfield a moment later. Then both officers observed that the cigar Bromfeld held in his left hand bore the same scarlet and gold band as the butt they found in room 187 at the Hollywood Hotel that morning.

Winfield said, "Good afternoon, Mister Bromfeld. This is Detective Sergeant Mackie and I am Detective Lieutenant Winfield. We are with the Los Angeles Police Department Homicide Division."

The lieutenant did not expect Bromfeld to extend his hand in an offer to shake and he didn't. He didn't offer them a seat, either. Instead, the man puffed his cigar, and moving his thick lips around it, said gruffly, "My man says you have something important to say. Say it."

Winfield had considered several ways to tell Bromfeld that one of his biggest box office attractions was dead. He decided on the one that most closely fit the man's attitude. He looked Bromfeld directly in his cold, brown eyes and said, "Lillian Lawrence was shot to death last night."

Bromfeld's reaction to the news was startling. He stood stock still for a moment, his eyes darting back and forth between Winfield and Mackie. Then his reddish complexion turned white as paper and he stumbled backward into his seat at the table. The woven wicker chair made a scraping sound on the tiled floor as it slid a few inches under the impact of Bromfeld's weight.

At the same time, both of the woman's hands went to her cheeks and she gasped, "Oh, no!"

Then Bromfeld shook his head and with his Polish accent thicker than before, said, "This cannot be so. We had dinner together only last night. You are mistaken!"

Winfield replied, "There's no doubt about it, Mister Bromfeld. The victim is Lillian Lawrence."

"But how? Where did this happen?"

"All we know so far is that she was found in her hotel room early this morning with a bullet in her brain."

The woman shivered and then sat staring at Winfield in stunned silence. The knuckles of both hands were white from gripping the red linen napkin in her lap. Bromfeld was still shaking his head and mumbling, "This is awful. Terrible! Who could be doing such a thing? Why?"

Winfield said, "Those are the same questions we're trying to answer, Mister Bromfeld. We hope that you can help us with a little information."

Bromfeld raised both hands as if to ward off Winfield's questions and said, "Not now. Please. This is such a terrible shock. Lillian was like my own daughter. I will answer your questions tomorrow."

"I'm afraid we can't wait that long, Mister Bromfeld. If we're going to catch Miss Lawrence's killer, we need answers right now."

Bromfeld groaned and said, "Okay, okay. What is it that you must know so urgently?"

Mackie already had his notebook out, and when Winfield nodded to him, the sergeant asked, "When did you last see Miss Lawrence?"

Without hesitation, Bromfeld said, "It was only last night. We were having dinner together."

"Where and when was that?"

"We met at the Hollywood Hotel where she was staying and ate in the dining room. I am getting there at around six-thirty and Lillian, she is already waiting for me in the lobby. We had a reservation, so we are sitting at our table right away."

"Was anyone with you or were you and Miss Lawrence alone?"

"No. There was just the two of us."

Jotting this in his notebook, Mackie asked, "What sort of mood was she in? Was she happy? Sad?"

"She was being happy. Very happy! We met to discuss her future at Western National. Lillian is saying she will stay with the studio. We are both very happy."

Glancing up at Bromfeld, Mackie said, "Isn't that something you would normally discuss in your office?"

"Yes. We had already been discussing at the studio. For a while Miss Lawrence is wanting out of her contract. I suggest we meet for dinner. For, you know, a change of atmosphere."

"I see," Mackie said, "Then she decided to stay. Why did she want to leave? Did she have a better offer from another studio?"

Bromfeld held his cigar half a foot from his face, studied it for a moment, and then said disdainfully, "Miss Lawrence was in love. Her head was filled with silly ideas about giving up her career in acting for to get married and have babies. But I knew when she had time to think about it, that she would be forgetting all of that nonsense."

"Alright. What time did you finish dinner?"

"I am not sure. Ruth . . . I'm sorry, gentlemen. I am so upset I am forgetting to introduce my wife. Ruth, what time was I getting home last night?"

Ruth Bromfeld frowned and twisted the red napkin in her hands while she thought about her husband's question. Then, as if suddenly remembering, she said brightly, "It was quarter past eight! I am sure because I was speaking to Dorothy Reid on the telephone and I could hear her clock chiming the quarter hour over the line at the same time our clock in the library chimed. We laughed about how close our clocks were, and I remember looking and seeing that it was quarter past eight. And just after that is when I heard L. A. come in the front door."

Bromfeld nodded and said to Mackie, "It would be taking me maybe half an hour to get my automobile from the parking place and to be driving home from the hotel. I must have left the dining room at quarter to eight."

Mackie wrote this down and asked, "Did you go straight from the dining room to your car or did you escort Miss Lawrence to her room first?"

Bromfeld stared at Mackie for a moment as though trying to decide if there was any hint at impropriety in the sergeant's question. Finally he said, "No. She was terribly tired, I think. Lillian left the table first. Then I am paying the bill and going to my car."

"Did you recognize anyone else at the hotel while you were there?"

"Oh, yes. There were several people of my acquaintance there last night."

"Did you speak with any of them?"

"Bromfeld hesitated a moment before saying, "Only one person. When I am coming out into the automobile parking area, I am seeing Miss Mae White. She is one of our players, so I am speaking with her for a while, maybe for five minutes."

Mackie looked up from his book again and said, "Did Miss White say why she was there at the hotel? Was she there to see Miss Lawrence?"

Bromfeld nodded and said, "I am not recalling if Mae is actually saying she was visiting Lillian, but I am sure that is why she was coming there. The two ladies, they were very close friends."

"You said Miss Lawrence was in love. Do you know the man she wanted to marry?"

Irritation was again evident in Bromfeld's voice when he answered, "Yes. His name is Bell, Tom Bell. He is a cowboy."

Mackie looked puzzled and said, "A cowboy? You mean he is a western actor?"

"No, no. He is a real cowboy. He is owning a ranch over on the coast—somewhere around Ventura, I am thinking. I don't know exactly where. Listen, officers, I have told you everything I know about this. You should now get busy and find out who is killing our lovely Lillian."

Winfield responded to this, saying, "That's what we're doing, Mister Bromfeld. Do you know the whereabouts of Miss Lawrence's family?"

Bromfeld shook his head and said, "There is no family that I am knowing about. Her mother has died several years ago."

Mackie was writing again, and Winfield asked, "What about her father?"

Bromfeld's earlier irritation turned to full-blown anger as he said, "Lillian's father was a bum! A drunk and a bum. He was always squandering away the money she is making in the gambling joints. They killed him and stole Lillian's money from him. The man was no good, and he got what he was deserving!"

Mackie asked, "How long ago was that?"

"It was only recently. Maybe two, three months ago."

Mackie noted this in his book and asked, "What was her father's name?"

"Harry Lee. Lee was being Lillian's real name, but we are choosing Lawrence for her film name. It is having more of an all-American sound."

Then, as if this reminded him of his studio's financial stake in Lillian Lawrence, Bromfeld said, "Officers, whoever has done this to Lillian is costing Western National Films a great deal of money. You cannot possibly be knowing how much. You must find her killer."

Winfield said, "Tell me, Mister Bromfeld, do you own a gun?"

Bromfeld's head jerked around from Mackie to Winfield. He glared at the lieutenant through narrowed eyes, and the pitch of his voice went up in proportion to his anger as he said, "What kind of stupid question is that to be asking? No, I am not owning any guns! What are you thinking? That I am killing Lillian? That I am killing that lovely girl who is like my very own daughter? Is this how you police are solving crimes?"

Quickly, Mackie said, "No, Mister Bromfeld. But it is our job to be thorough. If we didn't ask these questions of everyone involved, we might miss something important—a clue that might lead us to the killer more quickly."

The crimson coloring that spread over Bromfeld's face began to subside, and he leaned back in his chair, apparently somewhat placated by Mackie's explanation. Then Winfield asked, "Do you have any idea who might have killed Miss Lawrence? Can you think of anyone she argued with or someone who would benefit from her death?"

Bromfeld was still glaring at Winfield, but with less anger now. He said, "There is no one like that. Everyone is loving Lillian. She is the darling of the studio. There is nobody who would be wanting to kill her."

"Apparently there was at least one person who did. We're going to need your cooperation with this investigation, Mister Bromfeld. We'll want to talk to some of the people at your studio and perhaps look into any files or records you may have concerning Miss Lawrence."

Bromfeld waved his hand through the air in a gesture of dismissal and said, "Of course. Whatever you are needing. My secretary is Miss Shipman. I will tell her to be giving to you her full cooperation."

Mackie said, "One more thing, Mister Bromfeld. We would like to talk to Mae White since she may have been the last person to see Miss Lawrence alive. Do you know where she lives?"

Bromfeld frowned at that thought, and then said, "You know the Garden Court Apartments on Hollywood Boulevard?"

Mackie nodded and Bromfeld continued, "She is living there. Ruth, do you remember the number?"

Bromfeld's wife, apparently lost in her own thoughts about the tragedy of Lillian Lawrence's death, started at the sound of her name. Nervously, she looked up at her husband and said, "I'm sorry. What did you say, L. A.?"

Irritated, Bromfeld said, "Mae White's apartment number at the Garden Court, do you remember it?"

"No. It's . . . it's on the fourth floor. On the street side, but I don't . . .," her voice trailed off as though she knew her husband wasn't interested in anything else she might have to say.

He wasn't. Bromfeld had already turned back to Winfield and was saying, "There. You are now knowing everything I know. Please go and find this cold-blooded assassin who has taken our Lillian from us."

The butler, who was absent from the terrace during most of the conversation, suddenly reappeared through the French doors to escort Winfield and Mackie back to the octagonal foyer. He said only a terse, "Good day, gentlemen," as he closed the door behind them.

Mackie turned his Dodge around in Bromfeld's wide drive, and Winfield looked up at the terrace. He could see Ruth Bromfeld leaning across the table toward her husband. She seemed to be saying something important, but he was staring down at them, apparently paying no attention to his wife's words.

Turning right on De Mille Drive, C. K. said, "L. A. Bromfeld is quite a character, wouldn't you say?"

"I would, indeed. Of course you noticed the cigar he was smoking. Unless those El Panteras are more common than I think, it would seem he wasn't quite honest with us about going to Lillian Lawrence's room last night."

C. K. nodded, adding, "Yes, that is interesting, especially considering the fact that Mister Bromfeld seems to be left-handed. We need to find out how common those cigars really are. If they turn out to be a rare item, it might be even more interesting to ask him how one happened to end up in that hotel room."

Mackie turned left on Los Feliz heading back toward Hollywood and said, "There's something else bothering me about Bromfeld's story. He said they went into the dining room around six-thirty and left about quarter to eight. That's not much time for a dinner in the Dining Room of the Stars, especially if they were talking business."

"True, but he said Miss Lawrence was tired and left before he did. Maybe she didn't eat—just told him her decision to stay at the studio and left."

"Could be," Mackie said thoughtfully, "But it doesn't sound like the way a 'very happy' person acts, now does it? And remember what Missus Ackerman said about seeing Lillian crying while she was trying to unlock her door. None of that fits with Bromfeld's story."

Sounding surprised, Winfield asked, "You sound like you might be starting to suspect Bromfeld as our killer."

"I don't know, Bobby. Mister L. A. Bromfeld certainly qualifies as a suspect. He knew the victim, he was there, so he had the opportunity. The Maitre d' might be able to tell us more about that part."

"Even so, what motive could the head of Western National Films have for killing one of his most important actresses? Like he said, her death will cost the studio a fortune."

"That, Laddie, is one of the things we are paid to find out. Speaking of that, where are we headed? You want to stop for some lunch, or go on to see Mae White?"

Winfield looked at his watch and said, "It's just about one-thirty. Are you starving?"

"Not yet."

"Then let's go on and see Mae White. Where is this apartment house she lives in?"

"The Garden Court Apartments? Down on Hollywood Boulevard a couple of blocks west of the hotel, but I wouldn't call it an 'apartment house,' though."

"Why not? I thought Bromfeld said she lived in an apartment."

C. K. smiled and said, "Well, I suppose technically the Garden Court is an apartment house, but it's a far sight snazzier than most."

"How so?"

"For one thing, it's four stories high and looks more like a hotel than anything else. It's strictly the Ritz—fancy rugs, expensive furniture, and a grand piano in every apartment, that sort of thing. And the only folks who can afford to live there are the upper crust of the film business, like Mack Sennett, Lillian Gish, Mae Murray . . . they all seem to wind up there sooner or later."

As C. K. turned right onto Hollywood Boulevard, Winfield was thinking about the kind of people who were the upper crust of the motion picture business. He didn't really know any of them, but if L. A. Bromfeld was typical, he wasn't missing much. Somehow, though, he couldn't imagine Mae White and Lillian Lawrence coming from the same mold as Bromfeld. If fact, he was actually looking forward to making Miss White's acquaintance.

SIX

Winfield wasn't entirely sure of the correct architectural nomenclature to characterize the Garden Court Apartments, but Italian Renaissance seemed to come the closest. C. K. simply called the place gaudy and that fit as well as anything.

The massive four-story structure sat in the middle of a mostly residential block and fit in with its neighbors like a flapper at a temperance meeting. U-shaped with its open end facing Hollywood Boulevard, the building sat well back from the street behind a meticulously groomed lawn that was bordered here and there by spindly Italian cypress trees.

The open area between the two wings of the building that were perpendicular to the street was taken up by a raised forecourt behind an ornate curved railing. Entrance to the Garden Court Apartments was gained through a set of double doors at the rear of the forecourt. A stack of three massive and elaborately decorated balconies climbed the wall above the doors. The lowest of these was supported by four Doric columns and formed a portico over the entrance.

Inside, the lobby was furnished in the deco style with a couch and overstuffed chairs assembled around a large coffee table in front of a mock fireplace of white brick. A good quality oriental carpet and what Winfield thought looked remarkably like authentic Tiffany lamps completed the room's décor. The afternoon sun, filtered through filmy curtains, endowed the room with a peaceful, almost museum-like quality.

Next to the entrance a young woman with red hair of a shade that Winfield thought probably looked better on Clara Bow sat behind a reception counter. Only one dim amber light glowed on the complex telephone switchboard to her right. As the officers approached she laid down her copy of Saturday Night magazine and said in a well-rehearsed and slightly nasal tone, "Welcome to the Garden Court Apartments. May I assist you?"

Mackie said, "We're with the Los Angeles Police Department and we're here to see Mae White. Is she in?"

"I don't know, but I will be happy find out for you."

The receptionist turned to her switchboard and, picking up an earpiece, plugged a line into one of the many jacks. The board buzzed softly as she pushed a small lever. When a second amber light blinked on, the young woman leaned forward and spoke into a mouthpiece. Mackie and Winfield heard her say, "There are two gentlemen from the police down here at the reception desk. They want to see Miss White."

More than a minute passed before she said, "Okay, I'll send them right up."

Then the receptionist unplugged the line and turned to Mackie, saying, "Miss White is in. Her apartment is on the fourth floor, number 412. The elevator is down that hall."

Mackie and Winfield walked down the corridor she had indicated and found the elevator door open. As they stepped into the small wood and polished brass enclosure, an elderly Negro man in a brown uniform jumped up from his fold-down seat and asked, "What floor please, gentlemen?"

Winfield told him they wanted the fourth. The operator slid the doors shut with practiced skill and pulled his lift lever to the up position. They all watched a pointer mounted on the control panel slowly move around to the number four. When it finally got there, the operator proudly demonstrated his skill again by aligning the elevator within a quarter-inch of the fourth floor opening on the first try, without resorting to back and forth adjustments typically experienced in hotel elevators. Mackie followed Winfield into a carpeted hallway that was so quiet the sound of the elevator doors sliding closed behind them seemed unusually loud.

They were in a corridor that spanned the width of the building. At either end it met another hallway at right angles. Remembering that Ruth Bromfeld said Mae White's apartment overlooked Hollywood Boulevard, Winfield flipped a mental coin and followed the right-hand corridor toward the front of the building. It turned out to be a lucky guess. The hallway ended at a door on which an engraved brass plate bore the number 412.

A thin, stern-faced Negro woman who wore a white apron over her black uniform dress opened the door and invited them to take seats in the living room—Miss White would only be a moment or two. Then she quietly disappeared down a hallway leading to another part of the apartment.

While they waited, Winfield took advantage of the opportunity to survey the domain one of America's sweethearts called home. Her quarters were quite large, occupying the entire width of the Garden Court Apartments' east wing. The long, narrow living room in which he and C. K. sat ran through the center of the apartment, ending at a pair of arched French doors opening onto a small balcony overlooking Hollywood Boulevard.

A fine oriental carpet, similar to the one in the lobby, covered the hardwood floor to within a foot or so of the walls. The couch on which he and C. K. were sitting, like the other furnishings in the room, was deco in style and various shades of pale blue in color. From this comfortable vantage point, the intensely symmetrical painting of a woman encircled by something like radiating peacock plumes facing them from the long west wall looked enough like the work of Erte' to be the real thing.

To the left of the painting a mahogany-finished baby grand piano stood in a corner near the French doors. The piano's top was raised, and several pieces of sheet music lay on its music stand. Among them, Winfield recognized Yes Sir! That's My Baby and Don't Bring Lulu. These were two of the songs he most often heard through the floor of his room above the parlor in which Missus Haney's Victrola was enjoyed by her boarders.

While his own musical tastes ran more toward the traditional jazz of Bix Beiderbecke and Bessie Smith, Winfield didn't mind popular jazz music and wondered if Mae White actually played the piano or if the instrument was just here, along with its collection of sheet music, as part of the décor.

At the sound of a door closing somewhere behind them, both officers turned to watch Mae White enter the room. Winfield recognized her immediately, but he was struck by how different she looked in person. The Mae White he'd seen in motion pictures was a cute pixie sort of girl while this woman was endowed with a beauty that nearly took his breath away.

Mackie's impression of Mae White was slightly more objective. He gauged her height at about five-and-a-half feet and her weight to be average, around one-thirty-five. She appeared to be somewhere in her mid-twenties and wore her dark brown hair short in a fashionable marcelled style.

Winfield noted that, on the screen her face seemed much more pale. This Mae White had suntanned skin that almost glowed in the soft afternoon light, providing a radiant setting for her large, clear blue eyes. He also noticed that she looked quite trim in a navy blue pleated skirt that reached a point just below her knees, revealing shapely calves and ankles clad in dark hose. Above the skirt Miss White wore a loose, but slightly clinging cream-colored blouse which hinted at a shape that appeared somewhat less remarkable on the screen of San Francisco's Golden Gate Theater.

Both Mackie and Winfield were standing now, and after clearing his throat to make sure he still had a voice, the lieutenant said, "Good afternoon, Miss White. Ah, this is Detective Sergeant Mackie and I'm Bob Winfield. We're with the Los Angeles Police Department Homicide Division."

The fact that he introduced himself as Bob, rather than Detective Lieutenant did not escape C. K.'s notice. Apparently his young partner was rather smitten by Miss Mae White.

When she spoke, Mae White's voice—which, of course, Winfield had never heard—was soft and resonant. She said, "Please sit down, gentlemen." Then, with a hint of anxiety coloring her tone, she added, "What can I do for you?"

The officers returned to their seats on the couch, and Miss White sat in an armchair near Winfield's end of the couch. She crossed her legs and leaned forward slightly in apparent anticipation of learning why the police were visiting her on this Sunday afternoon.

It was at that point Winfield realized Mae White didn't yet know about the death of her close friend. He thought L. A. Bromfeld might have called to break the news, but she seemed not to have any idea of why he and Mackie were there. That left to him the unenviable task of telling her that Lillian Lawrence was dead. He said tentatively, "Miss White, are you aware that there has been some trouble involving Lillian Lawrence?"

She frowned and cocked her head to one side before saying, "Trouble? What do you mean? Has something happened to Lilly?"

Winfield took a deep breath and said, "I'm afraid so, Miss White. Miss Lawrence is dead."

He didn't know any kinder way to say it, but the shock on Mae White's face made him wish he'd been able to think of one. With tears already forming in her eyes, she said, "My God! What's happened?"

The lieutenant took another deep breath and said, "She was shot last night in her hotel room. A maid found her body this morning."

Tears were streaming down Mae White's face now and she shook her head in disbelief. "Oh God! Poor Lilly!"

Both Winfield and Mackie felt awkward and helpless as they watched America's favorite film actress surrender to her grief. Mackie said, "Can we get you anything, a glass of water or something?"

"No," she sobbed, "Just excuse me for a minute, please."

Then she ran from the room, her thin hands wiping the tears from her eyes so she could see her way. The detectives watched her disappear through a door that might have led to a bedroom or bath.

Both men stood as she ran past them. Now Mackie sat down again and Winfield walked to the French doors. He stared down at a tall man walking his eager German shepherd along Hollywood Boulevard. Behind him, C. K. said, "Sometimes it's like that, Bobby. You told her as easy as you could, but there just isn't any good way to break news like that."

"Yeah, I know," Winfield said, turning to face Mackie. "I've had to do it before. It's never easy and it's even worse when you have to tell a wife about a dead husband or the other way around."

C. K. nodded and the lieutenant sighed, "At least it's safe to say Miss White isn't our killer."

Mackie nodded again, but he wasn't quite as sure about Mae White's innocence as his lieutenant. She was, after all, an actress—a dramatic actress to whom portraying grief and crying on cue were all part of a day's work. He had no reason to suspect the woman, but neither was he willing to consider her above suspicion on the strength of what might simply have been a very good performance. In her favor, however, he noticed that she opened the door through which she had just disappeared with her right hand.

Returning to the couch, Winfield said, "I'm a little surprised Bromfeld didn't call her. He knew we were coming here. I would have expected him to call her as soon as we left if for no other reason, than to warn her against saying anything that might lead to a scandal involving the studio."

C. K. nodded and said, "That surprised me a little, too. Apparently he didn't, though. That might mean he isn't concerned about a scandal or maybe he was too busy calling someone else."

When Mae White returned to the living room a few minutes later, her large blue eyes were circled in red and still moist with tears. Clutching an embroidered hanky in her right hand, she sat in the armchair again and said, "I'm sorry, officers. This is just such a shock. I still can't believe it. I can't imagine Lilly dead. She was so . . . alive and . . . ."

Her voice trailed off into the silence of the room, and after a moment, Mackie removed the notebook from his breast pocked and said, "Miss White, I know this is a bad time for questions, but we're trying to find out who did this, and the faster we gather information, the sooner we're likely to find Miss Lawrence's killer."

Mae White wiped at her eyes and nodded. She said quietly, "I'll be glad to help in any way I can. What would you like to know?"

Mackie opened his book, and jotting a new page heading that would identify the following notes as resulting from their interview with Mae White, he said, "Miss White, when did you last see Lillian Lawrence?"

She thought for a moment and answered, "Well, the last time I actually saw her was Friday. We had lunch together. But I talked to her on the telephone early last night."

Mackie looked up. "What time was that? I mean that you spoke to her on the telephone?"

"It was around six. She was having dinner with L. A.—Mister Bromfeld—at six-thirty, and I thought Lilly might like some company after she met with him. L. A. can be a real . . . well, he can be upsetting. So, with Tom out of town . . . oh, my God! Has anyone called Tom Bell? Does he know Lilly is . . . ."

Winfield said, "Miss Lawrence's beau? No, we haven't called him. In fact, we didn't even know about him until we talked to Mister Bromfeld an hour ago, but Bromfeld didn't know where Mister Bell lives or how to get in touch with him. Do you know where we can reach him?"

"Oh, yes. I have his address and telephone number. I can give you all that, but Tom was away this weekend. He may not be back yet." She thought for a moment and added, "Is it okay if I call him and break the news?"

Winfield looked at Mackie, who nodded. Then the lieutenant said, "Sure, you can call him when we're through here. We'll wait and talk to him later."

Mae White nodded gratefully and said, "Thank you. I think it would be better for him to hear it from me than from a stranger."

Mackie was about to pick up his questioning again when Miss White, looking at Winfield, smiled thinly and said, "You know, you fellows are alright. It must be terribly difficult telling people about somebody dying, especially when they come all apart like I did. I'm sorry, Mister Winfield. I hope I didn't make it too hard on you."

Winfield was amazed. This famous, attractive woman was actually apologizing for making things rough on him. He said, "You didn't make it too hard. I'm just sorry we had to bring you bad news. I understand you were quite close to Miss Lawrence."

She nodded, and dabbing at her eyes, said, "I will miss Lilly a great deal. But you were marvelous under the circumstances. I really do appreciate your kindness."

The lieutenant was about to respond when he caught a glimpse of the impatience on C. K.'s face. The sergeant was obviously anxious to get back to his question, so Winfield simply nodded and Mackie jumped in before they started in all over again. He said quickly, "You were saying that you spoke with Miss Lawrence on the telephone last evening?"

Mae White looked at Mackie as though she'd forgotten he was in the room and said, "Oh, yes. We agreed to meet in her hotel room after she had dinner with L. A. She thought they'd be through by eight at the latest."

"So you went to the hotel later?"

"Yes. I got there a few minutes before eight, but I never saw Lilly. I put my car in the parking area behind the hotel. I usually do that instead of driving right up to the main entrance because it always causes such a fuss. Then I saw L. A. walking to his car. I figured, since he was leaving, they must be through with dinner, so I went straight to Lilly's room, but she wasn't there. I thought maybe she went for a walk or something, so I waited around a while, but she never showed up. Oh, Lord! Maybe she was already . . . ."

She left the sentence unfinished and tears began pooling in her eyes again. Mackie said quickly, "We're not sure when she died yet, Miss White. She was seen by another hotel guest going into her room sometime before eight o'clock, but we haven't found anyone who saw her after that. Did you hear or see anything outside Miss Lawrence's room while you were waiting for her?"

"No. I didn't wait in the hall. The gossips in this town find plenty to talk about without me loitering in hotel hallways. I went back to my automobile for a while. Then I tried knocking on Lilly's door again."

While Mackie wrote this down, Mae White leaned over and removed a cigarette from a leaded glass box on the coffee table. Winfield moved quickly to light it for her with a platinum table lighter from a receptacle at one end of the cigarette box. He noticed she smoked Player's, an English brand, and that even in this habit, which he had always found unattractive in women, Mae White's movements were graceful and pleasing to the eye.

Mackie finished writing and asked, "When did you go back to her room the second time?"

She thought about his question or a few seconds, and then said, "I'm not positive, but I imagine it was fifteen or twenty minutes after eight."

"What did you do then?"

Mae White took a long drag on her cigarette and answered simply, "I went for a drive and tried to think why Lilly hadn't kept our date."

"And," Mackie asked, "what did you decide?"

"I decided she probably just wanted to be alone. It wasn't like Lilly to stand up a friend, but L. A. put her through the ringer for the last few weeks, and I thought maybe she'd just gone to bed and didn't answer the door."

Winfield said, "What do you mean, 'L. A. put her through the ringer'?"

She looked at Winfield and said, "Lilly had decided to break her contract and leave the studio. She told Bromfeld that she would finish The Big Sister, and then she was through."

Mackie asked, "The Big Sister is a film Miss Lawrence was making?"

Mae White nodded and said, "Yes. It was just about wrapped up. I think they might have had a few close-ups left, but not much more than that."

Winfield asked, "Why was she leaving? Did she get a better offer from another studio?"

"No, no. Nothing like that. There wasn't enough money in the world to make Lilly stay in films. She just wanted out. She wanted to marry Tom and live on his ranch and just be a wife and mother.

"Lilly wasn't a city girl. She wasn't interested in the glamorous lives we movie people are supposed to have. In fact, she hated it. She hated being in the public eye all the time. She hated going to the fancy parties, and especially, she hated all the pressure at the studio. Making movies is really hard work in spite of everything you hear about this business. Lilly was just tired of it all. She really didn't belong here, and she wanted out."

"So," Winfield began, "Miss Lawrence just decided to quit?"

"Yes. It was when her father was killed. I think that was the last straw. It upset her so badly she had to take several days off. We talked about it a lot then. Tom had been after her forever to marry him, and I knew she really wanted to, but the studio was against it and they'd been keeping her so busy, she kept putting Tom off.

"Tom is a wonderful fella, and I told her she was going to lose him if she didn't say yes pretty soon. That's when she decided. When she went back after her father's death, Lilly told L. A. she was quitting, and of course, he told her she couldn't. Lilly even offered to buy back her contract, but L. A. wouldn't budge."

Mackie was writing feverishly, and when Mae White paused for a second, he asked, "How long did the contract have to go?"

"It was originally for five years, so there were about three years to go, but Lilly never would have survived that long. Tom might have waited three years, but Lilly would have been a complete wreck by then. So I said, 'to hell with Bromfeld and the studio.' I told her to just walk out and leave it all behind. If the studio sued, fine. Let them. She couldn't be any worse off than she was."

Winfield nodded as if agreeing with the advice Mae White had given Lillian Lawrence and said, "So she'd definitely made up her mind to quit?"

"Absolutely. She even sold her house. Lilly had a marvelous little cottage up in the hills just off Vista Del Mar, and she told C. E. Toberman, the real estate guy, to sell it for her and he did, practically the same day. That's why Lilly was living at the hotel. I offered to let her stay here, but she said she didn't want to crowd me. So she put all of her things in storage and moved into the Hollywood Hotel."

Mackie, looking a little puzzled, said, "Do you think there was any possibility that Miss Lawrence might have changed her mind about leaving? I mean, within the last day or so?"

Mae White shook her head emphatically. "Not a chance. She was really happy for the first time since I've known her. She and Tom were already making plans for their wedding."

Then, cocking her head a little to one side, she asked, "Why? Why did you ask me if Lilly changed her mind?"

Normally Mackie avoided telling one witness what another said, but this time he made an exception because Mae White's reaction to Bromfeld's story might help explain the contradiction. He said, "A little while ago, Mister Bromfeld told us Miss Lawrence had decided to stay at the studio. He said she told him that last night."

Anger flared instantly in Mae White's wide, blue eyes, and she started to say, "That lying son of a . . . ." Then she took a deep breath and, making an obvious effort to control her emotions, said deliberately, "Mister Bromfeld might have said that, but I can assure you he was mistaken. Even last night on the telephone, Lilly was sure she was doing the right thing. I can't think of anything he could have said to change her mind. In fact, at lunch on Friday, Lilly said L. A. had agreed to release her from her contract. She said he asked her to dinner last night to show there were no hard feelings."

Winfield thought about this while Mackie made his notes. Then the lieutenant said, "Is Mister Bromfeld like that? I mean . . . I mean is he in the habit of . . . stretching things a little to get people to do what he wants?"

Mae White looked directly at Winfield for several seconds before speaking again. "Mister Winfield . . . Bob, Mister Bromfeld is one of the most successful studio bosses in town. I believe he does what he thinks is necessary to make a profit for Western National. He also signs my paycheck, and it's a darn good paycheck. Beyond that, there's nothing more I can say about his methods."

Winfield stared back into Mae White's eyes and read there a good deal of what she had left unsaid. It mostly fell into the category of contempt. Her eyes also told him that there was no purpose in pursuing the subject further because she had said all she was going to say about L. A. Bromfeld.

After a long silence, Mackie said, "If you don't mind, Miss White, I'd like to get back to last night. You said you drove around for a while to think. What did you do after that?"

Mae White was still looking at Winfield. Slowly she turned to Mackie and said, "I went home."

"What time did you get here?"

She took a deep breath that might have expressed exasperation or just weariness. "I think it was about nine-thirty."

"You stayed in after that?"

"Yes. I was tired and a little worried about Lilly. I decided to try to get some sleep and call her this morning."

"And did you? Call her this morning?"

"Yes. I tried two or three times, but the operator said her room didn't answer."

"As he wrote, Mackie asked, "Did you leave a message for her to return your call?"

Wearily she said, "No. I figured Lilly would know that I was concerned about her and that she would call me when she was up to talking. It even occurred to me that Tom might have gotten back early and she might have driven out to his place."

"Did you try calling him?"

"No. If they were together, they didn't need me bothering them. Like I said, I figured Lilly would call me when she was ready to talk."

Mackie looked up at her and said, "But you also said Miss Lawrence wasn't like that—that she never stood up her friends. Weren't you concerned?"

"I said I was! Why don't you listen to me, damn it!"

Tears streaked down her cheeks again and Mackie was about to offer some sort of apology for having to ask such questions, but before her could, Mae White said in a calmer tone, "I was terribly worried about Lilly, but I'm not her mother. She has . . . had a right to her privacy. All I could do was wait and worry. Why, my heart nearly stopped when Adele told me the police were here. I just knew something had happened to Lilly."

Winfield changed his position on the couch, hoping the movement would attract C. K.'s eye. There was no reason for pushing Miss White this way, and he wanted to let the sergeant know that without having to actually say anything, but Mackie's eyes never strayed from Mae White's face.

Mackie sensed his lieutenant's displeasure without needing to look at him, and even though he still had some questions about the woman's behavior last night, the sergeant decided there was nothing to be gained by asking them now. Instead, he took a cue from Miss White's comment about not being Lilly's mother and asked, "We understand Miss Lawrence's parents are both dead. Do you know if she had any other immediate family?"

Dabbing at her eyes with the hanky, Mae White shook her head and answered, "She never mentioned anyone. I know she didn't have any brothers or sisters, so if she had any other family, I guess they weren't close."

Relieved that C. K. had pointed the questioning in a new direction, Winfield asked, "Miss White, do you happen to know when Miss Lawrence's mother passed away?"

"Yes. She died a little more than two years ago. That's when Lilly came to work at Western National. I guess Lilly's father was out of a job and her mother had been bringing in some money doing hand sewing, so when she died—I think she died of pneumonia or something like that—anyway, when she died, Lilly quit school and went to work in the studio's costume shop. That's where L. A. discovered her."

"I see. What about her father?"

Mae White looked a little bewildered for a moment, and then said, "Oh, you mean how did he die?"

"Well, yes."

"It was terrible—a real tragedy in Lilly's life, and it couldn't have come at a worse time for her. I don't know all of the details, but it happened late one night when Mister Lee was on his way home. Somebody beat him to death and robbed him at a little roadhouse way out on the Strip. The place has a Spanish name . . . Club Fiesta or something like that."

Mackie nodded and said, "I know the place. It's out a ways on the Sunset Strip. The County closed them down several times for Volstead violations, but they always manage to open up again."

Mae White continued, "Anyway, they found him all beat up and bloody in the parking lot behind the place. I don't know if they ever caught the men who did it or not. You'd probably know better about that than I would."

Mackie searched his memory for a recollection of the case and came up empty. That wasn't too surprising, though, because the Club Fiesta was outside the Los Angeles city limits so the case would have been handled by the county sheriff. He made himself a note to call the sheriff's office and get the details.

Reviewing his mental list of questions for Miss White, Winfield picked another subject and asked, "Did Miss Lawrence keep any expensive jewelry or large sums of money in her room?"

"Heavens, no! Lilly was very careful about that sort of thing. She kept her nice things in the hotel safe, and she never had more than twenty or thirty dollars in her purse. If she needed more, she could cash a check at the hotel any time."

Mackie nodded and asked, "What about enemies? Is there anyone you can think of who disliked Miss Lawrence enough to hurt her? Anyone she might have crossed or taken advantage of?"

"I can't think of anyone who disliked her, period. As far as the other part goes, Lilly was the kind of person who was taken advantage of, not the other way around. That's what I was trying to tell you before when I said Lilly didn't belong here. She was a good person, and good people just don't belong in the motion picture business."

Winfield was watching Mae White's face when she said good people don't belong in the motion picture business. The expression he saw there somehow went beyond the sadness he knew she felt for the loss of her friend. He wondered if she was relating the axiom to herself, and if so, which way did she think it applied to Mae White?"

Then her expression changed to thoughtful and she said, "There is one person who got into hot water over Lilly, but I can't imagine that he'd have it in for her enough to kill her."

It was the kind of statement that got Mackie's attention. In his experience, the one person people thought wouldn't was often the one person who had. He said, "Who would that be, Miss White?"

"Well, you're going to hear the story sooner or later, so I guess it's better if it comes from someone who was involved rather than second hand."

"And you were involved in this . . . ."

"Yes. It was just after the first of the year. Lilly and I were making our second film together. We hadn't done one since The Long Night, and L. A. thought pairing us up again was a good idea, so he got us a scenario with lots of comedy in it called Hello, Goodbye and he picked Ernst Frohmme to direct it.

"Ernst is one of those directors who yells and screams a lot. He thinks that fear is the best way to control actors. Of course, that's baloney, and those of us who have worked with him before just ignore his outbursts.

"The other thing about Ernst is that he's crazy about young women. He's a real smoothie, and there isn't a young actress on the lot he hasn't made a play for. And a lot of them bought his line, much to their regret."

Mackie interrupted to ask, "Why to their regret?"

Mae White thought for a moment, as though trying to think of a diplomatic way of answering Mackie's question. Finally, she said, "Well, the rumor is that Ernst has some . . . rather unusual tastes." Then after a quick glance at Winfield, she hastily added, "Mind you, I don't know this from personal experience or anything. It's just what I hear from some of the gals who've gone out with him.

"Of course, when Ernst got a load of Lilly, he went after her at full speed. He finally talked her into having dinner with him, and she told me she had to fight him off all night. I know she didn't encourage him, but that didn't matter to Ernst. He doesn't need any encouragement.

"Anyway, a few days after she went out with him, Ernst cornered Lilly behind a set during a break and . . . . Well, he put his hands where Lilly didn't want them. She tried to push him away, but he kept after her, so she screamed. Several of us were just around the corner, and we came running. We caught him red-handed.

"Ernst let go of Lilly and tried to laugh it off, but I gave him what for. I told him he was screwy and a menace to women. I told him I was going to tell L. A. to sack him or else."

Mackie stopped writing and asked, "Did you? Talk to Mister Bromfeld about him?"

"You bet I did! Of course, L. A. wouldn't fire him, but he promised to call Ernst in and warn him to stay away from Lilly and the other young women on the lot. And he did, too!

"Late that afternoon someone came by the set with a message for Ernst. He told us we were done for the day and stomped out. Later we heard that the message had been from Bromfeld and that they had a big shouting match in L. A.'s office. I guess the law was laid down because from that day on, Ernst was strictly business.

"But during the rest of the film, he harassed Lilly and me verbally every chance he got. Ernst would scream and holler at us and make us do scenes over and over again, even though we'd done them right. It didn't really bother me. I just gave it right back to him, but he really upset Lilly. She was in tears half the time. Once he even told her she was the worst actress he'd ever directed and he was going to see to it personally that she never made another film.

"It really amazed me that she was able to finish the picture under those conditions. I tried to get Lilly to go and see L. A. about it, but she wouldn't do it. She didn't want to make trouble for anyone is the way she said it. I think that episode probably had as much to do with Lilly deciding to quit as anything else."

Mae White looked as if the effort of telling the story had exhausted her. She slumped back in the chair and sat quietly staring off into space. Winfield looked at C. K., who nodded and said, "Miss White, I think we have just about everything we need for now. If you'll give us the information on how to reach Mister Bell, we'll be on our way."

She nodded and walked wearily down the hall. They heard her open a door and say, "Adele, please write Tom Bell's address and telephone number down for the officers."

A few minutes later Mae White returned with a slip of pale blue note paper. Mackie exchanged the blue paper for a white one from his notebook on which he'd written his and Winfield's name and the stationhouse telephone exchange. He said, "This is where you can reach Detective Lieutenant Winfield or myself if you think of anything else that might help us. We may want to ask you a few more questions; will you be available for the next few days?"

She said, "Yes. We just started a new picture and the location scenes are being shot on the beach near Santa Monica. I shouldn't be any farther away than that."

Mackie nodded and Winfield said, "Miss White, we appreciate your cooperation. I know this hasn't been easy for you."

Mae White's clear, blue eyes looked up into Winfield's face. She smiled briefly and said, "I hope I have been some help." Then offering her hand, she added, "Please call me if you have more questions."

Winfield grasped her small, warm hand gently and was surprised to feel her squeeze his hand more firmly. The feeling of surprise was renewed when Mae White held her grip for a brief second after he released his.

C. K., already waiting in the entryway, saw Winfield smile a little shyly and nod to Miss White. The sergeant shook his head and wondered about the young actress's apparent attraction to his lieutenant. He hoped for Winfield's sake that it was genuine.

SEVEN

L. A. Bromfeld eased up on the clutch pedal as he fed gas to the Packard's twelve-cylinder motor. At the same time he cranked the large four-spoke steering wheel around to the right. He performed these tasks automatically without conscious thought.

Bromfeld usually took great pride in his driving and under more normal circumstances, focused his concentration on controlling the automobile with precision and panache. Today, however, his mind was elsewhere.

The big phaeton didn't seem to notice this, though, and gracefully swung its long, dark green and nickel-plated nose into the light Sunday afternoon traffic moving east along Sunset Boulevard. Ruth Bromfeld, however, was painfully aware of her husband's distraction.

After the policemen left, L. A. disappeared into one of his contemplative trances. Sitting there at the table staring off into space, Bromfeld was so deeply engrossed in his thoughts that he was oblivious to the world around him. Ruth knew all too well the consequences of interrupting her husband during one of what she privately referred to as her husband's "spells."

The problem she faced was that they were expected at a Pickfair garden party in just over an hour. L. A. felt very strongly about what he described as their "social obligations," and to his delight, the frequency of these occasions had increased steadily in proportion to his prominence in the motion picture industry. When the Bromfelds reached the status of regulars on the Fairbanks' Saturday night guest list, L. A. was ecstatic. Now, with an invitation to one of Little Mary's intimate Sunday afternoon garden parties, Bromfeld repeatedly reminded her that they had arrived at the pinnacle of Hollywood society.

Doug Fairbanks and Mary Pickford were Hollywood's royal family. Their Beverly Hills mansion, Pickfair, was commonly known as the "White House," and the special guests attending their formal Saturday night dinners were easily on a par with those who frequented the other White House in Washington, D.C. They included an impressive parade of European and

Asian royalty mixed with a who's who of American notables such as Babe Ruth and Henry Ford.

While the Fairbankses were unquestionably the monarchs of Hollywood society, they weren't the only game in town. The Bromfelds now also regularly were invited to join the likes of Charles Chaplin, the Louis B. Mayers, and Hedda Hopper at the lavish soirees hosted by William Randolph Hearst and Marion Davies.

W.R., as Hearst was known to his motion picture acquaintances, loved costume parties. and L. A. delighted in raiding the Western National costume shop for the outfits he and Ruth wore to these festivities. His most favorite costume consisted of robes that turned him into a short, bald caricature of Valentino's Sheik. Those who found this transformation humorous—which included everyone who didn't find it grotesque—were careful to save their chuckles for times when Bromfeld could not hear them. That was because there were only a handful of individuals with sufficient preeminence to survive the inevitable repercussions of laughing openly at one of Hollywood's most influential and vindictive men.

Ruth Bromfeld often wondered at the delight her husband found in their blossoming social status. L. A. didn't seem to like most of the people he met at parties, and for the most part, they didn't seem to care much for him, either. Still, he insisted on attending many of the functions to which they received an invitation, but not all of them. He quickly rejected those from people he described as "peasants" and not worthy of his attention. Perhaps, she had concluded, L. A. found pleasure in social acceptance because it was new to him. For most of their lives together, she had felt as if they were the ones others viewed as peasants.

For her part, Ruth would not have minded missing Little Mary's garden party. It wasn't that she lacked refinement or felt awkward at social functions. Her parents sent her to the very best schools so she would be prepared for the role they intended her to assume. "Ruth," her mother would say, "someday you will be the wife of a rich and successful man. You want him to be proud of you, don't you? Of course you do!"

Her lack of enthusiasm for social functions was simply due to the fact that she was a quiet woman—a "homebody" as L. A. was fond of calling her—and keeping up with their increasing social obligations was a constant strain. It was, however, also part of being Missus L. A. Bromfeld, and that above all else was who Ruth strove to be.

All of those considerations left her wondering what she was to do on this Sunday. If she interrupted L. A.'s "spell," he would be very upset. If she didn't and they were late to the party or missed it, he might be even more upset. It was a tightrope that Ruth Bromfeld frequently walked. With time running out, she finally decided she must disturb him. She would do it as gently as possible.

Standing and gently placing her hand on his shoulder, she said quietly, "L. A.? L. A., it's getting late. We must . . . ."

Angrily, he spun around in his chair, pushing his wife away so violently that Ruth was knocked backward, first into her chair and then onto the hard tiles of the terrace. He yelled, "What do you want, woman? Go away! I must think! Leave me alone!"

"But, L. A.," she pleaded from the terrace floor, "we must get ready for Mary Pickford's party. It is almost time to go."

Bromfeld paused in the midst of cursing his wife. Looking at his pocket watch, he shook his head and stomped off into the library, leaving Ruth to pick herself up from the hard terrace floor and to bandage her leg where the chair cut it as she fell. Not much later, L. A. was standing at the bottom of the stairs yelling up to her, "Where are you, Ruth? We must go or we will be late!"

Now, as the Packard turned the corner and Ruth's weight shifted to the side of her buttocks that was bruised from her fall, she endured the pain silently, grateful that L. A. had not hit her in the face again. At least the bruise on her bottom and the cut on her leg didn't require a heavy layer of powder to prevent other party guests from noticing them.

A dozen or so blocks beyond Western, as the big Packard approached Gower Street, Bromfeld looked left. It was an automatic reflex—one he performed every day on his way to work. What he saw when he looked left from this particular intersection was the former home of Western National Films. For many months the buildings remained vacant with a for sale banner covering most of the old Western National sign.

Not long ago, however, the scene of Bromfeld's first Hollywood triumphs had undergone a change. The faded sign and tattered banner were replaced by a shiny new sign announcing the home of Columbia Pictures Corporation. Harry Cohn, Columbia's President and one of the few men in town whose reputation for rudeness and unethical behavior surpassed that of L. A. Bromfeld, also needed to expand his empire. Western National's old lot may have been small in comparison to Bromfeld's new facilities, but it was a step up for Cohn.

Unless it was out of his way, Bromfeld often took the Sunset Boulevard route to wherever he was going so he could catch a glimpse of his old studio. Seeing the place never failed to boost his morale because it reminded him he succeeded spectacularly where others failed dismally. Today, for some reason, L. A.'s usual glimpse became a prolonged stare, and it wasn't until Ruth gasped, that he returned his attention to the traffic ahead and saw the rapidly approaching rear bumper of a Chevrolet that stopped in the middle of the intersection for no apparent reason.

It was a testament to both Bromfeld's driving skill and Packard engineering that the big machine screeched to a halt before smashing into the

Chevrolet. Enraged, L. A. leaned on the horn button and launched a barrage of epithets at the stupid son-of-a-bitch who had nearly wrecked his beautiful automobile.

Then a brief memory of something that happened during the panic stop bobbed to the surface of Bromfeld's consciousness and made him look down at the floorboard. While the car was skidding to a stop, he thought he felt something bump the heel of his right shoe. Looking down, he saw that, yes, something had bumped his shoe. In fact, two somethings had slid from under the seat and come to rest against his foot: a shiny nickel-plated revolver and a small yellow cardboard box emblazoned with red letters that said, "Remington Small Arms Cartridges." For the second time in less than a minute, L. A.'s reflexes reacted quickly. He used his right foot to surreptitiously slide both objects back under the seat. Then, as the Chevrolet driver finally made up his mind to turn left onto Gower, Bromfeld moved the gear lever into first and glanced at his wife to see if she had noticed the pistol.

Ruth Bromfeld was staring straight ahead, apparently unaware that anything more unusual than a near collision had just occurred. L. A. got the Packard moving again, although somewhat less smoothly than normal, and breathed a sigh of relief that Ruth had not seen the gun and no explanations were necessary.

Before the panic stop, Ruth Bromfeld had been thinking about the party. Now her mind returned to those thoughts. She wondered what went on at one of Little Mary's garden parties. She wondered how long they lasted. She also wondered what in heaven's name a gun was doing under the front seat of L. A.'s automobile.

EIGHT

Their interview with Mae White took longer than Mackie and Winfield expected. It was nearly 3:00 p.m. when they finished, and by that time both men were more than ready for lunch.

Most days C. K.'s lunch consisted of a hefty sandwich, an apple, and when Helen had baked recently, a slice of cake or a few cookies, all of which he carried to work in a blue tin pail. Without a kitchen of his own, the lieutenant had to forego such luxuries as a homemade lunch and usually picked up a sandwich at Larry's Delicatessen on the east side of Vine just north of Hollywood Boulevard.

On his Sundays as watch commander, however, Mackie usually saved Helen the effort of packing a lunch and ate out somewhere. So upon leaving the Garden Court Apartments they made a beeline for Larry's. C. K. ordered a corned beef plate with German potato salad and Winfield picked pastrami on rye.

Larry's was located in a small store front, sandwiched between the Hollywood Pharmacy and the Bank of Hollywood. Inside, the town's largest selection of kosher meats and cheeses were displayed in cases running down one side of the shop. A lunch counter across the back of the store was equipped with half a dozen bar stools from which patrons could watch Larry and his son, Ike, assemble the sandwiches and cold plates for which the place was widely known. The rest of the deli was taken up with a collection of mismatched tables and chairs.

Mackie and Winfield carried their lunches to a table near a front window, and between mouthfuls of sandwich, Winfield reviewed the list of suspects Captain Royce would be expecting Monday morning. Holding up his fingers to count the possibilities, he said, "There's Bromfeld and the director, what's his name? Frohmme? That's two. I suppose we should throw Miss Lee's beau into the group, too—at least, until we talk to him. That makes three, so far."

C. K. looked up from his corned beef and asked, "Aren't you forgetting someone?"

"If you mean Miss White, I can't see her killing her best friend. What would her motive be?"

"For that matter, what motive could Bromfeld have for killing one of his most popular actresses? We've got a long way to go on this one, Laddie. I wouldn't be ruling anyone out just yet, no matter how blue her eyes may be."

Winfield glanced up sharply and said, "What is that supposed to mean?"

"I saw how you two were looking at each other. I just want you to keep a clear head, that's all."

With irritation obvious in his voice, Winfield said, "The way we did or didn't look at each other has nothing to do with this. You saw how the news hit her. She couldn't have faked that."

"Bobby, she is an actress by profession! The woman gets paid great God-awful gobs of money for making people believe she's happy or sad or whatever emotion the story they're filming calls for. You can't be ruling her out as a suspect just because she seemed upset. Remember, Mae White had the same opportunity as Bromfeld to kill Lillian Lawrence. They were both in the hotel at the right time."

Frowning, Winfield opened his mouth to speak, but C. K. cut him off. "Now don't be getting all churned up. For whatever it's worth, I don't think Mae White killed Miss Lawrence. For one thing, she's right-handed and our killer would seem to be a lefty. And you're right, she had no reason we know of for killing her friend. But we've got to consider all the possibilities. You know that."

The lieutenant sank back down in his chair and nodded. "You're right, C. K. We can't rule her out, but I just can't see Mae White blowing Lillian Lawrence's brains out."

"As I said, I don't think she did, but it wouldn't surprise me to find out she isn't telling us everything she knows about all this. It's just a feeling."

"Yes, I felt a little of that myself. Especially on the subject of Bromfeld."

Taking his notebook out, Mackie opened it and said, "Feelings and hunches can be useful, but they can also get us off the track. Let's look at what we've actually got to work with so far."

"Not much concrete except a dead woman and a cigar butt."

"We also have a handbag with twenty-some dollars in it and Mae White's statement that Miss Lawrence kept her valuables in the hotel safe. That would make it a fairly good wager that whatever the motive was, it wasn't robbery."

"All the same, I would like to peek into that hotel safe, just to see what's there. I'll bet Dennis Plant or Boyd would go along with that so we don't have to get a warrant."

Mackie made a note in his book and said, "I'll put that on my list for tomorrow. I'd also like to find the files on Harry Lee's murder and see what the investigating officers had to say. I may have to go to the sheriff's office for that since he died outside the city limits."

Winfield nodded and said, "Good idea. And while you're at the hotel, you'd better talk to that maid. We need to get her story before too much time goes by."

"True. If she isn't at work tomorrow, I'll go by her home. I also want to talk to the hotel manager," he shuffled the pages in his notebook and found the man's name, "Lloyd Harrison. He probably can't add much to what Plant and Boyd told us, but you never know."

"Another thing we need to find out is how common Bromfeld's cigars are. If they sell a million of them around here, the butt we found doesn't do us much good. On the other hand, if the things are as rare as I think they are, it could mean a whole lot."

C. K. wrote another note and said, "I know just where to find out. Back when I walked a beat downtown, there was a little newsstand that sold just about every kind of cigar ever rolled. An Eye-tie named Tony Marcelli owns the place. If anybody knows cigars, it's Tony. I've got him on my list for tomorrow."

"Good. If we get lucky and Bromfeld is the only guy west of the Mississippi who smokes them, we can be pretty sure he was lying about not being in Miss Lawrence's room last night. That would make three lies we've caught him in."

"Three? What are the other two? Oh, you mean him telling us he spoke to Mae White last night and her telling us they didn't speak, and Bromfeld saying Lillian Lawrence changed her mind about leaving the studio?"

"Yes. Miss White swears Lillian was determined to leave the motion picture business, so somebody is lying, and my money is on Bromfeld. But I still can't imagine why he would want to kill Lillian Lawrence. That would be like killing the golden goose. If she was set on breaking her contract, he could sue and the court would hold her to the agreement. Any way you look at it, Lillian Lawrence's death is going to cost Western National Films a bundle in lost revenue."

C. K. looked thoughtful for a moment and then said, "Unless he lost his temper and killed her in a fit of rage. Bromfeld strikes me as the kind of fellow who gets pretty upset when he doesn't get his way about things."

"The way the room was messed up, that's a possibility, but I can't see Miss Lawrence calmly sitting on the bed in the middle of a violent argument while Bromfeld put a gun to her head. For that matter, I can't see her allowing Bromfeld into her room dressed for bed as she was." Winfield shook his head and added, "There are just too many pieces of this puzzle that don't seem to fit the picture we're tying to make out of it."

"Maybe we're trying to make the pieces fit the wrong picture. I've had that feeling ever since this morning. You think it might be smart to take a look at Miss Lawrence's contract with Western National?"

Winfield pulled his own notebook out of a coat pocket and making a note, said, "I'll take care of that first thing in the morning. Going to the studio will also give me a chance to talk with some of the people she worked with. For one thing, I'd like to find out more about the incident with that director. Right now he's our only suspect with any kind of a motive."

"Because Lillian Lawrence rejected him?"

"That and because he got into trouble with Bromfeld over her. The whole thing must have been pretty humiliating."

C. K. said, "I suppose it might even affect his career. It would be interesting to know where he was last night."

The lieutenant added this to his list, and then he said, "We also need to see Tom Bell tomorrow."

"Absolutely. I'm going to call Mister Bell when we get back to the station. Mae White has had plenty of time to call him and break the bad news."

"Okay, while you do that I'll get started on our report for Captain Royce. I wish we had more to tell him. When do you think we'll get the coroner's report?"

"Don't expect it before Tuesday. I'll call the coroner's office first thing in the morning and ask them to put a rush on the autopsy, but it probably won't do much good unless the right guy gets the job. Most of those fellows are independent as hell over there."

"It will also be interesting to see what the Criminal Investigation Laboratory found in Lillian Lawrence's hotel room."

"Not much more than we found, I'll wager. Still, I'll give them a call tomorrow as well."

Winfield finished chewing the last bite of his kosher dill pickle and said, "When we get through at the station, you can drop me back at the hotel. My car is still there, and I can talk to the dining room maitre d'. Anything else you can think of?"

C. K. closed his notebook and scratched his chin with one corner of it. "Yeah, Bobby, what was the weather like last night?"

Puzzled, Winfield thought for a moment. Then he realized what Mackie was getting at and said, "It was a very warm night, and you're wondering why Lillian Lawrence kept her windows closed."

C. K. grinned, saying, "We might make a detective out of you after all."

Winfield grimaced and said, "Maybe she was one of those nervous types who are afraid to leave the windows open at night for fear someone will break in."

Mackie didn't look convinced. He just said, "Maybe."

"Something else about all this bothers me more than Lillian Lawrence's windows."

"What's that?"

"That both Lillian Lawrence and her father died violently within a few months of each other. That sort of thing doesn't happen very often without there being some connection."

Standing up from their table, C. K. said grimly, "Like I said, Bobby, we've still got a long way to go on this one."

NINE

The black hands of the large, white-faced clock on the wall behind the complaint desk pointed to three minutes past four when Mackie and Winfield walked into the stationhouse. Patrol Officer Otis was still on the desk since, like Mackie, his shift didn't end until five. When Otis saw them, he jumped to attention, saluted, and said, "Good afternoon, sirs!"

With more than a hint of exasperation coloring his tone, the sergeant returned Otis' salute and said, "Good afternoon, Otis. Relax, will you? One day you'll pop a gusset doing that. Anything going on?"

Looking a little confused, as if he didn't understand Mackie's remark about gussets, Otis answered, "No, sir. All quiet. There are two messages on your desk, Sergeant, neither of them urgent."

Suppressing a grin, but admiring Otis' enthusiasm, Winfield asked, "Captain Royce hasn't called, has he?"

The lieutenant was relieved when Otis said, "No, sir." Royce wanted answers, and all they had so far were questions. Putting that in a written report was bad enough; talking to the boss was something he'd rather put off until they had some concrete facts to work with.

Leaving the stationhouse lobby, Mackie and Winfield headed toward the detective room and C. K. called back over his shoulder, "As you were, Otis," fearing that if he didn't, the rookie would stand there at attention until hell froze over.

A "Yes, sir," followed them down the hall.

Winfield settled in at his desk while Mackie hung his uniform jacket and cap on a hook, complaining, "I swear that boy is going to drive me to drink."

The lieutenant laughed and said, "Aw, come on, Sarge. I bet you were just like him in your rookie days."

"I couldn't have been. I never would have lived to this ripe old age."

With that, Winfield buried himself in his initial Lillian Lawrence homicide report for Royce, and C. K. went across the hall to the assembly room so he could return his telephone messages and call Tom Bell without disturbing the lieutenant. When he was through on the telephone, Mackie filled out his Watch Commander's Report for Sunday, September 5, 1926.

By the time Mackie finished that chore, Patrol Sergeant Brian Sullivan, the night-shift watch commander, arrived and Mackie briefed him on the homicide and a few minor incidents that occurred during the day watch.

A few minutes before five, C. K. returned to the detective room. Winfield was leaning back in his chair re-reading his report to Royce for the third time. He looked up at C. K. and said, "I guess this thing is done. You want to look it over to see if I've dotted all the I's and crossed all the T's?"

Mackie sat at his desk and read the report. Finally, he handed it back to Winfield, saying, "Good job, Bobby. Very thorough. This ought to keep the good captain off our backs for a day or two."

"I hope so. Did you get through to Tom Bell?"

"Yes. The boy sounded genuinely upset. I guess he and another fellow were up in Fresno at a horse auction for the past few days. Said they'd just gotten back when Mae White called him. He's coming down here tomorrow. I asked him to meet us at the hotel around one o'clock."

"Think he'll show? Or should we drive up and see him tonight?"

"He sounds like an alright sort of chap. He'll be there."

Winfield stood to put on his jacket and said, "Okay, let's get out of here so you can get home for Sunday dinner and I can talk to that maitre d' at the hotel."

"Sure you don't want me to tag along?"

"Naw, I can handle this one. Just drop me off and go on home. Helen will have both of our hides if you show up late."

Winfield slipped his report into an envelope addressed to Captain Royce and handed it to Sergeant Sullivan with instructions to have a patrol officer take the report downtown and make sure it ended up on Royce's desk.

A few minutes later they were in C. K.'s Dodge and headed back to where the events of a long day had begun to unfold nine hours earlier. Hollywood Boulevard was even quieter at this hour than it had been at eight o'clock that morning. It was probably because of this that Winfield noticed the fellow. It was just a quick peripheral glimpse that wouldn't have registered anything out of the ordinary had there been more traffic and pedestrians on the street to distract him.

The guy was standing at the back of a narrow alleyway that split the block between Whitley and Cherokee to provide access to the service alley behind the businesses along the north side of Hollywood Boulevard. He wasn't doing anything, just leaning against the building with his hands in his trouser pockets, but the way he watched Mackie's car go by triggered an alarm somewhere in Winfield's beat cop instincts. He nudged C. K. and asked, "Did you notice that guy in the alley back there?"

Mackie glanced at Winfield and answered, "No. What was he up to?"

"Probably nothing, but he seemed very interested in us. There's a jewelry store in this block, isn't there?"

"Uh-huh, old man Kaplan's shop. We just passed it. Want to go back and take a look?"

"It's probably a waste of time, but turn right on Cherokee up here and let's take a look down the alley."

C. K. nodded and tapped the brake pedal just in time to swing onto Cherokee. Half a block later he braked again, pulling up at the service alley entrance. The guy was still back there, alright, but he'd moved. Now he was in the deep shadows of the alley itself, about halfway between Cherokee and the side alley where Winfield first saw him. When the fellow spotted them at the entrance to the alley, he hastily stepped out of sight into the empty space behind a couple of the shorter buildings facing Hollywood Boulevard. Part of the front fender and hood belonging to a gray automobile poked out into the alley from the same area.

This time Mackie saw him, too, and said, "Kaplan's is right about where that auto is parked."

Winfield nodded, adding, "Yeah. Something's going on down there. Let me off here and drive around to the other end of the side alley so we have him between us."

As soon as the lieutenant was out of the car, Mackie stepped the accelerator pedal and sped off. A moment later the black Dodge roadster turned right onto Yucca Street and disappeared.

Unbuttoning his suit coat, Winfield consciously sensed the weight of his police revolver in its shoulder holster under his left arm. He began walking down the unpaved service alley, staying close to the buildings on his right. Since the hard tires of the delivery trucks that plied the alley never rolled there, the dirt under his feet was soft and powdered his shoes with a fine coating of dust. It was so quiet he could hear the song of a mockingbird whose shape he could barely make out on a utility wire at the other end of the block.

Winfield had covered about half the distance to the jewelry shop when he realized the side alley off Hollywood Boulevard didn't go all the way through to Yucca. That meant C. K. would have to drive the full length of the block down to Whitley Avenue before he could turn into the service alley. The lieutenant slowed his pace accordingly. In spite of this, he was already close enough to see that the gray car was a Chevrolet sedan by the time Mackie turned into view at the far end of the alley. He waited for C. K. to pull up about twenty yards short of the space behind the jewelry store. As Mackie got out and pulled his billy from under the Dodge's seat, a slight movement of something brown on the other side of the gray car caught Winfield's eye. Apparently the sergeant also saw the movement. He yelled, "Police! Stay where you are!"

Winfield could now tell that the brown movement he'd seen was a tweed cap, and the young man wearing it—a different fellow than the guy he'd first seen—had been crouched on the other side of the Chevrolet to peek around the corner in Mackie's direction. Upon hearing Mackie's warning, the man stood and jumped back out of sight. The Chevrolet's self-starter whined and the car dipped slightly on its springs with the weight of someone climbing into it. Winfield wondered if the man had seen him as well as C. K.

A second later it was obvious he hadn't. When the car lurched out into the alley, its front wheels were cranked all the way over in Winfield's direction.

The reflexive movement that brought the lieutenant's revolver out of its holster took only an instant, but in that short time, the driver spotted him and slammed on the brakes. A clashing of misaligned gears drowned out Winfield's order to halt. A shower of loose dirt and pebbles squirted from under the rear tires as they changed direction and jerked the Chevrolet backward.

In that moment Winfield had a clear shot, but the target lined up in his sights was the driver's head. At that short range, even through the door's window glass, the impact of a .38 caliber slug on the man's skull would have been fatal. Winfield held his fire and hoped he wouldn't regret the decision.

The sedan's disappearance back into the area behind the jewelry store was followed immediately by a crash that sounded mostly of splintering wood. Looking over at Mackie, Winfield saw that the sergeant had dropped to the ground so his partner would have a clear field of fire. Getting back to his feet, he glanced at the revolver in Winfield's hand and gave one brief nod of what the lieutenant took to be approval.

The two officers sprinted from opposite directions toward the space into which the Chevrolet had disappeared, but stopped short and stepped into the opening cautiously. Three of the Chevrolet's four doors were open and the two men who'd just jumped from the driver's side were running toward an open door at the rear of a store. A sign above the door said, "Kaplan's Fine Jewelry."

The third man in the brown tweed cap had gotten out of the passenger side of the front seat, but found his escape route blocked where the sedan's rear bumper had smashed into the building. He was starting to scramble over this obstacle when Winfield shouted, "Police! Stop right there!"

The man froze where he was. Of the other two, the one closest to the doorway had disappeared through it. The driver, who was behind him, surprised both officers by spinning around in a crouch. The large revolver in his hand was aimed at Winfield. C. K. hollered a warning as he dove around the corner of the building on his side of the parking area.

Winfield clearly saw the pistol spit flame. He heard its percussive pop. He heard his own heartbeat as he instinctively dove for cover. He felt the sting of splintered brick on his cheek as the bullet smacked into the wall inches from his head. And as he landed on the soft dirt in the alley around the corner, he heard one of the men yell, "Come on, damn it!"

All of this was followed by scurrying sounds and the slamming of a door. Winfield stood up and looked over at C. K., who shouted, "You okay, Bobby?"

The lieutenant nodded, and in a softer voice Mackie said, "You keep 'em in there. I'll call for help and cover the front until someone gets here. Winfield nodded again and watched C. K. jog down the service alley, pausing at the Dodge long enough to pull his revolver from its hidden clips behind the dashboard. The lieutenant looked down at his own revolver and thought that, for all the good it had done them, the darn thing might just as well have been stashed with C. K.'s pistol.

Mackie disappeared down the side alley that led to Hollywood Boulevard and Winfield took a deep breath, trying to force some of the tension from his muscles. He'd just come very close to getting it. Much too close, he thought. Nearly gunned down in an alley by some two-bit punk with a big pistol who thought he was Billy the Kid—the same guy he had in his sights a moment earlier. Damn!

Then Winfield gave himself a mental kick in the seat of his pants. If he didn't start using his head here, he could still end up dead. He listened intently for the slightest sound from around the corner and rethought his situation.

It would take C. K. several minutes to reach the nearest police call box. Winfield couldn't remember for sure, but he thought the closest one was across Hollywood Boulevard at Cherokee. Then it would take several more minutes for someone from the station, probably Sullivan, to get there.

All told, he and the three men in the jewelry store had at least seven or eight minutes to kill before anyone else got there. They had to be figuring more cops would be showing up and that their odds of getting away were growing slimmer every second. When given time to think, men pinned down in situations like this usually did one of two things. They either got scared and gave up or they panicked and did something desperate. These guys, at least the guy with the gun, had already proven he didn't have any scruples about shooting cops, so it was very likely that something would happen in the next few minutes. Winfield needed to shift the odds more in his favor before it did.

The problem was he couldn't see the area between him and the shop without becoming a target. If they moved in his direction and did it quietly, he wouldn't know about it until they were already on him. He had to move into a better position, but where?

The opposite side of the alley was a blank wall. The only possible cover with a better view of the area behind the jewelry store was the robbers'

Chevrolet. He could see it—or at least part of it—from where he stood. They'd backed it into the area behind the shop at an angle with its hood toward him. If he could get to it, he'd have a clear shot at the back door. But getting to the car meant crossing nearly thirty feet of open space. The odds of making it were damned slim without some sort of diversion to distract the gunman. What the hell could he use as a diversion?

Winfield heard the mockingbird down the block again. It was too damned quiet. He had to know what was going on, and the only way to find out was to risk a look around the corner. Dropping to his knees so his head would be lower than the gunman would expect, he cautiously peeked around the building.

Two movements caught his eye almost simultaneously. The first to register was the swing of a gun barrel through an open window to the right of the jewelry store door. He'd already jerked his head back by the time another "pop" resounded through the alley and more brick chips exploded from where his head had been a split-second earlier. Winfield was sourly noting that the guy was pretty darn good with that revolver when the second movement he'd seen sank in.

C. K. was on the roof. But what did the sergeant have in his hands? He had two of them . . . large gray things. They looked those dome-shaped fans they put on roofs for ventilation. What the hell was he going to do with . . . . Of course! C. K. saw his problem and was about to provide exactly the distraction he needed to improve his position.

Winfield moved closer to the corner of the building, holstered his revolver, and got ready to move when the racket started. A few seconds later he heard a faint whistle. The sound was too far away to be Mackie on the rooftop, but it was immediately followed by a clatter that sounded like someone was dumping a truckload of tin cans in the alley.

By the time the second of Mackie's ventilators hit the ground, Winfield had covered three-quarters of the distance to the Chevrolet. He could see the gunman in the window. The guy had been looking right, in the direction of the noise, but now he saw the lieutenant and his gun barrel swung across the open space between them. Winfield dove across the last few yards and heard another shot followed by a "ping" as he hit the ground behind the sedan's radiator. The gunman really was good. He'd led Winfield by just the right distance, but the Chevrolet's fender had been in the way by the time he squeezed off the shot.

The lieutenant squirmed around on his belly so he could see most of Kaplan's back door between the sedan's front tires. Aiming his revolver at a point about knee-high in the doorway, he took a deep breath and was about to shout an order for the men to surrender, when C. K. beat him to the punch.

From the rooftop, Mackie shouted, "You fellows in the jewelry store, pay attention. There are now policemen guarding the front and back doors of the shop."

That explained, Winfield thought, the whistle he'd heard just before C. K. tossed the ventilator fans off the roof. It was someone letting Mackie know they were in position. But how in blazes did he get anyone here that fast?

C. K. continued from the roof, "Now boys, we can do this the hard way or the easy way. You fellows can throw out your weapons and walk through the back door with your hands in the air or you can try to shoot your way out, which will get you all killed. It's up to you. Decide what you're going to do, but don't take too long about it because I'm missing my Sunday dinner, and the longer I have to sit up here waiting on you, the crankier I'm going to get."

In spite of the serious situation they were in, the lieutenant couldn't help but smile at C. K.'s speech. Sunday dinner, indeed! Mackie had told them the truth, though. By moving behind the robbers' automobile, Winfield had cancelled out their only advantage. Unless there was another way out of the building, they were trapped. Several more seconds passed in silence, during which the lieutenant repeatedly forced himself to relax. This time, unless they gave up, he had no intention of holding his fire.

Finally a nervous voice from inside the jewelry store responded to C. K.'s ultimatum. "Okay, we give up. We're comin' out like you said. Here's the gun. Don't shoot."

The big revolver flew out of the dark doorway, bounced on the hard-packed dirt, and skidded to a stop near the left rear tire of the gray Chevrolet. Then the door hinges squeaked and three young men filed out with their arms held high above their heads. They stopped in a group just outside the door and looked apprehensively in the lieutenant's direction.

Winfield got to one knee in front of the sedan, but remained behind its protective cover and shouted, "Turn around and face the building. Keep your hands high where I can see them!"

They turned around as ordered and Winfield stood up, keeping his revolver aimed at the man in the center. With his free hand, he waved at C. K. on the roof. Mackie nodded back and moved out of sight. Then the lieutenant said to his captives, "Move to the right and spread out. Get at least two feet between each of you."

The three men shuffled their feet sideways until they were past the doorway and there were a couple of feet between them. Winfield said, "That's it. Now each of you take a step forward toward the wall."

When they had done this, he ordered, "Put your arms out in front of you and lean forward against the wall. Good. Now, don't anybody move a muscle until I tell you to."

With the situation more or less under control, Winfield chanced a glance to his left and his jaw dropped when he saw rookie patrol officer Otis jog around the corner into the area behind the jewelry store. He was expecting one of the evening shift patrol officers or maybe Sullivan. Otis was off duty. What the hell was he doing here?

Holding his revolver at the ready, Otis stopped alongside Winfield and said, "Good evening, sir."

The formal greeting drove some of the tension out of Winfield. With as much calm as he could muster Winfield said, "Good evening, Otis. If you wouldn't mind, please hand me that pistol over there on the ground and then search these fellows for any other weapons."

Otis snapped a, "Yes, sir," and holstered his revolver. Then, being careful not to step between the lieutenant and his prisoners, he picked up the pistol and handed it to Winfield before thoroughly and deliberately searching each of the men, using approved department procedures.

Otis' search took a minute or two, and just as he was finishing with the last man, Mackie strolled up. Otis turned to Winfield and holding a small pocket knife, he reported, "This was the only weapon they had on them, sir."

The lieutenant nodded and C. K. handed Otis three pairs of wrist cuffs he'd gotten from a box he kept in the luggage compartment of his Dodge. Mackie said, "Cuff 'em and sit 'em down against the wall. Sullivan's on his way over with the wagon to pick these fellows up."

With the prisoners properly restrained and Otis watching them like a hawk, Mackie and Winfield walked into the jewelry store. Inside, the lieutenant wiped the sweat from his forehead with the back of his hand and leaned against a workbench.

C. K. was busy examining the broken locks on several cabinets around the room. He said casually, "It got a little close back there, didn't it?"

Winfield sighed and said, "It sure did. Thanks for bailing me out."

C. K.'s gray eyes twinkled a little as he said, "That's what partners are for, Bobby."

Winfield walked over to the window the gunman had used and looked out. The thing that caught his eye immediately was a shiny spot about the size of a quarter near the edge of the gray sedan's left front fender. If the man had pulled the trigger a split-second sooner, Winfield realized, he would not be standing there now. He shook his head involuntarily and said, "What I want to know his how the devil you got help so quickly."

Mackie walked over to the window and said, "Oh, that was just dumb luck. As I came around the corner onto the Boulevard, there was Otis waiting for a bus. I explained the situation and told him to use the box down the street to call the station, and then to clear the area in front of this place. While he did that, I climbed up to the roof on a fire escape ladder I noticed as I went through the side alley. I told Otis to whistle when the area was clear and he was in position. The ventilator fans were just laying up there on the roof where somebody left them when they put new ones in. I figured they'd make a good diversion, so when I heard Otis whistle, I tossed 'em off the roof. They made quite a decent racket!"

Picking up a burlap sack from the floor, Winfield said, "Well, they did the job, and Mister Kaplan is going to be happy this stuff didn't get out the door."

C. K. looked over his partner's shoulder into the sack which held an assortment of watches, rings, and other jewelry the robbers had collected before they were forced to make a getaway. Mackie gestured around the room with a sweep of his arm and said, "Kaplan had best get himself a good, sturdy safe, because there might not be a sharp-eyed detective lieutenant around to spot the next bunch of thieves who decide to do some after-hours shopping in his establishment."

It was then that they heard the persistent clanging of a bell that signaled the impending arrival of Sergeant Sullivan and the paddy wagon. C. K. suggested Winfield go out and supervise the loading of the prisoners while he found old man Kaplan's telephone number and called him down to lock up his store.

A few minutes later Otis and another patrol officer who arrived with Sullivan were ushering the third prisoner into the enclosed back of the black Ford truck used for transporting prisoners. As they slammed and padlocked the door, Sergeant Sullivan walked over to Winfield and said, "You and C. K. landed yourselves quite a haul here. Nice work, Lieutenant. I'll take these fellows downtown. You going to come down and do the paperwork?"

Before Winfield could answer, C. K. walked up and said, "I'll take care of the paper, Sully. Bobby's got a homicide interview to do."

Sullivan said, "Okay. It's all the same to me as long as I don't have to do it. Bridges here can take their car to the garage."

Mackie nodded. "Good. I'll come down as soon as old man Kaplan gets here to lock up his shop."

The patrol sergeant gestured to Otis standing several feet away next to the paddy wagon and said, "Hell, why don't you leave the rookie here to do that?"

In a voice he knew was loud enough for Otis to hear, C. K. said, "Patrol Officer Otis is off duty. He volunteered to help us out of a jam here, and he did an exemplary job of it. He's earned his time off."

Winfield could see Otis beaming from the corner of his eye. Sullivan shrugged and headed toward the wagon, saying, "It's all the same to me."

After watching the truck pull away with Patrol Officer Bridges following in the robbers' Chevrolet, Winfield and Mackie heartily thanked Otis for helping them out. Then they were alone in the alley behind the jewelry store.

The lieutenant said, "Those guys aren't much more than kids. The fellow with the gun can't be twenty. What the hell got into them to make them wreck their lives like this?"

C. K. shook his head. "Beats me, Bobby. Maybe they were looking for an easy way to get their share of Hollywood glamour." Then after a long pause he added, "Maybe they'll get straightened out now. Thanks to you they still have a chance to do that."

Winfield looked puzzled. "What do you mean, thanks to me?"

"If you hadn't held your fire when they were in the car, the driver—the kid with the gun—would be headed for the morgue right now, instead of jail. He knows that as well as you and I. Maybe he'll think about it and figure out that he ought to take good advantage of the second chance you gave him."

Winfield said, "Maybe. I hope so, but I wouldn't bet that we won't be seeing him in trouble again when he's served his time for this one." Changing he subject, he said, "Well, I guess I'd better get over to the hotel before DeVoe gets so busy he doesn't have time to talk with me."

"If you'll wait a few minutes, until Kaplan gets here, I'll give you a lift."

"No thanks, C. K. It's only a few blocks and the walk will do me good. Oh, and tell Helen I'm sorry I made you late for Sunday dinner."

"Okay, Laddie, I'll do that."

After swatting the dust off his suit and straightening his cuffs, Winfield said, "Okay. I'm going straight over to Western National Films first thing in the morning, so I'll meet you at the hotel around one."

"Alright, Bobby. See you then. By they way, you handled yourself real well here."

"Thanks. You didn't do so badly yourself."

C. K. grinned and said, "It's all part of the job."

"Yeah," Winfield added sarcastically, "and when I signed on for this job, Royce told me nothing ever happened out here in the sticks."

TEN

There were three blocks of Hollywood Boulevard between Cherokee Avenue and the Hollywood Hotel at Highland. Winfield set a brisk pace, but his thoughts were elsewhere. They bounced back and forth between the events of the jewelry store robbery and the warning his mother repeated so often when he joined the department in San Francisco. She'd say, "Why don't you forget this foolish idea of being a policeman? No good will ever come of it, and you will end up being killed by some hoodlum in a filthy alley somewhere. Leave that sort of thing for men who are better suited to it."

Men like C. K. Mackie? Despite the fact that her dire prediction very nearly came true, he wondered what she would think made C. K. any better suited to dying in an alley than he.

At the intersection of Hollywood and Highland the lieutenant's thoughts were wrenched back to the business at hand by a newspaper boy who was holding up a copy of the Herald-Express and shouting, "Read all about it! Famous film actress murdered in Hollywood! Read all about it!"

Winfield handed the boy a nickel and accepted the newspaper he held out in his ink-smudged hand. Then the lieutenant followed the circular drive around to the hotel's main entrance and stopped under the portico to read what the Herald had to say about Lillian Lawrence's death.

The story was at the top of the first page under a banner headline: Famous Film Actress Shot To Death." Below that was a sub-headline in smaller type that said, "Popular Lillian Lawrence Killed at Hollywood Hotel." Below this the Herald had printed a two-column photograph of Miss Lawrence.

The story began, "The nude body of film actress Lillian Lawrence was discovered on the floor of her room at the Hollywood Hotel early this morning by a hotel maid. According to Captain Albert Royce, chief of the Los Angeles Police Department's Homicide Division, Miss Lawrence received one fatal shot to the right temple.

"From all indications the murder took place sometime Saturday evening. The actress's room showed signs of a violent struggle, but neither sounds of violence, nor any gunshots were heard by hotel guests staying in the rooms near Miss Lawrence's. Robbery has been ruled out as a motive for the killing because valuable jewelry and a large sum of cash were still in the room when detectives searched it this morning.

"In a meeting with members of the press early Sunday afternoon, Captain Royce said that no arrests had been made as of that time. He further stated that a crack team of detectives were interviewing suspects and he expected the killer to be brought to justice within the next 24 to 48 hours."

The rest of the story described Lillian Lawrence's overnight rise from studio seamstress to stardom. Her film roles were mentioned along with the fact that Miss Lawrence was under contract to Western National Films.

In a fashion Winfield knew to be typical of newspapers like the Herald and the Examiner, Lillian Lawrence's story was sensationalized by incorrectly reporting that her body was nude and that valuable jewelry, along with a large sum of money, was in her hotel room. He couldn't help smiling at the part about a "crack team of detectives," imaging how C. K. would react to that description when he read it. He also wondered what C. K. would think about Royce's optimistic prediction that an arrest was expected within the next two days. Winfield knew such predictions were typical of L.A.P.D. press conferences. Captain Royce would never admit to a room full of newspaper reporters that his crack team of detectives did not have the slightest idea who killed the famous Lillian Lawrence.

Folding the newspaper, Winfield walked into the lobby and asked a clerk behind the front desk for either Mister Plant or Mister Boyd. He was informed that Mister Plant had already left for the day, but that Mister Boyd would be with him shortly. The clerk then spoke briefly into a telephone, and a few seconds later Richard Boyd came through a door behind the registration counter. He surveyed the lobby through his thick eyeglasses and finally spotted the lieutenant. After shaking hands, Boyd gestured to the newspaper under Winfield's arm and said, "I guess you have already seen what the newspapers are saying about Miss Lawrence's death."

"Yes, and to tell the truth, the story isn't nearly as lurid or sensational as I expected."

"I assure you that was not from lack of trying. Dennis—Mister Plant—said we had more reporters here than guests this afternoon. They were trying to interview every employee in the hotel and demanding to see Miss Lawrence's room. Dennis said he had to station a bellboy in the hall outside the room after he caught one reporter trying to pick the lock on the door. The bellboy said later that he was offered some pretty tempting bribes to open the door."

Boyd squinted around the lobby and added, "I believe most of the reporters have left now, but I have given strict instructions for all night shift employees to direct any reporters they encounter to me. I have also instructed the hotel's night watchman to keep a close eye on room 187."

Winfield said, "It's too bad, but that's the nature of the press. I'd say you and Mister Plant have done an admirable job of keeping things under control."

"Thank you, Lieutenant. I sincerely hope Mister Harrison feels the same. Now, how can I help you this evening?"

"I came by to talk to your dining room maitre d'. I planned to get here earlier, before he got busy, but I was detained."

"I don't believe there will be a problem. The dining room is slow tonight, and I will cover his station while he speaks with you."

As they entered the dining room, Winfield counted a total of eight diners at three tables. Things were indeed slow, and he wondered if this was a typical Sunday night or if the newspaper reports of a murder in the hotel had kept people away. Then Boyd introduced him to Maurice DeVoe.

A friendly, but deeply lined face with some graying around the edges of DeVoe's curly, black hair gave Winfield the impression that the maitre d' was approaching middle age. The man was an inch or two shorter than average height and looked very much at home in his well-tailored tuxedo. He wore a thin mustache and his dark eyes were in constant motion, missing nothing of what went on around him. When he spoke, DeVoe's French accent was quite evident. Winfield wondered if the accent was real or something cultivated for the benefit of the Dining Room of the Stars' patrons.

DeVoe steered Winfield to a small table off one side of the large room and instructed an idle waiter to serve them coffee. They sat down and DeVoe offered the lieutenant a Camel cigarette from his pack and lit one for himself. Discarding his match into a spotless glass ashtray bearing the Hollywood Hotel's name in gold script, DeVoe said, "It is always so very sad when a lovely person such as Miss Lawrence meets with an untimely death. It is very difficult to believe that anyone would wish her harm."

"I take it you were fond of Lillian Lawrence?"

"Oh, indeed, yes. We all were. In this place," he gestured around the room, "we see many rich and famous people, but most, they are so full of self-importance. They disgust me. Miss Lawrence, though, she was always pleasant and friendly."

"Did she dine here often?"

"No, I'm sad to say. We only saw her occasionally, but we were always pleased when Miss Lawrence honored us with her presence."

"I understand she was here last night."

"Yes, she was. Miss Lawrence dined with Mister Bromfeld."

There was something in the way DeVoe spoke Bromfeld's name that gave Winfield an impression that the maitre d' didn't care much for the man. He asked, "When did they arrive?"

DeVoe thought about it only briefly before saying, "Mister Bromfeld's office made a reservation by telephone for 6:30 p.m. I saw Miss Lawrence waiting for Mister Bromfeld in the lobby a few minutes before that time. Then he arrived and I seated them at exactly 6:30."

Winfield jotted this down in his notebook and asked, "You said Bromfeld's office made the reservation. Do you know when that reservation was made?"

DeVoe excused himself from the table and returned a moment later with his reservation book, saying, "I always insist that when the reservations are made, the date and time of the call be noted in the book."

He flipped back a page or two and ran his finger down the carefully printed lines. "Here it is. The reservation was made at 11:35 a.m. on September third. That would have been last Friday. It was made by a Miss Shipman, whom I believe is the secretary to Mister Bromfeld."

"Did you happen to notice how Miss Lawrence behaved toward Mister Bromfeld?"

"Oh, yes. At first their conversation was friendly, and Miss Lawrence, she was cheerful."

"Then what happened?"

"The next time I pass their table, things are not so happy. I, of course, did not hear their conversation, but I could sense that Miss Lawrence was quite tense. Then she suddenly bolted from the table and left in a great hurry. When she passed me, Miss Lawrence had tears in her eyes. It made me angry that this pig, Bromfeld, should make her cry." After a pause, DeVoe added, "Please forgive my language."

"Did you happen to notice what time she left the table?"

"I did not look at the time. However, their entrees had not yet been served, so I would estimate that they had only been seated for maybe half of an hour."

Winfield noted this and said, "So it was around seven that she left?"

"Yes. Perhaps a few minutes later."

"Then what did Bromfeld do?"

DeVoe surprised Winfield by the vehemence of his answer, saying, "That horrible man! He sat there and finished with his supper as if nothing at all had happened. He was even smiling and cheerful as he ate!"

"What time did Bromfeld finally leave?"

"He eats his food quickly, like the pig. I am sure he was through with his meal and leaving by 7:30. Again, please forgive my way of speaking about Bromfeld, but I was happy to be rid of him."

"Did you happen to notice which way he went when he left the dining room?"

"No, I did not. We were very busy last night, not at all like tonight. However, I will tell you this much, if it is found that this Bromfeld is the one who has murdered Miss Lawrence, I would happily drop the blade of the guillotine on his filthy neck with my own hands!"

DeVoe's dark eyes flashed with his anger, and Winfield couldn't help but ask, "It's clear that you don't think very highly of Mister Bromfeld. Why is that?"

"Mister Winfield, it is my responsibility to provide hospitality and service to our dining room guests. This I must do whether, as you say, I think highly of the person or not. It is an unfortunate requirement of my position. But since you have asked of me the question, I do not like Mister Bromfeld in the least because he is so typical of his breed. Perhaps worse than most, but still typical."

"What does that mean?"

"The studio bosses, they are all cut from the same bolt of cloth. Zukor from Paramount, those Warners, Cohn at Columbia, and worst of all next to Bromfeld, Mayer at Metro-Goldwyn-Mayer—they are all the same. They are rude, ill-mannered peasants. Every one of them! Except," his tone softened slightly, "Mister Thalberg. He is a gentleman. The rest . . . peasants! Bah!"

Winfield couldn't help smiling at DeVoe's outburst, but he also knew there would be something to what the man was saying. He'd learned long ago that if you wanted to know who was who in any city, you talked to the maitre d's at the best restaurants. He also made a mental note of the names DeVoe had listed. These were names he should know if he ever expected to be as knowledgeable about Hollywood as C. K.

Winfield thanked DeVoe for his time, and Richard Boyd showed him to the hotel's front entrance. There Boyd said, "The newspaper said the police expect to make an arrest soon. Is that so?"

The lieutenant shook his head. "I wish it were. We have some suspects, but it takes time to dig out the answers."

"I wish you luck," Boyd said, "because the sooner you resolve this matter, the sooner things will return to normal here."

Winfield shook Boyd's hand and thanked him for his cooperation. Then the lieutenant walked out into the dusk of a balmy southern California evening.

His department Dodge sedan was parked on Highland near the corner, facing Hollywood Boulevard. He climbed into the driver's seat and looked at his watch. It was almost seven which meant he'd missed dinner at Missus Haney's. Winfield decided that was okay because he had a late lunch and wasn't really hungry. He glanced at the newspaper where he'd tossed it on the seat next to him and thought about going to his room and reading it.

That idea struck him as funny. Here he was in the most glamorous city in the country, and the most exciting thing he could think to do was go home and read the newspaper.

Well, he thought, to heck with that. If nothing else, he would drive around some, maybe up into the hills. He recalled Mae White saying that she had gone for a drive last night to think. He didn't need to think so much as to relax. Maybe driving was good for that, too. He was about to step on the starter when a brightly lit theater marquee a block-and-a-half down Hollywood Boulevard caught his eye. Suddenly he knew what to do with his evening.

The lieutenant made a left turn onto Hollywood and pulled to the curb in front of Grauman's Egyptian Theater. A moment later he handed the box office cashier one dollar in exchange for a ticket to see Fame and Fortune starring Miss Mae White.

ELEVEN

Monday - September 6, 1926

Monday morning arrived packaged in a thin layer of overcast extending from the coast to the inland hills surrounding the Los Angeles basin. Detective Sergeant Mackie welcomed the clouds because, even though the sun would burn them away before noon, they were a signal that fall was on its way, bringing with it some relief from several weeks of unusually hot summer weather.

Mackie's first stop of the day was Tony Marcelli's newsstand next to the Biltmore Hotel at Fifth and Olive in downtown Los Angeles. As he pulled his Dodge up to a loading zone in front of the newsstand, Tony Marcelli greeted him from the curb.

"Hey, C. K.! What are you doing in this neck of the woods? Last I heard they shipped you out to Hollywood."

"Hello, Tony. I'm still in Hollywood, but they let me come down to the big city once in a while so I don't forget what civilization looks like."

"Well, welcome to it. What can I do for you?"

"I'm looking for a cigar."

"I got all kinds. What kind you want?"

"It's called an El Pantera."

"Hell, and all this time I thought you was an honest cop."

Surprised, Mackie said, "What makes you think I'm not?"

"Because there ain't no way you're buyin' El Panteras on the money an honest cop makes."

"I take it they're expensive?"

"They are very expensive, my friend. I don't stock 'em because my trade can't afford high class cigars like them."

"Well, you'll be pleased to know that I'm still an honest cop. I just want to know who sells those things and who they sell them to."

"That shouldn't be too hard to find out. The only distributor I know who trades in expensive stogies like El Panteras is Pacific Tobacco Importers over to San Pedro. Since they probably don't sell many around here, they should be able to tell you which dealers handle 'em, and the dealers can tell you who buys 'em. Easy as that."

"Do you have a telephone number for Pacific Tobacco Importers?"

"Hell, no. Why would I have their number if I can't afford their products? But they ought to be in the book. I think the guy who owns the joint is named Humphrey."

"Okay, Tony. Thanks for the help."

"You're welcome, C. K., and come back downtown soon. We need a good cop around here!"

A few minutes later Sergeant Mackie walked into the lobby of the Central Los Angeles Police Station on First Street between Hill and Broadway. He asked the Sergeant manning the complaint desk where they were keeping telephone directories for outlying areas these days and was directed to a bookshelf in the main file room.

Mackie found the directories and opened the one that included San Pedro exchanges. He located the number for Pacific Tobacco Importers on Seventh Street and used the file room clerk's telephone to make the call.

When he got Mister Humphrey on the line, Mackie identified himself, and Humphrey said, "Sure Sergeant, how can I help you?"

"I'm interested in El Pantera cigars. I'm told they're imported from Cuba and they're very expensive. I'm also told that yours is the only company that imports them."

"Well, mostly that's correct. We are the sole west coast distributor for El Panteras. There's another importer in Florida that distributes them east of the Rockies. I think they are much more popular back there. Most men out here have never heard of El Panteras and wouldn't pay the price if they had."

"Can you tell me who you do sell them to around here?"

"We don't sell many of them. I can tell you that much right away, but I'll need to get the order book to give you the exact information. Shall I call you back in a few minutes or do you want to hang on the line?"

Mackie said he would hang on the line, and Humphrey went to get his order book. After a couple of minutes, Humphrey picked up the phone again and said, "I've got the book here, Sergeant, and it looks as though we only have three customers who regularly order El Panteras. One is the Market Street Tobacco Shop in Seattle, Washington. They're our only wholesale customer, and they order a box about once a month. The other two customers are private individuals. We take their orders because they both purchase large quantities."

"Who are they?"

"We ship two boxes each month to a Mister Harlow G. Ormsby in Denver Colorado, and we have a standing order for eight boxes a month from a Mister L. A. Bromfeld in Hollywood."

"What's the shipping address for that last customer?"

"Let me see . . . here it is. We send them care of Western National Films, 6320 Santa Monica Boulevard."

"I see. Tell me one more thing, Mister Humphrey. How many El Panteras come in a box?"

"They're packed twenty-five to a box. Fancy box, too, painted with bright red lacquer and made out of thicker wood than most. Costs more just to ship them because of the extra weight."

"Thank you for the information, Mister Humphrey. You've been very helpful."

"Glad I could help, Sergeant. Say, would you like me to send a box of El Panteras over to you? On the house, of course."

Mackie shook his head in disgust. The merchants of Los Angeles were so used to paying off cops that offers like this one were made automatically. He said, "No thanks, Mister Humphrey. I don't want to pick up any habits I can't afford."

"You sure now? I'd be happy to . . . ."

"Thanks anyway, Mister Humphrey. I appreciate your help."

C. K. hung up and returned the telephone directory to its shelf. After adding the information provided by Humphrey to his notebook, he asked the file room clerk to find the arrest record of Harry or Harold Lee of Hollywood. A few minutes later she returned with a bulging folder.

Mackie took the folder to a file room work table and opened it. There were a total of fifteen arrest reports, all of which were dated within the last two years. Six of them were for public drunkenness and four were charges of operating a vehicle in an unsafe manner—specifically, driving while drunk. There were also three arrests for illegal gambling and two for employing the services of a prostitute. Harry Lee had been a real man about town.

As amazing as the number of times Harry Lee had been arrested was the information C. K. found in the "Outcome" sections of the reports. In all of the public drunkenness cases the entries were "charges dropped for lack of evidence." The same was true for the unsafe vehicle operation arrests. The remaining five reports simply said, "Bail forfeited in lieu of fine." Lillian Lawrence's father had been arrested for a total of ten misdemeanors and five felonies during the past two years and never once went to court.

The only way that could possibly happen is if the "fix" was in for Harry Lee. Somebody in the department was receiving payoffs from Lee to keep him out of jail or perhaps the payoffs were from someone else who was interested in keeping Lillian Lawrence's name out of the newspapers. The latter possibility seemed more likely because it also took some clout to set up a fix, and Mackie doubted very much that a guy like Lee could pull it off by himself. It would take someone with connections—someone like the boss of a major motion picture studio.

The sergeant returned the file folder to the clerk and, on a hunch, asked her to locate any files they might have on Harry Lee's homicide case, explaining that the case was in county jurisdiction but that the sheriff might have requested L.A.P.D. assistance with the investigation.

Mackie was pretty sure she would come back empty-handed. Requests from the county sheriff for assistance with homicide cases were not uncommon due to the sheriff's limited manpower, but after going through channels, an official request for help in the Harry Lee investigation would have ended up at the Sixth Precinct because the victim lived in Hollywood. Since no such request had crossed his desk, the sergeant had no reason to think Central Division would have anything on it either.

That's why he was amazed when the file clerk returned about ten minutes later carrying a single folder. She told Mackie she'd found it in the Unsolved Homicides filing cabinet. Returning to the file room work table, he opened the folder. For a homicide file, the folder was surprisingly thin. Most murder cases generated an inch or more of crime scene descriptions, witness interviews, coroner's reports, and other investigation information. Harry Lee's file contained less than a dozen sheets of paper.

The top page was a letter from Captain Royce to Detective Lieutenant Brian Pierce, Winfield's counterpart at Central Division. In the sort of formal verbiage that was typical of Royce's communiqués, the captain informed Pierce that the Los Angeles County Sheriff was requesting assistance from the L.A.P.D. in investigating the death of Harry Lee. Royce instructed Pierce to provide such assistance as needed. That explained why the department had a file on the investigation, but it did not explain why it was never forwarded to the Sixth Precinct.

The next sheet in the folder was a standard Los Angeles County Sheriff's Department Homicide Investigation Report Form on which were summarized the details of the case. The entries on the form were handwritten and dated 3 July, 1926. Below the date came the victim's name followed by his address: 329 Hollymount Drive, Los Angeles, California. This was followed by the victim's age: 41; the next of kin: Lillian Lee (daughter); and a physical description: height, 5' 11"; weight, 175 pounds; hair, brown; eyes, green; and identifying marks, scars on left shoulder and left forearm.

The next section of the report described the circumstances of the victim's death. From this entry, Mackie learned that an anonymous call reporting a body in the parking area behind the Club Fiesta at 8345 Sunset Boulevard was received at the sheriff's Cahuenga Valley substation at 12:31 a.m. on Saturday, 3 July. Deputies responding to the call arrived at the Club Fiesta at approximately 12:45 a.m. and found the victim, who appeared to have been severely beaten and was missing his wallet, along with a pocket watch and a ring his daughter said he normally wore. No witnesses to the beating were found, but several patrons of the Club Fiesta knew the victim and said he'd been there since at least 9:00 p.m. and that he left the club a little before midnight. Witnesses hinted that Lee had been gambling and drinking steadily since he arrived at the establishment.

Mackie shook his head at the last part. Gambling was legal in the county, but consuming alcoholic beverages was not because it was a violation of the Federal Volstead Act, a result of the Eighteenth Amendment to the Constitution. Including witness statements that referred to drinking was, in effect, an admission on the part of the sheriff's office that they had failed to close down an illegal establishment. Such an admission would never, under any circumstances, have appeared in an official L.A.P.D. investigation document.

The first section on the back side of the form was labeled, "Cause of Death." After the coroner's file number were the words, "Victim died of cerebral hemorrhaging caused by repeated blows to the head. Weapon might have been a club or similar object." The report placed the time of death between 11:00 p.m. Friday night and 1:00 a.m. Saturday morning.

In the last section of the form, under "Investigating Officer's Comments," Mackie read, "Victim's record shows repeated arrests for public drunkenness and driving an automobile while under the influence of alcohol. The most likely motive for this murder is robbery by a person or persons unknown."

The next page in the folder was a handwritten note signed by Detective Lieutenant Pierce on 3 August, 1926, exactly one month after Royce referred the case to Pierce. It stated that the L.A.P.D.'s investigation of Harry Lee's murder was suspended on that date due, in Pierce's judgment, to a lack of adequate evidence and leads. He instructed that the case be placed in the Unsolved Homicide files and reviewed periodically or in the event new information was received.

Pierce's note was the last document in the Harry Lee homicide investigation folder. That came as no surprise to Mackie. He'd served under Lieutenant Brian Pierce a few times over the years and knew him to be barely competent. In fact, to the sergeant's mind, the only curious thing about the case was that Royce kept it within Central Division rather than forwarding it to the Sixth Precinct where it would have gotten the attention it deserved. Did the fix for Harry Lee extend all the way to the top of the Homicide Division? While Mackie didn't much care for Royce's tactics, he never before suspected the man of being a crooked cop. That possibility came as just one more disappointment in the department's lack of integrity.

As Mackie handed Harry Lee's homicide file back to the clerk, he wondered if she had instructions to report any interest in the file to someone upstairs. It might be interesting to hang around and see what she did next, but it was already close to ten o'clock and he still had a lot to do before his one o'clock appointment with Winfield at the Hollywood Hotel.

C. K.'s next stop was the Central Division detective room where he used a telephone to call the county coroner's office. When his call was answered, he asked to speak with Herman Geisler. Geisler was widely known as the best autopsy surgeon in Los Angeles, so celebrities showing up at the morgue usually ended up on his table. When Geisler got on the line, Mackie said, "Herman, this is C. K. Mackie. I was wondering if you were doing the Lillian Lawrence autopsy."

"Yes, they just handed me the paperwork. You handling the case at that end?"

"Yes. I'm working it with Bob Winfield. I don't guess you've met him yet. He took Ed Price's place out in the Sixth Precinct a few months back. What I wanted to know is when you figure we can see the report on Lillian Lawrence."

Geisler sighed and answered, "Will tomorrow morning do? Things are backing up around here, and that's about the earliest I can promise."

"Tomorrow morning is fine. Would you mind sending your report out to the Sixth?"

"Sure, C. K. I'll send a deputy over with it as soon as I get it typed up."

Leaving Central Division, Mackie turned his Dodge north on Broadway. To his right he could see the City Hall tower rising majestically behind the squat Hall of Records building. The magnificent white tower—the tallest building in town—was a Los Angeles landmark recognized far and wide. It was probably as well known as the city's reputation for crooked cops. That thought did nothing to alleviate the growing uneasiness he was feeling about Lillian Lawrence's murder.

TWELVE

Eugene "Tex" Clugman first saw the light of day through gaps in the canvas that covered a one-room shack in which his folks and two immigrant families were living while working on a farm along the Cimarron River near Kenton, Oklahoma. The next sixteen years of his life were lived out in similar places throughout the Oklahoma panhandle and northeastern Texas.

By the time Eugene was sixteen, somewhere 'long about 1918, he'd had enough of backbreaking farm labor and set out for west Texas where he heard there were jobs for cowboys. He was already six feet tall, and though on the lanky side, he was strong as a bull. In spite of his tender age and the fact that he'd never herded so much as a dairy cow, Clugman could stay on a horse and figured to learn the rest. He did and spent the next six years working cattle in the high country around Kermit, Pecos, and El Paso.

It wasn't a bad life, 'specially compared to farm labor. Once he learned his way around, the work wasn't too hard and the pay was pretty good. That meant there were also women and liquor. And when prohibition became the law of the land, west Texans pretty much ignored it, figuring the politicians hadn't meant it to include them anyway.

All in all, Eugene was doin' pretty good and probably would have stuck around longer if it hadn't been for old Jake Sterley. Jake was a Winkler County Deputy Sheriff, and he didn't much care for Eugene. It seemed that whenever Eugene was working around Kermit and came into town on a Saturday night, that old son-of-a-bitch Sterley would end up rousting him out of Red Darling's saloon for bein' drunk and disorderly. None of the other cowboys who were throwin' just as many punches as Eugene got arrested. Sterley always picked on him—said he was the instigator, whatever the hell that meant.

Still, old Jake always turned Eugene loose the next day after makin' him pay the night's damages and a stiff fine. It was a pain in the ass, but that's how it was. The real fuss got started when that damned lineman from over to San Angelo went and got himself killed.

Things were going about like they usually did on Saturday nights at Red's. Somebody riled somebody else, and there you were. It was just a way for the boys to let off a little steam. Nobody ever got killed or nothin', 'cept for that damned lineman.

Eugene didn't really mean to stick him. The fella was about as ornery as they come, and Eugene was just gonna scare him some. Who'd a-figured the guy was dumb enough to keep on comin' at a guy with a knife?

After it happened, Eugene was just sober enough to realize that the man was bad hurt, maybe even killed, and Deputy Sterley would sure as hell try to hang him for it. The brawl was still going strong when Eugene slipped out Darling's back door and borrowed Dud Welby's Model T truck. He only stopped long enough to pick up his goods at the ranch and leave off the truck. Then Eugene hiked over to the highway and stuck his thumb out in the general direction of California.

He celebrated his twenty-second birthday out on the road somewhere between Quartzsite, Arizona and Blythe, California. Eugene's birthday present turned out to be a ride all the way to his destination from an obliging truck driver.

Clugman decided on San Bernardino, about 70 miles east of Los Angeles, because he heard there were cattle ranches in the area. Eugene was already looking forward to working in southern California because winters never got as cold there as they did in west Texas and it hardly ever snowed.

By the time Tex, as he now introduced himself, had been in San Berdoo twenty-four hours, he'd discovered two things. Number one, none of the ranches in the area were hiring any help, and number two, it didn't much matter because he was on to something better. A fella he ran into at a roadhouse east of town told him about Gower Gulch.

It seemed this guy was just in town for the day visiting some hands he used to ride with before he got into the moving picture business. It wasn't as steady as ranch work, he admitted, but the pay was better and the work was a far sight easier. All you had to do was get down to the corner of Sunset and Gower in Hollywood first thing every morning and hang around. Pretty soon some fella from one of the picture studios showed up and hired hands to be extras or do stunts in their movies. They called the corner Gower Gulch because of all the cowhands hangin' around waitin' for work.

The guy said he was headed back there and if Tex wanted to ride along, he was welcome. Figuring that getting paid to ride a horse back and forth in front of a moving picture camera was better than pumpin' gasoline or diggin' ditches, Clugman accepted the offer of a ride into Hollywood.

The next day, wearing his best boots and ten-gallon Stetson, Tex Clugman joined the regulars of Gower Gulch. By the end of the week, he was a veteran with two film appearances to his credit. His earnings for the week tallied up to the grand sum of six dollars, but he was still learnin' the ropes.

Tex discovered that his greatest asset in the movie business was his appearance. His tall, lanky frame and a face weathered by six years of west Texas sun and wind gave him the rugged look of a cowboy. Clugman also learned that there were ways of making himself even more valuable. For example, if he was willing to take some "bumps," as the movie people called them, by falling off a horse or getting himself tossed through the plate glass window of a saloon set, he could earn stunt pay, which, depending on what he had to do, could be as much as twenty-five or thirty bucks for a single day.

Along with a fair number of cuts, scrapes and bruises, Tex Clugman quickly gained a reputation for being up to just about anything a director could throw at him. In one film he was shot off the roof of a two-story building. In another he ended up under the wheels of a fast-moving stagecoach. That one earned him $32.50 and two broken ribs that were quickly taped so he could go back the next day to dive off a fifty-foot cliff.

It wasn't long before the most common words associated with Tex Clugman's name around Gower Gulch were "dang fool" and "plum crazy." By that time, however, Clugman was livin' in his own apartment and had him a two-year-old LaSalle automobile which he was buyin' on time.

Tex survived all the punishment he got in front of the cameras because he discovered a few more natural talents in addition to his cowboy look. For one thing, the old cowhand who'd learned him how to work cattle back in El Paso also showed him how to take a fall without gettin' hurt. You had to kinda relax and get yourself lined up so you landed right. The other thing was that pain didn't seem to bother Clugman like it did other hands. He guessed as how he just didn't feel it as much. So with the confidence of knowin' how to land right side up and figurin' it wouldn't hurt all that bad if he didn't, Tex Clugman wasn't much afraid of anything.

One thing did tend to get him riled up, though. That was how the guys in suits made a whole lot more money for standin' around watchin' than he did for gettin' dirty and doin' all the work. It was the nature of things, and Tex knew there was no changin' it, so he made up his mind to get himself a suit job. He did, but the way it worked out was kinda funny.

Clugman was working at Western National Films, and he'd just finished a great two-bounce fall off the false front of a hotel on the studio's western street. He'd done it just right, but the Heinie director wanted him to do it all over again just to see if he could make it more dramatic.

Tex politely told the fella that the fall was plenty dramatic enough and that they ought to get on to the next shot. For some reason that got the director fella all bent out of shape, and he started in to hollerin' in Tex's face. In spite of the man's bad breath, all the yellin' didn't much bother him. Besides, Tex didn't know half the words the Kraut was usin'. Then he heard one he did know. The guy called him a son of a swine.

Now depending on Clugman's mood a fella might get away with callin' him just about any name in the book, but nobody was gonna call his ma a pig and stay standin' up for very long. Tex's right fist started out about waist high and lifted the Heinie clear off the ground when it connected with the funny little goat beard on the man's chin.

The director fella was still layin' in the dust with a bunch of his boys tryin' to wake him up as Tex walked off the set. He was passin' a whole gang of them suit fellas who was standin' around watchin' the shoot when one of them said, "Cowboy, come here for a minute."

Clugman stopped and looked at the fat little man with the big cigar who was callin' to him. Figurin' that he was in for another parcel of hollerin' and not bein' in the mood for it, Tex turned around and kept right on walkin'. A minute later the fat guy was huffin' and puffin' alongside him, tryin' to keep up, and sayin' in a high, whiny sorta voice, "Slow down, Cowboy. I am having for you a job."

Since that was about the last thing Tex expected to hear, he stopped and listened. The fat guy took the straw boater off his bald head and mopped up some sweat with his handkerchief. He said his name was Bromfeld, that he ran the studio, and that he wanted to give Tex a permanent job as his special assistant.

Clugman had no idea what a special assistant did, but he asked only two questions: How much would he make and did he get to wear a suit? Bromfeld said Tex would get two hundred a week to start, and the studio would buy him a whole closest full of suits. They shook on the deal, and Eugene "Tex" Clugman had himself a real suit job.

It turned out that a special assistant took care of special problems that came along. For example, Mister Bromfeld called Tex in one day and said they had a problem because the brother of a new actress at the studio showed up demanding money. He claimed that Heinie director had been messin' with his sister who, it turned out, was only seventeen. Mister Bromfeld wanted Tex to explain to the fella how things worked around there, which didn't include payin' off relatives. He did, and after the brother got out of the hospital, he went back to Portland and mindin' his own business.

Mister Bromfeld was so happy with the way Tex handled the job, he gave him a raise and his own little office out back near the studio's horse stable. And the raise he got was big enough that Tex got rid of his old LaSalle automobile and bought him a brand spankin' new Buick Master Six touring car—a blue one with all the trimmin's. Yes, sir, he was livin' in style.

Tex had been on the Western National payroll for about two years when Lillian Lawrence was killed. In fact, he'd just returned from a vacation to visit his ma and sister near Dallas the Friday before she died. Under the circumstances Clugman wasn't too surprised when he got an urgent summons from Mister Bromfeld on Monday morning. The boss was kind of excitable to start with, and this kettle of beans would have him in an uproar for sure.

When Clugman got to Bromfeld's office, he saw right off that he was right. The boss was even more riled up than usual, but the fuss didn't have nothin' to do with the little blonde actress. Instead, he was all lathered up about a bundle sittin' on his desk. It was about six by eight inches and maybe two inches thick. The package was all wrapped up in brown paper and tied real tight with string.

When the boss gave it to Tex, he handled the bundle like it was gonna bite him. Mister Bromfeld said, "You must be taking this up to my ranch and burying it. Bury it very deep in the ground and far away from the house. Do you understand?"

"Sure, Boss. What's in it?"

Bromfeld glared at Tex and said sternly, "This is nothing of your concern. And whatever you are doing, you must not be opening this. Just be taking it away from here and burying it deep in the ground like I am telling you."

"Sure, Boss. It's as good as done."

Clugman tucked the package into a side pocket of his suit coat and saw right away that Mister Bromfeld looked relieved. Tex asked, "Is there anything you want me to do about that Lawrence gal?"

"Yes, I want you should be very careful about what you are saying to the policemans about Lilly and her father. Two of them have already been to see me, and they will be coming here and snooping around also. If they are talking to you, you are to be watching carefully what you say. Do you understand that, too?"

"I got you, Boss. You don't have nothin' to worry about."

L. A. Bromfeld nodded grimly and looked like he was wishin' to Heaven Tex was right.

THIRTEEN

Lieutenant Winfield opened the door to L. A. Bromfeld's outer office and came face to face with a cowboy. Even allowing for his ten-gallon hat, the man matched Winfield's six-foot-two and then some.

The lieutenant took a polite step back and held the door open for the cowboy, who flashed a big grin on his deeply tanned face and said, "Thank you kindly, Pard."

Winfield watched him amble down the hallway, heard his high-heeled boots clack on the hardwood floor, and tried to place the fellow. His mannerisms and expensive suit with the spiffy western-style stitching around the pockets and lapels made him a caricature of the motion picture cowboy, but the lieutenant couldn't remember ever seeing the guy in a film. At the same time Winfield's cop eyes registered tiny inconsistencies in the picture they were seeing, like the bulging side pocket of the man's coat that held a parcel wrapped in newspaper and the slight limp that altered the rhythm of his footsteps. None of the inconsistencies meant anything; they were just little flaws in an image the fellow obviously worked hard to maintain.

Walking into Bromfeld's outer office, Winfield came face to face with another caricature, that of a stern, no-nonsense school marm with graying hair pulled back into a bun that made her sharp features more severe than they probably were. A neatly carved wooden name plate on the desk said, "Miss Bessie Shipman." The woman looked up from her desk, glared at him for a moment, and then turned back to her work, commanding, "Sit down. I'll get to you as soon as I'm done here."

Her tone perfectly matched her appearance in the same way the cowboy's wide grin and mannerisms so perfectly portrayed a western movie character. Winfield wondered if the dramatic aura surrounding motion picture studios was so overwhelming that everyone who worked in such an environment, regardless of their actual job, was somehow drawn into portraying fantasy roles just as the real actors performed their assigned roles in front of the cameras.

For a moment the lieutenant was tempted to respond with rudeness equal to the woman's, but thought better of it. Instead, he sauntered over to the wall on his right and contemplated the gallery of framed photographs displayed there. A dozen or so film scenes were arranged in a loose circular pattern around a large color rendering of the studio's logotype, a stylized motion picture reel trailing a length of film that spelled out "Western National Films."

In the first photo that caught Winfield's eye, Nigel Pierce was standing on a railway platform portraying Phileas Fogg in a scene from the motion picture adaptation of Jules Verne's Around the World in Eighty Days. There were also individual photographs of Lillian Lawrence and Mae White, including one of Miss White in a costume he recalled seeing in Fame and Fortune the night before. In another photo he recognized the western hero with blazing six-shooters as Tom E. Colt.

Then he came to a photo of Lillian Lawrence and Mae White together. It was from their film, Hello, Goodbye. Miss Lawrence, costumed in overalls and a straw hat, stood gawking at a sophisticated Mae White in a sequined evening gown. Studying the photo, he saw the camera had captured something in their expressions that made them appear to be enjoying the moment beyond the facades of their characters—like two close friends mugging for a snapshot in the family photo album.

These thoughts were interrupted by the stern voice behind the desk that said, "Young man, will you please sit down! I cannot concentrate with you pacing back and forth.

Winfield decided he'd cooled his heels long enough. Turning to face the woman, he casually opened his jacket and took out the wallet that contained his badge. The secretary's eyes were still registering some slight surprise at what he thought might have been the sight of his shoulder holster when he said, "Miss Shipman—that is your name isn't it?"

She nodded, staring slightly cross-eyed at the badge he held inches from the end of her sharply pointed nose. He continued, "Miss Shipman, I am Detective Lieutenant Robert Winfield of the Los Angeles Police Department Homicide Division, and I am certain the good people of our fair city would appreciate it if you stopped wasting my time and their money. I presume Mister Bromfeld told you to expect me this morning?"

Bessie Shipman recovered quickly and making it abundantly clear that she was not impressed by public servants, even those with guns, said, "Yes, Mister Bromfeld did say something about the police coming around to investigate Lillian Lawrence's murder. A tragedy, I might add, that would not have occurred had you been earning that salary the good people of our fair city so generously pay you."

Ignoring her remark as if it were never spoken, Winfield said, "Perhaps I should direct my questions to Mister Bromfeld personally."

"I am so sorry," she purred, "but Mister Bromfeld is in conference all morning and cannot be disturbed."

"In that case, would you be so kind as to tell me where I might find Ernst Frohmme?"

"I'm afraid he isn't available, either. Mister Frohmme is directing a location filming in Santa Monica."

"Then I presume Miss Mae White is also unavailable?"

"Oh my, yes. Miss White's maid called early this morning to say Mae would be staying home today. As any sensitive person might expect, she is terribly upset over the loss of her dear friend, Miss Lawrence."

Smiling his most ingratiating smile, Winfield said, "Well, then, Miss Shipman, I'm afraid that means we are stuck with each other this morning. So let's begin with Lillian Lawrence's contract with Western National. I would like to see it please."

Then thinking it might be useful to have another example for the sake of comparison. He added, "I would also like to see Mae White's contract."

Miss Shipman seemed to consider the second part of Winfield's request for a moment and then apparently decided it was within the bounds of her boss's instructions. She said, "Certainly, Mister Winfield. Mister Bromfeld asked me to cooperate in whatever small way I could with your investigation. If you will please be seated, I'll try to locate those documents."

Bessie Shipman stood and painstakingly assembled all the loose papers on her desk into a neat stack she tucked away in a drawer. Then without so much as another glance at Winfield, she left the room.

Nearly twenty minutes passed before Miss Shipman returned. She began to hand the papers she carried to Winfield, but stopped, leaving the lieutenant standing there with has hand outstretched while she admonished, "I'm sorry, Mister Winfield, but studio policy prohibits me from allowing these documents to leave this room. I'm afraid you will have to look at them here." Then, smiling in a way that was clearly not intended to convey any degree of friendliness, she thrust two sheaves of paper into Winfield's hand and returned to her desk.

The lieutenant sat on a leather couch near the door and began looking at the documents. The first thing that struck him was that Lillian Lawrence's contract consisted of a much thinner stack of paper than Mae White's. Winfield began deciphering the legal language in Miss Lawrence's contract first. It was dated July 16, 1924, and in a nutshell said that Lillian Lee was to be employed as a motion picture actress by Western National Films, Incorporated for a period of five years. While Miss Lee was bound to remain in the studio's employ during that time, Western National reserved the right to renew their option on her services at six-month intervals.

She was to be paid an initial salary of $650.00 per week. The contract further stipulated that her salary was to be increased by an amount not exceeding $250 per week at the end of each six-month period of employment. So, Winfield figured, if Lillian Lawrence received all of the maximum increases allowed for in her contract, her weekly salary during the final six months of the agreement could have been as much as $2,650 per week. A rough calculation gave him a mind-numbing total of nearly $138,000 for her annual salary at that rate.

Then it struck Winfield that at the time of her death Lillian Lawrence was making around $200 more in a week than he made in an entire year as a police lieutenant with a college education. It was a sobering indication of their relative importance in the eyes of the public. Folks would wait in line to pay fifty cents or a dollar for the privilege of seeing Miss Lawrence act on film, but they screamed bloody murder if their taxes were raised by a few pennies in order that police officers might earn a decent wage.

The contract's remaining paragraphs clearly spelled out what was expected of Miss Lawrence. They required her to accept any role assigned to her and further allowed the studio to "loan" her to another film company at any time. Should she refuse to comply with any of the contract stipulations, Western National had the option of suspending her employment indefinitely without pay. Furthermore, she was forbidden to accept employment from any other studio during such periods of suspension.

Winfield turned to Mae White's contract and discovered several major differences. For example, he noted that on the subject of billing, which wasn't even mentioned in Lillian Lawrence's contract, Miss White's agreement required that her name appear first in all advertisements and film credits "in letters larger and of greater prominence than the name of any other player." Further clauses stipulated that Mae White would not be required to make more than six motion pictures per year and that she retained the right to reject any parts or films she deemed inappropriate. Also, her work day was to begin no earlier than 9:00 a.m. and end no later than 5:30 p.m.

When he came to the compensation and benefits section of Mae White's contract, the lieutenant shook his head in complete amazement. The vast sum earned by Lillian Lawrence was a mere pittance compared to the amount Mae White earned. In addition to specified benefits, which included clothing and automobile allowances, Mae White was paid $19,000 per week!

It was almost beyond comprehension that for each picture she made Mae White earned more than twice the annual salary Calvin Coolidge received for running an entire country. Winfield had to wonder how many dollar bills had to pass through theater box offices across the country for Western National to pay Mae White that kind of money in addition to its other production costs and still make a profit. Making movies was obviously a much bigger business than he ever imagined.

The lieutenant copied a few of the pertinent details from Lillian Lawrence's contract into his notebook and returned the documents to Bessie Shipman's desk. She made a show of examining them to be sure they were complete and said, "Now, Mister Winfield, if there is nothing else you need . . . ."

"Just a few questions, Miss Shipman. Mister Bromfeld had dinner with Miss Lawrence Saturday night at the Hollywood Hotel. Do you know if a dinner reservation was made for that meeting?"

"Yes, of course. I made the reservation myself."

"When did you make that reservation?"

"I called the hotel dining room just before noon on Friday."

Winfield noted in his book that Bessie Shipman's description of how and when the dinner reservation was made jibed with Maurice DeVoe's. Then he asked, "Do you know the purpose of that meeting?"

Miss Shipman thought about the question for a good deal longer than Winfield thought should have been necessary before saying, "No, I do not."

The lieutenant watched her for several seconds hoping the long pause might illicit further comment on the subject, but it did not. The secretary simply sat there staring back at him. Finally, he asked, "Can you think of anyone who disliked Miss Lawrence enough to kill her? Or anyone who might have benefited somehow from her death?"

This time the answer seemed to come much too quickly. "No, Mister Winfield, I cannot."

"Was she liked by people here at the studio? Did she get along with everyone?"

"I don't spend much time out on the lot, so I really can't answer that question."

In spite of feeling as if he were beating his head against a brick wall, Winfield continued his questions. "I understand Miss Lawrence was a seamstress in the studio's costume shop before she started making films. Is that correct?"

"Yes. Miss Lawrence worked in the costume shop for three or four months before Mister Bromfeld discovered her there and arranged for a screen test."

Sensing a small victory in finally finding a line of questions the cautious Miss Shipman was willing to answer, he pressed her further on the subject. "How did he happen to discover her?"

"As I understand it, Mister Bromfeld noticed her through a window in the costume shop and thought she had the sort of face that would photograph well."

Noting this in his book, Winfield asked, "Who did Miss Lawrence work for in the costume shop?"

Bessie Shipman hesitated again as though she was trying to recall a name, and then she said, "Our head costume designer is a woman named Viola Wiebe. She would have supervised Miss Lawrence's work."

"And where can I find Viola Wiebe?"

There was another long pause while Miss Shipman thought about her answer or perhaps whether she should answer the question at all. Finally she said, "Miss Wiebe would be in the costume shop over on the new lot. Go back out the main gate to Santa Monica Boulevard and turn right. Cross Cole Street and turn right again through the gates in the middle of the block. The commissary parking area will be on your left. Go past that and turn left at the next street. The costume shop is the first building on your left after the commissary."

Winfield was still writing these directions in his notebook as he said, "Thank you, Miss Shipman. Is there anyone else here at the studio who knew Miss Lawrence well or worked closely with her?"

"Mister Bromfeld anticipated that you might ask that question and suggested you speak with Oliver Stephens. He was the camera operator on Miss Lawrence's films. Also, Mister Bromfeld thought you might want to talk to a Miss Fanny DeWitt who did Miss Lawrence's makeup. You will most likely find her in the makeup studio behind Film Stages One, Two and Three directly opposite this building. I don't know where Stephens would be, although you might try the camera shop across the street from the makeup studio."

The lieutenant finished adding this information to his notebook and then smiled at Bromfeld's secretary. "Thank you, Miss Shipman, you've been most helpful."

Bessie Shipman glared at him again and said curtly, "You are most welcome, I'm sure."

FOURTEEN

Winfield stood on the front steps of Western National Films' administration building after interviewing Bessie Shipman and took a moment to get his bearings. The austere two-story office building behind him faced east and sat in the southwest corner of the studio's east lot on Santa Monica Boulevard between Cahuenga and Cole.

The high concrete wall isolating Western National's world from the real world traffic on Santa Monica Boulevard was on his right just beyond the south end of the administration building. The wall was interrupted only once that he could see, and the opening was protected by the studio's heavy iron entrance gates and a security guard. Directly in front of him was a paved parking lot provided for visitors and the studio's administrative staff. On the far side of the parking lot, a two-lane street led north past the administration building before disappearing into the maze of buildings on his left.

Across the street from the administration parking area there was a massive, cream-colored barn-like structure that was larger and even less ornate than the administration building. Its exterior wall on Winfield's side had neither doors, windows, nor any other kind of opening. From Bessie Shipman's description, he presumed this structure housed film stages one, two, and three, which meant the makeup studio and camera shop were somewhere beyond it.

Winfield descended the administration building steps and turned left to walk diagonally toward what he guessed was the back of the film stage building. He paused briefly, however, to look at an automobile parked near the administration building entrance. It was the movement of his reflection in the glossy depths of the open phaeton's dark green paint that caught his attention and drew him closer. Even under an overcast sky, nickel plating sparkled on running lights, bumpers, and a hundred other trim pieces that decorated the machine like Christmas ornaments. From the center of each huge, wire-laced wheel, a bright red octagon informed those in the know that this was no ordinary automobile; it was a Packard.

A small sign just visible beyond the Packard's gleaming radiator indicated that this parking space was reserved for L. A. Bromfeld. That made perfect sense to Winfield. An employer of people who earned hundreds of thousands of dollars a year would drive no less an automobile than this gleaming behemoth.

Winfield crossed the main street to follow a secondary road that led off at an angle behind the film stages. A triangle-shaped wooden building that had been stuffed into the sliver of land created by the junction of the two streets bore a small sign identifying it as "Property Warehouse #2." Beyond the warehouse, the street jogged right again in front of a smaller building labeled, "Camera Shop." He followed a well-worn dirt path to the three wooden steps leading up to its door. Inside he found a gloomy room that seemed to occupy most of the building's interior space. What light there was came from a narrow window in the wall to his left and a bare light bulb hanging from the ceiling over a large worktable at the room's center. With the exception of the wall space occupied by the window, the entrance door, and another door to his right, all four walls were lined with floor-to-ceiling shelves filled to overflowing with wooden cases, cardboard boxes and lose piles of what the lieutenant thought were camera parts. Large wooden tripods were stacked three and four deep in each corner of the room, and the worktable was cluttered with more camera parts and an assortment of screwdrivers, pliers, and wrenches.

There were no signs of life in the room, but Winfield could hear movement through the closed door on his right. A neatly painted sign on the door read, "Dark Room." A sheet of yellowing paper tacked below the sign bore the hand-printed words, "Don't open this door, all the dark will leak out!" Smiling at what was apparently darkroom humor, he said loudly, "Hello? Anybody here?"

A male voice behind the door shouted back, "I'm loading film. Be with you in a minute."

Winfield wandered around the room looking at the tools of the motion picture camera operator's trade for a few minutes, and then the darkroom door opened and a slender man several inches shorter than the lieutenant came through it. He wore round, metal-framed spectacles and a brushy mustache that might have been grown to compensate for the fact that the man's head was otherwise bald. He was carrying what looked like the top half of a motion picture camera—the part with two large round shapes that held the camera's film supply. In spite of its gloom, the outer room must have been much brighter than the darkroom because the man blinked several times while his eyes became accustomed to the change in light before he spotted the lieutenant and said, "What can I do for you?"

"I'm with the Los Angeles Police Department. I'm looking for Oliver Stephens."

The man carefully set his film canister on the worktable and cautiously said, "I'm Oliver Stephens."

The lieutenant put Stephens at ease by offering his hand and saying, "Mister Stephens, I'm Bob Winfield. I'm investigating the death of Lillian Lawrence."

Stephens shook the offered hand and said with a smile, "Glad to meet you, Bob. Call me Ollie."

"Okay, Ollie. Mister Bromfeld gave me your name as one of the people here at the studio who worked with Miss Lawrence."

"That's true, and I'm going to miss her. Lilly was one of the few sane people in this asylum."

Stephens had returned to the worktable and was attaching the film canister to the top of a black box with a nickel-plated crank sticking out of one side and four black and silver tube-like lenses mounted on a circular disk attached to its front panel. Watching the man's slender fingers twist and snap fasteners that held the film canister to the camera body, Winfield said, "I was hoping you could tell me a few things about Miss Lawrence and her work here."

As Stephens stretched a thin, rubber drive belt around a small silver pulley on the canister, he said, "Sure. I'm happy to help in any way I can, but I've got a crew waiting for me out back. Would you mind talking on the way over there?"

"Not at all."

Stephens carefully fitted the camera into a wooden carrying case and snapped the lid down. Then he went to a corner and selected a tripod. Tucking its bulk under one arm, he grabbed a round metal gizmo sprouting an assortment of levers and knobs from a shelf, and stooped to pick up the camera case. Winfield stepped forward and said, "You've got quite a load there. Can I help carry some of that?"

Stephens handed him the round gadget with all the levers and knobs, saying, "Thanks. You can carry the camera mount if you don't mind. My assistant was supposed to load the camera and move all this stuff out to the set early this morning, but Al Tinker's helper didn't show up and Al has location shoots out in Santa Monica this week, so I made him the loan of my man."

Outside, Winfield followed Stephens through a narrow gap between the camera shop and another building marked "Electrical Shop" to a well-traveled dirt road. Turning right, then left, and then right again, they followed the dirt road around a barn complete with a corral and four horses who observed their passing with only mild interest. Two young women in heavy makeup and snug-fitting costumes that looked appropriate to a western saloon setting bustled by. Both were barefoot, carrying their satin high-heeled shoes to keep them from getting dusty or so they could walk faster, Winfield wasn't sure which. They each greeted Stephens with a cheerful, "Hi, Ollie!"

He returned their greetings, and the taller of the two girls—a redhead with green eyes and a beauty mark on her right cheek—shot an appraising glance and a smile over her shoulder at Winfield as they hurried along.

Up ahead, at the far end of the barn, some workmen were manhandling an elaborately painted Roman chariot down a makeshift ramp they'd rigged against the back of a flatbed truck. Winfield found the incongruity of people and objects in this bizarre movie world fascinating. With some effort he forced his attention back to the business at hand and asked, "Ollie, how did Miss Lawrence get along with people here? I mean, did she have any particular friends or enemies?"

"Lilly got along with just about everybody, and she was naturally friendly, unlike some people around here. A lot of actors get swelled heads once they're successful and figure themselves better than everyone else. Lilly was just the opposite. She actually seemed grateful to be here and worked like the dickens to please everybody from her directors on down."

"It seems as if she made it to the top awfully fast. Was she really that good an actress?"

Stephens thought for a few steps, and then stopped and turned to face Winfield. "Bob, let me tell you something. I came out here to Los Angeles back in 'thirteen on the train from New York with the great Mister Cecil De Mille. Since then I've cranked film for the best actors in the business—little Mary Pickford, Bill Hart, Valentino . . . all of them—and I can tell you that none of those people worked any harder or had one ounce more talent than Lilly Lawrence. The only difference is the others wanted fame and fortune; Lilly was just trying to make a living. I really believe she would have been happier going back to her old job in the costume shop."

They started walking again and Winfield said, "That's interesting. You wouldn't think someone who felt like that would work so hard."

"That's the way Lilly was. She knew that a lot of people would give their right arms to be in her shoes. I think she felt some kind of responsibility because of that. To tell you the truth, most of us were glad to hear she was quitting the business—not because we didn't like working with her, but because this business was too hard on her. In spite of all the glamour, movie actors are under a lot of pressure, and she wasn't cut out for that kind of life. Even in the short time she was here you could see how it was wearing her down."

The left side of their route, opposite the horse barn, was bordered by a tall board fence. Through occasional gaps, Winfield caught glimpses of several wooden buildings that looked to be under construction. He could also see that the road they were on dead-ended up ahead at the concrete wall which guarded Western National's eastern boundary along Cahuenga Avenue.

"Ollie, would you say Miss Lawrence was particularly close to anyone here at the studio?"

"I guess you'd say her closest friend was Mae White. Lilly was close to Viola Wiebe, too, but that was different. Viola was her boss in the costume shop, and she was more like a mama to Lilly than a pal."

"What can you tell me about the relationship between Mae White and Miss Lawrence?"

Stephens smiled. "I can't think of two people who were less likely to end up as bosom buddies than those two. Lilly was shy and . . . I guess 'innocent' is the word. Mae White, well, I'll just say she's more the opposite kind of person."

"You mean the opposite of shy and innocent?"

"Take it easy on me, Bob; I'm trying to be diplomatic here. I don't believe in talking behind other folks' backs. Let's just say they were different kinds of people."

After a moment, Stephens added, "I'll say this for Mae White, though. She's got more balls than most of the men around here when it comes to standing up for herself and her friends."

"Oh? How's that?"

"I just mean she doesn't stand for any nonsense."

"You mean like from a director?"

Stephens glanced at Winfield and said, "Oh, I guess you already heard about that."

"I heard there was a problem between Miss Lawrence and a director named Frohmme. Where you around when it happened?"

"Yes. Unfortunately, I was."

"Tell me what you saw?"

"Like I said, I don't like to talk about people behind their backs."

"I appreciate that, Ollie, but we're really in the dark on this case. If we're going to find Miss Lawrence's killer, I need every piece of information about the people in her life I can get. Like, what sort of fellow is this Frohmme?"

They had come to an opening in the wooden fence on their left. Stephens headed through it and Winfield followed him into the midst of a carpenter's nightmare. The half-finished buildings he glimpsed through the fence were actually the backs of false-fronted movie sets—facades held up by cobwebs of two-by-fours. From that perspective, they looked as if they wouldn't survive a stiff breeze. From the front, however, the sets looked remarkably like substantial buildings complete with shop windows, doors, and signs. And they seemed to go on forever, lining a maze of streets that apparently covered the entire northeast corner of the studio property.

As they walked through a deserted urban neighborhood, Winfield noticed there seemed to be something slightly out of whack with the scale of things. Everything looked a little smaller than real life. The doorways and windows seemed right, but the sidewalks were narrower and the upper floors of the buildings seemed shorter than they should have been. He concluded that the camera saw things differently than his eye because he had never noticed a discrepancy in the proportions of buildings he saw on the movie screen. Winfield was still contemplating this feat of illusion when Stephens finally answered his question.

"Ernst Frohmme is a hard man to work for, so naturally people don't take to him. He's a different sort of person than most of us are used to—kind of aristocratic, if you know what I mean."

"What makes him a hard man to work for?"

"Well, for one thing, Frohmme is a perfectionist. He wants things just so, and if an actor isn't doing something exactly that way, he gets upset. He screams and hollers like it was a personal insult. Frohmme can be moody, too. He goes from one mood to another just like you turn the dial of a radio set. One minute he's charming and all smiles, and the next he's Captain Bligh, throwing things around and cursing everyone on the set. And he can be real . . . I guess you'd say sadistic. Sometimes he seems to enjoy abusing people—the ones who will take it. That's the secret to working with Frohmme. If you don't let him bother you, it takes the fun out of it and he doesn't pick on you as much."

"We've heard that Frohmme is fond of young women and that he has some unusual sexual interests. Any truth to those stories that you know of?"

Stephens thought about his answer as they turned a corner and left the urban neighborhood to enter an old French village. "You've got to remember, there are always going to be stories about fellows like Frohmme—guys who are different than the average person. I know from working for him that he goes for the young girls, so that part is true. I've heard the rumors that he has some funny ideas about sex and that the studio has had to pay off actresses to keep them quiet, but I don't know if any of that is true or not."

Winfield nodded his understanding of Stephens' disclaimer and said, "So what was Frohmme's relationship to Miss Lawrence?"

"I guess you'd have to say he was very interested in her. I worked on Hello, Goodbye, which Mae White and Lilly made together. Frohmme directed it, and from the moment Lilly walked onto the set, you could tell he was attracted to her. I heard she went out with him once, but I never saw anything happen between them that would indicate they were even friends. The problem was she never learned to ignore his tantrums, so he picked on her more than the others, especially after he got in trouble with Bromfeld over her."

"How did that come about?"

"We were shooting scenes around a barn set over on the other lot, and Frohmme gave us a break while the property guys moved some things around. Everybody sort of wandered off in different directions. I moved the camera for the next scene and was just sort of watching the prop guys when we heard Lilly scream.

"Well, everyone dropped what they were doing and ran behind the set where the screams came from. Mae White and a couple of other gals—offhand, I don't recall who—got there first. When I got there Miss Lawrence was off in a corner crying and Mae White was cussing Frohmme up one side and down the other. It was the only time I've ever seen the man at a complete loss for words. Mae was poking her finger into his chest and telling him that Bromfeld was going to hear about what he'd done. He just kept shaking his head and trying to back away from her. Finally, he pushed her hand away and stormed out."

"What happened then?"

Miss White took Lilly off somewhere, and everybody stood around trying to figure out what happened. The general consensus was that Frohmme had cornered Lilly and tried something funny. Anyway, after a while Frohmme came back and set up the next scene as if nothing had happened. Neither Miss White, nor Lilly were in the scene, so we went ahead and shot it.

"A little while later Miss White and Lilly returned to the set and they acted like nothing had happened, too. Then while we were setting up for another shot, a messenger boy showed up and talked to Frohmme for a few minutes. I found out later that Bromfeld had ordered Frohmme to his office. Frohmme looked madder than hell. He told us to strike the set, that we wouldn't be shooting anything more that day, and then he stormed off."

"Do you know what went on in Bromfeld's office when they met?"

Stephens shook his head. "I have no idea. The story was that Miss White complained to Bromfeld and he called Frohmme on the carpet. I don't know if that's what happened or not, but it fits because Bromfeld runs this place with an iron hand and he couldn't let anything like that happen to one of his most promising players without doing something about it.

"Whatever happened, it didn't make Frohmme happy. From that point on he was twice as hard on Lilly and Miss White both. He made them re-shoot a lot of scenes for no reason that I could see, and he did everything he could to make their lives miserable. That sort of stuff never got to Miss White, but you could see that it was really upsetting Lilly. Several times I felt like taking a poke at him myself."

They rounded another corner and Winfield found himself on the main street of Dodge City or some such western locale. Several people were milling around in the middle of the block, including a couple of cowboys and the two saloon girls who greeted Stephens on the way over. They were all apparently waiting for the camera to show up because when somebody spotted Stephens, everybody got busy doing things and a tall man wearing a white shirt and tweed trousers tucked into knee-high riding boots started shouting instructions through a megaphone.

Winfield said, "It looks like you're the man of the hour here."

"Yeah, and the director—the guy with the megaphone—isn't happy about me keeping everyone waiting. I'm gonna be busy for a while, so if you've got more questions . . . ."

"Just one, Ollie. Do you think Ernst Frohmme is capable of killing Lillian Lawrence for revenge or anything like that?"

Stephens set the camera case and tripod down. Then he took the camera mount from Winfield and looked the lieutenant in the eye. "Most of the time, no, but if he got into one his rages . . . ." He shrugged and left the sentence unfinished.

Winfield nodded his understanding and thanked Ollie for his cooperation. Then the lieutenant stepped back out of the way to watch. Stephens moved the tripod into a position in front of the Silver Dollar Saloon and quickly mounted the camera and its attachments. Two young men moved a four-foot square white sheet stretched around a wooden frame into position, apparently for the purpose of reflecting sunlight into an area of the scene that needed more light. When all was ready, the director raised his megaphone and said, "Places, everybody."

Cowboys and saloon girls scurried around for a few seconds, moving into their assigned locations. Then everyone stood quietly watching the director.

The man in the tweed pants stood behind Stephens and surveyed the tableau before him. He pointed to the redheaded saloon girl and gestured her to the right a foot or so without a word. Then he slowly raised the megaphone to his lips, paused a second, and quietly said, "Camera."

Stephens, who was already squinting through the camera's viewfinder, began turning the crank with what seemed to Winfield like clockwork precision. The director waited a moment longer and then calmly uttered the word, "Action."

It was as if a switch had been thrown somewhere. Two cowboys standing in front of the swinging saloon doors suddenly began throwing punches at each other, and the two women instantly looked shocked at the proceedings. Then the director said, "Now, Tom!"

The swinging doors swung outward and Tom E. Colt burst through them. He was wearing his signature all-black costume, just as in the photo on Bromfeld's office wall. Colt quickly stepped between the brawling cowboys to break up the fight. He ducked a punch from one of them and then threw a fist that sent the cowboy reeling. At the same time, the other cowboy, who was behind Colt, drew his gun. Somehow sensing this, Colt spun around, drawing one of his own pistols. Guns blazed and the second cowboy flew backward through the saloon's window. Glass shattered, the women shrieked, and the director quietly said, "Cut! Nice work, Tom. Next set-up."

That was it. The switch had been flipped off again, the saloon women wandered off, Ollie Stephens began moving his camera to a new location, and Tom E. Colt offered a hand to help the cowboy he'd just shot climb back through the broken saloon window.

It had taken just moments to capture a life and death struggle on film to be projected thousands of times for millions of people in theaters all over the world. After seeing it in person, Winfield had the feeling that sitting in one of those theaters would never be the same for him.

He waved a final thanks to Ollie Stephens and looked at his watch. It was not quite ten-thirty. He still had plenty of time to interview the woman that had done Miss Lawrence's makeup. He began retracing the route they'd taken from the camera shop, and passing through the French village, it occurred to Winfield that his job would be a lot easier if real life were like the movies. If it were, Ollie Stephens and his camera would have been there in room 187 of the Hollywood Hotel Saturday night to capture Lillian Lawrence's murder on film. On the other hand, he realized, if life were like the movies, Lillian Lawrence would have simply gotten up off the floor of her room to do the next scene instead of taking a one-way trip to the morgue with Eddie and his helper.

- - -

Even though he had himself a suit job now, Tex Clugman was still a cowhand at heart. He missed sittin' around with other hands swapping tales about the good old days down on the Pecos. He was also bored. The boss man, that Bromfeld fellow, set Tex up with his own little office place, but he didn't have much to do most days because the boss said he was savin' Tex's talents for special jobs. That was all fine and good, but Tex wasn't the kind to just set around all day. He needed to be doin', not settin'.

As things turned out, though, the solution to his dilemma was right close to hand. It seemed that the place where the boss man set up his special assistant's office was in a little ol' shack way back by the horse barn. With the barn right next door and all, Tex just sort of appointed himself overseer of the wranglers. He wasn't bossy about it or nothin'. He just stopped in at the barn every so often to be sure the hands was takin' good care of the stock.

Well, Monday morning, when Tex was on his way back from the boss's office with that package he was supposed to bury up at the ranch, he decided look in on the hands. Besides, the boys would be wantin' to hear about the vacation he took to see his kin down in Texas.

They sat around the coffee pot for a spell, and then this guy from the property department stuck his head in and said he was there with the chariot and would they come out and give him a hand gettin' it off the truck. So the boys and Tex went out and put up a ramp so they could roll this horse cart thing down into the barn and rig some harness for the horses to pull it.

That chariot was sure enough a funny lookin' outfit. Hell, there wasn't even a seat on the dang thing so the driver had to stand up all the time. Anyway, they was a-pushin' and a-pullin' to get the cart off the truck when Tex noticed one of them camera fellas comin' down the road with that stranger he'd seen goin' into the boss's office. Clugman remembered Bromfeld sayin' how the law would be snoopin' around about that little actress gal that got herself killed, and he had a feelin' that maybe the stranger was a cop.

Since the boss had said they had to watch what they said to the law, and the camera fella looked like he was givin' the cop an earful, Tex figured the boss might like to know what stories his people were tellin' the law. So when the cop and the camera guy turned into the place with all them pretend building they used in the movies, Clugman left the boys to finish gettn' the cart into the barn and trotted off behind the camera guy and the cop.

Actually it was pretty easy. They was walkin' down what everybody called the New York street, and Tex just kinda moseyed along with 'em behind the false fronts. He couldn't hear everything they was sayin', but he heard enough to get the idea. The camera fella was bendin' the cop's ear about that Heinie director, sayin' how he was hard to work for and that he had funny ideas about sex. That seemed to Tex like a whole lot more than the cop needed to know.

About then the two guys turned down another street where Tex couldn't very well follow them without gettin' caught at it, so he went on back to his shack to do some thinkin'. Tex flopped into the fancy swivel chair the boss had put there for him and felt the package in his pocket thump against the chair arm.

He took the package out and tossed it on his desk. It landed with a loud thud that made him wonder what was in the package to make it so heavy. But the boss told him not to open it, so Tex left it on the desk and wondered why the cop was askin' questions about the Heinie director. Did the law think he killed that actress gal? Why else would they be askin' questions about him?

Well, that was about as much thinkin' as Tex liked to do at one time, so he put the whole business aside to think about it again later. Since lunch was a ways off yet, he took the most recent copy of the Police Gazette magazine out of his top drawer and propped his boots up on the desk.

FIFTEEN

Sergeant Mackie didn't recall ever seeing the Hollywood Hotel lobby as quiet as it was when he walked in a few minutes past ten-thirty Monday morning. The unusual tranquility combined with dozens of large wicker flower baskets that traditionally decorated the space gave him a momentary sensation of stepping into a huge funeral parlor.

The room was two to three times as wide as it was deep. A line of four massive baroque chandeliers, complete with gold tassels, crossed the lobby between two rows of large rectangular pillars supporting the high ceiling. Area rugs in a dark green pattern covered the marble floor between the pillars. The baskets with their bright bouquets of white and yellow blooms sat on the floor between and around an assortment of chairs and small couches.

Several sets of French doors with their dark green drapes tied back to help brighten the big room were set into the back wall opposite the main entrance and opened onto the central courtyard. Visitors using the main entrance from Hollywood Boulevard passed through a short foyer on their way to the lobby. Turning left brought them to the registration desk which crossed the front of the lobby on that side. The assistant manager's office, along with two or three other small rooms, was located behind the registration counter. The bell captain's podium, the concierge desk, and a stairway shared the front wall on the opposite side of the main entrance. The Dining Room of the Stars' ornate double wooden doors set into the left wall near the back of the lobby were closed.

Upon entering the lobby, Mackie became the fourth person in the large room. The bell captain, resplendent in his gold-braided, gray uniform, leaned against the wall chatting with a man sitting at the concierge desk. The young man behind the registration desk was so intent upon some task involving small slips of paper with numbers on them he didn't notice the sergeant step up to the counter. When Mackie said, "Excuse me," the startled clerk jerked into an upright posture that was apparently reserved for guests. When he noticed the sergeant's uniform, he relaxed a little and answered the question

Mackie put to him by gesturing toward the stairway and explaining that the hotel manager's office was on the second floor above the lobby.

Climbing the stairs, Mackie looked down on the deserted lobby and wondered if Lillian Lawrence's death had anything to do with the room's lack of activity. On the other hand, he couldn't remember ever being there on a weekday morning before. Perhaps this was simply a quiet time between morning checkout and lunchtime.

The windows behind Lloyd Harrison's desk overlooked the courtyard, and Mackie stood before them impatiently watching an orange tabby stalking birds among the shrubbery below. Harrison's secretary had showed him into the manager's office, explaining that Mister Harrison would only be a minute. Her minute, however, had already turned into ten, and he was very near to going out and asking the woman to hunt down her boss when the door opened and the manager of the Hollywood Hotel walked in.

Harrison was about average height with shock-white hair that made him look older than he probably was. Mackie guessed the fellow didn't get out much because his pale face looked almost chalky next to the dark blue of his tailored three-piece suit. The thick gold watch chain stretched across his vest drew attention to the beginnings of a paunch.

The manager gave Mackie a grim smile that was hardly welcoming and motioned toward one of the two straight-backed chairs facing the desk. Then Harrison dropped into his own chair and said, "Have you seen the morning papers, Sergeant? Both the Examiner and the Times smeared Lillian Lawrence all over their front pages. The Examiner even ran a photograph of what they claimed was room 187 with an outline of Miss Lawrence's body drawn on the floor. Of course, it wasn't 187. It wasn't even a room in the same wing, but little details like that don't matter to a Hearst newspaper."

Mackie opened his notebook and started to speak, but the manager interrupted. "I just hope you're here to tell me you've found the killer so we can let this thing die down and get back to some degree of normality around here."

The sergeant waited a few seconds to be sure Harrison was finished, and then said, "I sincerely wish that were my reason for being here, Mister Harrison, but I'm afraid we've got a way to go yet on this one."

Harrison looked even grimmer. He sighed in apparent resignation and asked, "Okay, Sergeant, how can I help?"

"According to Mister Plant you were in the hotel most of the day on Saturday. Did you see Miss Lawrence during that time?"

Harrison must have been expecting the question because he answered without hesitation. "Yes. I saw her twice. The first time was just after lunch. I was down at the front desk speaking with a guest when she came in. I imagined Miss Lawrence had been shopping because she was carrying a small bundle tied with string."

"You think this was around one?"

"Yes. One or one-thirty, and I glanced out the window here a little later and noticed her sitting in the courtyard. That struck me as unusual. We aren't used to seeing her around the public areas of the hotel."

"Was anyone with her either time you saw Miss Lawrence?"

"No, she was alone. She did have a book with her in the courtyard, but I don't believe she had much interest in it. In fact, she seemed rather bored, as though she didn't have anything to do and was just killing time. When I glanced out the window a little later she was gone, and I didn't see her again before I left the hotel.

A moment of silence passed while Mackie finished an entry in his notebook. Then he asked, "Do you recall what time you saw her in the courtyard?"

"I can't say with any accuracy. It was the middle of the afternoon, perhaps three or three-thirty, but I wouldn't wager on that."

"Do you happen to know if Miss Lawrence had any visitors on Saturday?"

Harrison stared at Mackie for a moment and then answered, "Well, I understand she had dinner with L. A. Bromfeld."

"I mean besides that."

The manager shook his head and said, "There were none that I know of, but that's hardly conclusive since I certainly don't see everyone who comes through the door. It would be more productive to ask the desk clerk who was on duty Saturday. That would be Mister Bascomb, who happens to be here today, as well.

"Thank you. I'll do that on my way out. Can we find out if Miss Lawrence received any telephone calls on Saturday or Sunday morning?"

The manager opened his top desk drawer and removed a sheet of paper that was mostly blank and handed it to Mackie, explaining, "We don't keep track of guests' incoming calls unless they are out and the caller wishes to leave a message. I checked the telephone message record this morning, and this is the last message we received for Miss Lawrence. You may keep that."

Three neatly printed lines on a piece of hotel stationery said, "Telephone message for Miss Lawrence—Rm. 187. Friday, 9/3/26, 4:45 p.m. Message: Please call Mister Grant of the Hollywood News at Holly 291 regarding an interview."

Sergeant Mackie folded the page into his book and said, "Thank you, Mister Harrison. By the way you anticipated my questions, you seem to have given this matter a good deal of thought."

Glumly the manager said, "How could I not give it a great deal of thought? The Hershey family pays me a lot of money to think about things that affect the Hollywood Hotel. In fact, I have already received a long distance telephone call from Pennsylvania this morning asking what was being done to clear this up. Miss Lawrence's death has already made the east coast newspapers."

Mackie nodded and asked, "Is it possible that your telephone operator might remember if anyone called Miss Lawrence Sunday morning and did not leave a message? Especially someone who might have called more than once?"

"We can certainly ask her."

Harrison lifted the handset of his telephone and waited several seconds. Then he said, "This is Mister Harrison. Who am I speaking with, please? Miss Parsons, who was working the switchboard Sunday morning? You were? Do you recall any incoming calls for Miss Lawrence in room 187?"

After a longer pause he said, "Thank you, Miss Parsons." He hung up the handset and told Mackie, "Miss Parsons works days, Friday through Tuesday. She says she doesn't remember any calls, and she thinks she would remember them if there had been any because Mister Plant left strict instructions to tell callers for Miss Lawrence that she was out."

Entering this in his notebook, Mackie said, "I see."

Harrison added, "Again, Sergeant, that information may not be conclusive. When our telephone operators get busy or have to leave the switchboard for a moment, the front desk people sometimes take incoming calls. From what I gather, Sunday morning was quite chaotic, what with Miss Lawrence's death and our weekend guests checking out. It is possible that a call or two might have come in without Miss Parsons' knowledge."

Mackie glanced down his current page of notes. The circles he'd drawn around each occurrence of the words "inconclusive" and "can't say for sure" made the page look like a slice of Swiss cheese. He changed the subject, asking, "In general, what can you tell me about Lillian Lawrence's stay here?"

This time the manager thought about the question for a moment before answering. "I make it a practice to personally greet our celebrity guests when they check in. I was pleasantly surprised when I met Miss Lawrence. She was quite unlike most of the actors I encounter. She was quiet and quite friendly, although somewhat less sophisticated than most."

"Did she mention why she was staying here? I mean, she owned a home in Hollywood, so why was she checking into the hotel?"

"Yes. Miss Lawrence mentioned she had sold her home and would be staying with us while she finished a motion picture. I believe she expected to be here about a month."

"Did she say what her plans were when the motion picture was finished?"

"No, I don't recall that she did."

Mackie finished his notation and said, "Well, Mister Harrison, I think that's all of my questions. Would it be possible for you to let me look at whatever belongings Miss Lawrence might have left in the hotel safe?"

Frowning, Harrison contemplated the sergeant's request for several seconds and then said, "Technically I'm not supposed to allow that without a court order, but under the circumstances, I can't see that it would hurt anything. And if it will help your investigation along . . . . I can't allow you to remove anything from the hotel, though."

The large safe occupied most of a small room behind the front desk next to the assistant manager's office. Harrison was careful to shield the combination dial from Mackie's view as he spun it from one number to the next. When the lock clicked open, the manager selected one of several small wooden boxes neatly arranged on the safe's top shelves. As he removed it, Mackie noticed the number 187 on a small white tag tied to a brass handle on the box's hinged lid. Harrison pushed the safe's door closed and set the box on a small table in the middle of the room. With care that seemed almost reverent, he lifted the lid and stepped to one side.

Mackie tipped the box and spread its contents on the table. There were four items: a white business-sized envelope and three small, leather-covered jewelry boxes. He examined the boxes first. The smallest box contained a gold pin in the shape of a heart with what appeared to be small diamonds spaced around its edge and a larger stone Mackie thought might be a sapphire at its center.

The remaining boxes were both long and narrow. The first of these held a delicate gold necklace with a solitary diamond mounted in a setting that resembled flower petals. The last box contained a string of pearls that seemed almost iridescent against the black velvet lining of its box. Mackie noticed Harrison's eyebrows go up at the sight of the pearls and asked, "Expensive?"

"I would say so. I'm not a jewelry expert, but I did purchase a similar strand of pearls for my wife last Christmas, and I hate to say how much they cost. And these are larger and more perfectly matched. Sergeant, I would estimate that you hold at least two thousand dollars' worth of pearls in your hand."

Mackie simply nodded and closed the box. Then he picked up the envelope. It was not addressed and had no stamps, so it hadn't been mailed. The return address printed on the envelope was that of C. E. Toberman Real Estate. Inside, he found a bill of sale marked "duplicate." It specified the details involved with the sale of property located at 329 Hollymount Drive. Mackie recalled the address as being the same as the one in Harry Lee's homicide report.

Mackie wrote a brief description of the jewelry and real estate document in his notebook and then said, "I'm finished, Mister Harrison. Thank you."

Harrison carefully checked the contents of each jewelry box before replacing them in the wooden safe deposit box and returning it to the safe.

The door clicked shut and he spun the combination dial. Then he asked, "Is there anything else I can help you with, Sergeant Mackie?"

"How many keys do you have for each room?"

"We generally have two so if more than one guest in a room requires a key we can provide it. There is also, of course, a set of passkeys that will open any guest room in the hotel."

"So there are two keys to room 187?"

"Yes. I understand you have one of them—the one that was in Miss Lawrence's possession when she died. The other was in her room box behind the desk until this morning. When I discovered it was still there, I removed the second key and put it in my desk for safe keeping."

Mackie leaned over the small table and added this to his notes. As he did this, he said, "I would like to talk with the maid who found Miss Lawrence. Is she here today?"

"No. That was one of the first things I checked when I arrived this morning. The housekeeping supervisor said she hadn't come in, so I had my secretary call her home. Actually, it turns out that the telephone number we have for her belongs to a neighbor. The woman who answered had just seen Missus Brown and said she was still very upset and couldn't come in today."

Mackie flipped back several pages in his notebook to be sure he had the address Dennis Plant gave him for Hattie Mae Brown. Then he thanked Lloyd Harrison for his cooperation. As Harrison headed back up the stairs toward his office, Mackie spoke briefly with the young desk clerk, Bascomb, who was on duty Sunday.

The young man remembered seeing Miss Lawrence in the lobby at one point on Saturday, but he didn't recall any guests she might have had during the day. He quickly added that he might not have seen any guests she might have had who went directly to her room without stopping at the desk to be announced.

Mackie added another hole to the Swiss cheese in his notebook and walked out to his Dodge. The interview with Harrison accomplished little more than confirming facts he already knew or surmised. About the only new knowledge he gained furthered the impression that Lillian Lawrence did not expect trouble on Saturday. The manager said she seemed bored when he saw her in the hotel's courtyard. People who were worried or scared didn't usually strike witnesses as being bored. This added some credence to Mae White's statements that Bromfeld had agreed to release Miss Lawrence from her contract.

The most disappointing part of the interviews at the hotel was the inability of anyone to confirm or deny Miss White's claim that she tried to reach her friend by telephone Sunday morning. Of course, even if she'd already known that Lillian Lawrence was dead, Mae White might have thought to call the hotel just to avoid suspicion, but if that had been her angle, she would have left a message so there would be no doubt about her calling. It was a loose end that bothered Mackie more than he thought it should. He wondered why.

Starting his Dodge Brothers police car, Mackie turned his attention to the route he would take to Hattie Mae Brown's home. She lived on Carlton Way, which he recalled as being a block south of Hollywood Boulevard between Gower and Western. As a neighborhood, it was a far cry from the mansions along De Mille Drive a short distance to the northwest.

SIXTEEN

Figuring his next stop to be the makeup studio, Winfield retraced the meandering route he and Ollie Stephens took from the camera shop. Bromfeld's secretary said the makeup department was next to the sound stage building which, if Winfield had his directions straight, ought to put it across the street from Stephens' shop.

Recalling Bessie Shipman's directions put Winfield in mind of her belligerent attitude. She'd been downright rude from the moment he walked into her office. He wondered why. Was that just the way she treated everyone or did she have some reason for disliking him in particular? Either way, it probably didn't mean anything, but the incident peaked his curiosity.

Back at the camera shop, Winfield studied the three wooden buildings nestled against the sound stages across what passed for a street in this fantasy world. The largest, to his left, bore a sign that said, "Dressing Rooms." The smallest building, to the right, had no sign and its lack of windows gave him the impression it was used for storage of some kind. The sign on the middle building simply said, "Makeup."

Inside, the makeup studio resembled nothing more than a barbershop, except it was brighter than any barber shop he'd ever seen. Multiple lights affixed to the ceiling and walls brightly illuminated three barber chairs. On the wall next to each chair were a porcelain sink and a mirror. The spaces between the mirrors were covered with floor-to-ceiling glass-fronted cabinets filled with all manner of bottles, jars and toothpaste-like tubes.

What the makeup studio did not have, Winfield observed, was any sign of life. Since a door leading from the back of the room was ajar, he guessed the people who worked there might be in the back somewhere. Hoping the sound of the front door opening and closing when he came in might bring one of those people out, he killed a minute by looking at the bottles and jars in the nearest glass-fronted cabinet. One shelf slightly below his eye level was lined with a neat row of identical squat, opaque white glass jars with black lids. Each jar bore the legend "Max Factor Shading Cream." Below that the labels carried a number from one to twelve. He noted that the jars were carefully arranged in order according to these numbers.

He was looking at an assortment of tiny brushes and tubes of pigment on the next shelf when his peripheral vision caught a movement at the back of the room. Looking up he saw a young woman in a white smock come through the back door. Winfield noted that she was short—barely five feet—with a round, cherub face framed in platinum blonde hair he was pretty sure couldn't be natural. She was carrying what looked to be a human head with long, shaggy black hair. She was intent on arranging the strands of black hair as she walked, and when he moved to announce his presence, she jumped and nearly dropped the mannequin head.

Recovering quickly, she said, "Can I help you with somethin', mister?"

"Hello. I'm sorry I startled you. I'm Detective Lieutenant Bob Winfield with L.A.P.D. Homicide. I'm investigating the death of Lillian Lawrence. Mister Bromfeld's secretary, Miss Shipman, suggested I talk with Fanny DeWitt. Is she here?"

Setting the straggly-haired head down, she slowly walked toward Winfield, saying, "I'm Fanny. I heard about poor Lilly this morning when I came in. It's awful! That's what it is, just awful!"

"Yes, it is. Do you have a few minutes to answer some questions about Miss Lawrence?"

By this time she was standing a few feet from Winfield, leaning on the back of the nearest barber chair. From there he could make out the woman's features more clearly. Her wide eyes, long lashes, and bright red cupid's bow lips were almost a caricature of the popular "flapper" girl style. While a bit overly made-up for Winfield's taste, she was certainly attractive in a cute sort of way. Unfortunately, her enthusiastic gum chewing was somewhat less than endearing.

Answering his question, she said, "Sure. I'll be happy to, 'specially if it will help you find the monster that killed poor Lilly."

"Thank you, Miss DeWitt." Taking his notepad and pencil out, Winfield continued, "How would you describe Miss Lawrence as a person?"

"Oh, she was a peach. That's what she was, a real peach."

"Could you be a little more specific?"

Fanny DeWitt thought for a moment and then said, "Lilly was prob'ly the nicest, friendliest person on the lot. Some of these movie celebrities are all full of themselves, but not Lilly. She was as sweet and down to earth as they come."

"So you would say she got along well with everyone here?"

"Posilutely! Everyone loved Lilly." After a brief pause, she added, "Well, everyone but that jerk director."

"You mean Ernst Frohmme?"

"I sure do. What a creep! I get the heebie-jeebies just being in the same room with him!"

"Why didn't Mister Frohmme like Miss Lawrence?"

"Oh, he liked her plenty at first. Lilly even went out to dinner with him . . . once." Winfield noted the emphasis Fanny DeWitt put on the word "once."

She continued, adding, "Trouble was, he liked her too much in the wrong way if you get my meaning. He couldn't keep his hands to himself on their dinner date and Lilly let him know in no uncertain terms that she didn't want no part of what he was dishin' out.

"I guess he couldn't take no for answer, though, cuz he tried to put the make on her between takes on a movie they were making. Lilly had to fight him off, and he got in big trouble over it."

Winfield looked up from his notebook and asked, "How did Frohmme get into trouble?"

"Mae White and some of the other people near the set heard Lilly scream and came a-running. They caught that pig red-handed! After that, Mae White took Lilly to see the Big Cheese. When old man Bromfeld heard about it he popped his cork. He called Frohmme on the carpet and gave him an earful!"

"Did Frohmme leave Miss Lawrence alone after that?"

"Yes and no. He didn't try anymore funny stuff, but he treated Lilly and Mae real bad from then on. He was always yellin' at 'em and makin' 'em reshoot scenes that there was nothing wrong with."

"Do you think Ernst Frohmme was angry enough to kill Miss Lawrence?"

As Fanny DeWitt thought about his question, she pulled a pale blue packet of Blackjack gum from her smock pocket and added another stick to the wad already in her mouth. Finally, she said, "I don't think so. He comes off like a real tough guy, but I don't think he's got the balls . . . ah, the nerve to actually kill anyone. Forgive my language."

Changing the direction of the interview slightly, Winfield said, "You mentioned Mae White. Were she and Miss Lawrence close?"

"Just like peas in a pod! Lilly was lost like a fish out of water when she first got here. Mae sort of took Lilly under her wing . . . showed her the ropes and made her feel more comfortable-like. We all tried to do that for Lilly, but she and Mae just hit it off real good and got to be close friends."

"Does that strike you as unusual? I mean, Miss Lawrence and Miss White seem like exact opposites."

"Haven't you heard that opposites attract? Besides, they weren't really all that different, unless you've heard the rumors about Mae being 'easy.' Is that it?"

"Well, I have heard something to that effect."

Fanny DeWitt surprised Winfield with the vehemence of her response. "That's a lot of hooey! Mae is not easy! Yes, she dates a lot, but she's a lady. She doesn't even pet!"

Winfield smiled and said, "You seem very sure about all that. How do you know so much about Miss White?"

"Jeepers! I ought to know all about Mae; we grew up together."

Surprised again, Winfield said, "Is that so?"

"Yes, it is. She lived two doors down from me on Rivington Street in the Lower East Side of New York when we were kids. Mae and me—of course, her name wasn't Mae White back then—were even in the same drama club at school. We both wanted to be famous stage actresses—that was our dream. Only she had the looks and the talent to really do it. When we got out of high school, she landed a job making movies for Vitagraph in New York, and I ended up working in a beauty salon.

"But Mae didn't forget her best friend! When she came out here to work, she talked them into giving me this job. In spite of the tough times she's had, Mae is the genuine article; I can vouch for that."

"Tough times?"

Fanny DeWitt hesitated a moment before saying, "Well, that part is kind of personal. You see, Mae got engaged to be married a while back. Her beau was an actor here by the name of Louis Hogan. He was a swell guy, and they were made for each other like in a storybook romance."

"What happened?"

Putting on a sad expression, the young woman said, "Louis committed suicide. His movies were doing really well, and he and Mae were all set to tie the knot when Bromfeld fired him for no reason. I don't know what Bromfeld told Louis, but whatever it was really upset Louis. That night he parked his car in his garage and left the motor on so the garage filled with fumes and he was afixitated."

"Are they sure it was a suicide?"

"Oh yes. He even left Mae a note. Of course, she was heartbroken. For a while I was afraid she might do herself in, too. But she hung on and got okay again."

"And you think Louis Hogan committed suicide because Bromfeld fired him?"

"I'm sure of it."

"What makes you so sure? Did he say that in his suicide note?"

"I don't know what the suicide note said. Mae never showed it to anyone after the police gave it back to her. I know it because Mae told me so. She said Bromfeld was against them getting married, and when he couldn't talk them out of it, he fired Louis and told him he would never work in Hollywood again. Louis got all balled up about his career being over and not being worthy of Mae, so he killed himself. That's what Mae told me."

"That sounds rather vindictive of Bromfeld. Would he really do something like that?"

"I don't know what vind . . . what that word means, but Bromfeld is a real stinker when he doesn't get his way. It was a really mean thing he did to Louis and Mae, but there was nothing anyone could do about it."

Winfield closed his notebook and said, "Miss DeWitt, you've been a great deal of help. Thank you for answering my questions so frankly."

"You're most welcome, I'm sure. And I hope you find that rat who killed Lilly and give him what he's got comin' to him."

"We're working hard on doing just that. Oh, one more question if you don't mind?"

"Sure."

"What was Mae White's name back in New York?"

Fanny DeWitt hesitated and then said, "Well, that's supposed to be a secret, but since you're a policeman and such a nice guy, I guess it would be okay to say. Her name was Millie Glaum."

"Thank you, Miss DeWitt. The secret is safe with me."

SEVENTEEN

Mae White was on Winfield's mind as he turned right out of Western National's east lot and drove a block on Santa Monica Boulevard to the gate at Western National's west lot. If there was truth to the story told him by Fanny DeWitt, Mae White had indeed been through a tough time. The only part he found questionable was her beau's suicide. It seemed a rather drastic reaction to being fired from a job. Perhaps there was more to the story.

Once past the guard at Western National's west gate, the lieutenant followed Bessie Shipman's directions to the costume shop, making a left turn just past the large building labeled "Commissary." About a block later he spotted a sign that said "Costume Shop" attached to a large wooden building squeezed in between the back of the commissary and another structure that looked like it might be a carpentry shop.

Pulling his Dodge up near the costume shop door, he got out and walked into a huge cavernous space as dark and gloomy as the makeup studio was brightly lit. The place was bustling with the activity of what he guessed must be twenty or more women working at sewing machines. Bolts of cloth in every hue imaginable lined both side walls of the room.

After standing inside the door for a while without anyone paying the slightest bit of attention to him, Winfield approached a young woman sitting at a table near one of the few windows in the building. She was hand-sewing some sort of beadwork to a gown, and when he approached, she glanced up at him with something of a fearful expression on her face. Winfield said, "Is this where I can find Viola Wiebe?"

The young woman nodded, turned in her chair to face the room, and pointed to an older woman walking briskly in their direction. Viola Wiebe appeared to be on the far side of fifty and dressed accordingly in a long black dress and a severe white blouse with a high collar and long sleeves.

"May I help you, young man?" Her voice was firm and clear. Winfield got the immediate impression that Viola Wiebe tolerated no nonsense.

He said, "Yes, if you don't mind. I'm Detective Lieutenant Robert Winfield with the Los Angeles Police Department Homicide Division. I was sent here by Mister Bromfeld's office to speak with Viola Wiebe."

"I am Viola Wiebe. May I assume that you are here to discuss the death of Lillian Lee, or Lawrence as she was more recently known?"

"That is exactly correct, Miss Wiebe." Winfield took a guess at addressing the woman by the title of "Miss." Apparently it was a good guess because she did not correct him. Instead, she said, "Then I suggest we step outside where it is more conducive to conversation."

Winfield followed her through the costume shop door. The light outdoors seemed blindingly bright in comparison to the dim room they just left. Viola Wiebe seemed oblivious to the change, though, and got right down to business. "What is it you would like to know, Detective Lieutenant Winfield?"

"I understand Miss Lawrence worked in your costume shop before she became an actress."

"That is correct."

"How would you describe Miss Lawrence?"

Viola Wiebe hesitated only for a second before answering. "Lillian was a sweet, innocent young woman who was figuratively thrown to the wolves."

Winfield waited for more, but when Miss Wiebe simply stared at him, he asked, "In what way was she thrown to the wolves?"

"That tyrant, Bromfeld, forced Lillian to leave the costume shop, where she was happy earning a decent wage, and compelled her to become an actress, a job she despised."

"I see. Would you mind being more specific about how that happened?"

"Not at all. About two years ago Lillian was doing handwork by the window there when Bromfeld happened by. He spotted Lillian through the glass and came charging into my shop like a bull elephant, demanding that Lillian come with him for a screen test.

"Lillian was terrified by Bromfeld. I immediately intervened on her behalf, but that man would not accept no for an answer. In the end Lillian was forced to go with him and perform the test.

"The next day one of Bromfeld's lackeys came here to tell Lillian that Bromfeld liked her screen test and wanted her to play a small role in Mae White's movie, The Long Night. Lillian explained to Bromfeld that she didn't want to be an actress, but that wicked man told her she would be fired from her job in the shop if she didn't accept the role. She was the sole support of herself and her father, so she had no choice."

Winfield looked up from his notebook and asked, "You say she was the sole support of her father? Didn't he have a job?"

Viola Wiebe looked disgusted. "That man was a drunken lout! He lived off of his daughter's labors as if she were his slave."

Winfield nodded and said, "What happened next, Miss Wiebe?"

"The situation grew worse for Lillian in every possible way. The public loved her performance in The Long Night, and that man, Bromfeld, prepared a five-year acting contract for Lillian. Again she told him she did not want to act, she just wanted to return to the costume shop. That monster, Bromfeld, told her returning to the costume shop was impossible.

"Then Lillian learned that her father owed many thousands of dollars in gambling debts. And again she had no choice but to do what she so desperately did not want to do. You know, Detective Lieutenant Winfield, it would not surprise me in the smallest bit to learn that Bromfeld encouraged Harry Lee to drink and gamble Lillian's money away so she would have no choice but to make motion pictures for him. Those men, Bromfeld and Harry Lee, they ruined little Lillian's life, and now she is gone."

Winfield detected a quiver in Viola Wiebe's voice that didn't seem to fit her nature. He asked, "Miss Wiebe, I have the feeling that you were very close to Miss Lawrence. Am I right about that?"

Now tears were forming in the woman's eyes. She said shakily, "Little Lilly was like a daughter to me."

"I'm sorry I have to ask you these questions, Miss Wiebe. I can see this is difficult for you."

Viola Wiebe dabbed at her eyes with a handkerchief that appeared from somewhere on her person and said, "Yes, it is difficult, but I will gladly answer questions all day if it will help bring the person who took Lillian from us to justice."

"I assure you your answers will help make that happen. I have just a few more questions. Do you know of anyone else here at the studio who was close to Lillian?"

"Everyone loved little Lillian because she was so friendly and good-natured. I think, however, that Lillian was closest to Mae White. Miss White was kind to Lillian and helped her with her acting."

Winfield said, "I've heard that from others. What is you personal opinion of Mae White?"

The woman was quiet for a moment as if she were carefully deciding how to answer the question. Finally she said, "In her heart, I believe Mae White is a good person. Sometimes she acts boldly in ways that are not attractive for women. Some might call her 'brassy' or 'pushy.' I do not judge her for these things. It could very well be that in her position pushy behavior is necessary. I do not know. I do know she was a good friend to Lillian, and that is all that matters."

"Do you know Tom Bell, and if so, what was your impression of him?"

Again Viola Wiebe seemed to frame her answer carefully. "I only met Mister Bell once. Lillian brought him here because she wanted to introduce us. Based on that short meeting, Mister Bell seemed to be a very kind and caring person . . . a gentleman.

"I do know that Lillian was very much looking forward to becoming his wife. To her, Tom Bell was a knight in shining armor, and marrying him was a dream come true. Lillian was so happy and excited to be making plans for the wedding. It was all she talked about the last few times I saw her before . . . before she died."

"Miss Wiebe, can you think of anything—any possible reason—that would have made Miss Lawrence change her mind about leaving the studio?"

Viola Wiebe looked up sharply. "What makes you ask that question? Did someone tell you such a thing?"

"I can't say who said it at this point, but yes, I was told Miss Lawrence changed her mind and agreed to stay on and fulfill her contract with Western National Films."

Her eyes flashed angrily as she said, "They were lying to you Mister Detective Lieutenant Winfield! I tell you this for true and sure . . . nothing in this world could have made Lillian change her mind about leaving this place and marrying Tom Bell."

"Thank you, Miss Wiebe. You've been a great help."

Viola Wiebe stared intently into Winfield's eyes and said, "I think you are very good at what you do, Detective Lieutenant Winfield. Having met you, I now have a great deal of faith that you will find the man who took Lillian from us and see that he is punished. I thank you in advance for that."

They said their goodbyes, and as Viola Wiebe returned to the gloom of her costume shop, Winfield climbed back into his Dodge and considered driving around Western National's west lot just to see it. Looking at his wristwatch, however, he realized there wasn't enough time for that before his one o'clock meeting with C. K. and Tom Bell.

EIGHTEEN

Detective Sergeant C. K. Mackie parked in the Hollywood Hotel's circular drive at twelve-forty. He knew Winfield had a lot of ground to cover at Western National Films, so he wasn't concerned when he didn't see the lieutenant's car at the hotel.

Mackie walked through the hotel's main entrance and stopped at the front desk to see if there were any messages for him. There weren't, so he settled into a comfortable chair near the entrance to wait for Winfield and Tom Bell.

The lobby was nearly as quiet as it was before he left to interview Hattie Mae Brown. Aside from hotel employees, the only other lobby occupants were two men in suits seated on a couch outside the Dining Room of the Stars entrance, which was now open. He recognized neither of the men on the couch and guessed their enthusiastic conversation might be about some business deal. From where he sat most of the tables in the dining room appeared to be empty.

Again Mackie wondered if the lack of activity around him was the result of Lillian Lawrence's murder. Since there were now three other fashionable hotels in Hollywood, visitors who might have otherwise stayed at the prestigious Hollywood Hotel had alternatives if they were squeamish about staying where someone famous was murdered.

He glanced toward the entrance just in time to see Winfield's Dodge roll past the glass doors. According to the clock over the front desk, the lieutenant was five minutes early for their meeting with Tom Bell.

"Hello, C. K. I take it Tom Bell isn't here yet?"

"Not yet. How did it go at Western National?"

Winfield smiled. "It was quite an experience. The world of motion pictures is definitely different."

"Yes, it is, Laddie. You can understand why picture celebrities sometimes have difficulty telling fantasy from reality."

"I surely can. They certainly live different lives from the rest of us. I'm beginning to see why you aren't particularly enthusiastic about movie people. They are a strange bunch."

Mackie grinned. "I'm glad to hear you say that, Bobby. I was afraid you might get star-struck over there and decide to give police work up for the glamorous life of a picture celebrity."

"Don't hold your breath waiting for that to happen! Those folks may make buckets full of money, but I would rather keep my sanity."

"They probably feel the same way about police work. It's all in how you see things."

It was four minutes past one by the front desk clock when a tall young man in a well-fitting brown suit, a tan Stetson hat, and dressy cowboy boots walked through the lobby entrance. He removed his hat and stood in the entrance foyer looking around the lobby.

Guessing the new arrival was Tom Bell, Mackie and Winfield stood and walked toward him. The young man spotted them and immediately moved in their direction. When they were within speaking distance, Mackie said, "Would you be Tom Bell?"

The man replied solemnly, "I would."

Offering his hand, Mackie said, "Hello, Mister Bell. I'm Detective Sergeant Mackie and this is Detective Lieutenant Robert Winfield. I'm the one who spoke with you on the telephone yesterday."

Shaking Mackie's hand and then Winfield's, Tom Bell said quietly, "Howdy, gentlemen."

Winfield said, "Hello, Mister Bell. I'm sorry we have to meet under such sad circumstances."

Bell merely nodded his acknowledgment of Winfield's greeting, and Mackie suggested they sit out in the courtyard for their conversation. Walking across the lobby, Winfield mentally recorded his first impressions of Tom Bell. He was a good-looking young man in his late twenties with light brown hair, blue eyes, and a tanned complexion that said he spent a good deal of time outdoors. Judging by the quality and style of his clothing, Bell had money, and yet the conservative cut of his suit indicated he was not one to flaunt his wealth.

They sat at the first in a row of small round tables below windows that overlooked the courtyard from the dining room. Mackie began the interview by saying, "Thank you for coming in to meet us."

"You're welcome. What can I do to help your investigation?"

Mackie said, "We're trying to learn as much about Miss Lawrence as possible so we get some insight as to who could have killed her."

"I'll do my best to answer whatever questions you have."

Mackie gave a slight nod to Winfield and the lieutenant said, "We understand you and Miss Lawrence were engaged to be married. Is that correct?"

"Yes, we were planning to have the wedding as soon as Lilly finished the picture she was working on. We hadn't set the actual date yet, but we were figuring on the end of this month or early October."

"How long had you known Miss Lawrence?"

Bell thought a moment before saying, "We met at a Christmas party last December. We began seeing each other whenever possible soon after New Year's. So the answer to your question would be a little more than eight months."

As Mackie jotted notes in his book, Winfield continued his questions. "How long had you been engaged?"

"I first asked her to marry me around the beginning of last summer, and she turned me down. We continued to see each other, and I kept asking. She finally said yes a few weeks ago. That was right after her father was killed."

Winfield cocked his head inquisitively and said, "Do you think that was a coincidence or are the two events related?"

"I'm not entirely sure. It was difficult to understand Lilly's feelings about her father's death. Of course she was grief-stricken, but I kept thinking she was also feeling some relief . . . just a little. I've wondered if there was some connection. I only met her father once, and quite honestly, I didn't care for the man."

"Why was that?"

Before Bell could answer, a waiter from the dining room appeared at their table asking if they would care for something to eat or drink. Bell and Winfield ordered coffee, and Mackie said he would be fine with a glass of water.

The waiter left to get their orders and Bell said, "To answer your question, I don't like to speak ill of the dead, but Harry Lee struck me as a four-flusher—a lazy fellow who never held a job for long and was perfectly willing to let his daughter support him. Lilly talked about her mother often, but never had much to say about her father, however, others have told me Mister Lee drank and gambled a great deal. I never saw any evidence of that personally."

"Mister Bell, how would you describe Miss Lawrence as a person?"

Tom Bell seemed to contemplate his answer for a moment and then said, "She was a lovely woman. I think if I had to pick one word to describe Lilly, it would be wholesome. At first I thought she was a little naïve, but after getting to know her, I came to realize she was just an honest, friendly woman without a phony bone in her body. Lilly was a hundred percent real.

"She also had a bit of tomboy in her. When Lilly could get away from her work for a day or two, we would go riding on the beach near the ranch. She loved being outdoors with the wind in her hair. I always thought Lilly was at her most beautiful on those days."

Bell sounded as if he was getting a little choked up as he answered Winfield's questions about Lilly, so the lieutenant changed his line of questioning. "Mister Bell, you strike me as a well educated man. How did you get into the ranching business?"

The young man appeared to be taken aback by Winfield's question. He said, "Lieutenant Winfield, there is no law that I know of saying a man can't be well educated and still enjoy working outdoors with his hands."

"You're right, of course. I apologize for implying that ranchers are uneducated. I meant no offense."

Bell seemed to be smiling a little as he said, "None taken. Actually, I sense a lot of people thinking along the same lines, especially fellow ranchers. To answer your question, my granddaddy started up a horse ranch out near the coast somewhere along about 1885. He knew good stock when he saw it, and he taught my father to recognize it, too. Then Dad took over the ranch when Granddaddy passed. That was about the time I was born.

"The ranch has always done very well, and Mom and Dad had the wherewithal to send me to college, which they both felt was important to my future. So I went off to Leland Stanford University for four years and came home with an education.

"Dad died soon after that when a horse he was breaking tossed him into a corral fence. After that, I took over the ranch. Mom is still with us, thank goodness, but she pretty much leaves things at the ranch to me."

As Tom Bell completed his story, the dining room waiter returned to their table and distributed the orders of coffee and water. When the young man picked up his coffee cup with his right hand, Mackie and Winfield glanced at each other briefly. Winfield was actually a little relieved to discover Bell was right-handed. He was taking a liking to the man. Getting back to the interview, he asked, "What kind of horses do you raise on your ranch?"

"Quarter horses especially trained for handling stock and rodeos. Four of the winners at last year's Pendleton Round-up rode Bell Ranch horses. We're pretty well known throughout the west."

"Winfield nodded and returned to the subject of Lillian Lawrence, asking, "Getting back to Miss Lawrence for a moment, how did she feel about acting and working for Mister Bromfeld?"

Bell looked vehement when he said, "She hated it. Lilly spoke often about how much she enjoyed working for Miss Wiebe in the studio costume shop, and she told me how Bromfeld dragged her away kicking and screaming to make her a nationally famous picture celebrity. Lilly said that in a joking way, but I'm certain there was a lot of truth to it. She honestly didn't want to be an actress."

He paused for a moment and then continued, "Once, Lilly made a point of taking me to meet Miss Wiebe, and I liked her from the moment we met. You know, Lilly's mother passed while Lilly was still in high school. It seems her mother brought in most of the family's income doing fancy sewing work, so when Missus Lee passed away, Lilly was forced to pick up the slack by leaving school and working in the costume shop. That was mostly because her father wasn't working or worked very seldom. So I think in many ways Miss Wiebe took over the role of Lilly's mother by caring for her and giving her good advice."

Winfield said, "So it came to you as no surprise that Miss Lawrence was eventually willing to walk away from her career in motion pictures to become your wife?"

"That's right."

"Tell us something about that, like her decision to leave Western National."

"Well, as you may already know, the life of a motion picture actor is not all it's made out to be. They work very long hours, and a great deal of stress goes along with the job.

"Don't take me wrong about this. Lilly was not afraid of hard work, but the stress upset her from the beginning. I'm not sure Lilly would have survived the work as long as she did without Mae White's help. For example, there was an incident with a director—I believe his name is Frohmme or something like that. As I understand the story, this director cornered Lilly on the set of a movie she was making and . . . well, he behaved in a very ungentlemanly manner toward her. Mae, along with several other people, heard her cry for help and saw what this Frohmme fellow was up to. Apparently Mae took the man down a peg or two verbally and then went with Lilly to make a complaint with Bromfeld. I understand the director was in quite a bit of hot water over the matter.

"All that happened right after I came on the scene, and when I heard about it, I was naturally very concerned for Lilly's welfare. From what Mae told me about that director, I concluded he wasn't a straight-shooter and he might have been angry enough over the incident to hurt Lilly or Mae. I even gave Lilly a small pistol to protect herself in case it came to that."

Winfield shot a quick glance at Mackie, who returned a short nod. Winfield asked, "You gave her a gun? What sort of gun was it?"

Bell gave Winfield a curious look before answering the question. "It was just a little nickel-plated 'purse pistol' Dad gave Mom as a gift the Christmas before he passed. Mom never had much use for guns of any kind, so she put it away on the top shelf of her closet. I don't think it had ever been fired, and Mom was happy to have it gone, although it concerned her that Lilly might actually need such a thing. Mom and Lilly were already becoming good friends by that time."

Winfield quickly asked, "Can you be more specific about the pistol? What caliber was it?"

Again Tom Bell looked curiously at Winfield. "It was a twenty-two caliber Smith and Wesson revolver with a short barrel. I believe they called the model 'Ladysmith.' I gave Lilly the pistol and a box of ammunition while she was visiting at the ranch. Then we went up into the hills and I taught her to fire it. Lilly took to shooting right away, and her aim was surprisingly good for someone who never fired a gun before."

As Mackie finished noting the pistol's details, Winfield said, "I apologize for interrupting your story. You were telling us about Miss Lawrence's decision to leave Western National."

"Well, to shorten a long story, when the grief of her father's passing was added to the load of stress she was already carrying, I think Lilly just decided she had taken all she could take. I believe that decision also had a lot to do with Lilly accepting my proposal of marriage. She desperately wanted to start a new life as a wife and, eventually, a mother. Lilly's mood improved considerably once she finally decided to leave the studio."

Winfield nodded and said, "I can understand that, but what about Miss Lawrence's contract with Western National Films?"

Bell sighed and said, "That was the fly in the ointment. Lilly went to Bromfeld and asked to be released from that contract. Bromfeld said no. Then Lilly offered to buy out her contract, but Bromfeld said no to that as well.

"Lilly was getting desperate, and that's when Mae told her to just walk away. In spite of Bromfeld's threats, Mae was certain the studio wouldn't really take any legal action because of the bad press it would cause. So Lilly told Bromfeld she was leaving the studio when she finished shooting The Big Sister and he could do as he pleased with her contract. Then Lilly put her house up for sale and moved here to the hotel until the picture was done."

Winfield waited a moment for Mackie's pencil to stop moving and then asked, "Would you say Miss Lawrence was definitely determined to follow that course of action?"

"There's no doubt in my mind that she was."

"Can you think of any possible reason she might change her mind and stay on at the studio?"

Bell gave the question a moment's thought before saying, "Absolutely not. Lilly was as excited as a kid about moving out to the ranch. She and Mae were already making the wedding plans." After a brief pause, the young man looked Winfield in the eye and said, "What makes you ask that question?"

Winfield hesitated before saying, "We were told by someone close to the studio that Miss Lawrence changed her mind and planned to stay on at Western National."

Tom Bell looked genuinely surprised. Leaning forward, he said, "That's not possible. Who on earth told you such a story?"

"I can't really say at this point in the investigation. Do you happen to know if Miss Lawrence had any special plans for Saturday night?"

Bell leaned back in his chair again and said, "None that I know of. Lilly told me during a telephone conversation before I left the ranch Thursday morning that since I was going to be out of town, she might have dinner with Mae and work on the wedding plans some more."

"Then it would surprise you to know that she had dinner with Mister Bromfeld here at the hotel Saturday night, ostensibly to celebrate her staying on at the studio?"

"Well, when Mae called to tell me the terrible news about Lilly Sunday afternoon, she said something about Bromfeld being here to see Lilly Saturday night. I'm afraid I wasn't paying too much attention to that part after learning that Lilly was dead, but I just can't imagine anything like that happening. Lilly was definitely through with Bromfeld and his studio."

Again noticing that Bell was getting emotionally upset, Winfield said, "Okay, Mister Bell, just a couple more questions. We understand you were up in the Central Valley over the weekend. Is that right?"

"Yes, that's correct. I left the ranch around ten Thursday morning and drove up for a horse auction in Fresno. I stayed there through Saturday night and got back to the ranch a little before four Sunday afternoon."

Adopting an apologetic tone, Winfield said, "I hope you understand that I have to ask this question. Is there anyone who can verify that you were in Fresno for those days?"

"I understand. Actually, there are several people who will verify I was in Fresno. I ended up buying two horses at the Saturday afternoon auction session. The bills of sale are back at the ranch, but you could place a telephone call to the Central Valley Livestock Auction Company out of Visalia, California. They'll have records of the sales with dates and my signatures. Or the easiest way to confirm that I was in Fresno would be to talk with Asa Stewart. He owns a horse ranch in Santa Maria. We drove up to the auction and came back together. Oh, you could also check with the Hotel Californian in Fresno. That's where we stayed."

"I'm sure those sources will verify what you've said. Do you happen to know Mister Stewart's telephone exchange?"

As Mackie wrote Stewart's telephone number in his book, Winfield said, "I only have one more question for you, Mister Bell. Can you think of anyone at all who might have a reason for wanting to kill Lillian Lawrence?"

Bell frowned for a moment, and then said, "No I can't. I mean, there's that director who accosted Lilly, but that was a while ago. I can't imagine he would still be holding a strong enough grudge to do anything that drastic. I guess Bromfeld must have been angry at Lilly. He's ruthless and vindictive, but mostly his motives seem to be driven by financial gain. Killing Lilly wouldn't earn him a dime."

"Okay, Mister Bell, unless Sergeant Mackie has any questions, I think that's all for now."

Winfield and Bell looked at Mackie, and C. K. said, "Actually, I do have one question. Did Miss Lawrence have a will?"

Bell said, "Yes, she did. Lilly told me her father insisted on her having one drawn up when she started making money in films. Then, when her father was killed, Lilly updated it with an attorney Mae recommended."

"Do you know who will inherit her estate?"

Bell hesitated a moment before saying, "Actually, I do. The only reason I do is that when Lilly updated her will, she wanted to include me in it. I told her that wasn't right. She ought to leave her money to someone who might need it. So she left a few pieces of jewelry to Mae, but the most of her estate will go to Viola Wiebe."

Tom Bell leaned his forehead on his hand and said in a choked voice, "I remember when we had that conversation. I never for a minute ever thought she would actually need a will." After a few seconds, he looked at Winfield with tears forming in his eyes and said, "I know it won't bring Lilly back, but please find the person who killed her so she can rest in the peace she deserves."

Winfield took a deep breath and said, "We will, Mister Bell. We will."

Mackie and Winfield watched Tom Bell reenter the lobby from the courtyard and then looked at each other. Winfield broke the silence, saying, "He's quite a guy."

C. K. nodded and said, "I think you're right, Bobby. Looking at him, you don't see much evidence of the grief, but it's there. It's deep, but it's definitely there."

Winfield said, "Okay, what's next?"

C. K. grinned at him and said, "That's up to you. You're the boss. If you want a suggestion, though, I move we go back to the station and have some lunch while we catch up on what we've learned today. That will give you more to put in your report to Captain Royce."

Winfield grimaced at Mackie's subtle reminder that Royce was expecting daily updates on their progress. Oh, well, he thought, it's all part of the job.

NINETEEN

After a quick stop at Larry's Deli for a Reuben to go, Winfield arrived in the detective office at the Sixth Division station on Cahuenga to find Mackie already at his desk munching a hearty sandwich of baloney between slices of fresh home-baked bread. Of even more interest to Winfield was the delicious-looking slice of homemade cherry pie on C. K.'s desk.

Between bites of his sandwich, Mackie said, "Well, we might as well start comparing notes on this morning's interviews. You want to go first or shall I?"

Unwrapping his sandwich, Winfield said, "You go first, I need to get a little of this lunch in me."

"Okay. My first stop this morning was Tony Marcelli's newsstand downtown next to the Biltmore to ask about those El Pantera cigars. We got a break there because it turns out they are very expensive, so expensive that only one company west of the Rockies imports them from Cuba. I talked with the owner of that company, and he told me the only El Pantera customer he has in the Los Angeles area is one L. A. Bromfeld. Mister Bromfeld has a standing order for eight boxes a month shipped to Western National's address. That adds up to 200 cigars a month or an average of six or seven cigars a day.

"While that evidence is circumstantial, there's a good chance Mister Bromfeld was fibbing when he told us he wasn't in Miss Lawrence's hotel room Saturday night."

"Interesting, but if he committed murder in that room, you'd think he would have been more careful about leaving clues behind."

Mackie nodded his agreement and continued, "The next item on my list was looking into Harry Lee's murder. The sheriff requested our help on the investigation, so some of the paperwork is on file at Central Division. Interestingly, Royce sent it to Brian Pierce instead of us.

"Anyway, Lee was found beaten to death in the Club Fiesta's parking area on Sunday, July four. The time of death was fixed at around two a.m. Sunday morning. The motive was put down as robbery because his wallet, a ring, and a watch were missing. No arrests were made and the investigation was suspended due to lack of leads.

"Next I took a look at Harry Lee's record. It showed fifteen arrests for drunkenness, gambling, and employing the services of a prostitute during the past two years, but no convictions. I have no evidence for this other than a feeling, but the record stinks to high heavens of a fix. And since the arrests were made after Lillian Lawrence became a successful actress at Western National Films, I've got a pretty good idea who did the fixing."

Winfield agreed, saying, "It certainly sounds as if Bromfeld or somebody at Western National was making sure their star's father stayed out of the newspapers."

"My thoughts exactly. While I was downtown, I also checked with Herm Geisler in the county coroner's office. He said he'd do his best to get an initial report to us by tomorrow morning. I'm not expecting much new information from his report, but you never know. We should also receive the Criminal Investigation Lab's report tomorrow. I don't expect any earthshaking revelations from them, either."

"Good work, C. K. Were you able to talk with the hotel manager?"

Mackie flipped through some pages in his notebook and said, "Yes, that was the next stop on my list, although I'm afraid it wasn't too fruitful. Harrison saw Miss Lawrence twice on Saturday. The first time was around mid-morning. He saw her coming into the hotel with a small package, probably the package of items she picked up at the drugstore.

"The second time he saw her was between three and three-thirty in the afternoon. She was sitting out in the courtyard with a book. He said she looked bored."

Consulting his notes, Mackie continued, "With regard to telephone calls to Miss Lawrence or telephone messages for her, Harrison could find no record of either since Friday, but that may not mean anything. Based on how telephone messages are handled at the hotel, it's entirely possible calls for Miss Lawrence could have been received but not recorded. I also spoke with the desk clerk who was on duty Sunday morning. He told me the same story.

"I then got Harrison to open Miss Lawrence's box in the hotel safe. It held three pieces of expensive jewelry and an envelope. The envelope contained a duplicate bill of sale for Miss Lawrence's home.

"The last tidbit of information I got from Mister Harrison is a little disturbing. It seems there were two keys to Miss Lawrence's hotel room. She had one of them—the one now in my pocket. The second key was sitting in her room box behind the front desk until Harrison arrived at the hotel this morning, at which point he took possession of the key and put it away in his desk drawer."

Finishing the last bite of his sandwich, Winfield said, "If that key was there Saturday, it means somebody could have entered Miss Lawrence's room without her having to open the door."

"True. Of course, many of the employees also have passkeys that will open any guestroom in the hotel, so it's hard to say how significant the second key to room 187 really is."

Winfield contemplated the information for a moment before saying, "I guess that's right. I wish those hotel room doors had a second lock that could only be released from the inside. That would eliminate some of the questions about how the killer got into Miss Lawrence's room. Did you talk to the housekeeping maid?"

"That was the last item on my list. She took the day off, so I drove out to her home. That poor women is still in shock, so it took some doing to get anything coherent out of her. The way Hattie Mae Brown remembers Sunday morning, she knocked on the door to room 187 and got no answer. Then she tried the doorknob and found the door unlocked. That's probably the most important part of her story, and she's certain of it.

"Next she picked out some fresh towels and entered the room. It was dark because the curtains were pulled, so she couldn't see very well. She says she tripped over something just inside the door and ended up on the floor, face to face with the victim."

Winfield chimed in, "She probably tripped over Miss Lawrence's purse. It was just inside the door."

"That's my guess. Anyway, that is the last thing Hattie Mae remembers before waking up out in the hall. She swears she touched nothing in the room."

"The part about the door being unlocked might be important. It seems to indicate the murderer didn't have a room key or he probably would have locked the door on his way out. That, in turn, supports our initial theory that Miss Lawrence knew the killer and let him into her room."

"Perhaps, but all of that is speculation at this point. It's nothing we can rely on. We need facts that will stand up in court."

Winfield nodded his agreement. "I'm afraid my interviews didn't provide many of those facts you're talking about. Mostly what I got were confirmations of things we already knew."

Mackie said, "Confirmations are important, Bobby. A corroborated fact is generally twice as reliable as an unconfirmed fact. Tell me what you got."

Winfield began by summarizing his interview Sunday night with the dining room maitre d', Maurice DeVoe. "The fellow made it clear that he has very little love for Bromfeld. Other than that, I learned Bromfeld's secretary made the Saturday night dinner reservation before noon on Friday—she confirmed that herself this morning. DeVoe said Bromfeld and Miss Lawrence arrived in the dining room about 6:30 and their conversation seemed friendly at first.

Then the talk got tense and things came to a head when Lillian Lawrence left the table in tears just before seven. According to DeVoe, Bromfeld was still in good spirits and finished his dinner before leaving around seven-thirty."

"Interesting. That sort of shoots a hole in another of Bromfeld's stories—the one where he told us they had dinner to celebrate Lillian Lawrence changing her mind about leaving the studio. If that were true, it seems unlikely she would leave the dining room in tears."

"Yes, that's what I made of it, too. On the other hand, if things went the way Mae White anticipated, Bromfeld would have been the one who was unhappy. So we can probably conclude things didn't go as Miss Lawrence planned."

Mackie added, "I think that's a safe assumption. Maybe Bromfeld found something to hold over Miss Lawrence's head that convinced her she couldn't leave Western National."

"It would sure be nice to know what that was."

Mackie agreed, "It would indeed. How did your interviews go at Western National this morning?"

Winfield launched a concise summary of the studio interviews beginning with his comparison of Mae White's and Lillian Lawrence's contracts and ending with Viola Wiebe's poignant plea for them to find Miss Lawrence's killer. When he was done, Mackie said, "Good police work, Laddie. What you learned this morning confirms most of what Mae White told us and some of what Tom Bell said."

"Yes, it does. I think the most interesting parts were the stories I heard of Ernst Frohmme accosting Miss Lawrence. In spite of Tom Bell's doubting Frohmme was still angry enough to harm Miss Lawrence, I think Frohmme is still a strong suspect."

"I agree. What's next on our agenda?"

Winfield thought for a moment before saying, "I need to get started on my report to Captain Royce. How 'bout you make a few telephone calls to confirm Tom Bell's alibi while I start typing."

"Sounds good to me."

With that, Mackie left the detective room so Winfield could concentrate on his report. The lieutenant rolled an official L.A.P.D. Investigation Report Form into his typewriter and began filling in the blanks.

Los Angeles Police Department
HOMICIDE INVESTIGATION REPORT

```
VICTIM: Lawrence (Lee), Lillian
DATE: 6 September, 1926
INVESTIGATOR: Det. Lt. Winfield, Robert
```

SUMMARY OF PERSONS INVOLVED

NAME: Bell, Thomas
RELATIONSHIP: Victim's fiancé
MOTIVE: None known
MEANS: None known
OPPORTUNITY: None
NOTES: Subject has concrete alibi for time of murder
STATUS: Cleared

NAME: Bromfeld, L. A.
RELATIONSHIP: Victim's employer (W/N Films)
MOTIVE: ?
MEANS: ?
OPPORTUNITY: Subject is known to have been at the Hollywood Hotel at the time of the crime.
NOTES: Subject is left-handed, which coincides with crime scene evidence. Subject smokes expensive Cuban cigars, which coincides with crime scene evidence. Subject was in conflict with victim prior to murder.
STATUS: Under investigation

NAME: Frohmme, Ernst
RELATIONSHIP: Directed victim in films at W/N Films
MOTIVE: Career was threatened by victim
MEANS: ?
OPPORTUNITY: ?
NOTES: Subject accosted victim sexually during filming. Victim and Mae White complained to L. A. Bromfeld, who reprimanded subject. Subject harassed victim vindictively after incident.
STATUS: Under investigation

NAME: White (Glaum, Mildred), Mae
RELATIONSHIP: Actress and close friend of victim
MOTIVE: ?
MEANS: ?
OPPORTUNITY: Subject is known to have been at Hollywood Hotel around time of murder.
STATUS: Under investigation

Winfield was nearly done with the report when Sergeant Mackie returned to the detective room with news that he confirmed Tom Bell's alibi with both the auction company and Fresno's Californian Hotel. He added that he was unable to reach Asa Stewart, but talking with him didn't seem necessary with the other confirmations.

The lieutenant rolled the form out of his typewriter and handed it to Mackie for his review. C. K. read the report carefully. When he finished, Mackie said, "You write a thorough, and concise report, Bobby. I see you even included Mae White's real name. How did you happen upon that that tidbit of information?"

"It turns out the woman who does Miss Lawrence's make-up grew up with Miss White. She sort of let Miss White's real name slip out."

Mackie grinned. "You do seem to have a way with the young women in this case, Laddie. I shall leave all such interviews to you from here on."

Winfield grinned back at his sergeant, and then flushed slightly when it dawned on him that he overlooked the same information when examining Mae White's contract. She surely signed such a document with her legal name, just as Lillian Lawrence signed her contract, "Lillian Lee." He was pretty sure the same thought occurred to Mackie. The lieutenant gave himself a swift mental kick in the seat of his pants as a reminder to be more thorough in the future.

With Mackie's blessing Winfield sealed the report form in an envelope addressed to Captain Royce. He then handed the envelope to the desk sergeant with instructions to have a patrol officer hand deliver it directly to Captain Royce's office.

When Winfield returned to the detective room, Mackie said, "Okay, Boss, where do we go from here?"

Winfield sat back in his desk chair and thought for a moment. Then he said, "We seem to have two major holes in our investigation to fill in at this point. The first hole is Bromfeld and his inconsistencies. I would also like to know if anyone besides him has access to his fancy cigars.

"The second hole has to do with Ernst Frohmme. We really need to get a handle on him and his whereabouts Saturday night."

Mackie said, "You want to do those interviews yourself or do you want me along?"

"Bromfeld and Frohmme seem to be our prime suspects, so I think it would be beneficial for us to do the interviews together."

"Alright. Shall I call Bromfeld's office and get us on his schedule for first thing tomorrow morning?"

"Good idea, but watch out for that secretary of his. I've known rattlesnakes that were easier to get along with!"

Mackie grinned. "That I will, Laddie. Anything else?"

"I guess I need to make my call to Captain Royce. Other than that, let's call it a day."

"Okay by me. Meet you here at the usual time in the morning?"

"Sounds good."

With that, Mackie went off to call Bessie Shipman. Winfield took a deep breath and dialed Captain Royce's office number. Winfield gave the captain a complete and accurate summary of the investigation's progress, and even though they hadn't made an arrest yet, the captain surprised Winfield by complimenting him on their progress. He did, however, make it very clear to the lieutenant in no uncertain terms that Lillian Lawrence's murder was a "headline case" that needed to be closed within the next few days.

That night in his room at Missus Haney's boardinghouse, Winfield figured he'd fall asleep the minute his head hit the pillow. He didn't. Instead, the name Millie Glaum came drifting into his mind along with the vision of a perfect piece of homemade cherry pie. He wasn't sure why those two thoughts popped into his head simultaneously, but Winfield almost laughed out loud at the ridiculous notion of America's motion picture sweetheart in her kitchen baking pies.

TWENTY

Tuesday - September 7, 1926

It was precisely ten minutes before eight a.m. by Winfield's wristwatch when he and Detective Sergeant Mackie rolled up to the Western National Films east lot gate. Jake Blore was manning the gate, and as he signed them onto the studio grounds, he asked Mackie, "You see the Times this morning? Lillian Lawrence is all over the front page again."

"Yeah, I saw it. They said about what I expected them to say."

"Tell me, just between us old warhorses, is what they claim Captain Royce said right? Do you really expect to make an arrest any minute or is that just the usual newspaper hooey?"

Mackie smile at Blore. "You know how these investigations go, Jake. It takes time to put together a good case that will stand up in court."

Blore nodded knowingly. "That's what I thought. Well, I wish you luck with it."

Mackie nodded thanks and drove his Dodge onto the studio grounds. As he pulled into a parking space in front of Western National's administration building, Winfield noticed that L. A. Bromfeld's reserved parking spot was empty. He said, "Looks like we'll have to wait for Bromfeld. He isn't here yet."

Climbing down from the driver's seat, Mackie said, "We're a few minutes early, but that's okay. I've got a few questions for Bessie Shipman."

"Good luck getting anything useful out of that old battleaxe."

Mackie grinned at Winfield and said, "You really got off on the wrong foot with her, didn't you?"

Bessie Shipman was already at her desk when Mackie and Winfield entered Bromfeld's outer office. She looked up and after glaring at Winfield, said, "Good morning, Sergeant Mackie. I'm afraid you're a little early. Mister Bromfeld hasn't arrived yet."

"Good morning, Miss Shipman. I realize we're early. Perhaps you can answer a couple of questions while we wait for Mister Bromfeld."

Bessie Shipman smiled at Mackie and said, "Why, certainly, Sergeant. What would you like to know?"

The secretary's cooperative attitude left Winfield wondering if they were in the right office. C. K. said, "Well, it's just a matter of curiosity, but I've been wondering about those cigars Mister Bromfeld smokes. They're imported, aren't they?"

"Oh, yes. They come all the way from Havana, Cuba. Mister Bromfeld has a standing order with the company that imports them. They send him eight boxes right here to the studio every month."

"Really? Those cigars must be worth their weight in gold!"

"Oh, they are! Mister Bromfeld even had a custom humidor cabinet made with a locking door to keep them safe in his office."

"Is that so? I wager he doesn't give many of them away to visitors and the like."

"You win that bet. Mister Bromfeld keeps a box of less expensive cigars in his office for guests. He . . . ."

The office door flew open and L. A. Bromfeld bustled into the room with a cheerful, "Good morning to all!"

Bessie Shipman said, "Good morning, Mister Bromfeld. Sergeant Mackie here is with the police. He called for an appointment yesterday afternoon after you left the studio."

"I am remembering the sergeant and Mister Winfield from when they are coming to my house on Sunday and bringing us the terrible news about our poor little Lilly." Then, opening the door to his inner office, Bromfeld continued, "Come in, gentlemen, and tell me how I can help you."

Now Winfield was certain he was in the wrong office. Not only was Bessie Shipman friendly, but Bromfeld's attitude had changed completely from what they witnessed two days earlier.

After Bromfeld closed the door and offered them seats in two comfortable chairs facing his desk, Mackie said, "We need a little more background information on Miss Lawrence. I understand she worked in your costume shop before she became an actress."

Sitting at his desk and looking exactly like the stereotypical motion picture executive, Bromfeld bit the tip off an El Pantera, spit it into a trashcan next to his desk, and after lighting the cigar with great pomp and ceremony, he said, "This is correct. I am walking by the costume shop one day and I am seeing her through the window. I am knowing right away that little Lilly was going to be a big star. We are doing a screen test and that is proving me right.

"Then we are putting her in a small role in Mae White's picture, The Long Night. The public is loving her and demanding to see more of her!"

Mackie, jotting notes in his book, said, "How did Miss Lawrence feel about that?"

Bromfeld took a long, satisfying drag on his cigar and said, "Lilly was a shy young woman. She was not liking all the attention, but she is putting her shoulder to the wheel and working very hard on that picture. I cannot deny that her acting skills were needing some improvement, but I am knowing without a doubt that little Lilly was going to be our next star, and she was!"

"So Miss Lawrence didn't care for acting?"

Bromfeld took another drag on his cigar and thought about the question a moment before answering. "It was not so much that she did not care for acting, but that she was having no confidence that she could act. In spite of the wonderful reviews she received for appearing in The Long Night, she was being . . . how I should say, reluctant to be making more pictures. I offered her a five-year contract, but she is turning it down at first."

"But she eventually signed the contract?"

"Yes. I am thinking it was about two weeks later when she came back to my office and is saying she will accept my offer. I am being completely delighted!"

"I see. Do you have any idea why she changed her mind?"

Mackie and Winfield waited while Bromfeld removed a piece loose tobacco from his tongue. Finally, he said, "I am not being sure about this, but I am thinking she changed her mind because of her father, Harry Lee."

"He encouraged her to sign the contract?"

"It was more than that. You must understand, gentlemen, that Harry Lee was not a good man. I am not liking to speak badly of a dead man, but I am feeling I must be completely honest with you, and the honest truth is being that Harry Lee was a drunken bum and a bad gambler. After Lilly was paid a great sum of money for her appearance in The Long Night, this man is spending the money like it is water. Soon he is having big gambling debts.

"Poor little Lilly is wanting nothing more but to be working at her old job in the costume shop, but Harry Lee's debts are being too much for the small salary she is making there. So I am believing Lilly is accepting my offer of a contract so she will be having money to pay her father's debts."

Mackie finished noting this in his book and asked, "Did Mister Lee continue to run up large gambling debts after Lilly signed the contract?"

Bromfeld hung his head in an overly dramatic gesture of sadness and said, "Sadly, yes. Lilly is trying her best to change him, but he is gambling and drinking more than ever. I am even having to bail him out of jail many times, and . . . and I am begging with the police to keep Harry Lee's name out of the newspapers. It would not be good for the fans of Lillian Lawrence to know she was the daughter of a drunken bum."

Winfield mentally substituted the word "bribing" for "begging." Mackie was right. The fix was definitely in for Harry Lee. At least fifteen times Lee had been arrested without ever once going to court or serving more than a night in jail. And heaven only knows how many times that scene was replayed without an official arrest being made. The lieutenant found himself agreeing with Viola Wiebe's thought that Bromfeld might have even encouraged Harry Lee's gambling. What better way to force Lillian Lawrence to sign a contract than to create an impossible financial situation for her? He jotted a reminder in his notebook to look into that possibility.

Mackie said, "So you must have felt some relief when Harry Lee was killed."

Bromfeld stared at Mackie for a long moment. "If I am being completely honest with you, the answer is yes. Poor little Lilly was heartbroken when her father died, and I would not be wishing such sadness on her for anything, but I am knowing in my heart that she is better off without Harry Lee."

As Bromfeld spoke, he waved his cigar around as if he were leading an orchestra. Winfield could not help but notice its ragged, soggy tip resulting from a habit of chewing on the cigar as he smoked.

C. K. sat quietly for several seconds. Then he said, "People who knew Miss Lawrence say it wasn't long after Harry Lee's death that she asked to be released from her contract with Western National Films. Is that true?"

A momentary look of surprise passed over Bromfeld's face before he said, "Well, yes, that is the truth. She was being suddenly alone and very upset. It is only natural that Lilly should be confused about what she should be doing next."

"And you refused her request?"

A slight edge of defensiveness colored Bromfeld's words. "I am having no choice, gentlemen. I must always be looking out for the interests of this company's investors. Lillian Lawrence was making for the studio a great deal of money. We could not afford to be releasing her from her contract. Besides, I am also knowing that little Lilly was not thinking clearly and she would be regretting it if I was giving into to her whim."

"We have also been told that Miss Lawrence didn't enjoy acting—that she was very unhappy doing it."

Now anger began creeping into Bromfeld's tone. Poking the burning end of his now short cigar at Mackie, he said, "Who is telling you such lies? Lilly loved acting. She was working very hard at being a successful actress!"

"Then why did she offer to buy out her Western National contract?"

"I have already been telling you! She was upset and confused because of her father's dying. I knew she would be changing her mind, and she did."

"Did she?"

"Yes! After a short time she is telephoning me to say she is deciding to stay on with Western National."

"When was this?"

Bromfeld thought about the question and then said, "I am thinking she is calling me on the Thursday before her tragic death. I am suggesting to her that we celebrate her decision by having dinner at her hotel Saturday night. She is accepting my invitation."

"So that was the purpose of your dinner Saturday night? To celebrate her decision to honor her contract? What was her mood at dinner?"

"She was happy—excited to be going ahead with her acting."

Mackie made a show of flipping through the pages of his notebook before saying, "Witnesses tell us she seemed quite the opposite at dinner. In fact, they say she left the table in tears without touching her dinner. Do you recall that happening?"

Bromfeld was frowning as he answered. "Well, yes. I am not recalling that she was crying, but she is saying that she is not hungry and asking to be excused from the table. Little Lilly was still being under a great deal of strain about her father dying, so it is understandable, her behavior. I am telling her to be going and getting some rest."

"What did you do after she left the table?"

Sounding as if he was giving the obvious answer to a dumb question, Bromfeld said, "I am eating my dinner."

"I see. What time did you leave the dining room?"

"I am already answering these questions on Sunday. It was around quarter before eight."

"By any chance did you stop by Miss Lawrence's hotel room—say, to make sure she was okay?"

"I did not. It would not be being appropriate for me to visit her hotel room. Besides that, I am not wanting to disturb her rest."

"So you left the dining room and went straight to your automobile?"

"Yes."

"And that's when you spoke with Miss White? In the hotel parking area?"

"Yes."

"How long did you talk with Miss White?"

The way he was chewing on the end of his cigar more vigorously gave Winfield the impression Bromfeld was becoming increasingly uncomfortable with Mackie's questions. He said, "We are talking only for a minute—just a few words. Why are you asking these questions? I am telling you all of this on Sunday."

Mackie replied calmly, "I just want to be sure we have the information right because you were quite upset over Miss Lawrence's death Sunday. So you went straight home from the hotel and arrived around eight-fifteen or eight-twenty. Is that correct?"

"Yes, that is correct."

Mackie turned to Winfield and said, "Do you have any questions for Mister Bromfeld?"

Winfield nodded and said, "Yes, I do. Mister Bromfeld, we understand that Miss Lawrence and Miss White were close friends. Is that right?"

Looking somewhat relieved at the change of subject, Bromfeld said, "Yes, they were being bosom buddies. Mae is being very helpful to Lilly by helping with her acting techniques and such."

"What is your general impression of Mae White?"

Bromfeld hesitated only a second before saying, "Mae is a wonderful actress—very beautiful and talented. We are fortunate to be having her under contract."

"We have heard that Miss Lawrence was having some difficulty with one of your directors—a man named Ernst Frohmme. Can you tell us what happened?"

Bromfeld took another drag on his cigar and discovering it had gone out, relit the stub before saying, "Yes, that was a terrible misunderstanding. At one time, Lilly is going out to dinner with Ernst. I am afraid Ernst is mistaking that occasion for that she is being interested in him romantically. Soon after they are having dinner, he is approaching her on the set of a movie they are making together and he is being . . . romantic toward her. Lilly is not feeling the same way and is being scared by Ernst. She is getting upset and screaming at him.

"It is then that Mae and others are coming to see what the matter is. Mae is being very protective of little Lilly and bringing her here to me for to telling me what happened. I am also being upset, so I am calling Ernst here and telling him he must not be behaving as he did toward Lilly. That was that."

Winfield said, "Not quite. We've been told Mister Frohmme was very hard on Miss Lawrence during filming after that incident."

"Mister Winfield, let me please be telling you about Ernst Frohmme. He is starting out in pictures as an actor before discovering that his real talents are for directing. He is doing directing with great flair and is getting wonderful performances from the actors. His pictures always receive great acclaim. This is because he is being a perfectionist and having a strong temper. He is expecting actors to be doing things exactly as what he says. When they are not following his direction, Ernst is losing his temper and going about yelling and screaming at them. It is how he is.

"Some actors, like Mae White and Estelle Fontaine, are understanding this and not letting it bother them. But Lilly is being naïve and too much sensitive. She is thinking he is picking on her because she is making him in trouble with me. This is not so."

Winfield jotted a note in his book and said, "I see. We've been told that Mister Frohmme has a liking for young women and that he has some unusual sexual interests. What can you tell us about that?"

"I can be telling you that some people who are not knowing what they are talking about should be keeping their mouths shut! Ernst is being very hard on actors, and they are sometimes telling stories about him that are not true. I am personally talking with some actresses who have accused Ernst of doing unspeakable things, and after I am calming them down, they are telling me they are making more of what has been happening than it is really being."

"Mister Bromfeld, we would like to speak with Ernst Frohmme. Can you arrange that?"

Bromfeld thought for a moment and then said, "Ernst is filming over on the coast near Santa Monica this week. If you must be talking to him right away, then you must be going there. I am understanding he is filming on the beach north of the municipal wharf. You should be having no trouble finding them."

With that, Mackie stood and said, "We appreciate your cooperation, Mister Bromfeld. We're making progress with our investigation, and I hope to have news of an arrest in the case before much longer."

Bromfeld dropped what remained of his soggy cigar into the large glass ashtray on his desk without stubbing it out and said, "I am hoping you are bringing me that news soon. We are needing to put this tragedy behind us."

As Mackie and Winfield stepped into the outer office, Bessie Shipman turned, and speaking to Mackie, she said, "Oh, good, you're through. I thought I might have to interrupt the conference because your office just called and said you have an urgent message. The gentleman who called asked that you call in right away. You may use the telephone on my desk if you wish."

Mackie took the slip of paper Bessie Shipman held out and said, "Thank you, Miss Shipman. We are driving directly back to the stationhouse, so we'll just wait until we get there for the message."

Riding up Cahuenga toward the Sixth Precinct Station, Winfield said, "I wonder what the urgent message is."

"I can't imagine. Geisler's autopsy report might have arrived already, but that wouldn't constitute an 'urgent message.' We'll find out in a couple of minutes. In the meantime, what did you think of Bromfeld?"

"Well, his mood has certainly improved since Sunday. He was downright friendly, as was Miss Shipman. More important, Bromfeld is sticking to the story he gave us Sunday, and that's a problem. Unless Miss White and DeVoe, the maitre 'd at the Dining Room of the Stars, are both wrong, fifteen to twenty minutes of Bromfeld's time is unaccounted for on Saturday night. That's plenty of time to commit murder."

Mackie nodded. "Yes, indeed, it is. Anything else?"

"Yes. Did you notice Bromfeld's cigar?"

C. K. chuckled. "The way he waved the thing around, it was hard to miss!"

"I meant did you notice how he chews the end until it's a soggy blob?"

"Yes, but what . . . oh, I see what you're getting at. The cigar in Miss Lawrence's hotel room wasn't chewed up that way."

"Exactly. I'm not sure what that means, but it seemed worth remembering. Did you catch anything else I missed?"

C. K. thought for a moment. "No, you mentioned the main concern I have—Bromfeld's missing time on Saturday night. There is something else that's nagging at me a little, though."

"What's that?"

"In both of our interviews Bromfeld claims he spoke with Mae White as he was leaving the hotel Saturday night, but Mae White said only that she saw him leaving the hotel. She didn't mention talking to him."

Winfield said, "Bromfeld said they only exchanged a few words—sort of a hello-goodbye conversation. Maybe Mae . . . Miss White didn't think it was important enough to mention."

As Mackie U-turned across Cahuenga into an empty parking space in front of the stationhouse, he said, "Maybe. And as you say, it might not be important, but if we're going to do a thorough job of this investigation, it is a point we ought to clarify."

TWENTY-ONE

Patrol Officer Paul Otis was manning the complaint desk at the Sixth Precinct stationhouse when Winfield and Mackie arrived. Upon seeing the detectives come in, he jumped to attention, offered a crisp salute, and said, "Good morning, sirs."

In his peripheral vision, Winfield saw Mackie roll his eyes in exasperation at Otis' military protocol. To spare C. K. the effort, Winfield returned Otis' salute and said, "Good morning, Otis. As you were."

Otis relaxed his ramrod-straight posture and said, "I have an urgent telephone message for you, and a patrol officer from Central Division just delivered this envelope for you."

Winfield accepted the folded telephone message form and an envelope from Otis and then followed Mackie down the hall toward the detective room. Unfolding the message form, he read it and said, "Now, this is interesting."

Over his shoulder, Mackie said, "What's interesting?"

"This telephone message. It's from Ruth Bromfeld."

"Is it now? What does Missus Bromfeld have to say?"

"She asks that we call her as soon as possible. Even more interesting is that we are supposed to ask for her at Hotel Knickerbocker. What do you suppose Ruth Bromfeld is doing there at this hour of the morning?"

Mackie leaned back in his desk chair and said, "I can't imagine. This sort of thing is what makes our jobs interesting. You never know what will happen next. What's in the envelope?"

Winfield looked at the return address on the official-looking white envelope and read, "Office of the Coroner of Los Angeles County."

"Good. That must be Geisler's preliminary autopsy report. Let's open it up and see what Herm found."

The lieutenant settled into his chair and used a letter opener from his desk drawer to slit the top of the sealed envelope. Inside he found printed forms with several additional typewritten pages. Across the top of the first page were the words, "County of Los Angeles – Office of the Coroner." Below that it said, "Preliminary Autopsy Findings."

Winfield said, "That's what it is, alright. Let's see . . . Date: Seven, September, '26. Subject Name: Lillian Lee (Lawrence). Description: Caucasian female approximately twenty years of age; height: five feet-four inches; weight: 117 pounds; hair: blonde; eyes: green. Subject was in good physical condition."

Scanning down the page, Winfield read, "Time of Death: Between 7:30 PM and 8:30 PM Saturday, Four, September, 1926. Cause of Death: Cerebral hemorrhage resulting from bullet wound to right frontal lobe of brain. Additional Explanation: It is likely subject lost consciousness immediately and died within two to four minutes after receiving wound."

Mackie said, "No surprises so far. What else did Herm find?"

"Under 'Wounds' it says there was a single bullet wound in the area of the subject's right temple. Additional Explanation: Bullet was .22 caliber fired at close range as indicated by powder burns surrounding the wound. Bullet was lodged in brain and recovered for possible comparison. No other wounds were found.

"Under 'Other Details' it says there were no signs of sexual molestation. Grains of cordite were found on subject's right hand. Stomach contents indicate subject had not eaten for approximately six hours. Blood tests showed no signs of alcohol or other foreign chemicals were present.

"Under 'Crime Scene Evidence' it says the Criminal Investigation Laboratory report (attached) showed no evidence was found that the subject was moved after death. Victim appears to have been sitting on the edge of the bed at time of shooting. Dozens of fingerprints were found in the victim's hotel room; many were smudged. The victim's prints were the only ones found on personal items such as cosmetic bottles.

"That's it. The rest of the pages contain measurements and chemical analysis results."

Winfield handed the report to Mackie. After glancing at it briefly, the sergeant put a Bostitch staple into the upper-left corner of the report pages and slipped them into the case file folder on his desk. Settling back into his chair, Mackie said, "Any of Herm's findings interest you?"

"Mostly it confirmed what we concluded Sunday. I did find the presence of cordite on Miss Lawrence's right hand interesting, though."

Mackie nodded. "That does give cause to wonder. Cordite grains usually indicate the subject was holding a gun when it was fired."

Winfield added, "Or that the subject's hand was near the gun when it was discharged. It's possible she was grabbing at her assailant's hand to push the gun away."

"Or Miss Lawrence committed suicide."

"Yes, or that. But if Lillian Lawrence killed herself, where is the gun? And what about a suicide note? Lillian Lawrence was engaged to be married. If she committed suicide, surely she would have left a note for Tom Bell explaining why she was killing herself."

"All good questions, Bobby. Since her hotel room was apparently unlocked between the time of death and when the body was found, I suppose someone might have entered and removed evidence, but who and for what purpose?"

"I have no idea."

Winfield noticed the telephone message from Ruth Bromfeld on his desk. He picked it up and said, "I guess we ought to find out what Missus Bromfeld wants. You want to call her?"

Mackie said, "Sure."

After the hotel operator connected his call to a guest room, Mackie had a brief conversation with Ruth Bromfeld. Hearing only C. K.'s side of the conversation, Winfield didn't get much of what they were talking about until Mackie concluded the call by saying, "Certainly, Missus Bromfeld. Detective Winfield or I will be there within half an hour. Yes, ma'am."

Returning the telephone handset to its cradle, Mackie said, "Missus Bromfeld says she needs to speak with us."

Winfield asked, "Did she say what she wants to speak to us about?"

"No, only that she needs to see us this morning because she is leaving town by train this afternoon."

"That sounds a little mysterious."

"That's why I told her one or the other of us would be there soon."

Winfield frowned. "I don't think we ought to put off seeing Ernst Frohmme much longer, though. He's still on our list of suspects. You want to see Missus Bromfeld while I head out to Santa Monica to see Frohmme?"

"Alright. You probably won't be back here until afternoon, so unless I need to follow-up on whatever Ruth Bromfeld has to say, I'll come back here and catch up on our paperwork."

"Deal."

TWENTY-TWO

Situated in the first block of Ivar north of Hollywood Boulevard, the Hotel Knickerbocker was only three blocks from the Sixth Precinct stationhouse. It would have been an easy walk for Sergeant Mackie, but he chose to drive to the hotel so his automobile would be handy for whatever might be required of him after meeting with Ruth Bromfeld.

The hotel was a ten-story cube with a grand triple-arched entry facing Ivar Avenue. The exterior always struck Mackie as being rather garish, even for Hollywood. The front of the ground floor was white, while the rest of the structure was finished in a reddish-brown topped off with white bands below and above the top floor. Sitting on a framework atop the hotel's roof was a giant electric sign that spelled "Hotel Knickerbocker" in brilliant red letters. Even strangers to Hollywood would have a hard time missing the Knickerbocker.

Mackie pulled to the curb in front of the hotel and walked through the main entrance into a huge lobby that, compared to the Hollywood Hotel's lobby, was modern and bustling with activity. Ruth Bromfeld told Mackie she would meet him in the lobby, and it only took a moment for the sergeant to spot her seated in a back corner of the room.

As he approached her, Ruth Bromfeld got to her feet. Mackie guessed by the slow, careful way she moved that Missus Bromfeld was in pain, a fact further evidenced by a plaster cast on her left wrist and a large, dark bruise on her left cheek that was only partially concealed by the shawl she wore.

"Good morning, Missus Bromfeld. I'm Detective Sergeant Mackie."

"Yes, Sergeant, I remember you from your visit on Sunday."

"Please sit down and be comfortable, Missus Bromfeld."

She slowly lowered herself back into the chair, and after seating himself in the chair next to hers, Mackie said, "Forgive me for mentioning it, but you look as if you've had an accident. Are you alright?"

"Yes, Sergeant, my injuries will heal. They always do."

"I certainly hope so. Now, how can I help you, Missus Bromfeld?"

"I want to register an official police complaint against my husband."

Of all the things Ruth Bromfeld might have said at that point, registering a complaint against L. A. Bromfeld was the last thing Mackie expected. After pausing a moment to let the thought sink in, he said, "I see. What is the charge?"

"Assault and battery, Sergeant."

Nodding, Mackie said, "I take it then that your injuries were caused by your husband?"

"Yes. He hit me and knocked me down last night in a fit of rage."

Mackie raised his hand in a stop gesture and said, "Missus Bromfeld, if you want to make this an official complaint, I need to get a form from my automobile so I can record the details of the incident as you describe it."

"Please do, Sergeant."

Mackie walked quickly out to his Dodge to retrieve a leather briefcase from the trunk. Back in the lobby, the sergeant removed a clipboard and attached an L.A.P.D. Citizen Complaint form to it. Then, while filling in the name and date blanks at the top of the form, Mackie said, "Okay, Missus Bromfeld, tell me what happened in as much detail as you can."

Without hesitation, Ruth Bromfeld said, "It happened last night shortly after dinner. We were sitting in the library with our coffees when the telephone rang. Clarence, our butler, took the call. He came into the library and told L. A. that Miss Shipman, L. A.'s secretary, was calling. L. A. picked up the receiver of the library telephone extension and spoke with her for a few minutes. Then he hung up the telephone and flew into a rage."

Mackie held up his hand in the stop motion for a second while he neatly printed the pertinent details on the form. When he finished, Mackie said, "Okay, Missus Bromfeld, please continue."

"I don't know what Miss Shipman told him, but it must have had something to do with the police because L. A. was yelling incoherently about 'the ignorant police wasting his valuable time.'"

As the sergeant wrote, he wondered if Bessie Shipman called Bromfeld to warn her boss about the appointment Mackie had scheduled for the following morning. He couldn't imagine what else the police might have done to raise Bromfeld's ire.

"Then L. A. grabbed a heavy book from one of the library shelves and threw it across the room. It hit a table lamp and caused a terrible racket that startled me so much I dropped my coffee cup and saucer on the floor. They broke into pieces, and that made me the target of L. A.'s rage. He came at me hollering that I was stupid and clumsy.

"I stood up quickly, intending to leave the room, but L. A. got to me before I could take a step." Mackie saw her hand go to the bruise on her cheek as she continued, "He hit me across the face with the back of his hand so hard that I stumbled backward into an end table, knocking it over and falling on top of it.

"The next thing I knew, L. A. was standing over me looking as if he was going to hit me again. At that moment, Clarence came running into the library to see what the ruckus was about. The moment L. A. saw him, it was as if a switch was thrown. His rage was gone, and he calmly told Clarence to call the doctor because 'Missus Bromfeld has had an accident.'

"Clarence went off to do as he was told, and L. A. offered his hand to help me up. That's when I realized I must have broken my wrist in the fall."

Mackie paused Ruth Bromfeld again to catch up with his notes on the complaint form. Then he said, "Alright, Missus Bromfeld. What happened next?"

"The doctor arrived about half an hour later and set my wrist with this cast." She held up her left arm. "While I was waiting for the doctor, I made up my mind that this was the last time L. A. would ever hit me. I decided to pack a bag and take the first train I could get for my sister's home in New York."

Mackie asked, "Mister Bromfeld has hit you before last night?"

"So many times I've lost count. L. A. has always had a strong temper, but he was never violent toward me until we moved to Hollywood a little more than three years ago. I have always thought that it was the strain of running the studio that caused L. A. to become so violent, but that is no excuse for hurting me."

Mackie nodded agreement, saying, "No, it certainly isn't. You said you were seen by a doctor. What is his name?"

"Doctor Phillip Mason. His office is on Franklin Avenue just beyond the Methodist church."

"Has doctor Mason treated you for injuries caused by your husband in the past?"

"Yes, at least three or four times when my injuries were serious enough to require his attention."

Mackie added Mason's name to that of Clarence, the butler, in the "Witnesses" section of the complaint form. Then he asked, "Did you leave last night or this morning?"

"I left this morning. I got up early, and while L. A. was still asleep in his bedroom, I packed my bags with enough clothes for a few weeks. As soon as L. A. left for work, I called a taxicab and had them bring me here. After having the concierge make my train reservation for this afternoon, I checked into a room so I would have someplace safe to wait until my train leaves. I'm taking the Santa Fe Chief to Chicago and then the Twentieth Century Limited into New York."

Mackie looked at his pocket watch and asked, "What time does your train leave?"

"At twelve-thirty."

"It's eleven now, so you'll need to leave for the station soon. May I give you a ride?"

"No, thank you, Sergeant. I've already made arrangements for a taxicab."

"Alright, Missus Bromfeld. What are your future plans with regard to your husband?"

Sounding as if her answer should have been obvious, Ruth Bromfeld said, "I plan to divorce him as soon as possible. I will make arrangements for that to happen with our family law firm in New York. I will then make arrangements for the rest of my belongings to be shipped back to New York. With any luck at all, I will never have to set foot in this town again as long as I live."

Surprised, Mackie looked up at Ruth Bromfeld and said, "If we arrest your husband for assault and battery, you will have to be here to testify at his trial."

"I don't expect you to arrest him, Sergeant. It would serve no purpose. L. A.'s conniving lawyers would easily get him out of it on some technicality or other."

"Then why are you filing this complaint?"

"Simply to have an official police report to support my claim for a divorce on the grounds of physical cruelty. I'm sure my lawyer in New York will be writing to you for a copy of the report before too long."

Mackie nodded. "I see. Okay, Missus Bromfeld, please read through this complaint form and then sign and date it at the bottom where it says, 'Complainant.'"

Ruth Bromfeld read the form carefully and signed it with Mackie's fountain pen. Mackie took the form back and placed it in his briefcase. Then he said, "Okay, Missus Bromfeld, I think we're done. Have a safe trip to New York."

"There's one more thing, Sergeant Mackie."

Mackie had started to get up, but sat back in his chair, "What would that be, Missus Bromfeld?"

"You have been so prompt and friendly about helping me with my problem, I would like to offer you something that might help solve one of your problems."

"Oh?"

"Yes. Do you recall asking L. A. if he owned a gun while you and that other officer were at the house on Sunday?"

"Yes. If I remember correctly, your husband said he didn't own any guns."

"That is what he said, but it was not the truth. After you left, we went to a party in Beverly Hills. L. A. drove us there in his Packard automobile, and the traffic was quite heavy. At one point he was forced to brake sharply to avoid hitting another automobile, and as he did, something caught my eye on the floorboard in front of L. A.'s seat. Apparently the abrupt motion of braking the car caused it to slide out from under the seat."

"And what did you see?"

"A gun, Sergeant Mackie."

"You don't say. Can you describe the gun?"

At that moment a young man in bell captain livery approached and said, "Missus Bromfeld, your taxicab is here to take you to the train. I've already loaded your bag."

Ruth Bromfeld looked up and said, "Thank you, young man. Please tell the driver I will be there in a moment."

As the young man went off to deliver her message, Ruth Bromfeld turned to Mackie and said, "I'm afraid I know nothing about guns except that they kill. All I can tell you about this one is that it was small and shiny. Oh, and there was a small yellow box next the gun that must have slid out from under the seat at the same time. I believe the box label said, 'Remington.'"

Mackie was already adding the information to his notebook as he asked, "Have you ever seen this gun before?"

"No, I have not. Nor have I seen it since Sunday. Now, I'm afraid I must go. I hope I've been of some help to you."

"You certainly have, Missus Bromfeld. Thank you."

After escorting Ruth Bromfeld out to her waiting taxicab, Mackie sat in his car for a few minutes thinking about what he'd just learned and wondering why Bromfeld had lied about owning a gun. He could think of only one reason.

TWENTY-THREE

Detective Sergeant Mackie watched the taxicab carrying Ruth Bromfeld to the railroad station disappear around the corner onto Hollywood Boulevard. Her disclosure of the gun in Bromfeld's Packard was enlightening to say the least. Now he had to figure out what to do about it.

His first thought was to visit Western National Films and look under the front seat of Bromfeld's automobile, but he rejected that idea for two reasons. First, he didn't want to tip Bromfeld off to the fact that he was rapidly becoming a prime suspect for the murder of Lillian Lawrence, and second, if Bromfeld had any sense at all, the gun his wife saw in the car was long gone by now.

Mackie's next thought was that good police procedure required that he corroborate Ruth Bromfeld's story about Bromfeld assaulting her. Even if she didn't expect or necessarily want them to arrest her husband for assault and battery, Missus Bromfeld's complaint was going to end up in a courtroom sooner or later, and the sergeant didn't want to give some high-priced lawyer any reasons to claim shoddy police work. Since he also had a few questions pertaining to the Lillian Lawrence case that needed to be cleared up, Mackie decided the witness he would see was Clarence, the Bromfelds' butler.

Twenty minutes later Mackie parked his Dodge in Bromfeld's driveway. He clipped a Witness Statement form to his clipboard and climbed the steps to the mansion's elaborate entrance.

After giving the brass door knocker a second rap, the door finally opened far enough for Clarence to stick his head out and say, "Neither Mister or Missus Bromfeld is at home."

Before the butler had a chance to close the door, Mackie blocked it with his foot and said, "That's okay, Clarence. You're the one I came to see."

The butler looked surprised. "Me? Then you are wasting your time. I know nothing about the death of Miss Lawrence."

"I'm not here about Lillian Lawrence. Now either you open that door and invite me in for a few minutes of conversation or I will kick the door in and drag you off to the station as a material witness. You decide which it's going to be."

Apparently deciding he couldn't buffalo Mackie, Clarence accepted the inevitable and opened the door, asking, "A material witness to what?"

Stepping past the butler, Mackie said, "The trouble that occurred here last night."

Closing the door, Clarence said, "What trouble? There was no trouble here last night."

"Even if you don't consider wife beating trouble, the Los Angeles Police Department takes a very dim view of such goings-on."

The butler's expression took on a look of concern and he said, "Oh, that."

"Yes, that. Let's go to the library where we can sit for a minute or two."

Clarence said, "Alright, officer," and led Mackie down the hall to the library.

In the library Mackie seated himself in a comfortable wingback chair and began filling in the initial blanks on his Witness Statement form, leaving the butler standing in the middle of the large room looking extremely uncomfortable. Finally the sergeant said, "We have a report that L. A. Bromfeld assaulted Ruth Bromfeld in this room last night and that you witnessed part of the crime. I want you to tell me exactly what happened from the time you received the telephone call from Bessie Shipman. Let's begin with the time of that telephone call."

Clarence cleared his throat and said, "I didn't notice the exact time. It was right after the Bromfelds finished dinner, and dinner was served at exactly seven p.m. in accordance with Mister Bromfeld's standing order. If I had to make a guess, I would say the telephone call came in around eight."

Noting that Clarence's superior demeanor had deflated like a punctured automobile tire, Macke said, "What did Miss Shipman tell you?"

"She just asked to speak with Mister Bromfeld."

"Miss Shipman didn't say what the call was about?"

"No, sir. She just said it was urgent that she speak with Mister Bromfeld."

"Okay, what did you do then?"

"Well, Mister and Missus Bromfeld were in here having their after-dinner coffee, so I came in and told Mister Bromfeld that Miss Shipman was calling for him. Then I closed the door and went back to clearing the dinner table."

"What happened next?"

"Several minutes later I heard Mister Bromfeld yelling about something—I didn't catch his words—and then there was a crashing sound, like breaking glass."

"And?"

"Well, hearing Mister Bromfeld raising his voice isn't uncommon, but the crashing sound concerned me. I went to the library door and listened to find out what was happening."

"Go on."

"As I arrived at the library door, I heard Missus Bromfeld screaming something like, 'No! L. A., please don't!' Then there was another loud crash. This time it sounded like furniture falling or breaking. Fearing that something terrible was happening, I opened the library door and looked in."

"What did you see?"

"Missus Bromfeld was on the floor there by where you're sitting, and the end table that used to be next to the chair was toppled and broken."

"Where was Mister Bromfeld?"

"He was standing over Missus Bromfeld looking . . . ah, very angry."

Mackie took a moment to catch up with his entries on the Witness Statement form. Then he said, "What happened next?"

"When Mister Bromfeld looked up and saw me in the doorway, his anger seemed to disappear, and he said something to the effect of, 'Ruth has had an accident. Call the doctor.'

"I went to the kitchen telephone extension and placed a call to the Bromfelds' family physician."

"That would be Doctor Mason?"

Clarence nodded. "Yes. Of course, at that hour, I got his exchange. I asked the exchange operator to have Doctor Mason hurry to the Bromfeld residence because there had been an accident. The woman had me stay on the line while she called the doctor. After a few minutes, the operator came back on the line and told me Doctor Mason was on his way. He arrived here about twenty minutes later."

"Alright, what was going on in here while you were calling the doctor?"

"When I came back to say the doctor was on his way, Missus Bromfeld was seated in the chair in which you are seated. Her eyes were closed, and she was holding her left arm in her lap. She appeared to be in a great deal of pain. Mister Bromfeld was pacing around the room."

"What happened when Doctor Mason arrived?"

"He accompanied Missus Bromfeld upstairs to her bedroom in order to treat her injuries. Mister Bromfeld went into his study and closed the door. Doctor Mason was here for about an hour. I saw him to the door when he finished treating Missus Bromfeld. He told me Missus Bromfeld would be okay, but that she needed to be still and rest for a few days."

Mackie added a few more details to the form and asked, "Mister Bromfeld didn't come out of his study when the doctor left?"

"No, sir. He stayed in the study for quite a while. I believe he was still there when I finished my evening chores and retired for the night an hour or so later."

"When did you see either of them again?"

"I served Mister Bromfeld his usual breakfast at quarter to seven this morning, and after that he left for the studio just as he always does. Soon after that I heard Missus Bromfeld come downstairs. She stopped in here for a moment to make a telephone call—apparently to a taxi company. Then she instructed me to go to her bedroom and bring down some suitcases she packed. When I came back, she was standing out in the foyer. She instructed me to carry the suitcases down to the driveway. I did so with Missus Bromfeld following me down the steps.

"After that Missus Bromfeld thanked me and said I should go about my usual duties. She also told me in no uncertain terms that I was not to inform Mister Bromfeld of her departure until he got home tonight.

"A few minutes later I saw a taxicab pull into the drive. The driver got out, helped Missus Bromfeld into the backseat, put her suitcases into the cab's luggage compartment, and drove off. That's it until you arrived."

"Did you call Mister Bromfeld to tell him Missus Bromfeld had packed up and left?"

Clarence, still standing in front of Mackie, hesitated for a moment before saying, "No, sir."

Noting the butler's hesitation, Mackie asked, "Why not?"

"Because Missus Bromfeld specifically told me not to call him."

"Mister Bromfeld is your employer. I should think he would expect you to inform him right away if his wife packed her bags and left."

"As I'm sure you can understand, Sergeant, this is an extremely awkward situation for me. If I may be quite frank, Missus Bromfeld is a very nice woman. She has always treated me with kindness and respect. Mister Bromfeld, however . . . ."

When the butler hesitated, Mackie finished his sentence for him, "Mister Bromfeld treats you like crap. Is that it?"

"Yes, sir."

"Tell me, Clarence, have there been other instances when Mister Bromfeld has lost his temper and taken it out on his wife?"

"Yes, sir. That sort of thing happened with some frequency."

"Do you recall the last time it happened?"

"Yes, sir. It was day before yesterday. After you and the other officer left, Mister Bromfeld knocked Missus Bromfeld to the ground out on the terrace. I don't believe she was seriously hurt, but I did notice her limping as she went up the stairs later."

"Anything else you think I should add to this Witness Statement form before you sign it?"

Clarence looked surprised. "I have to sign that statement?"

"Yes, you do. I realize that puts you in an even more awkward position, but I think I can assure you no one, especially Mister Bromfeld, will see this form for some time—at least long enough for you to find another position, which might be a wise course for you to follow."

Looking thoughtful, the butler simply said, "I see, sir."

After Clarence signed the Witness Statement, Mackie stood and said, "I do have a few more questions pertaining to Mister Bromfeld's actions last Saturday night."

"Yes, sir?"

"Missus Bromfeld said he got home about eight-fifteen. Does that coincide with your recollection?"

"More or less. Actually, I recall that it was just a little later, perhaps twenty or twenty-five minutes after eight."

Mackie noted Clarence's reply in his notebook and asked, "Did you happen to notice what sort of mood Mister Bromfeld was in when he arrived home?"

"Well, yes. Because of his . . . shall we say, temper, we on Mister Bromfeld's staff are particularly conscious of his moods. Saturday night he seemed in unusually good spirits."

"I see. Did anything out of the ordinary happen after he got home?"

Clarence considered the question for a moment before saying, "No, I don't recall . . . well, there was one unpleasant incident."

"What was that?"

"As is my custom on Saturday nights, I was polishing the silver when Mister Bromfeld arrived. It is also my job to move Mister Bromfeld's automobile from the drive and lock it in the garage. I intended to do that as soon as I finished the silver. Just as I was finishing, however, Mister Bromfeld noticed that his Packard was still in the drive, which upset him. He ordered me to move his automobile in immediately so dew would not damage the upholstery. There was no dew Saturday night, but I did as he instructed."

Mackie thought about that for a few moments. Then he asked, "What time was it when you finally moved his automobile?"

"It was probably a few minutes after nine."

"So Mister Bromfeld's automobile was out in the drive for thirty to forty minutes before you locked it in the garage?"

"Yes, sir."

Mackie made another note in his book and said, "Just one more question. Mister Bromfeld told us on Sunday that he doesn't own any firearms. Have you ever seen any guns in his possession?"

"No, sir, I have not. It is possible there might be some firearms out at his ranch, but I have not seen them."

"Ranch? Where is Mister Bromfeld's ranch?"

"Out near the coast in the area known as Decker Canyon, sir."

"Does Mister Bromfeld go there often?"

"No, sir. He occasionally holds weekend parties there, but the last one was in June. I don't believe he's been there since. At least if he has, I don't know about it."

"Is anyone at the ranch on a full-time basis?"

"Not any longer. When Mister Bromfeld bought the property, it was a working cattle ranch, but he decided the cattle were more trouble than they were worth, so he sold the stock and dismissed the people who worked there. Now when Mister Bromfeld plans to visit the ranch, he sends some of us out there a day or two before to prepare the ranch house. Otherwise, it's locked up."

"If someone wanted to visit Mister Bromfeld's ranch, how would they find it?"

"It is relatively simple to find. One would go a few miles north of Malibu on the coast highway and turn right on Highway Twenty-Three. The route is also known as Decker Canyon Road. Roughly half a mile up, Decker Canyon Road intersects Decker-Edison Road. One would turn right there and Mister Bromfeld's property is the first gate on the left. The sign over the gate says, 'Rancho Bromfeld.'"

Mackie restrained himself from laughing at Bromfeld's attempt to give his "Rancho" a Spanish-California name. After jotting down the ranch's location for future reference, the sergeant said, "Thank you, Clarence. You've been most helpful."

Seeing Mackie to the door and resuming his butler persona, Clarence said, "You are entirely welcome, sir."

Returning to the stationhouse, Mackie contemplated what he'd learned. Clarence's recollection of the time his boss got home Saturday night confirmed the time gap in Bromfeld's story. It even widened the gap by a few minutes.

Then there was Bromfeld's ranch. The ranch would probably prove to be insignificant, but you never knew when a little piece of knowledge might prove useful. Finally, there was the seemingly minor matter of Bromfeld's car sitting in the drive for a period of time before Clarence moved it to the garage. For no particular reason he could think of, that detail nagged at Mackie's mind.

TWENTY-FOUR

It was a few minutes short of nine-forty-five when Detective Lieutenant Winfield set out on the route C. K. gave him for the drive to Western National's film location in Santa Monica. Actually, C. K.'s directions were pretty simple. Just head south from the Sixth Precinct stationhouse on Cahuenga and turn right on Santa Monica Boulevard. Stay on Santa Monica Boulevard until he actually arrived in Santa Monica, and then turn left on Lincoln. After that Mackie said to take a right on Colorado and keep going until he couldn't go any further without getting his tires wet in the Pacific Ocean. C. K. said the route was about fifteen miles and would take forty to forty-five minutes to drive.

Traffic was heavy with automobiles and delivery trucks for the first part of the drive through Hollywood and on past Beverly Hills and Westwood, but after he passed Sepulveda Boulevard, traffic thinned out. So did the homes and businesses along his route. It was hard for Winfield to believe there was so much open country just a few miles from the bustling metropolis of Los Angeles.

When he saw Santa Monica's Municipal Pleasure Pier ahead at the end of Colorado Avenue, Winfield turned right onto the coast highway and began watching for signs of Western National's filming location on the beach to his left. He found what he was looking for in less than a mile—several automobiles and a large truck parked along the road next to the beach. The truck was black with a canvas cover over its load area and "Western National Films" painted on its doors. Winfield made a U-turn and pulled off behind the truck.

Looking down on the beach from his driver's seat, there didn't appear to be much happening—just a lot of people milling around a couple of cameras and some other movie-making paraphernalia. Winfield guessed the weather conditions might be responsible for the inactivity. It was chilly because the sun was late in burning through the usual morning fog that arrived around dusk every night to shroud the beach in its heavy mist. The lieutenant didn't know much about the motion picture business, but he was pretty sure it took light, and plenty of it, to make movies. At the moment, the lingering fog was allowing little of that particular commodity to reach the beach.

Making his way down an incline between the road and the sand, Winfield began to see some degree of organization to the scene before him. About halfway down the beach toward the surf, a group of men in work clothes were clustered around the cameras, having a discussion that involved a lot of gestures. He guessed they were the camera operators and other crew members. Behind them, and to his right more men—this group in suits—were standing around a couple of folding wooden camp chairs. At the center of this group was a tall man dressed in a belted, brown leather jacket, knee-high riding boots, and a German-looking Alpine hat. Judging by the man's air of authority, Winfield concluded he was getting his first look at the notorious Ernst Frohmme.

Directly ahead of Winfield there was another group consisting of chilly-looking young women with bare feet and legs below jackets they'd pulled snugly around their bodies as insulation against the cold. This group was gathered around another young woman sitting on a camp chair. As he got closer to the shivering bathing beauties, he could make out the letters across the canvas back of the seated woman's chair. They spelled out "Miss Mae White."

It was then that a couple of the young women noticed Winfield. One of them pointed in his direction and Mae White turned to look. Her recognition of the lieutenant was instantaneous. She quickly stood up, and as he got within speaking distance, Mae White smiled broadly and said, "Bobby! How wonderful to see you again!"

Pleased that Miss White remembered his name, Winfield took the hand she offered, and trying not to stare at the shapely legs below the hem of her jacket, he said, "Hello, Mae. How are you?"

Looking up into his face with her clear blue eyes, she said frankly, "I think I might be getting frostbite out here, but other than that, I'm good. How about you?"

Smiling back at her, Winfield said, "I'm doing fine. You ladies should get someone to build a driftwood fire to warm you up."

Still smiling, Mae White said, "That would be the gentlemanly thing to do, wouldn't it? Unfortunately there seem to be very few gentlemen among this crowd. Now, tell me what brings you all the way out here to our sunny beach location."

Taking his eyes off of Mae long enough to glance around the beach, Winfield noticed that the half-dozen or so bathing beauties who'd been clustered around Miss White were now watching them intently. Winfield guessed they might be wondering if he was Mae White's latest beau. Finding some small delight in that thought, he said, "I'm here for two reasons. I need to ask Ernst Frohmme some questions. I also have a few points I would like to clarify with you about Saturday night."

Instantly putting a pout on her lips, Mae White said, "Aw, gee. I was hoping you just came out to see me in a bathing costume."

Laughing, Winfield said, "That's the frosting on the cake!"

Mae chuckled in response to his comment, and looking up at the brightening sky, she said, "Golly, Bobby, I don't know if there will be time for all of that. The fog is burning off quickly now. By the time you finish with Frohmme, he'll be anxious to start shooting."

"Well, maybe we could talk when you take a lunch break."

She shook her head sadly. "With this late start, our lunch break will be short if we even get one."

"Okay, how about this afternoon when you finish up here?"

"That won't work, either. As soon as we wrap up here, we're going back to the studio for more filming." After a short pause, she said, "Say, I've got an idea. How would it be if I answered your questions over dinner tonight?"

Winfield felt a twinge of excitement at the prospect of having dinner with the beautiful Mae White, but he said, "I hate to take up your time off with a lot of questions."

"Nonsense. I would enjoy having dinner with you, questions or not."

"Alright. What time and where?"

"Why don't you pick me up at my place around six-thirty? We'll go over to Musso and Frank or somewhere."

"That would be fine."

"Understand, though, that I'm buying dinner."

"Oh, no. That's not . . . ."

"Yes, it is. I don't know for sure, but I suspect policemen don't make nearly as much money as famous motion picture celebrities, and you shouldn't be stuck with the price of two dinners just because my schedule is so busy."

"Well, we can discuss that when the time comes."

Looking stern, Mae White said, "There will be no discussion on that subject, Bobby Winfield." Then the smile returned to her face as she added, "Come on. I'll introduce you to our resident tyrannical director."

As they hiked across the sand to the group of men in suits, Winfield shook off the pleasant thoughts of having dinner with Mae White and mentally reviewed his plan for interviewing Ernst Frohmme. Based on what he already knew about the man, the lieutenant figured he needed to take command of the situation from the very start. That would require a no-nonsense, hard-boiled approach. Putting himself into the right mood for questioning Frohmme, Winfield wondered if what he was doing was something like the way an actor prepared for a role. In that sense, he thought, actors and police detectives were not all that different.

Approaching the group surrounding Ernst Frohmme, Winfield sized the man up. He appeared to be in his thirties with dark hair framing equally dark features composed into a permanently stern face. Frohmme was gesturing with a long cigarette holder in his left hand while he impatiently slapped the side of his boot with the riding crop in his right hand. All Frohmme needed, Winfield thought, was a monocle to complete the stereotypical image of an aristocratic grand duke from some east European kingdom.

Seeing Mae White, the men in suits stepped aside to clear a path, and she said, "Ernst, I want you to meet Detective Lieutenant Winfield. He's with the Los Angeles Police Department investigating Lilly Lawrence's murder." Then Mae White turned to Winfield and with a barely perceptible wink, said, "See you later, Detective." Then she was gone, leaving the lieutenant face to face with Ernst Frohmme.

Winfield flashed his badge and said, "I need to ask you some questions, Frohmme."

Ernst Frohmme looked disdainfully at Winfield and said with a thick Germanic accent, "We are now about to begin filming. You must come to see me some other time. I have no time for questions now."

"Then you will make time, Frohmme."

The surprise on the director's face said he wasn't used to being contradicted. "How dare you speak to me in such a manner, you impertinent public servant!"

"That's right, Frohmme, I'm a public servant—one with the authority to haul your butt off this beach and take it downtown to a police interrogation room. I'd be happy to do that, but it seems to me your time would be much better spent answering my questions here."

Frohmme literally sputtered with anger for a few seconds, but then he saw the wisdom in what Winfield said. "Okay, okay. We will talk, but you must make it quick so I do not lose the light."

Apparently sizing the situation up as one they wanted no part of, the suits gathered around Frohmme quickly scattered in various directions, leaving Winfield and the director alone. Winfield gestured to the camp chairs and said, "Let's sit a minute."

Frohmme sat stiffly. Taking his notebook in hand, Winfield sat in a second chair and said, "Let's start with your impressions of Miss Lawrence."

Without hesitation, Frohmme responded, "Quite frankly, I do not know what Bromfeld saw in that girl. She was an unsophisticated child possessing neither the talent nor the temperament of an actress."

"That may be true, but the public liked her."

"The public, bah! What do they know? The success of her films is due entirely to my directing skills. I assure you those films made money in spite of Miss Lawrence, not because of her."

Using a doubtful tone, Winfield simply said, "I see." After making a show of flipping through the pages of his notebook, he said, "We have been told by witnesses that you were caught red-handed molesting Miss Lawrence on a movie set not long ago. What do you have to say about that?"

Winfield ignored the glare Frohmme directed at him and calmly waited for a response. Finally, Frohmme said, "It was a misunderstanding that became blown completely out of proportion. I did not 'molest' Lillian Lawrence. She mistook friendly conversation for something else and began screaming, which attracted a bunch of meddlers who saw nothing of what actually happened. She embarrassed me in front of the cast and crew. Unforgivable!"

"A couple of those meddlers are quite positive about what happened. So, apparently, is L. A. Bromfeld. He said he was forced to intervene on Miss Lawrence's behalf and reprimand you for your behavior."

"Bah! Bromfeld called me in to make a show of placating Lilly and Mae White. It meant nothing."

Again Winfield simply said, "I see." After another pause he said, "Speaking of Miss White, how do you get along with her?"

"We get along, as you put it, amicably. Miss White has some small degree of acting talent, which fortunately I am able to enhance with directing skill. I am afraid, however, that the woman is also a tramp. One day we will lose her to scandal."

Winfield resisted the urge to smack Frohmme right then and there. Instead he said, "Frohmme, are you left-handed?"

The question surprised the director. After a slight hesitation, Frohmme said, "Actually, I am ambidextrous. I do tend, however, to favor my left hand. Yes. Why is it that you ask such a question?"

"Just curious. Where you were between seven-thirty and eight-thirty last Saturday night?"

Frohmme hesitated a little longer over this question. Finally he said, "Why? Is that when Lilly Lawrence was killed? Are you implying I am suspected of committing her murder?"

"I'm implying nothing. Just answer the question."

"I spent the entire evening Saturday from about six o'clock until well after midnight in the company of Estelle Fontaine at a party she hosted."

Staring intently into Frohmme's eyes as if he could see into the man's mind, Winfield asked, "Did you leave the party at any time?"

"I did not."

"Miss Fontaine will vouch for that?"

"Yes, she will, as will several of my other film colleagues who attended the party."

"Name two."

Frohmme thought for a second before saying, "The director, Oscar Darmond, and Douglas Ives, the well-known actor."

Deliberately jumping from one subject to another, Winfield said, "I am told that on numerous occasions L. A. Bromfeld has been forced to bail you out of trouble with other actresses besides Lillian Lawrence."

"Bah! More lies! Those were no-talent women who were desperate to become actresses. They told lies about me to blackmail Bromfeld into giving them money or work. He never should have given into them!"

Winfield jotted a few notes and said, "What about the claims that you have unusual sexual habits?"

Frohmme jumped to his feet and shook his cigarette holder in Winfield's face. "That is enough! We are through with this conversation, Mister Public Servant. I have a film to direct."

With that, Frohmme picked up the megaphone from the sand next to his chair and stomped off, yelling instructions to the crew and actors. Winfield watched him for a few minutes and then put his notebook away. Frohmme, he decided, was an interesting character, one he suspected was perfectly capable of murdering people he saw as having offended him.

Trudging through the sand on the way back to his automobile, Winfield caught Mae White's eye and waved. She blew him a kiss in return. He thought about that gesture while he emptied the sand from his shoes before climbing into the Dodge for his drive back to Hollywood.

TWENTY-FIVE

Winfield got back to Hollywood around noon, and after a quick stop at Larry's Deli for a roast beef sandwich and an apple, the lieutenant headed for the stationhouse. He found C. K. in the detective room already enjoying the meatloaf sandwich Helen had packed for his lunch.

"Hello, Bobby. You find Santa Monica alright from my directions?"

"Sure did. It couldn't have been easier. Did you find out why Ruth Bromfeld needed to see us so urgently?"

"I did. It seems she wanted to file a police complaint against her husband."

Winfield looked up from his sandwich in surprise. "I sure didn't expect that! What's the charge?"

"Assault and battery."

"No kiddin'?"

"No kidding. Apparently Bromfeld's temper gets the better of him on a regular basis, and he's taken it out on Missus Bromfeld several times during the past few years. Monday night was the most recent of those times, and it was the straw that broke the camel's back for Ruth. She packed up and left to stay with her sister in New York."

"Well, how about that!"

Mackie continued, "She said a telephone call from Bessie Shipman set him off last night and he ended up breaking her wrist and giving her some nasty bruises. She listed her doctor and Clarence, their butler, as witnesses to the incident. After interviewing Missus Bromfeld, I drove over to the house and talked to the butler. He confirmed her story."

Winfield said, "Then I guess we need to go arrest L. A. Bromfeld."

"Nope. Ruth Bromfeld said she wouldn't come back to California to testify at the trial. She figures Bromfeld's lawyers would get him off, anyway."

Confused, Winfield said, "Then why did she file the complaint?"

"She plans to divorce Bromfeld on grounds of physical cruelty, and she wants an official report on file to support her claim."

"Too bad. I would enjoy throwing Bromfeld in jail."

"I would, too. But there's more to the story. Ruth Bromfeld says she saw a pistol in L. A.'s automobile Sunday afternoon. She doesn't know much about guns, but her description pretty much matches the pistol Tom Bell gave Lillian Lawrence."

"Well, how about that!"

Mackie grinned at Winfield's enthusiasm. "Yeah, that's sort of what I thought."

"Did the butler give you any confirmation of the gun?"

"No. However, he did confirm Ruth Bromfeld's statement that her husband didn't get home Saturday night until eight-fifteen. In fact, he thinks it was actually five or ten minutes later than that."

"Interesting. That expands the time gap in Bromfeld's story a bit. Now there may be twenty minutes or more of his time Saturday night that are unaccounted for. Were you able to get anything else useful out of the butler?"

"Not much. Just a couple of details that probably don't enter into the case. For one thing, he told me Bromfeld owns a ranch out in a canyon north of Malibu. For another, he mentioned that he didn't get around to parking Bromfeld's Packard in the garage until around nine Saturday night. That means the automobile was out in the drive unattended for forty to forty-five minutes. I'm not sure why, but that little detail bothers me."

Winfield thought about the possible significance of the car being unattended for a period of time. Then he said, "I don't see the significance unless you think someone planted the gun in his automobile."

Mackie frowned. "I suppose it's a possibility, but that could happen anywhere, even at the studio. How did you do with that director, Frohmme?"

"I had to give him the hard-boiled cop routine, but in the end he grudgingly answered most of my questions. Frohmme is a first-class SOB. He's completely full of himself and has nothing good to say about anyone else, especially Lillian Lawrence and Mae White. Frohmme claims his directing is the only reason their pictures are successful."

Mackie said, "Sounds like a typical motion picture big shot. I don't know what gives them such giant egos, but most of them think they're God's gift to the world."

"That fits Frohmme to a T. About all I got out of the interview is that he has an alibi for Saturday night. He claims to have been at a party given by . . ." Winfield turned a couple of pages in his notebook and continued, "Estelle Fontaine, the actress. He also gave me the names of two other people he says will verify he was at the party between six and midnight—a director named Oscar Darmond and Douglas Ives, the actor.

"Oh, I also found out Frohmme is left-handed—well, he claims to be ambidextrous, but he definitely favors his left hand."

"Okay, I guess we need to locate these people to find out if Frohmme was really at the party. I wonder if my new best pal, Bessie Shipman, can tell us where to find them."

Winfield frowned. "I don't know how you did it, but Miss Shipman seems to think you're the cat's pajamas. Give her a call."

While Mackie made his call, Winfield killed a few minutes looking through the growing stack of mail in his in-basket. About the only thing he found of any interest was an envelope from the headquarters of the Texas Rangers in Austin. Inside the envelope he found two wanted circulars, one for a fellow named Eugene Clugman, who was wanted by the Rangers for murder, and the other about a guy named Luke Bremmer, also wanted for murder. The Bremmer circular included a photo; the one for Clugman did not.

Circulars like the two from Texas were not uncommon. Most states sent out wanted notices for suspects they were unable to capture after a period of time. The murder, for example, for which Clugman was wanted occurred in 1924. That the Texas Rangers were just now sending out a circular on him meant they'd run out of local leads. This likelihood was confirmed by a comment on the circular saying it was thought that Clugman may have headed west to find employment on a cattle ranch.

Winfield had just shuffled the Texas wanted circulars to Mackie's in-basket when C. K. hung up the phone. He said, "That anything I need to look at right away?"

"No, just a couple of wanted circulars from Texas. What did you find out from Miss Shipman?"

Consulting his notebook, Mackie said, "Fontaine and Darmond work at Western National. Ives is under contract to the Warner brothers. The first two are supposed to be at the studio today. Fontaine is shooting on film stage four and Darmond should be on film stage six. Bessie says those film stages are on the west lot."

Winfield nodded. "Okay, let's split up and get the interviews done so we can find out whether or not Frohmme is a legitimate suspect. Which do you want, Western National or Warner Brothers?"

"Since you already know your way around Western National a little, why don't you go there, and I'll take Warner Brothers."

As the lieutenant stood up, Mackie said, "By the way, did you get a chance for a second interview with Mae White out there in Santa Monica?"

"No. Frohmme was behind in his shooting schedule, so there wasn't time. I set up an appointment to see Miss White tonight."

With a twinkle in his eye, Mackie asked, "Do you want me to go with you, Laddie?"

Slipping into his suit coat, Winfield said, "No, I think I can handle it."

Mackie may have thought, "I bet you can," but didn't say it. Instead, he said, "Okay. Meet you back here when we're done with these interviews?"

"Yeah. I need to update our suspect list and give Royce a report. Maybe we'll be able to rule out Frohmme as a suspect by then."

- - -

It took Winfield several minutes of winding through the maze of buildings on Western National Film's west lot before he finally found what he was looking for tucked away back in the northwest corner of the lot. The large, rectangular building's sign said, "Film Stages 4, 5 & 6."

Winfield pulled into a small parking area adjacent to the stages and walked through a pair of large, barn-like doors. Inside, the place reminded Winfield more of a huge, cluttered warehouse more than anything else. The three stages were lined up in a row along the length of the building with low walls separating them. A sign on the wall next to the first stage he came to informed him he'd found stage six.

The stage area was brilliantly lit by spotlights mounted on the ceiling and on roll-around stands with long electrical cords trailing behind them. On the stage itself, two actors in what Winfield guessed were supposed to be medieval costumes were emoting in front of a backdrop depicting a castle interior. Just in front of the stage, a camera operator slowly and methodically turned his camera's crank while a man standing next to the camera calmly gave the actors direction in a quiet tone. The director was a balding fellow who looked to be in his early fifties. He was wearing baggy tweed trousers and a white shirt with the sleeves rolled up to his elbows. Off to one side, a woman at a piano played a haunting classical piece to enhance the mood of the performers on the stage. Between Winfield and the director, about a dozen people, a few in costume, watched the performance.

Winfield joined the onlookers for about a minute before the director said, "Cut! We'll use that one. Players, take a fifteen minute break while we set up for the next scene, but hold on a minute." The director picked up a sheaf of papers from a wooden camp chair behind the camera and studied them for a moment. Then he added, "The next scene will be number twenty-seven—same set, new props. Let's go everyone."

With that, everyone—actors, crew and on-lookers alike—scurried off in different directions, leaving the director standing there studying his shooting script. Guessing the director was the man he'd come to see, Winfield approached him and said, "Would you be Mister Darmond?"

The man looked up with a pleasant expression on his face and said, "I would. Who might you be?"

Winfield held up his badge. "I'm Detective Lieutenant Winfield, L.A.P.D. Homicide. I'm investigating the murder of Lillian Lawrence. Can you spare a moment for a couple of brief questions?"

"If they're really brief. What would you like to know?"

Notebook in hand, Winfield said, "Can you tell me where you were last Saturday night?"

Darmond frowned and said, "Goodness! I hope I'm not suspected of killing Miss Lawrence!"

"No, sir. I'm here to verify the alibi of someone else in the case."

Relief passed over Darmond's face as he said, "I'm certainly glad of that! Let's see . . . Saturday night I attended a party at the home of Estelle Fontaine. She's a new actress here on the Western National lot."

"Do you recall what time you arrived at the party and when you left?"

"Well, I got there around six-thirty, and I left fairly early. I remember the clock on my bureau said nine-thirty when I got home, so that would mean I left around nine, give or take a few minutes."

Winfield added this to his notes, and then said, "Did you happen to see Ernst Frohmme at Miss Fontaine's party?"

Darmond showed no surprise at the question. In fact, Winfield thought he detected a slight knowing nod before the director said, "Lieutenant, it's hard to miss Ernst Frohmme in any situation. He seems to enjoy being the center of attention. So, yes, I saw Ernst at the party. He was holding court in one corner of the living room the entire time I was there."

"Is it possible Mister Frohmme might have left the party for a period of time, say half an hour or so?"

"Not while I was there. I'm certain of that."

The lieutenant made note of Darmond's statement, saying, "Good. We're almost through. Please give me your impressions of Ernst Frohmme."

Darmond gave the question some thought before answering, "Despite the fact that his pictures make the studio a great deal of money, his work tends to be overly elaborate and too . . . ," he searched for a word and came up with, "flashy. And the performances of his actors strike me as mechanical and sterile. I like to see actors portray honest emotion; Ernst is more concerned with the precision of their movements and the fit of their costumes."

"I see. What about Frohmme as a person?"

"Well, if you're asking if I would want him as a friend, the answer would be no. He's not someone with whom I enjoy spending my time."

"We've been told that Mister Frohmme has an eye for young women and that he may have some rather unusual sexual tastes. Can you elaborate on either of those aspects of his personality?"

"Not really. I've heard the same rumors and more, but I don't recall ever actually seeing anything personally that would support them."

"Okay, Mister Darmond, one last question. My next interview is with Estelle Fontaine. Can you tell me a little something about her?"

"Only that she shows a lot of promise as an actress. I've never directed her myself, but I've seen some of the work she did before coming to Western

National. I think the only films she's worked on here are The Long Goodbye and a couple of comedy shorts."

Winfield looked up. "The Long Goodbye is the film Lillian Lawrence was making when she died, isn't it?"

"Yes. Miss Fontaine has a small part in it, which is unfortunate because I don't know if the studio will finish the film without Miss Lawrence. They might finish it for the box office value of its being Lillian Lawrence's last film. That would depend on where they were in the shooting and if they have enough on film to complete it without Miss Lawrence."

"Alright, Mister Darmond, I think that's all of my questions. So unless you have something to add to what we've talked about, I'll get out of your hair."

"No, I don't think there's anything . . . well, yes, there is. I don't want to speak out of turn, but it would probably be helpful if you knew that Miss Fontaine and Ernst Frohmme are . . . ah, romantically involved. She has quite a crush on Mister Frohmme, and that might tend to color her answers to your questions, if you understand what I'm getting at."

"I believe I do. Thank you, Mister Darmond. You've been very helpful."

"You're welcome, Lieutenant. Good luck with your investigation. Oh, you'll find Miss Fontaine down at the other end of this building—film stage four. They're shooting an Eddie Smith comedy short down there."

Winfield shook hands with Oscar Darmond and headed for the opposite end of the film stage building. As he walked, Winfield couldn't help smiling at his recollection of the last Eddie Smith comedy he saw. The man was a comic genius, easily on a par with Mack Sennett of Keystone Kop fame. Like Sennett, Smith kept theater audiences howling with laughter at a variety of gags like exploding cigars and pie fights.

There were, however, no exploding cigars or flying pies in view when Winfield arrived at film stage four. Instead Smith, dressed as a down-and-outer, was on his knees, apparently proposing marriage to a young woman who seemed to have no interest in his proposal.

The scene ended abruptly when Smith, who seemed to be directing the film as well as acting in it, yelled, "Cut." Getting back on his feet with some assistance from his costar, Smith said, "We'll keep that take. We have to. My knees won't take any more of this!" Limping off the stage, Smith added, "That's it for today, folks. We'll pick it up tomorrow morning at eight sharp. Good job today, everyone!"

Pausing to pick up a towel from his camp chair, Smith wiped the sweat from his face and hastily limped from the building. The rest of the cast and crew began milling around, seemingly in no hurry to leave. Winfield interrupted a conversation between two young men in work dress and asked, "Excuse me, gentlemen. Is an actress by the name of Estelle Fontaine here?"

Both men looked around the film stage, and then one of them said, "Yeah, that's her over there."

The man was pointing at the young woman who was in front of the camera with Smith a few minutes earlier. Winfield thanked the men and walked over to Estelle Fontaine. She was talking with another woman who also wore the greasepaint and make-up of an actress. Estelle Fontaine struck the lieutenant as a natural beauty with raven-black hair in sharp contrast to her pale skin. Her voice, however, wasn't nearly as pleasant. She spoke in a loud, whiney tone that reminded Winfield of fingernails scraping a blackboard.

"Excuse me, Miss Fontaine. May I please have a word with you?"

The woman smiled broadly and said, "Sure thing, handsome. What can I do you for?"

As the other actress drifted away, Winfield said, "I'm Detective Lieutenant Winfield of the L.A.P.D. Homicide Division. We're investigating the death of Lillian Lawrence, and I would like to ask you a few questions."

Estelle Fontaine immediately put on a sad face and said, "Oh, my. Poor Lilly. Her death is such a tragedy! She's only been gone a few days now, but I already miss her so terribly!"

"Yes," Winfield responded, "Her death is certainly a tragedy. Can you tell me . . . ."

"It seems like only yesterday we were up on that stage together. Lilly was so sweet. She treated me like a sister."

"Ah, yes, Miss Fontaine, like a sister. If you don't mind, please tell me where you were last Saturday night."

"Why, that's the night poor Lilly was killed, isn't it? I feel simply awful. We were all having a gay time at my party while poor Lilly was suffering at the hands of her killer. I will never . . . ."

"You say you were having a party? Was Ernst Frohmme at your party?"

Estelle Fontaine started to answer, but her sad face was suddenly replaced with a look of suspicion, and she said, "Surely you don't suspect dear Ernst of killing poor Lilly! Ernst wouldn't hurt a fly. He's an utter sweetheart of a man."

For a second Winfield wondered if they were talking about the same Ernst Frohmme. He asked, "We would just like to know of his whereabouts Saturday night. Was he at your party?"

"Oh, yes. Ernst and I are, you know, a couple. He wouldn't have missed my party for the world!"

"Did you happen to notice if he left the party at any time during the evening?"

Estelle Fontaine's expression changed again; this time she put on a mask of sincerity. "Ernst was at my side all night. He never left me, even for a teensy moment. I simply don't understand how you could possible suspect

Ernst. He's a darling and a brilliant director. Ernst was directing me and poor Lilly in The Long Goodbye. Do you know if the studio plans to finish The Long Goodbye? In spite of poor Lilly's death, I do so hope they will finish the film. The Long Goodbye is my first feature film here, and my career will suffer a terrible setback if they don't finish the picture. It's a wonderful story about . . . ."

Fearing the sun would set before Estelle Fontaine finished expounding on "dear Ernst," "poor Lilly," and every other darn subject that came up, Winfield interrupted her, saying, "Thank you for your time, Miss Fontaine. You've been most helpful."

– – –

Back at the Sixth Precinct, Winfield was just rolling a fresh Homicide Investigation Report form into his typewriter when C. K. walked into the detective room. Winfield greeted him and asked, "How did you do with Ives?"

"I'm afraid Mister Ives was so drunk Saturday night, he doesn't even remember for sure that HE was at the party, let alone if Ernst Frohmme was there."

In mock shock, Winfield said, "They were serving alcoholic beverages at the party? Heavens! Don't they know that's a violation of the Volstead Act?"

Mackie grimaced. "Yeah, imagine that! How did you make out?"

"I got two confirmations that Frohmme was at Estelle Fontaine's party Saturday night. One was from Fontaine, who apparently is romantically involved with Frohmme. The other was from a more reliable witness."

"That would be the director. What was his name?"

"Oscar Darmond. He strikes me as a straight-shooter, and he's certain Frohmme was there between six-thirty and about nine. That's when Darmond left the shindig."

Mackie sighed, "Well, that's another suspect we can cross off the list. You working on your report for Royce?"

"Yeah. If you can give me a couple of minutes to finish the form so you can look it over, you can get out of here a little early for a change."

"That would be a change! Have at it, Bobby. I'll go through some of this mail."

Copying the basic information from the previous day's report, Winfield incorporated changes resulting from the day's investigation:

Los Angeles Police Department
HOMICIDE INVESTIGATION REPORT

```
VICTIM: Lawrence (Lee), Lillian
DATE: 7 September, 1926
INVESTIGATOR: Det. Lt. Winfield, Robert
```

SUMMARY OF PERSONS INVOLVED

NAME: Bell, Thomas
RELATIONSHIP: Victim's fiancé
MOTIVE: None known
MEANS: None known
OPPORTUNITY: None
NOTES: Subject has concrete alibi for time of murder
STATUS: Cleared

NAME: Bromfeld, L. A.
RELATIONSHIP: Victim's employer (W/N Films)
MOTIVE: While a specific motive is not yet known, subject is known to have been in conflict with the victim over her fulfillment of her contract with the subject's studio.
MEANS: Subject's estranged wife says subject was in possession of a firearm similar to the murder weapon on Sunday, 5 September, 1926. Firearm was seen to slide out from under the driver's seat of subject's Packard automobile.
OPPORTUNITY: Subject is known to have been at the Hollywood Hotel at the time of the crime. The subject's account of his time there is at odds with statements made by witnesses.
NOTES: Subject is left-handed, which coincides with crime scene evidence. Subject smokes expensive Cuban cigars, which coincides with crime scene evidence.
STATUS: Under investigation

NAME: Frohmme, Ernst
RELATIONSHIP: Directed victim in films at W/N Films
MOTIVE: No motive is known for certain, but the subject's career may have been threatened by victim.
MEANS: ?
OPPORTUNITY: None
NOTES: Subject has confirmed alibi for the time of the murder. Alibi is substantiated by two witnesses.
STATUS: Cleared

NAME: White, Mae (Glaum, Mildred)
RELATIONSHIP: Actress and close friend of victim.
MOTIVE: None known
MEANS: None known
OPPORTUNITY: Subject is known to have been at Hollywood Hotel around time of murder.
STATUS: Under investigation

Winfield rolled the form from his typewriter and handed it to Mackie. The sergeant took his time, reading the document carefully. When done, he said, "Well, it looks as if we've crossed three suspects off our list. That leaves us two that we know of: Mae White, who was the victim's best friend; and L. A. Bromfeld, who appears to have had both the opportunity and the means to kill Miss Lawrence."

Winfield nodded. "Yeah, that's pretty much it. With any luck, maybe we can narrow it down to Bromfeld after my interview with Miss White tonight."

Mackie looked up at Winfield. "Are you sure you don't want me in on that interview?"

Winfield anticipated that Mackie might ask again about coming with him to interview Mae White, and he had an answer ready. "I'm sure. I seem to get along pretty well with Miss White, and the main thing I want to accomplish is shedding some light on the differences between her story and Bromfeld's about what happened in the hotel parking area Saturday night. Beyond that, I'll just try to get her talking. If she has any guilt in this case, she might let something slip, like a possible motive."

Mackie looked at him for a long moment and then said, "Alright, Bobby. That sounds like a good plan. Our primary suspect at this point, however, is Bromfeld. All we need to make an arrest is the gun Tom Bell gave the victim and a reason why Bromfeld would want to kill one of his studio's biggest money-makers."

"That's a tough one unless he killed Miss Lawrence in a fit of temper. I suppose he could have gone to her room and threatened her. If that happened, Miss Lawrence might have gotten the pistol out to defend herself. If Bromfeld took the pistol away from her and if he was in a rage, he might have shot her."

"That's a whole lot of 'ifs'."

"You can say that again. That scenario doesn't seem very likely, does it?"

Mackie shook his head, but said, "I wouldn't reject that idea entirely, but I also wouldn't want to be the one who has to sell it to a jury in front of the kind of lawyers Bromfeld can afford."

"Speaking of lawyers, we should check with the D.A.'s office tomorrow and see if we can get a warrant to search Bromfeld's home and ranch for that gun his wife claims she saw in his automobile."

"With what we've got already, that shouldn't be a problem. You want me to take care of that detail?"

"Sure, but meet me here first so we can plan the rest of the day."

Mackie nodded. Then he stood and reached for his uniform jacket. "Okay, Bobby, it's all yours till mornin'. I'm goin' home to put on the feedbag. Good luck with Miss White tonight."

It crossed the lieutenant's mind to wonder what manner of luck Mackie was wishing him, but he said, "Thanks, C. K. Enjoy your dinner."

After sending his Homicide Investigation Report off to be hand-delivered to Royce, Winfield checked his wristwatch. It was four-forty-five, so Captain Royce was probably still in his office. The lieutenant dialed Central Division and asked for Royce. When the captain came on the line, Winfield said, "This Detective Lieutenant Winfield, sir. I'm calling with our daily progress report on the Lillian Lawrence case."

"Alright, Winfield, go ahead with your report."

The lieutenant began by telling Royce that a paper copy of his Homicide Investigation Report was on its way to the captain's office. Then Winfield launched into a brief summary of the report's contents. He finished by saying, "At this moment in time, L. A. Bromfeld is our strongest suspect, but we're lacking a motive for him killing one of his studio's biggest stars."

Royce was quiet for quite a while. Then he said, "You know, Winfield, with Bromfeld as your suspect, this becomes an even bigger headline case. You must proceed very cautiously. I've met L. A. Bromfeld, and he carries a lot of weight out there in your part of the city. We do not want to alienate him without just cause. Do you understand what I am telling you?"

"I do."

Royce reinforced his point by saying, "If Bromfeld turns out to be innocent and you arrest him, it will surely mean your job and quite possibly mine, too!"

"We won't be arresting Bromfeld without a solid motive and the murder weapon. Sergeant Mackie will be talking to the D.A.'s office tomorrow morning about a search warrant so we can look for the murder weapon at Bromfeld's office and home and at a ranch he owns out near the coast."

Royce was quiet again. Finally, he said, "I'm not sure that's such a good idea right now. If you get your warrant, Bromfeld will know we think he's a suspect. The repercussions from that could be nearly as bad as arresting him. Hold off on the search warrant until you have a motive. Got that?"

Shaking his head in frustration, Winfield said, "Yes, sir. I've got it."

"Okay, Lieutenant, keep up the good work and find us a killer!"

Returning the telephone handset to its cradle, Winfield said to himself, "It's going to be damned hard to find you a killer with our hands tied behind our backs!"

TWENTY-SIX

Standing outside the door to number 412 at the Garden Court Apartments, Detective Lieutenant Winfield expected Mae White's maid, Adele, to answer his knock as she had done on Sunday, so he was surprised when Mae herself opened the door. She greeted him enthusiastically, saying, "Good evening, Bobby. Come on in for a minute while I get my coat. Then I'm ready to go."

Winfield couldn't help smiling in admiration of Mae's eveningwear. She was draped in a dark blue sleeveless dress made of a material the lieutenant guessed was silk. Her hem ended precisely at the mid-point of her knees, and the neckline dipped in a deep V to a point that almost, but not quite, threatened modesty. Pleated below a pale blue sash with an offset bow at her hips, the dress was clearly designed to flow with the wearer's movements and, Winfield noted, it did.

Mae's outfit was complemented by black stockings, black shoes Winfield thought were a style known as 'Mary Janes,' a long strand of authentic-looking white pearls, and a white cloche hat with a turned-down brim and a pale blue ribbon band.

Turning from a cloak closet off the entry foyer, Mae caught Winfield's smile of appreciation and said, "For goodness sake, what are you grinning at, Bobby? Is my hem crooked?"

Feeling his face redden at being caught staring, Winfield said, "Oh, no! You look great."

Handing the lieutenant a knee-length white cloth coat with a soft fur collar, Mae said, "Why, thank you, sir. I'm pleased you approve."

Holding the coat as Mae slipped her arms into the sleeves, Winfield said, "There is one thing we ought to discuss before we go."

Straightening the fit of her coat, Mae said, "Sure, what's on your mind?"

"Well, I'm afraid the only vehicle I have at the moment is the automobile the department provides for my use, and it occurs to me that . . . well, that you might not be comfortable driving around town in a police car."

Grinning, she said, "Why, Bobby, how considerate you are to think of my reputation! You're probably right. Seeing me pull up in front of Musso and Frank in a police car would certainly start tongues to wagging. It might even be fun to see the reactions, but I guess it would be prudent to put off my first ride in a police car for another occasion."

"Then if I may use your telephone, I'll call a taxicab."

"Or, if you wouldn't mind, we could go in my car."

"That would be fine. I'm sorry . . . ."

"Hush, Bobby. There's no need for apology."

After an elevator ride to the ground floor, Mae led the way to the Garden Court Apartments' rear entrance. Out in back, a low structure with six sets of barn-like doors spanned the width of the property behind a concrete extension of the driveway that ran down the west side of the apartment building. Winfield surmised that the outbuilding was where residents who owned automobiles garaged their vehicles.

Mae handed him a key ring, saying, "Mine is the last one on the right. The little silver key opens the padlock."

Winfield unlocked the hasp and opened the doors. Then he stood there for a moment admiring one of the most beautiful machines he'd ever seen. Winfield immediately recognized the gleaming cream over light brown automobile as a brand new Chrysler Imperial roadster. He knew this because he had admired its sporty lines in magazine advertisements. Seeing the new Chrysler model in person for the first time, however, he realized the magazine photos didn't do the car justice. To his mind, the automobile in front of him was the pinnacle of automotive design.

Mae couldn't help noticing his admiration. She said, "You like it? I just got it two weeks ago."

Offering the key ring back to Mae, he said, "You have excellent taste in automobiles."

"Oh, no. You drive. Every time I take it out, I'm afraid of scratching the fenders!"

Excited at the prospect of actually driving the beautiful Chrysler, Winfield held the passenger door open and offered Mae his hand to assist her over the running board and onto the rich, brown leather seat. After pulling the car out and locking the garage doors, he carefully guided it out to Hollywood Boulevard, where he joined the light flow of east-bound traffic for a distance of three blocks. At Cherokee he made a U-turn and pulled into an empty parking spot near the entrance to the Musso and Frank Grill.

After shutting off the Chrysler's powerful six-cylinder engine and setting the handbrake, Winfield trotted around to the passenger door and assisted Mae's graceful exit from the car. Then she took his arm and they strolled into Hollywood's oldest and most popular eatery.

Aside from a huge electric sign across the front of the building, Musso and Frank's Grill wasn't much to look at—just an arched façade framing a large window on either side of the entrance. Inside, Musso and Frank was something else entirely. Dark wood paneling covered the walls from floor to ceiling, with wall sconces softly illuminating booths running down both sides of the main dining room. A pattern of heavy, dark beams crisscrossed the high ceiling creating rectangles of indirect lighting for the tables filling the center area of the dining room. Overall, the effect was simultaneously posh and comfortable.

They waited for the maitre 'd at the podium just inside the entrance. Winfield was prepared to tell him they wished a table for two, but he never got the chance. When a distinguished-looking fellow in a short red jacket, white shirt, and black bowtie arrived, he ignored Winfield entirely and addressed Mae directly in a basso voice slightly tinged with an Italian accent. "Good evening, Miss White! Welcome to Musso and Frank. Will you be needing a table for two or will there be others joining you for dinner this evening?"

Mae smiled briefly at the maitre 'd and then turned to Winfield, politely putting the fellow on notice that her escort was the person to whom he should be addressing his question. Without missing a beat, the maitre 'd switched his attention to Winfield, who said, "There will just be the two of us this evening."

"Very good, sir. Please follow me." Selecting two menus from a holder attached to the side of his podium, the fellow turned and led the way down the length of the dining room to a comfortable, secluded booth in a back corner. Turning to Winfield again, the maitre 'd said, "Will this booth be acceptable, sir?"

"It will be fine. Thank you, Jesse." Addressing the man by name elevated Winfield's status considerably. Mae had whispered it in Winfield's ear on the way to their table.

Addressing Mae again, the maitre 'd asked, "May I take your coat, Miss White?"

Mae said, "Yes, thank you," and the fellow moved quickly to help Mae out of her coat, which he draped over his arm.

Standing there watching this ritual, Winfield decided escorting one of America's most popular screen celebrities would definitely take some getting used to. Of course, he anticipated their arrival would attract some attention, but he did not expect the hush that spread throughout the entire restaurant nor the stares that followed their passage through the dining room.

Feeling a little under-dressed for the occasion in his work suit, Winfield found himself wishing there had been time to go home for a fresh change of clothes. Even more he wished he'd had the presence of mind to leave his shoulder holster and thirty-eight caliber police revolver in his patrol car, thus eliminating the slight bulge in his jacket under his left arm.

As they slid into seats facing each other in the booth, Jesse said, "Mario will be serving you tonight. Please enjoy your dinner."

As the maitre 'd left their table, Winfield watched him intercept a young woman brandishing a menu and a fountain pen. The maitre 'd politely, but firmly, turned her around and directed the disappointed autograph-seeker back to her table. Yes, Winfield thought, escorting Mae White to public places would certainly require some adjustment on his part if it were to become a frequent activity.

Still taking in his surroundings, Winfield felt Mae's gentle touch on his arm. When he turned and looked into her eyes, he saw her apologetic expression as she said, "I'm sorry for not giving you fair warning of what to expect here. I've grown accustomed to all the attention, but I can still remember my initial experiences in public after my first successful films. It can be very annoying."

Nodding, Winfield said, "I guess it can be, at that. I expected you would attract some attention, but this is amazing. These people really love you."

Smiling, Mae said, "Well, I'm not sure love is the word for it. I think it is more of a fascination. They're all imagining what it's like to be rich and famous."

Returning her smile, Winfield said, "If you say so."

"I do. Love is a word I reserve for someone very special to me." The warmth in her eyes made Winfield wonder who that very special person might be.

Mario, a younger edition of Jesse, arrived at their booth and asked if they would care to place drink orders. Mae turned to Winfield and said, "I think I would like iced tea."

Looking up at Mario, Winfield said, "The lady will have iced tea, and I'll have coffee."

Mario hesitated a moment as if he was expecting something more. Winfield realized he was waiting for some code that indicated they wanted their drinks with a little something extra. When Winfield just stared at him, Mario rushed off to fill their drink orders.

Turning to Mae, the lieutenant said, "I gather they aren't above doctoring the beverage orders here?"

Laughing lightly, Mae said, "Why, Detective, what on earth do you mean?"

"Don't worry; I won't raid the joint tonight."

"Well, I should hope not! That would be most embarrassing, although I see you are armed and ready for action."

Winfield grinned sheepishly. "I meant to leave my sidearm in the patrol car. I guess my mind was on other things."

Smiling coyly, Mae said, "If by that you mean you were thinking about being with me this evening, I will take it as a very thoughtful compliment."

Matching her smile, Winfield said, "I ain't admittin' nothin', lady." Opening his menu, he added, "Now, what's good for dinner at this joint?"

"My favorite is the fillet of sole Normande with rice pilaf and a green salad with Roquefort cheese dressing. In fact, I think I'll have that tonight, but almost anything on the menu that suits your fancy will be good."

Closing his menu, Winfield said, "Sole sounds good to me, too."

After Mario delivered their drinks and took their dinner orders, Winfield decided it was time to get back to being a detective. He said, "If you don't mind, I guess we should take care of some business."

"I don't mind. I guess that's why we're here."

Winfield resisted the temptation to say something about having more personal reasons for being there and said, "First, I would like to clarify a point. You told us you saw L. A. Bromfeld in the hotel parking area Saturday night but that you didn't speak to him. Is that correct?"

"Yes. He was getting into that big circus wagon of an automobile he drives. I don't know if he saw me or not, but I didn't feel much like talking with him."

"I see. And that was a few minutes before eight?"

Mae gave the question a moment's thought and said, "I think so. I remember looking at my wristwatch when I knocked on Lilly's door. It was exactly eight o'clock then, so figuring it took about five minutes for the walk to her room, L. A. must have driven off about seven-fifty-five, or so."

Flipping a few pages in his notebook, Winfield said, "See, that's where this gets confusing. Bromfeld says he spoke with you for several minutes in the parking area. It's an important point because if you did not have a conversation with him, there's a time gap in his story of fifteen to twenty minutes. I don't mean to imply you aren't being truthful, but are you absolutely certain you didn't speak with him?"

Smiling again, Mae said, "I'm absolutely certain. L. A. was the last person I wanted to talk to Saturday night."

"Alright. I just wanted to be sure I had it right. Now my next question concerns Miss Lawrence's relationship with her father. You and other witnesses have tied her decisions to leave the studio and marry Tom Bell to the death of Harry Lee—I mean, she turned down Bell's proposals before that and then she seems to have changed her mind right after her father died. Do you have any idea why her father's death might have caused her to make those decisions?"

Mae was quiet for a few minutes while Mario delivered crisp green salads to their table. Finally, she said, "Yes, I know why Harry Lee's death caused Lilly to accept Tom's proposal. This is difficult to explain, and I don't want to leave you with the impression that Lilly didn't love her father. She loved him dearly, but . . . well, to put in bluntly, Harry Lee was an embarrassment.

"Frankly, he was a bum. He seldom held down a job for more than a few weeks. That's why Lilly left high school and went to work in the costume shop. Most of the family income came from her mother's work as a seamstress. She made lovely gowns for some of this town's most influential women and was paid well for her skill. When her mother died of pneumonia, Lilly had to quit school and find a job in order to put food on the table."

Noting how closely Mae's thoughts about Harry Lee paralleled those of Viola Wiebe, Winfield nodded and said, "Then it must have pleased Harry no end when Miss Lawrence began earning a large salary as an actress."

Mae laughed softly. "Pleased is hardly the word for it! He went nuts, throwing Lilly's money around as fast as she made it."

Winfield swallowed a particularly tasty bite of salad with a large chunk of Roquefort cheese in it and asked, "What did he spend it on?"

"The high life—fancy clothes, booze, and mostly, gambling."

Recalling Harry Lee's arrest record and L. A. Bromfeld's story about having to bail the man out of jail to avoid bad publicity, Winfield said, "I understand the drinking and some of his other habits got Lee into trouble with the authorities."

"That's another understatement. Lilly's father ended up in jail more times than I can remember. I've even heard that L.A had . . . ." She paused for a second, and then continued, "I mean no offense to your profession, but I heard that L. A. had an 'arrangement' with the police to keep Harry's name out of the newspapers."

"No offense taken. I will not deny there are dishonest officers on the force." Returning to his original question, Winfield said, "So how did Lee's death affect Miss Lawrence?"

"She was grief-stricken; there's no doubt about that, but she was also relieved in a way. You see, she turned down Tom Bell's proposals because she was afraid Tom wouldn't approve of her father. Knowing Tom, I don't think Harry's behavior would have changed his feelings for Lilly one bit, but Lilly couldn't see that.

"When she began to move on past the sadness of losing her father, Lilly realized she was free. Harry couldn't embarrass her anymore, and she no longer had to work to pay his debts, so she could quit acting, which she disliked terribly, and marry Tom."

"I see. It almost sounds as if her father's death was the best thing that could have happened to Miss Lawrence."

Mae appeared to think about Winfield's statement for a moment before saying, "In a sense, yes. Lilly would never have said that because she loved her dad, but it really was a blessing in disguise for her." As an afterthought, she added, "And for Western National."

Winfield was pretty sure he knew what Mae meant, but wanting to hear the explanation in her words, he asked, "How so?"

"That's pretty obvious, isn't it? I mean, Harry's bad behavior was a constant threat to the studio's investment in Lilly. I'm sure Bromfeld breathed a huge sigh of relief when he got the news about Harry's death. Sure it meant Lilly missed a few days of work, but in the long run, L. A. could stop worrying about how Harry was going to embarrass the studio next."

Writing surreptitiously so other diners wouldn't be aware that he was questioning the famous Mae White, Winfield added a few lines of notes to his book. Then Mario arrived to clear away their salad plates and present their entrees with a flourish.

The lieutenant noted that Mae missed Mario's presentation of their sole Normande. She appeared to be deep in thought, as if she were trying to make a decision. Finally, when Mario left them to their meals, Mae said, "Bobby, there's something else I need to tell you—something I learned only a few days ago."

Winfield set his fork down and leaned forward slightly. "What's that, Mae?"

Pausing for a moment, as if choosing her words carefully, she said, "I found out that L. A. had Harry Lee killed, and what's more, I can prove it."

Surprised, Winfield said, "What makes you think that?"

Taking a bite of her sole, Mae chewed it daintily, and then said, "It's kind of complicated, but the first clue was a watch chain. You see, Lilly gave her father a beautiful pocket watch and custom-made chain for his birthday last year. The chain was gold and had a distinctive design of long, rectangular links with an intricate design engraved into them. Lilly had it made at Kaplan's, and it cost her plenty. She showed the watch and chain to me before she wrapped it. The chain was quite heavy and very masculine—the sort of thing Harry would appreciate."

Wondering how she was going to get from a watch chain to Bromfeld killing Harry Lee, Winfield simply said, "I see."

"Well, Harry loved the watch and wore it constantly. He was wearing the watch and chain the night he was killed, but it was missing when the police found his body."

Remembering the murder investigation report Mackie dug up, Winfield recalled that robbery was given as the apparent motive. "If I remember the sheriff's report correctly, Lee was also missing his wallet and a ring."

Mae nodded. "Right. To the best of my knowledge, the ring and wallet have never turned up, but the watch and chain have. I saw them or, more accurately, I saw the chain."

"Oh?"

"I saw it last Friday at the studio. I was walking down the main hallway in the administration building and I met this fellow, Tex, going the other way.

He fancies himself quite the lady's man, so of course he had to stop and talk to me. While I was trying to get rid of him, I noticed he was wearing Harry Lee's watch chain."

"No kidding? Are you certain it was the same chain?"

"I have no doubt about it. It's one of a kind."

Busily adding notes to his book, Winfield asked, "Who is this Tex?"

"I understand he started out at the studio as a Gower Gulch cowboy doing stunt work in western films. Then L. A. hired him as a special assistant, which is a fancy title that means L. A.'s personal errand boy. L. A. even gave Tex a private little office all his own out by the horse stable on the east lot."

Pausing with pencil poised, Winfield asked, "Does this Tex have a last name?"

Mae shook her head. "I've never heard it. He's just known as Tex around the lot."

"What does he look like?"

"He's tall and lanky and dresses like a dude cowboy—you know, boots, ten gallon hat, and fancy western piping on his custom-made suits. He puts on a Texas drawl—always saying things like, 'Howdy, ma'am'—like that."

A memory flashed in Winfield's mind of the cowboy he met in Bromfeld's office on his first visit to the studio. He said, "I think I've seen the fellow you're describing. He was coming out of Bromfeld's office as I was going in."

"That was probably him. Tex is always hanging around L. A.'s office."

"Okay, so you saw Tex wearing Harry Lee's watch chain. How do we get from there to Bromfeld being behind Lee's death?"

"Well, for one thing, Tex is L. A.'s right-hand man when it comes to fixing problems around the studio. For example, I heard about L. A. sending Tex to beat up the brother of an actress who claimed Ernst Frohmme raped her. The brother showed up from out of town and was making things hot for L. A., and then he suddenly ended up in the hospital.

"But there's more to the story. Of course, I thought a lot about why Tex had the watch and chain that were stolen from Harry. It just didn't make any sense that Tex would have killed Harry just to rob him. I'm pretty sure Tex gets paid well for his services, so he can afford the things wants.

"Anyway, I decided to go to the Club Fiesta out on Sunset Friday night to see if I could find out why Tex had Harry's watch and chain. One of the waitresses there looked familiar, but I couldn't place her right away. Eventually I realized I saw her at Harry's funeral. I remembered her for two reasons. One is that she is quite attractive in a bawdy sort of way. The other reason I remembered her from the funeral is that she was terribly upset and crying during the service. I figured that meant she was close to Harry.

"Thinking she might shed some light on the situation, I went to my automobile and waited for the woman to come out for a break or at the end of her shift.

"She finally showed up a few minutes after midnight and started hiking east on Sunset. I pulled up and offered her a ride to wherever she was going. I gave her the 'woman-alone-at-night' story.

"She accepted the ride, probably because she was tired from being on her feet all night. So once I got her in the car, I introduced myself. Of course, she was surprised and immediately figured I was up to something. It took a few miles of driving and talking like a Dutch uncle, but I finally got her to open up.

"She told me her name was Maria Skouris and that she and Harry were planning to get married. That was a shocker because Harry never said anything to Lilly about some woman he was going to marry. Lilly would have mentioned it if he had.

"To make a long story short, Maria said she and Harry fell in love, and I think she was sincere about what she told me. The real shocker came a few minutes later when she told me she'd witnessed Harry's murder."

Winfield looked up from his notebook and said, "If she knew who killed Lee, why didn't she tell one of the deputies investigating the murder? The sheriff's report said they had no solid leads."

"Maria didn't tell them because she was afraid of the man who killed Harry. Apparently Harry was waiting for her in the club's parking area, and when she came out to meet him, she saw the whole thing. Maria told me she saw three men beating Harry. One of them was using a club, and her description of that man fits Tex perfectly. So add Maria's story to the facts that Tex is L. A.'s trouble-shooter and he was wearing Harry's watch and chain, and you've got Harry's murderer, or murderers."

Winfield stopped writing again. "So you think Tex killed Harry on Bromfeld's orders and took his watch, ring, and wallet to make the murder look like a robbery?"

Mae grinned. "You catch on pretty quick for a cop."

The lieutenant grinned back at her and said, "I do my best. Do you know where I can find this Maria Skouris?"

"Well, you could find her at the Club Fiesta, but it might be smarter to talk Maria at her home. Friday night I dropped her off in front of the Sunset Court apartment building at Sunset and Western. It's on the southeast corner. I don't know how much she will tell you, though. Tex has her scared out of her wits. I hope she will talk to you so you can arrest L. A. and Tex and put them in jail where they belong."

After noting Maris Skouris' address in his book, Winfield said, "If Miss Skouris' testimony fits the facts we already know, we can certainly arrest this fellow Tex. Bromfeld is another matter. The problem is, without solid proof that Bromfeld ordered Tex to kill Harry Lee, we don't have a case that would stand up in court. Yes, Bromfeld was no doubt glad to be rid of Lee, and yes, this fellow Tex works for Bromfeld, but that's what's lawyers call circumstantial evidence, and it doesn't hold much water with a jury."

Cocking her head to one side, Mae said, "I suppose that's true. You know more about such things than I do. But I'm sure there's something around the studio that would tie L. A. to Harry's murder. All we have to do is find it."

Winfield shook his head. "'We' are not going to look for it. Sergeant Mackie and I will investigate this, but I want you to promise me you won't do any more digging on your own. You took a real chance going out to the Club Fiesta. This fellow Tex obviously doesn't have any qualms about murdering people, so he's not the sort of guy who will react kindly to someone snooping into his business."

Smiling her coy smile again, Mae said, "Tell me, Mister Detective, are you just saying that as a policeman or could it be that you are developing a personal interest in my welfare?"

Winfield hesitated a moment, not sure how to answer her question. Then he looked into Mae's eyes and saw the same warmth there he'd seen when she talked about love being something she was saving for someone very special. He said, "Both, but right now I'm talking as a cop. We've got two murders that may be related on our hands now. This is very serious business." He paused a moment, and then in a softer tone, he added, "I really need to know that you are staying clear of danger. Now please promise that you'll let me handle this from now on."

Mae placed a hand on his and looked into his eyes. "I promise, Bobby. And thank you for caring about me."

Winfield gave her a brief smile and a nod. Then he said quietly, "I think you have already figured out that Bromfeld is a prime suspect in Miss Lawrence's murder."

She nodded, but said nothing. Winfield went on, saying, "We think he had the opportunity, and we found out earlier today he may have had the means to kill Miss Lawrence. The missing part is a motive. Unless he killed her in a fit of rage, why on earth would L. A. Bromfeld murder one of his biggest stars?"

Mae looked up from her plate and said, "That's an easy question, and the answer is insurance."

"Insurance?"

"Yes. Like most major studios, Western National takes out life insurance policies on its most profitable players. I'm insured for a cool million dollars. So if something happened to me—if I were to die in an accident or I was murdered—the studio gets a million bucks to make up for the loss."

"Wow! Are you really worth that much to Western National?"

Grinning, Mae said, "You better believe it, buster! Actually, I'm worth a lot more. My last picture, Fame and Fortune, cost a little less than two hundred thousand to produce, but the box office receipts to date are more than one million, seven hundred thousand, and the film is still on release. That means Western National will net at least a million-and-a-half on Fame and Fortune."

Astonished, Winfield said, "I had no idea there was that kind of money in motion pictures."

"There surely is, and my talent agent keeps close tabs on those numbers because if they are high, they make good bargaining chips when my contract with the studio comes up for renewal."

"Did Western National have a policy like yours on Lillian Lawrence?"

"I don't know that for a fact, but I would be surprised if they didn't. Her films were doing very well."

Thinking out loud, Winfield said, "So if Miss Lawrence walked away from her contract, the studio gets nothing more out of its investment in her, but if she died, they get a million-dollar payday."

"That's about the size of it."

"I guess that sure qualifies as a motive. How would I go about finding out if Western National has an insurance policy on Lillian Lawrence without tipping our hand and letting Bromfeld know we're looking into the studio's affairs?"

"Well, I could . . . ." Noticing Winfield's expression, she started over, "I suggest you ask Marty Goldstein. Marty is Western National's chief accountant, and I know he has no great love for L. A. They are always at loggerheads over the way Bromfeld spends the studio's money."

"He sounds like the man to talk to. How should I approach Mister Goldstein?"

Mae thought about her answer for a moment and said, "It would probably be best to contact him after working hours. In fact, you might be able to see him tonight. He lives up Beachwood Canyon in the new Hollywoodland development. I attended a party he and his wife put on when they moved into their new house, and I'm pretty sure I could find it again."

Smiling, Winfield asked, "I don't suppose you happen to know his telephone number?"

Mae said, "No, I'm afraid I don't, but I'll bet a telephone operator will give it to us. Get Mario's attention and ask him to bring a telephone to our booth and we'll find out."

Surprised, Winfield said, "They'll do that?"

Mocking a haughty air, she said, "They will for me. I'm special."

A few minutes later Winfield found out she was right. Mario promptly brought a modern-looking telephone to the booth and plugged it into an outlet on the wall next to their table. A few minutes later he had Marty

Goldstein on the line and was explaining why he needed to see the man. At the conclusion of their brief conversation, the lieutenant returned the telephone handset to its cradle and said, "Thank you, Mae. I have an appointment to see Mister Goldstein in thirty minutes, at eight o'clock."

"Good. That gives us plenty of time to find the place in case my memory isn't as good as I think it is."

Well, I'm not sure . . . he gave me his address, so I think I can find it by myself."

Looking disappointed, Mae said, "Bobby, please let me come along. I'll wait in the automobile while you talk to Marty. I just don't want this evening to end quite so quickly."

Winfield looked at Mae for a long moment, torn between wanting to spend more time with this attractive young woman and his responsibility as a policeman to remain objective during an investigation. Finally finding justification in the thought that letting her ride along to Goldstein's wasn't really compromising his objectivity, he said, "Alright, Mae. I'll ask for our check so we can get started."

While they waited for Mario to deliver the dinner bill, Mae surreptitiously reached across the table and pressed two twenty-dollar bills into his hand. Surprised, he asked, "What's this for?"

"Remember? I said dinner was on me tonight."

"I know you said that, but . . . ."

"No buts. A deal is a deal. Besides, if you don't take the money, I'll make a fuss and embarrass the devil out of you!"

Knowing that the woman across the table from him was perfectly capable of making good on her threat, Winfield accepted the bills, saying, "Okay, but next time dinner is my treat."

Mae White put on her coy smile again and said, "That's fine with me. And, Bobby, just so you know, I'm already looking forward to next time."

TWENTY-SEVEN

With Mae White sitting pleasantly close beside him on the leather seat, Winfield steered her Chrysler through a right turn onto Las Palmas and repeated the maneuver onto Franklin. While he knew the route, Winfield didn't recall ever actually being to the Hollywoodland development.

In fact, all he really knew about the place was that the developers spoiled everyone's view of the hills behind Hollywood by erecting a gigantic sign with fifty-foot-tall, white letters spelling out the name of their development across the side of Mount Lee. Then, adding insult to injury, they outlined the letters with light bulbs to be sure their advertisement wouldn't be missed after dark.

Glancing up at the dazzling eyesore looming above them, Winfield had to agree with Mackie's assessment that the sign was ugly and detracted from the otherwise pleasant surroundings of Hollywood. He hoped C. K. was right when he said a strong wind would blow the damned thing down one day soon and that would be the end of it.

When they came to Beachwood Drive, Mae instructed him to turn left. From there the street led them past a few apartments and craftsman-style cottages as it wound its way up Beachwood Canyon. Then, immediately after they drove between a pair of sandstone pillars announcing their arrival in Hollywoodland, the street split in three directions. Mae told him to take the middle road which continued up the canyon.

A block or so later, Mae said, "Okay, slow down. I think we make a right turn up here . . . there. Turn right on that little street."

Winfield negotiated a sharp right turn onto a narrow road that curved around to parallel Beachwood back down the canyon, and Mae said, "Marty's place is right along here somewhere on the left."

Noting that there were no houses anywhere in sight and remembering that Mae grew up in New York City where there was very little open countryside, Winfield said, "You sure? All I see is empty space."

"Just keep following the road, ye of little faith."

A moment later, as they rounded a bend in the road, a brilliantly lit, two-story stone castle with tall Moorish turrets loomed up before them. Mae said excitedly, "There it is! I knew I could find it!"

Slowing the Chrysler and leaning forward so he could take in the entirety of the monstrosity ahead of them through the windshield, Winfield said, "You did, indeed. You did not, however, warn me that Mister Goldstein is afflicted with delusions of grandeur."

With a giggle, Mae said, "I think it is Missus Goldstein who has the delusions. Their drive is just up here on the left."

Winfield turned in to a cobblestone drive that ended in a flagstone parking area adjacent to the castle's grand entrance—a pair of heavy, oak-plank doors trimmed with wrought iron and set back under a peaked arch entryway. Pulling to a stop, he looked at Mae and said, "Where's the moat?"

With a grin, she said, "They probably have one somewhere. Be careful you don't fall in."

"I most certainly will." Then he added, "You sure you don't mind waiting out here by yourself?"

"I'll be fine. Go ask Marty your questions."

Stepping under a brilliant chandelier illuminating the massive doors, the lieutenant gave one of them a wrap with its black iron knocker and then fished his badge out of a coat pocket while he waited for an answer to his knock. The doors swung open a moment later to reveal a short, portly young man with receding black hair. "Good evening. You must be the detective."

Winfield held up his badge and said, "Yes, I'm Detective Lieutenant Winfield."

The man, dressed in a maroon paisley smoking jacket over neatly pressed black trousers, said, "Come in, Mister Winfield. I'm Marty Goldstein."

Stepping over the threshold, Winfield found himself in a round foyer with marble flooring, similar to L. A. Bromfeld's entry except that here, the curved wall was made of stone. Goldstein said, "My wife is entertaining a few of her friends this evening, so we'll talk in my study if that's okay with you."

Assuring the man that anywhere would be fine, Winfield followed him down a long hallway and into a large room with a massive oak desk at its center. The paneled walls were covered with a hodge-podge of paintings and photographs. Most of the latter prominently featured Goldstein with celebrities and well-known politicians, including a group photo with President Calvin Coolidge at the forefront.

Stepping behind the desk, Goldstein gestured to a comfortable wingback chair and said, "Have a seat, Mister Winfield. Make yourself comfortable. Can I offer you a refreshment of some sort? Coffee, brandy . . . ."

"No, thank you. I'll make this as brief as I can so as to take up as little of your time as possible."

Looking a little disappointed that Winfield didn't seem interested in his hospitality, Goldstein sat in the large leather chair behind his desk and said, "Alright, how can I help you?"

Goldstein listened with interest as Winfield explained that he was investigating Lillian Lawrence's death and that his questions concerned any insurance policies Western National might hold against the death of Miss Lawrence. When the lieutenant finished his explanation, Goldstein said, "Mister—or Detective—Winfield, if you prefer, I can and will answer your question because it is in Western National's best interests that you find Miss Lawrence's killer in a timely fashion, but before I do, kindly explain how the existence of such an insurance policy figures into your investigation."

To Winfield's ear, Goldstein was now speaking more like an attorney than a financial executive—an observation that made the lieutenant give even more cautious consideration to the approach he took with the man. He said, "Mister Goldstein, this investigation is more complex than most. When large amounts of money are associated with a homicide, it is understandably important to determine who, if anyone, might benefit from the victim's death."

Goldstein leaned forward in his chair. With a frown, he said, "I hope you are not suggesting that the studio is in any way responsible for Miss Lawrence's untimely passing."

Putting what he fervently hoped wasn't too much stock in Mae's opinion that there was no love lost between this man and L. A. Bromfeld, Winfield decided to take a risk. He said, "No, not the studio, but perhaps an employee of the studio."

Goldstein relaxed in his chair again. He appeared to be giving Winfield's words thoughtful consideration. Finally he said, "I don't suppose you are willing to reveal the name of that employee."

"Not at this time. We are dealing with some very influential individuals in this investigation, and it is not my intention to make any accusations until we are absolutely certain of our facts."

Winfield thought he saw a slight smile cross Goldstein's lips before the man said, "I see. I suppose that is a wise precaution. Let me make my position clear here so that all of our cards are, as the saying goes, on the table.

"I am, in effect, the second-in-command at Western National Films. I answer only to Mister L. A. Bromfeld directly and, through him, to our New York investors. In this instance, it is therefore incumbent upon my responsibility to those investors that I be prepared to protect their financial involvement in the studio should some catastrophic event affect Western National's normal operation.

"For that reason, I am asking, Detective Winfield, for your assurance that you will provide me with as much warning as possible if you foresee such a catastrophe in the studio's future. Is that condition agreeable to you?"

"It is."

"Thank you. Now to answer your original question, yes, Western National Films holds an insurance policy on Miss Lawrence's life in the amount of one million dollars. It was issued approximately one year ago by the Motion Picture and Theatrical Indemnity Company of New Brunswick, Connecticut.

"Briefly stated, the policy pays Western National the stated amount of money in the event Miss Lawrence dies as the result of illness, an accident, homicide, or act of nature. However, the policy does include the customary suicide clause so that if Miss Lawrence's demise was intentionally caused by her own hand, the insurance company is, as they say, off the hook. Does that information adequately answer your question, Detective?"

"Quite adequately, Mister Goldstein. Can you also tell me if Western National has put in a claim with the insurance company concerning Miss Lawrence?"

Goldstein hesitated a moment before apparently deciding there was no harm in answering Winfield's question. "In effect, yes. I started the wheels in motion this morning by placing a long distance telephone call to M.P. and T. Indemnity informing them of Miss Lawrence's passing. I was told we could expect a prompt payment as soon as the company reviewed Miss Lawrence's death certificate and, since her death may be the result of a homicide, a copy of the final investigation report from the Los Angeles Police Department. I imagine your headquarters will be receiving an inquiry from M. P. and T. Indemnity sometime within the next week to ten days."

Winfield nodded his understanding and said, "I am hopeful that our investigation will be concluded by that time." Standing, he offered his hand to Goldstein, saying, "Thank you for your cooperation."

Holding his grip on Winfield's hand, Goldstein said, "You're welcome, Detective Winfield. I trust you will remember our agreement regarding any warning you can give me of the . . . involvement . . . of a Western National employee in Miss Lawrence's death. In exchange for that warning—even though you have not asked me to do so—I will refrain from mentioning our conversation to anyone at Western National."

"I appreciate that, Mister Goldstein. You can count on hearing from me under the circumstances you laid out."

As Winfield walked across the flagstone parking area to Mae's Chrysler, he marveled at Goldstein's shrewdness. The man darn well knew Bromfeld was the employee they were investigating, and he had taken care to insure his own longevity with Western National by insisting on a promise from Winfield to give him fair warning if Bromfeld was going down. Very shrewd indeed.

As he settled into the Chrysler's seat, Mae said, "Judging by the happy look on your face, I'm guessing Marty was helpful."

Turning to face her, Winfield said, "He was very cooperative. And, yes, Western National does have an insurance policy on Lillian Lawrence."

Grinning, she said, "Don't keep me in suspense! Is she worth more than I am?"

Winfield couldn't help laughing at her question. "I can assure you that Western National held both of you in equal regard."

"Good! I was going to give those rats a piece of my mind if Lilly's policy was for more money than mine."

Then, as Winfield stepped on the Chrysler's starter, Mae said quietly, "I'm sorry. That was in very poor taste. I didn't mean to make light of Lilly's death. It's just that I still find it so hard to believe she's gone—that I can no longer pick up the telephone and talk with her. She was so . . . so alive, so wonderfully alive and real."

Winfield sensed rather than saw the tears in her eyes. He held out his hand and said, "I know, Mae; I know."

He felt her take his hand in hers and squeeze it for a moment before letting go so he could shift the transmission as they turned left onto Beachwood Drive. No more was said until they reached Mae's apartment door. There she said, "Please come in for a minute, Bobby. I want to discuss a couple of things before you leave."

Assuming Adele was somewhere in the apartment and thus they would be properly chaperoned, Winfield said, "Sure, Mae."

After unlocking her door with the key she handed him and helping her out of her coat, Mae said, "Come into the living room. Let's sit on the couch. Would you like some coffee or . . . anything?"

Settling into the pale blue couch, Winfield said, "No, thanks; I'm fine."

Mae then leaned back on the couch and crossed her legs. After demurely smoothing the hem of her dress so it revealed only an appropriate amount of knee, she began to speak in what sounded to Winfield like a somewhat rehearsed tone. "Bobby, I'm sure it will come as no surprise to you that gossip travels quickly around a studio lot, and knowing that, I'm sure you will also not be surprised to learn that I know you were asking questions about me at Western National."

Winfield started to explain that those questions were just part of his job, but Mae shushed him. "I know, Bobby, it's your job to ask questions, and that's okay because there's nothing about me I want to hide from you. I do have a concern, though.

"Sad as it may be, I have an undeserved reputation in some circles for being a . . . well, I guess 'loose woman' is the best description."

"Don't worry, Mae, I didn't put any stock in . . . ."

She shushed him again, saying, "Please, Bobby, let me say this my way. I've put a lot of thought into what I want to tell you and how I was going to say it because it is important to me that you understand this."

Winfield resolved to keep his mouth shut and listen. Mae seemed to collect her thoughts for a moment before saying, "It's important to me for you to know there is no truth to those rumors about me. The people who spread such lies base them on the fact that I seldom go out with the same man twice.

"That's because I don't have a steady beau, and I haven't wanted one until . . . well, until very recently. Going out and being seen at parties and such is part of my job, and it is expected that I have an escort when I do so. At the same time I've been trying to avoid entanglements, especially with the sort of men I meet in the motion picture business. So I've made it a point to date different men to avoid the sort of gossip that comes from being seen frequently with the same escort. Unfortunately, my cleverness seems to have backfired on me.

"The point is, as a celebrity it is impossible to avoid being talked about, and when jealousy and egos become involved, the talk can be malicious, especially when what is being said isn't true. I mean, look at poor Louise Brooks. She is forced to date men I'm sure she doesn't care for just to avoid being branded as a lesbian. I don't know if she is or she isn't, but that doesn't matter to me because what she does in the privacy of her own bedroom is her business. But because she is a film celebrity, some people say things they know nothing about just to sound important and like they're in the know. Does that make sense?"

"Yes, it makes perfect sense, and I assure you I put absolutely no stock in rumors and gossip. Even if I did, your friend, Fannie, set me straight in no uncertain terms on the subject of your virtue."

"Oh, she did, did she? Fannie is a treasure and I love her dearly, but she does have a tendency to say more than she should sometimes."

"Don't worry. Fannie didn't give away any skeletons from the closet. She just wanted to be sure I got the straight dope on one Mae White."

Smiling, Mae said, "Bless her heart. That sounds just like Fannie. Now, there's one more thing I want to tell you."

"Okay, shoot."

After pausing another moment, apparently to gather her thoughts again, she said, "As I suspect you already realize, I've grown quite fond of you during the short time we've known each other. That's partly because you are so different from the men I see on a regular basis. I mean, you are obviously intelligent, but more than that you are considerate and thoughtful. Most important to me, you are a real person, just as Lilly was. You don't put on airs and try to impress people. You are just you, and I find that your most endearing quality of all."

Feeling his face redden, Winfield said, "Well . . . thank you, Mae. I hope you know I'm quite fond of you as well."

"Yes, that shows even through your shyness. What I want you to know, though, is that I understand the situation you are in. I mean, you have a job to do, and that job includes being objective about everyone involved in your investigation of Lilly's murder. I haven't made that easy for you, and I suppose that's wicked of me, but sometimes I find it difficult to hide my feelings.

"So the thing is, I want you to know I don't expect any special treatment from you in your investigation. At the same time, I will do my best not to put any undo stress on you by . . . well, by expecting you to spend your time with me or expecting you to express whatever feelings you may have for me. Do you understand what I'm trying to say?"

"I do, Mae. And I appreciate that."

"Thank you for understanding, Bobby. Now, please understand this: When you finish this investigation and all this is over and done with . . . ." Mae paused for a second to put on a big grin, "when this is over and done with, look out buster, because this gal has her eye on you in a big way."

Winfield couldn't help grinning back at her. "Alright, Mae, you've given me fair warning, and I promise to be prepared for whatever I need to look out for."

"Okay, Bobby, now you'd better get out of here because I've got to get up early tomorrow morning, and I need my beauty sleep."

Standing by the apartment door, Winfield found himself looking into Mae's eyes. He said sincerely, "Thank you for dinner, Mae. And thank you for putting me in contact with Marty Goldstein." Winfield paused long enough to take a deep breath, or maybe it was a sigh, and then he said, "Especially, thank you for explaining things for me tonight."

Looking back into his eyes, Mae said softly, "You're welcome, Bobby."

Then as if it were the most natural thing in all the world, she slipped into his arms and he kissed her gently on the lips. They continued to hold onto each other for a long moment after the kiss ended.

Finally, Winfield took a step backward toward the door and said, "Goodnight, Mae."

"Goodnight, my dear Detective Lieutenant."

TWENTY-EIGHT

Wednesday - September 8, 1926

The sun was just beginning to cast its first shadows Wednesday morning when Detective Lieutenant Winfield started out for the Sixth Precinct stationhouse. He looked forward to the day with enthusiasm. Thanks to Mae White, he finally felt as if they were getting a handle on the Lillian Lawrence homicide investigation.

In the detective room, Winfield put the extra time his early arrival gave him to good use by reviewing his notes from Tuesday night's interviews. When Sergeant Mackie arrived an hour or so later, he found Winfield jotting thoughts on a pad of yellow legal paper.

C. K. said, "Well, look who's up with the chickens this morning! Good morning to you, Bobby."

"The same to you, C. K. I trust you had a good night."

Hanging his uniform jacket on the coat rack, the sergeant said, "It was quiet, just the way I like it. More to the point, how was your evening? Did you learn anything new from Mae White?"

"Actually, it was a very productive evening. I picked up some interesting pieces of our puzzle, but before I get into that, we need to talk about my conversation with Captain Royce yesterday afternoon."

Mackie pulled his chair up to his desk and said, "Let me guess. Captain Royce told you to hold off on the search warrants until we have more evidence because he doesn't want to upset Bromfeld's applecart prematurely."

"You hit that nail on the head. How'd you know?"

"When you've worked for a man as long as I've worked for Captain Royce, you get to know him pretty well. For all his tough crime-fighting talk, the captain is . . . well, let's just say cautious."

"That isn't exactly the way I would put it."

"Remember, Laddie, the captain didn't rise to his lofty rank by ruffling the feathers of influential people, and you can't really blame him for protecting his position."

"You mean protecting his butt."

"Yes, well, that too."

"Well, the good captain might be singing a different tune when I tell him we're a big step closer to having the goods on Mister L. A. Bromfeld this morning."

C. K. looked surprised. "Are we now?"

"We are indeed. We now have a solid motive for Bromfeld killing Lillian Lawrence."

"And what would that be?"

"In a word, insurance. Last night, Miss White told me it is common practice for motion picture studios to take out hefty life insurance policies on their most valuable players. Both Mae White and Lillian Lawrence are insured by Western National Films for one million dollars."

Mackie whistled softly. "That certainly qualifies as a motive. Have you confirmed this with anyone else or are we taking Miss White's word for it?"

"It's confirmed. After my interview with Mae White, I followed her suggestion and contacted the number two man at Western National—a fellow named Martin Goldstein. I paid him a visit around eight o'clock last night at his home up in that Hollywoodland subdivision. He's a cagey fellow, but he did give me a verbal confirmation that the studio does carry a one million dollar life insurance policy on Miss Lawrence."

"Well, isn't that nice for the studio?"

"Sure is. What it comes down to is this: If Lillian Lawrence walked away from her contract with Western National, the studio got no more return on their investment in her without a messy legal battle that was sure to put them in a bad light with the public. If, on the other hand, Miss Lawrence died, the studio collects a cool million dollars and goes on about their business."

Mackie looked up from adding the new information to his notebook and said, "If Bromfeld couldn't change Miss Lawrence's mind about leaving, that million might have seemed like an acceptable alternative despite having to kill her to get it. Tell me, Bobby, is this Goldstein going to tell L. A. Bromfeld you questioned him about the life insurance?"

"I'm pretty sure he won't. I learned from Miss White that Goldstein and Bromfeld are not the best of pals, and as I said, Martin Goldstein is a cagey fellow. Even though I never mentioned Bromfeld's name, I'm pretty sure he figured out who our suspect is. If I had to guess, I would say Goldstein sees this as a way to get Bromfeld out of his hair and maybe take over the top job at Western National."

"Now that sounds like what I would expect from somebody in the wonderful dog-eat-dog world of motion pictures."

"Goldstein asked for my promise to give him advance warning if we did something that, as he put it, would cause a catastrophic change in the normal operation of the studio. I gave him that promise, ostensibly in exchange for his promise not to mention our conversation to anyone at Western National."

"Very shrewd indeed. Do you plan to keep that promise?"

"Yes, but only to the extent it doesn't interfere with our investigation or the conviction of a suspect."

Mackie smiled. "Sounds fair to me. Did you pick up any other useful tidbits from the glamorous Miss Mae White?"

"I certainly did. The matter of the studio life insurance policy is only one of two big bombshells Miss White dropped last night."

C. K. leaned back in his chair and said, "Okay, I'm all ears."

"Before I get to the second bombshell, she gave me a couple of smaller items worthy of note. For one, Miss White is sticking to her story that she did not talk to L. A. Bromfeld in the Hollywood Hotel parking area Saturday night. She's quite definite about that."

Mackie nodded. "I figured she would be. And when you combine that with the statements of the other witnesses to Saturday night's events, you end up with at least twenty minutes of Bromfeld's time that is unaccounted for."

"Plenty of time to commit murder. Another point worth noting is Miss White's belief that Harry Lee's death is the reason Miss Lawrence changed her mind about leaving the studio to marry Tom Bell. As we already know, Harry Lee was spending his daughter's money faster than she made it. His gambling debts and the money he spent living the high life were the main reasons she was forced to continue playing in motion pictures.

"In addition to that, Miss White said even though Miss Lawrence loved her father—she must have in order to put up with his behavior—she was ashamed of him and turned down Tom Bell's proposals because she was afraid of what Bell would think of her if he knew about her father's bad habits.

"When Lee was killed, Miss White thinks Lillian Lawrence was relieved in a way. It meant she was free to leave the studio and marry Bell."

Mackie said, "That pretty much confirms the stories you got from the folks at Western National. What's the second bombshell Miss White dropped last night?"

Winfield grinned. "Patience, Sergeant Mackie, I'm just getting to that. The second bombshell is that we've got ourselves a second murder to investigate."

C. K. leaned forward in his chair. "A second murder? Who else is dead?"

"Harry Lee."

"Hell, Bobby, we already know about that one. It's a dead end case."

"Not anymore more." Winfield held up his notebook for emphasis. "Last night Mae White gave me a very promising lead in the Harry Lee murder, and what's more, she claims that our prime suspect in the Lawrence case is also responsible for Lee's murder."

Mackie leaned back and tossed his pencil on the desk. "That certainly is a bombshell. What makes her think Bromfeld killed Harry Lee?"

"It goes like this: Miss White believes an employee of Western National Films—a dude cowboy who goes by the name of Tex—killed Lee with the help of two accomplices and that he did so under orders from Bromfeld. The murder was made to look like a robbery to cover the real reason Bromfeld wanted Lee dead."

Sounding dubious, C. K. said, "Which was?"

"At first, Harry Lee's gambling and other expensive habits were beneficial to Bromfeld because they forced Lillian Lawrence into a position of having to make more films for the studio to pay her father's debts. Bromfeld may have even encouraged Lee's gambling in the beginning. By the time of Lee's death, though, Bromfeld had Miss Lawrence's signature on a five-year contract and Harry Lee had outlived his usefulness.

"To make matters worse, Lee's behavior was getting out of hand, and Bromfeld feared he would do something the studio couldn't keep under wraps by paying off the department. If that happened, Lillian Lawrence's reputation would be ruined, making her worthless to Western National."

Mackie shook his head. "Now hold on, Bobby. This is getting pretty damned farfetched. Does Mae White have any evidence to support this story or did she get it from her Ouija board?"

"An eyewitness to Lee's murder seems like pretty strong evidence to me."

Still sounding skeptical, C. K. said, "Okay, I'll bite. Who is this eyewitness?"

"A woman by the name of Maria Skouris. She's a waitress out at the Club Fiesta. Mae White saw the woman at Lee's funeral and got curious, so she went out to the club and talked to her. It turns out Miss Skouris and Harry Lee were romantically involved. Lee was waiting for her outside the club the night he was attacked. Miss Skouris came out just in time to see the whole thing."

A little less skeptically, Mackie said, "Is that so? How is it she didn't come forward with this revelation when the sheriff was investigating Lee's murder? You'd think she would want the man who killed her lover to be punished."

"Mae White says Maria Skouris is scared to death of this guy Tex. She was afraid he would kill her, too, if she talked. Apparently Tex is a pretty bad hombre."

Leaning back in his chair again, C. K. looked to be mulling this information over before saying, "Okay, for the sake of argument, let's say this waitress's story is true. Aside from the theory that Harry Lee had outlived his usefulness to Bromfeld, what actual evidence do we have that this Tex was doing Bromfeld's bidding when he killed Lee?"

Winfield flipped a page in his notebook and recited what Mae White told him about Tex, including the fact that she saw him wearing the unique pocket watch chain taken from Harry Lee the night he died. In conclusion he said, "I'll grant you most of that is speculation or circumstantial evidence at best, but the connection between Bromfeld and Lee's death seems plausible and worth pursuing."

Mackie still looked skeptical. "And if we can prove the connection, we clear the books on an unsolved homicide, but is solving that one worth diverting our attention from Lillian Lawrence's murder right now? I'm not sure Captain Royce would think so."

"I disagree. Proving Bromfeld's involvement in Harry Lee's murder would open some new doors for our Lawrence investigation. At the very least, it gives us an undeniable reason to arrest Bromfeld which in turn gives us leverage for search warrants and anything else we need to prove Bromfeld's guilt in Lillian Lawrence's murder. Plus, it gives us this Tex character who might very well provide us with additional evidence in the Lawrence case, especially under the threat of a second murder conviction."

"Okay, you're the boss. What do we know about this Tex? Do we have a last name?"

"No last name yet. Miss White only knows him as Tex, but we do have a pretty good description. Even better, I'm pretty sure I met him coming out of Bromfeld's office when I was there to do my first round of interviews. The guy is a real character. He's tall—at least my height—and kind of lanky, with brown eyes and dark brown hair. He dresses in custom-made suits with cowboy-style stitching on the lapels and pockets. He completes the western look with a big-ten gallon Stetson hat and fancy cowboy boots. He also talks with a Texas drawl. The man looks and acts for all the world like a western movie actor."

"It also sounds like he makes pretty darn good money for a hired hand. How do you propose we proceed from here?"

Having already given the question a good deal of thought, Winfield said without hesitation, "The first thing we need to do is confirm some of this information. The best way to do that is talk to Maria Skouris. Depending on what we learn from her, our next step might be to do a little snooping around the Club Fiesta. After that, we need to weigh it all out and see if we've got enough to arrest Tex. If we've got a provable murder case against him, I'm betting he'll be willing to implicate Bromfeld to save some of his own hide."

After several moments of thought, C. K. said, "Okay, that sounds like a reasonable approach. Do we know where to find Maria Skouris?"

"I have the address where Miss White dropped Miss Skouris off the night she talked to her. It's an apartment building out at the west end of Sunset called the Sunset Court Apartments."

C. K. nodded, indicating he knew the place. Then he said, "You know, if this woman was too scared to talk to the sheriff's deputies at the time of Lee's murder, she may not be willing to talk to us now. If that's the situation, we're up against another brick wall."

"That's a possibility, but it shouldn't take us long to find out. I'm hoping we can convince her she'll be safe when we get Tex put behind bars. If not, we set the Harry Lee murder aside for now and go back to the Lillian Lawrence case, although without a search warrant, we really don't have much to go back to."

Mackie looked thoughtful again, and then said, "I'm beginning to see the sense in your decision to switch our attention to Harry Lee's murder. Without the search warrants we need, we don't have any solid leads left to pursue in Lillian Lawrence's murder. In a roundabout way, that gives us a convincing argument for Captain Royce if he questions the wisdom of going after Lee's killer in the middle of our Lawrence investigation. When do we go see Miss Skouris?"

It bothered the lieutenant that Mackie seemed more concerned about keeping Captain Royce happy than he was about solving murders, and Winfield wondered if he might be missing a lesson C. K. wanted him to learn. Looking at his wristwatch, he said, "The woman works a nightshift at that club, so I'm thinking she might be more receptive to our visit a little later in the day. It's only about nine-thirty now, so how 'bout we stick around here for a while and clean up some paperwork, and then go see her about lunchtime?"

Mackie looked forlornly at his overflowing inbox and said, "I was afraid you were going to suggest something like that. Okay, hand me the shovel, Laddie, and I'll dig into this mountain of paper."

TWENTY-NINE

By eleven-forty-five, Detectives Winfield and Mackie were finishing up the filing, report-reading, and other chores necessary to clear out their in-baskets. At that point, C. K. suggested it might be a good idea to stop for lunch because it was likely to be a long afternoon if things turned out as they hoped.

Winfield agreed and told Mackie he would run over to Larry's for a sandwich. C. K. said that wouldn't be necessary. His wife, Helen, thought it was sad the lieutenant always had to eat store-bought lunches, so she put a second sandwich and an extra apple into C. K.'s lunch pail that morning. Unwrapping a thick sandwich piled high with slices of roasted beef, Winfield told Mackie to tell Helen she was an angel.

At twelve-fifteen, they climbed into Mackie's Dodge and headed for the Sunset Court Apartments. When they got there, Winfield observed that the name of the place was far grander than its rundown appearance deserved.

After gingerly negotiating two rotting wood front steps to the porch, Winfield studied the mailboxes sagging from the wall near the front door. The name, "M. Skouris," was barely legible on a small white card attached to the mailbox for apartment number two.

Apartment number two turned out to be the first door on their right down a main hallway with a threadbare maroon carpet that was badly frayed along its edges. Winfield knocked on the door. After a moment's wait brought no reply, he rapped on the door again, this time more firmly. It took a third knock that was hard enough to rattle the tarnished brass doorknob to get a response from inside the apartment. A woman's voice came faintly through the door. Nervously it asked, "Who is it?"

Winfield glanced at Mackie and said, "Los Angeles Police Officers, ma'am. Please open the door."

Another long moment passed before the door opened about eight inches. Through the narrow space, Winfield saw a woman in her late thirties who under different circumstances might fit Mae White's description of "attractive." At the moment, however, she looked up at him from under tousled black hair, her dark eyes puffy from sleep. The woman said, "Yes?"

"Miss Maria Skouris?"

"Yes."

Holding up his badge, Winfield said, "I'm Detective Lieutenant Winfield, L.A.P.D. Homicide Division, and this is Detective Sergeant Mackie. We would like a few words with you."

A brief glance at the lieutenant's badge and Mackie's uniform changed the woman's expression from nervousness to fear. "What about?"

"Harry Lee."

"I already told the sheriff's deputies all I know."

In the calmest voice as he could muster, Winfield said, "We know, Miss Skouris, but we're conducting a follow-up investigation, and we have a few new questions. May we come in?"

Accepting the inevitable, Maria Skouris opened the door to allow the detectives into her apartment. The living room was about what Winfield expected based on the building's exterior. A small coffee table, a sagging couch with cushions that had been reupholstered more than once, and an overstuffed chair with a tear in its arm just about filled the tiny room. A small table barely supported an old fashioned radio set beneath a window overlooking a fence that was missing a couple of boards. In spite of the disheveled furnishings, Maria Skouris's living room was otherwise neat and tidy.

In bare feet and a bathrobe that wasn't in much better condition than the couch upholstery, Miss Skouris closed the door behind them and said, "What do you want to know?"

Winfield said, "Do you mind if we sit down while we talk?"

She nodded silently and sank into the overstuffed chair. Mackie and Winfield took seats on the couch, which groaned audibly under their combined weight. The sergeant removed the notebook from his breast pocket, and Winfield said, "We're sorry to interrupt your day. We'll make this as brief as possible. We understand you were close to Mister Lee."

Quietly, Maria Skouris said, "Yes."

"How did you know him?"

"Harry used to come into the club where I work a lot."

"That would be the Club Fiesta on Sunset?"

The woman nodded, and Winfield asked, "How well did you know Mister Lee?"

"Pretty well. We went out sometimes on my nights off."

"Were you and Mister Lee in love?"

Winfield watched tears forming in Maria Skouris's eyes as she nodded. He said, "I know this is painful for you, Miss Skouris. I'm sorry we have to ask these questions."

A tear rolled silently down her cheek, but she said nothing. Looking into her eyes, Winfield thought he could see the conflict between fear and sadness there. Sadness appeared to be winning the battle.

Keeping the tone of his voice calm and quiet, the lieutenant said, "Please tell us what happened on the night Harry was killed."

Maria Skouris took a deep breath and began to recite words that sounded as if she'd repeated them a hundred times. "I came out of the club's back door at the end of my shift and found an ambulance and some sheriff's cars in the parking area. Two men in white coats were kneeling next to someone on the ground. One of the deputies was standing next to them. I walked over to where they were for a better look and saw that it was Harry on the ground. He was all bloody. That's all I remember."

"About what time was that, Miss Skouris?"

"My shift ends at midnight, so it was a few minutes after that."

Glancing at C. K., Winfield noticed the sergeant had his notebook open, but wasn't writing anything. It was clear he knew as well as Winfield that what they were hearing wasn't the truth, so there was no sense in writing it down.

Winfield said, "I see. Well, Miss Skouris, that's where we have a little problem with your story. You say you saw sheriff's deputies and an ambulance at the club a few minutes after midnight, but the official report says the call about a body at the Club Fiesta didn't come into the sheriff's office until twelve-thirty."

After a long hesitation, during which her expression resembled that of a kid who'd been caught with his hand in a forbidden cookie jar, Maria Skouris said, "Well, maybe I was wrong about the time. Maybe I didn't get away until later that night."

Quietly, Winfield said, "Or maybe you came out of the club and witnessed the attack on Harry."

The woman stared at Winfield and looked as if she was going to deny his accusation, but she never got the words out. Instead tears pooled in her eyes again, and she broke down, sobbing incoherently.

The lieutenant looked over at Mackie and got a slight nod. Winfield stood and leaned over Maria Skouris's chair. Putting a gentle hand on her shoulder, he said, "It's okay, Maria. We know you are afraid of the men who killed Harry. That's certainly understandable, but with your help, we intend to put those men in jail where they will never hurt anyone again.

Maria Skouris shook her head violently. Between sobs she said, "I can't . . . they'll kill me like they killed Harry . . . please, go away!"

"We can't do that, Maria. It's our job to catch men who hurt people. Those men killed the man you love. Don't you think Harry would want you to help us catch them?"

Slowly, and with more encouragement from Winfield, Maria Skouris began to calm down. Finally she said, "I just can't tell you anything more. The men who killed Harry will get me; I know them."

Winfield said, "They won't touch you because the Los Angeles Police Department can and will protect you."

Looking up at the lieutenant through large, tear-filled eyes, she said, "How can you do that?"

"There are several things we can do. For example, do you have a close friend or relative in the area you could stay with for a few days?"

"My aunt Rosie lives in Long Beach, but I can't go there. I have to work. I really need the money, and if I don't show up, Ricky will fire me!"

"No, he won't. I will talk to your boss this afternoon. I'll tell him you are a material witness in a murder investigation and that we have placed you in protective custody. Under the circumstances, I'm certain he will allow you a few days off, perhaps even with pay."

With her sobs dying away, Maria Skouris said, "Are you sure?"

"I'm sure." After glancing at Mackie, Winfield added, "I will also arrange for a police officer to take you to your aunt's in Long Beach." Turning to Mackie again, Winfield said, "Sergeant, will you please use the pay telephone out in the hall to call the stationhouse and arrange for a patrol officer to come over here and escort Miss Skouris to her aunt's home?"

Mackie nodded and let himself out the apartment door to make the call. Returning a few minutes later, C. K. resumed his seat on the couch and said, "Patrol Officer Otis will be here within the next half-hour with a patrol car to drive Miss Skouris to Long Beach."

Still standing next to Maria Skouris's chair, Winfield said, "Thank you, Sergeant. Now, Maria, please tell us what you saw when you left the Club Fiesta a few minutes after midnight on Saturday, July third."

She heaved a great sigh, and said, "I left through the back door and started to walk around to the parking area where I was supposed to meet Harry. When I got to the corner, I saw Harry in the middle of a group of men. They were hitting him."

Returning to the couch, Winfield asked, "How many men were hitting Harry?"

"There were three of them."

"Was there enough light to see them clearly?"

"Yes. There's a big electric sign on that side of the building. I could see the men clearly in the light from the sign."

"Could they see you?"

Maria Skouris paused for a moment, apparently imagining the scene in her mind. "I think they could have at first, but none of them looked at me. They were too busy with Harry. When I realized what was happening, I stepped back and peeked around the corner so they couldn't see me."

"Okay, what happened next?"

"Harry was trying to fight them off, but one of the men had a club of some kind. He kept hitting until Harry fell down." Her tears returned, streaming down her cheeks as she said, "He just kept hitting Harry with that club, over and over. It was awful!"

"What did you see then?"

Sniffling, she said, "After a little while, Harry stopped moving. The man with the club hit him a few more times, and then they went though Harry's pockets, taking things. After that, they got into a car and left the club."

"And you say you know the three men?"

Maria Skouris paused a moment to wipe her eyes on the sleeve of her bathrobe and then said, "Yes. They spend a lot of time at the club."

"Okay, let's start with the man who was beating Harry with the club. What is his name?"

"Everyone calls him Tex. I've heard his last name, but I can't remember it for sure. It begins with a K, like Klingerman or Klubman."

Winfield and Mackie looked at each other, and Mackie asked the question that occurred to both of them. "Could the man's name be Clugman?"

"Yes! That's it."

The mental image of a Texas wanted circular for Eugene Clugman was still in Winfield's mind as he asked, "Can you describe Tex Clugman?"

"Yes. He dresses like a fancy cowboy—you know, in western clothes with a big cowboy hat and boots. He's kind of tall and thin."

As C. K. added her description to his notes, Winfield asked, "What about the other two men?"

"One of them is called Cubes. His last name is Conway. I think they call him Cubes because he likes to shoot dice. He's short and kinda fat. He's got a red face and he's almost bald. He sweats a lot.

"The other man is called Lou. He's Italian. His last name is Rossini or something like that. He's about average size and kind of dark—I mean, he has dark hair and dark eyes. He acts kind of nervous all the time, like a cat—always looking around like somebody is going to jump out and get him."

"Do you know if Harry knew these men?"

"Oh, yes, he knew them. He was always playing cards with Cubes and Lou. Harry should have known them; they took enough money off him. Harry would drink too much, and then he always lost at cards. I can't prove it, but I think Cubes and Lou might have been cheating when Harry got so drunk he didn't notice."

"And these men are regulars at the Club Fiesta?"

"Yes. Well, Cubes and Lou are there all day, every day. It's almost like they live there. The other man, Tex, isn't there so much. He comes in one or two nights a week, mostly to drink and talk. He doesn't play cards—at least, not that I've seen."

"You're doing great, Maria. Just one more question. You said all three men left the club that night in an automobile. Can you describe it?"

Maria Skouris thought for a moment. Finally she said, "I'm not very good about cars. It's a big one, though, with a cloth top like one of those big touring cars with four doors. The top was up that night."

"Do you remember the color of the automobile?"

"Well, the top is black. The metal part is a dark color, maybe dark blue."

Winfield looked at Mackie and said, "Can you think of anything we've missed, Sergeant?"

C. K. finished the last note he was adding to his book and said, "I think that covers everything for now. We'll need the address of Miss Skouris's aunt in Long Beach and her telephone exchange, if there is one."

Seemingly much calmer, Maria Skouris stood and said, "I have all that written down in my address book."

Winfield also stood. He watched the woman open a small drawer in the table below the window. She drew out a small personal address book and thumbed through the pages. When she found the entry she was looking for, she held the book out to Mackie.

As Mackie copied the aunt's information, Maria Skouris turned to Winfield and said, "I'm sorry, Mister . . . ."

"Winfield."

"I'm sorry, Mister Winfield, for getting so upset. I just loved Harry so much, and I miss him terribly. Ever since that night I've been terrified that those men saw me and were going to hurt me."

"That's certainly understandable. It's sad that you had to see what you saw, but I'm glad you did. With your testimony we can put the men who killed Harry behind bars where they belong."

Maria Skouris paused for a moment, and Winfield thought maybe the idea that she would be required to testify against the killers in court was just sinking in. If it was, she said nothing about it. Instead she asked, "What will happen to those men?"

"Well, murder is a capital offense in California, so they will very likely hang for their crimes." Changing the subject, Winfield said, "Your police escort will be arriving pretty soon. Why don't you go freshen up a little and pack a bag for your visit to your aunt?"

She simply said, "Okay," and disappeared into a room Winfield assumed to be the bedroom.

Closing his notebook, Sergeant Mackie stood and handed Maria's address book to Winfield. "It might not be a good idea to leave this behind. Miss Skouris really ought to take it with her."

Before Winfield could agree, they heard a knock on the apartment door. The lieutenant opened it, and Paul Otis snapped to attention on the other side of the threshold. "Patrol Officer Otis reporting as ordered, sir."

"Glad to see you, Otis. Come in. Sergeant, do you have some instructions for Patrol Officer Otis?"

"I do. Otis, your assignment is to drive Miss Maria Skouris to Long Beach. She will give you the address. Miss Skouris is a crucial witness in the Harry Lee murder case, and we are taking her out of town for her protection while we round up the guilty parties. I want you to keep a sharp eye on the other cars around you on your way to Long Beach to be sure you are not followed. If you think you are being followed, you are to drive straight to the nearest L.A.P.D. stationhouse and call me. Then stay put until you hear back from me. Understood?"

"Yes, sir."

"Good. When you've delivered Miss Skouris to her aunt's house, come back to the stationhouse and resume your normal duties."

"Yes, sir."

A few minutes later, Maria Skouris returned to the living room carrying her handbag and a small overnight case. With her hair brushed and a little too much lip rouge on, Winfield could see why Mae White described the woman as attractive in a sort of bawdy way. He said, "Miss Skouris, I would like you to meet Patrol Officer Otis. He will escort you to your aunt's. You should stay there until you hear from us. We'll send another officer to pick you up when it's safe for you to come back here."

Otis stepped forward and taking her bag, said, "Good afternoon, Miss Skouris. I'm pleased to meet you."

Maris Skouris nodded to Otis and turned back to Winfield. "Thank you for all you're doing to help me, Mister Winfield. I don't know how much longer I could have gone on if you hadn't come to talk to me."

"You're entirely welcome, Maria. And please don't worry anymore. We'll take care of everything from here on. Oh, and here's your address book. I put one of my cards in it in case you want to call us."

She slipped the address book into her handbag, and Winfield turned to Otis. "Okay, you two had best be going."

A few minutes later the detectives were in Mackie's Dodge. The sergeant executed a U-turn and headed back in the general direction of the stationhouse. He said, "Laddie, once again I must compliment you on some good police work. I seriously doubted we were going to get a word out of that woman, but you put her at ease. Well done."

"Thanks, C. K."

"Okay, what's our next step?"

"How about heading out to the Club Fiesta?"

"Sounds good to me, but first we need to make a quick stop at the stationhouse to make some telephone calls."

"Who are we calling?"

"First, we ought to make a courtesy call to the Long Beach Police Department to let them know we're stashing a material witness in their fair city. And we need to call the sheriff's office."

Winfield said, "That's right. The Club Fiesta is outside our jurisdiction."

"It is indeed, Laddie. I will request a deputy to meet us there. Then if we're lucky enough to find anyone to arrest, it will be done all legal and proper."

THIRTY

To the minds of most Hollywoodians, the downtown area of their fair community is a rectangle on the map bordered by Franklin Boulevard on the north, Sunset Boulevard to the south, Vine Street on the east, and Highland Avenue to the west. It is within this area that they shop, dine, and see moving picture shows.

North of Franklin are the swank residential developments like the Hollywoodland tract nestled against the Hollywood hills. Just east of Vine and south of Sunset are the tree-lined streets of the community's middle-class neighborhoods. Further to the east and south property values drop off to provide affordable housing for working-class residents like Maria Skouris. These are also the industrial areas of Hollywood where small manufacturing plants and woodworking shops compete for space with land-hungry motion picture studios.

The region west of Vine, however, is something altogether different, for in this area are the last vestiges of orange orchards, vineyards, and other agricultural crops upon which the first settlers of the Cahuenga Valley relied for their livelihoods. And if you drive west on Sunset, as Winfield and Mackie were doing, to the point where the road jogged southwest to avoid the fringes of the Hollywood hills, you come to the virtual no-man's land known locally as the Sunset Strip.

To the best of anyone's memory, the term "strip" was first used by a newspaper reporter bemoaning the terrible condition of Sunset Boulevard along the mile-and-a-half section between Hollywood and Beverly Hills. He referred to this barely paved section of the boulevard that deteriorated into a dustbowl in summer and a swamp in winter as the "county strip of Sunset" because it was outside the Los Angeles city limits and thus maintained by undermanned and overworked county road crews. Ultimately, the name was shortened to the "Sunset Strip."

Road conditions aside, the primary reason the Sunset Strip is of any significance whatsoever to Hollywoodians is found in differences between the laws of the city of Los Angeles and the county of Los Angeles. The county, it seems, takes a more casual stand on vice. Gambling casinos, for example, are strictly forbidden within the city limits but are quite acceptable in the county. And as all law-abiding citizens know, one sin fosters others, such as prostitution and the consumption of alcohol, which are illegal even in Los Angeles County. This factor, along with an overburdened sheriff's department, and perhaps the willingness of deputies to overlook certain infractions in exchange for compensation, resulted in the establishment of many dens of iniquity along the Sunset Strip. The Club Fiesta was well known to law enforcement officers as one of the most iniquitous of those dens.

Since Mackie asked that a deputy sheriff meet them a few hundred feet down the road from the club so as not to alert the suspects of their arrival, he drove past the Club Fiesta. Having not visited the notorious establishment before, Winfield paid close attention to its layout as they passed.

The club sat all by itself between two vacant lots on the south side of Sunset. It was a long, narrow building sitting perpendicular to Sunset with its parking area to the left. A large neon sign overlooking the parking area spelled out "Club Fiesta" in bright red letters between a pair of fading sombreros painted on the wall. From what Winfield could see as they passed, the club's entrance appeared to face the parking area.

About two hundred feet further along Sunset, Mackie spotted a black, Chevrolet four-door sedan on the shoulder of the road. The white star on its door identified the automobile as belonging to the L.A. County Sheriff's Department. C. K. made a U-turn and pulled up behind the Chevrolet. As he and Winfield climbed down from their Dodge, two uniformed deputies got out of the black Chevrolet. The man emerging from the driver's side wore three chevrons on his shoulder and appeared to be about the same age as Mackie.

As they approached each other, the man with the sergeant's stripes held out his hand and said, "Hello, C. K., you old hound dog. How have you been?"

Mackie shook the man's hand, saying, "No complaints, Dick. How about you?"

"The same as always, just trying to stay a jump ahead of the do-badders out here in the hinterlands. C. K., shake hands with my partner here, Jimmy Hernandez. Jimmy, this is Sergeant C. K. Mackie, the best of L.A.'s finest."

Mackie shook hands with the second deputy, a solidly built man of Latin heritage sporting a mustache and a no-nonsense expression. Gesturing toward Winfield, Mackie said, "Boys, meet Detective Lieutenant Bobby Winfield. Bobby, this is Sergeant Dick Blake."

Once the introductory handshakes were out of the way, Blake got down to business. "How do you fellows want to handle this?"

C. K. deferred to Winfield and the lieutenant said, "Well, we're here to arrest a couple of fellows who were involved in the murder of Harry Lee a few months back. We interviewed an eyewitness to the killing this morning, and she identified two of the three men who murdered Lee as regulars at the Club Fiesta."

Blake said, "You don't say. I'd kind of given up on the Lee case because we couldn't get a lead to save our souls."

"We realize Harry Lee's homicide occurred in your jurisdiction, but we're looking at one of the killers for another murder, so we wanted a crack at him before you fellows take over. Is that agreeable?"

"Sure. We're happy to cooperate, especially since you guys seem to have solved a homicide for us. Who are the guys you're looking for?"

Winfield said, "One of them is a short, fat fellow who goes by the name Cubes Conway. The other one is an Italian named Lou Rossini or something like that."

Blake nodded. "I know both of them, and your witness is right. They hang out at the Fiesta most of the time. Lou's last name is Rossellini. Which of those two are you interested in for your murder case?"

"Actually, we're interested in the third guy, a fellow named Tex Clugman. We're hoping to pick up the other two and get one or both of them to roll over on this Tex character. Then we have a reason to pick him up and put some pressure on him about the other case."

Blake said, "Got it. One more thing before we go in. You want to watch out for Lou Rossellini. He's quick and mean. He also carries a switchblade pig-sticker, usually in his right-hand coat pocket."

"Thanks, Sergeant, I'll bear that in mind. We were told this place has two entrances, the main entrance and a back door. Is that right?"

"Yup, you've got it straight."

"Then, unless you've got a better suggestion, I think two of us—C. K. and Deputy Hernandez—should cover the exits while you and I go in and see if our suspects are there. If they are, you can do a legal arrest and take them to the Hall of Justice. We'll follow you and interrogate them there. That sound okay?"

"Sounds like it ought to work. Let's get to it. Hey, C. K., I don't see your sidearm. Maybe you'd better get it."

Mackie simply said, "Don't think I'll need it, Dick. Let's go."

Blake and Winfield gave Hernandez time to jog around to the club's rear door, and then they walked through the front door. Inside, the Club Fiesta was so dark it took a few seconds for the officers' eyes to adjust. When they did, Winfield saw a bar with empty shelves to his right and a dining room to his left. At the far end of the dining room a pair of swinging doors led to what the lieutenant guessed was the kitchen.

The dining room's décor made a meager attempt at festiveness with a few piñatas hanging from the ceiling and some colorful serapes tacked to the walls between faded travel posters advertising exotic Mexican destinations like Mexico City and Tijuana. Straight ahead from the main entrance Winfield saw a hallway, and about halfway down the hall, an arrow pointing to the left with the words "Card Room" painted on it hung from the ceiling.

The only dining room table in use was occupied by a couple of young men in work clothes. They looked up from their coffee cups and watched the officers with interest. Blake said, "If they're here, Rossellini and Conway will be back in the card room."

Walking down the hallway with Blake close behind, Winfield noted a stairway on his right leading to the club's second floor and a pair of doors on his left marked "His" and "Hers." Entrance to the card room was gained through two old-fashioned, saloon-style swinging doors on the left beyond the restroom.

Winfield and Blake looked over the tops of the swinging doors before going into the card room. Four men at a table just inside the doors were deeply involved in what appeared to be a penny-ante game of five-card stud poker. The only other occupants of the card room were two men sitting at a table in the far corner. There were no cards on their table, and they seemed to be just sitting there smoking cigarettes and drinking what looked like beer from tall Pilsner glasses. They fit Maria Skouris's description of Conway and Rossellini to a T.

Confirming Winfield's observation, Blake said quietly, "Those are our boys at that back corner table."

At that moment the Italian man looked up and made eye contact with Winfield. The lieutenant said, "Yeah, and Lou has made us. Let's go."

Side by side, the two officers pushed the swinging doors open and walked into the card room. Conway stared at them but remained seated. Rossellini stood quickly and, shoving his right hand in his coat pocket, began edging his way to Winfield's right. Winfield, who was on Blake's right said, "You take Conway; I'll deal with Lou."

With that the two officers separated, Blake walking directly toward Conway's table and Winfield moving to his right toward Rossellini. The lieutenant saw the man's dark eyes darting around the room, sizing up his situation. Lou continued moving to Winfield's right, and when only one table separated the two men, they heard Blake say, "Conway, you are under arrest for the murder of Harry Lee. Stand up, turn around, and put your hands over your head."

Winfield watched Rossellini's eyes shift in Blake's direction for a second. Then his right hand came out of his pocket and the lieutenant heard a distinct metallic click as a switchblade stiletto knife flashed in his hand. Winfield said,

"Don't be stupid, Lou. We've got the exits covered. Drop the knife and put your hands over your head."

Rossellini glared hatred at Winfield and said, "You ain't getting me that easy, copper."

Winfield picked up a wooden chair from the table between them and held it in front of him with its legs pointed at Rossellini in the fashion of a circus lion tamer. Moving quickly as a cat, Rossellini upended the table and made a running break for it to Winfield's left. Reacting with equal speed, Winfield stepped back and to his left to avoid the table careening toward him. At the same time he thrust the chair he was holding toward Rossellini's legs.

As Winfield hoped, Lou's legs became entangled in the chair's legs and the man sprawled forward, landing hard on the card room floor. Rossellini still held the knife, though, and as he turned quickly to fend Winfield off, he found himself looking directly into the barrel of the lieutenant's thirty-eight caliber revolver. Rossellini froze and dropped his knife.

Winfield said, "Okay, Lou, now you're getting smart. Stand up slowly and raise your hands."

Still glaring at the lieutenant, Rossellini did as he was told. When he was upright, Winfield said, "Turn around and put your left hand behind your back."

Rossellini complied, and exchanging his revolver for a pair of handcuffs, Winfield fitted one of the bracelets snugly to the man's left wrist. Then he pulled Lou's right hand down and cuffed it. After patting Rossellini down, Winfield picked up the man's knife and glanced toward Blake, who had cuffed Conway and was pushing the man toward the card room doors. The excitement apparently over, the men playing stud returned to their game.

Outside the Club Fiesta, Blake and Winfield sat their prisoners down on the ground, and Deputy Hernandez sprinted down Sunset to fetch the sheriff's automobile. The lieutenant handed Rossellini's knife to Blake and said, "Good call on the switchblade, Sergeant. Lou would have caught me off guard if you hadn't told me what to watch out for."

Blake smiled at Winfield. "I'm not so sure about that, Lieutenant. You moved pretty quick in there." Turning to Mackie, Blake held up Rossellini's knife and added, "You've got yourself quite a partner there, C. K. The Eye-tie pulled this on him, but the lieutenant put him on the floor as slick as you please."

Mackie glanced at Winfield and said, "Oh, the lad has his moments."

With the prisoners stowed in the back of their Chevrolet sedan, the deputies headed for the County Hall of Justice on Temple Street in downtown Los Angeles. Mackie went to recover his Dodge, and Winfield went back into the Club Fiesta for a brief conversation with the club's manager, Ricardo Mendez, who'd come down from his upstairs office to see what all the fuss was about.

Facing Mendez in the empty bar, Winfield said, "I'm sorry for the interruption to your business this afternoon. I'm afraid it couldn't be helped."

Mendez nodded, but said nothing. The lieutenant continued, saying, "I wanted to talk with you about Maria Skouris."

The man's expression remained solemn. "What about her?"

"We have taken her into protective custody, so she's going to miss a few days of work. I want to be sure Maria will still have a job when she comes back."

Mendez shrugged. "Maybe she will, unless I find someone better to replace her."

"Mister Mendez, I don't think you understood me. Miss Skouris will have a job when she comes back. Does that make my meaning clearer?"

The man blinked and said, "If you say so, Lieutenant."

"I do say so. And what's more, being the good, civic-minded citizen you are, I'm sure you won't dock Miss Skouris's pay for the days she misses while helping us bring murderers to justice."

Mendez frowned. "You are awfully pushy for a city cop who has no authority here."

Winfield gave Mendez a friendly smile. "Oh, there is a strong spirit of cooperation between us and the county sheriff's office. You have a pretty sweet deal here because some deputies choose to overlook your violations of the Volstead Act and a few other laws. One telephone call from me, however, and the eyesight of those deputies will suddenly improve."

Mendez's eyes narrowed. "Okay, Lieutenant. We do things your way this time. Maybe next time things will be different."

"Mister Mendez, it is very unlikely there will be a next time for either of us. Good day, sir."

It took about thirty minutes for Mackie to drive from the Club Fiesta to the Hall of Justice. Driving down Western Avenue toward Beverly Boulevard, C. K. said, "I gather things got a little sticky back there at the club."

"A little. Lou doesn't care much for policemen. He pulled his trick knife and tried to leave the party early."

"And you taught him some manners, I take it?"

"I guess you could say that. How do you think we should handle the interrogations of Mister Conway and Mister Rossellini?"

After a moment's thought, Mackie said, "Well, based on what little I observed of them, I'm not hopeful for much cooperation from your friend, Lou. As you pointed out, he doesn't seem to care for policemen. Mister Conway, however, strikes me as someone who might be very cooperative if he sees that his other option is the hangman's noose."

"That's what I was thinking. You want to take the lead?"

"If you like. We need to be sure Blake or Hernandez is in the room, though. Technically, this is their case, and they will be the ones taking it to the district attorney. Also, I will fill Blake in about what Maria Skouris told us, and I'll give him the address of her aunt in Long Beach so they can question her officially."

"Okay, just be sure Blake understands that Maria is scared out of her mind. He needs to protect her. Okay?"

"That I will, Laddie. Dick Blake is a good cop. He'll handle it correctly and by the book."

When they got to the new Hall of Justice building—a ten-story, granite, beaux arts edifice—Mackie pulled into a parking space reserved for official vehicles. Entering through a rear entrance, the detectives made their way down a flight of stairs to the sheriff's lock-up in the basement.

Blake was waiting for them in the booking room. He said, "We split Rossellini and Conway up so they won't have a chance to compare stories. Jimmy is handling the booking."

Mackie said, "Thanks, Dick. I'll write up a report of everything we have on the Harry Lee case and get it to you first thing in the morning. The long and the short of it is we need to get either Conway or Rossellini to corroborate the witness's story that this fellow, Tex Clugman, was the ringleader in the attack on Harry Lee. It turns out Clugman is also involved in the Lillian Lawrence murder investigation, but we don't have anything connecting him to the Lawrence case except that Harry Lee was Miss Lawrence's father."

"We don't think Clugman killed her, but he works for our prime suspect, so we need all the leverage we can get to make him spill what he knows about Lillian Lawrence's death." Mackie showed Blake the Texas wanted circular on Clugman and continued, "Clugman is already wanted for murder in Texas, so if we can get one of those guys from the club to give him up, we should be able to convince him to cooperate."

Blake shook his head. "This is a big one, isn't it? No wonder you were so anxious to nail Conway and Rossellini. They're the little fish that will help you catch the whale. Which one do you want to talk to first? I'd suggest Conway."

Mackie nodded. "That's what we're thinking. Obviously you need to be in on the interrogation, but do you mind if we take the lead?"

"Not at all. If you get what you want out of either one of them, I'll have a stenographer write up the statement so we can add it to the evidence against these birds."

Mackie, Winfield, and Blake entered a small windowless room that contained a table, four chairs, and one Cubes Conway. Despite being less than a year old, the interrogation room already reeked of stale tobacco smoke.

It was also stuffy, but Mackie was pretty sure that fact only accounted for part of the sweat covering Conway's face.

The sergeant sat down opposite Conway while Winfield and Blake took up positions behind the man, adding to his uneasiness. C. K. just stared at Conway for a while. Dressed in a pinstripe suit, the man appeared to be in his late thirties. After staring at Conway for a while, making the man even more nervous, Mackie finally said, "Okay, Mister Conway, here's the situation in a nutshell. We have an eyewitness who says you and Rossellini killed Harry Lee out in the Club Fiesta's parking area. That in itself earns you a trip to the gallows. We also know another man was involved. What you tell us about that man might just get you off the gallows and into prison for a life sentence. Now, life in prison might not be a pleasant thought, but it is a far sight better than dangling from a rope until your neck snaps. Are you following me here?"

Wiping the sweat from his face with his shirt sleeve, Conway said quietly, "Yeah, I follow you."

"Alright, Mister Conway, who was the third man with you when you killed Harry Lee?"

"You got that part all wrong. Me and Lou didn't kill Harry. The man you want is Tex Clugman. The whole thing was his idea. He killed Harry. He kept beating him with a piece of shovel handle until Harry was dead. Me and Lou just held Harry so he couldn't get away. Tex killed him."

Winfield and Blake were jotting notes as quickly as they could, but in his eagerness to shift the blame for Harry Lee's murder to Clugman, Conway was going too fast for them. Winfield signaled C. K. to stop for a minute so they could catch up.

Mackie leaned back in his chair and watched the man across the table from him sweat. After a minute or so, when Winfield nodded, Mackie said, "Why should I believe your story, Mister Conway?"

"Because it's the truth. Tex told us he needed to teach Harry a lesson. He said he'd pay me and Lou a hundred bucks each to help him out and keep our traps shut. We only went along with it cuz of the money. I swear that's the honest truth."

"Okay, suppose I believe you for a minute. Why did Tex Clugman want Harry Lee dead?"

Conway shook his head. "We didn't know Tex was gonna kill him. He just said he was gonna teach Harry a lesson."

"Did he tell you why?"

"Tex said Harry was being a pain in the ass to his boss, so he needed to teach the guy a lesson."

"Did Tex say who his boss was?"

Conway thought for a moment. "No, he didn't say. But Tex works at one of them places where they make motion pictures, so it would be somebody there."

"If Tex only wanted to teach Harry a lesson, why did you fellows take his jewelry and wallet?"

"Jewelry? Oh, you mean Harry's ring and watch. That was Tex's idea, too. He said taking Harry's stuff would make it look like a robbery instead of what it really was."

Mackie paused again to let Winfield and Blake catch up with their notes. "You claim you didn't know Tex Clugman was going to kill Harry Lee. Do you think that was his intent all along or did things just sort of get out of hand?"

"Oh, he meant to kill Harry, alright. I didn't think so at first, but the way he kept beating on Harry with that shovel handle . . . I mean, I thought maybe Tex was just angry and got carried away, but I could see his eyes out there. He was cool as a cucumber, just hitting Harry over and over as hard as he could."

"Okay, Mister Conway, let's see if I've got your story straight. You say Tex Clugman hired you and Lou Rossellini for one hundred dollars each to help him 'teach Harry Lee a lesson,' but you believe Clugman planned to kill Lee all along. Is that right?"

"Yeah, that's right. Me and Lou, we wouldn't have had nothin' to do with it if we'd knowed Tex was gonna kill Harry. Hell, I liked Harry. We played poker almost every night at the club. He was an okay guy."

Picking up on Conway's comments, Mackie changed the direction on the interrogation. "We understand Harry wasn't a very good gambler. He ran up some pretty big gambling debts, didn't he?"

Conway nodded. "Yeah, Harry lost a bundle nearly every night. Some nights, when he got into a big game, he dropped a couple of grand. Ricky Mendez—he's the boss of the club—he gave Harry credit because he knew Harry was good for it."

"Tell me, Mister Conway, was Harry really that bad a gambler or was something else going on?"

Conway hesitated. "I don't get what you mean."

"Sure you do, son. Those games at the club were rigged so Harry Lee would lose, weren't they?"

"Well, they might have been. I don't know nothing about that. I always played fair and square with Harry."

Mackie stared Conway in the eye and said, "Cubes, you've already confessed to being an accessory to murder. You can't get into much more trouble than that. Now would be a good time to confess the rest of your sins. That's the only thing that's going to keep you off the gallows."

Conway wiped his face with his sleeve again. "Okay, okay. You gotta understand, I don't know any of this first-hand, but I heard that Tex wanted to make sure Harry lost a lot of money, so he set things up with Ricky to make sure that's what happened. I don't know if they used rigged dice or what, but nobody could lose as much money as Harry did on legit games. But it was Harry's fault, too. He drank too much. Drinkin' and playin' don't mix. If he'd been sober, Harry woulda knowed he was being cheated."

Mackie sighed. "I don't suppose it ever occurred to you to tell an okay guy like Harry that he was being taken for a ride."

"Well, I thought about it I guess, but if Ricky found out I spilled the beans, I might've got banned from the club or beat up or somethin'. I didn't want that to happen!"

"You're a real pal, aren't you, Cubes?"

Conway just stared back at Mackie with a hurt look on his face. Finally Mackie looked up at Winfield and Blake and said, "You fellows have any questions you want to ask Mister Conway here?"

Winfield shook his head and Blake said, "No, C. K., I think I've got all I need for now."

Standing, Mackie said, "Then let's get out of here. This place stinks."

A few minutes later Winfield and Mackie were on their way back to Hollywood. Winfield said, "Nice job of interrogation, C. K. You got Conway to spill his guts in no time at all."

Without taking his eyes from the road, Mackie shook his head. "Not much of a challenge in that. Conway is no killer. He was so scared I probably could have gotten him to admit being Jack the Ripper."

"But you bought his story about Tex Clugman, right?"

"Yeah, I think he was telling the truth. Maybe not the whole truth, but all the truth we need. What's our next step?"

Winfield looked at his wristwatch. "It's four-fifteen. Let's head back to Western National's east lot. Maybe we can catch Clugman before he leaves for the day."

"You planning on arresting him tonight, are you?"

"Is there any reason not to? We've got Maria Skouris's story confirmed by Cubes Conway that Clugman murdered Harry Lee, plus we've got that wanted circular from Texas. There's no sense in giving Clugman a chance to catch wind of what we're up to and vamoose before we can arrest him."

"There's no reason to wait that I can think of. I just wanted to make sure we were both on the same track, but if we're going to get to the studio before he leaves, we'll have to step on it. I guess I'll have to use that God-awful siren gadget to move some of this traffic out of our way. Hang on."

With that, C. K. pushed a button on the dashboard and his siren began to scream. As the automobiles in front of them gave way, he stepped down harder on the accelerator pedal and the black Dodge roadster demonstrated why the L.A.P.D. patrol officers who drove Fords were jealous of the detectives who got Dodges.

THIRTY-ONE

Detectives Mackie and Winfield signed onto Western National's east lot at four-thirty-five by the lieutenant's wristwatch. Winfield instructed Mackie to follow the road ahead straight back until it jogged around the scenery shop about two thirds of the way toward the back of the lot.

Just after passing the scenery shop, Winfield told Mackie to make the right turn that would take them to the horse stable and, if the lieutenant was remembering correctly, to the tiny shack Tex Clugman used as an office. They made the turn and Winfield studied the buildings ahead. He spotted the horse stable coming up on their left and the point where the road turned right just beyond it. Clugman's shack had to be right at the point where the road turned.

It was then that he saw a dark blue touring automobile pull out onto the road ahead. The car turned onto the road in the same direction Mackie and Winfield were going which would take it to the main gate. Winfield said, "That might be Clugman."

Slowing, Mackie said, "It matches Maria Skouris's description of the auto Harry Lee's killers used to leave the Club Fiesta alright. Where does this road end up?"

"Back at the main gate. If that's Clugman, he's leaving the lot."

"You want me to catch up or do you want to see where he's headed?"

"Let's see where he's going."

Mackie followed the road around to their right, and they saw the touring car ahead. It was approaching the large building Winfield remembered housed film stages one, two, and three. The lieutenant said, "The road turns right again just after that big building. From there it joins the road we came in on. A left turn there takes us back to the main gate."

The sergeant hung back until the touring car made its right turn around the film stage building, and then he increased his speed. Slowing again where the road turned right, they saw the automobile ahead turn left toward the lot gate.

Mackie sped up again, and they got to the main road just in time to see the dark blue touring car turn right onto Santa Monica Boulevard from the gate. Mackie hit the accelerator and swung his Dodge up to the gate. The security guard stepped up to sign them out, but the sergeant interrupted him, saying, "Was that Tex Clugman in the car that just left the lot?"

The guard nodded and started to hand Mackie his clipboard to sign out, but the sergeant pulled past him and swung right onto Santa Monica, accelerating hard as he made the turn. Winfield watched the traffic ahead intently. Mackie asked, "Do you have him in sight?"

"I think so. He just went through the intersection at Cole."

The sergeant kept his right foot down hard on the accelerator pedal until they passed Cole. Winfield said, "He's still up there."

By the time the detectives reached the intersection at Las Palmas, Mackie had closed to within two hundred feet of the touring car, which was close enough for Winfield to identify it as a Buick. Leaving a couple of cars between them and Clugman, the sergeant slowed to the speed at which traffic was flowing and said, "This is about as close as we can get without taking a chance on him seeing us."

"This is fine. Now we can just sit back and see where Tex is headed."

- - -

Tex Clugman took his eyes off the traffic beyond the long nose of his big luxurious Buick long enough to take a quick glance at the string-tied, brown paper package on the seat beside him. He'd lied to Mister Bromfeld a few hours earlier when the boss man asked if he took care of burying the package out at the ranch. Tex saw no sense in upsetting Mister Bromfeld by saying he hadn't gotten around to it yet. Besides, the job was as good as done now anyway.

It would only take an hour or so to get to the ranch, and Tex figured when he got there it wouldn't take long to find some soft dirt out behind the ranch house and bury the package with a shovel he'd borrowed from the stable. After that, an hour back to town and by seven-thirty he'd be all set to dig into a big ol' steak at the Club Fiesta.

Of course, Tex had peeked inside the package even though Mister Bromfeld told him not to, and Tex couldn't figure for the life of him why the boss man wanted to bury a perfectly good shootin' iron. True, it wasn't much of a gun, just a little twenty-two—more of a lady's gun than somethin' a man would carry. But it looked brand spankin' new, and there was even a mostly full box of cartridges for it. Bromfeld was a strange fella; there was no gettin' around that.

That's when Tex had a thought. Maybe the boss man wanted him to bury the little gun cuz he didn't want nobody to know he had it. Sure, that was it. Maybe Mister Bromfeld shot somebody with it and . . . . Well, Tex thought, that was none of his business. The boss man paid him good, so what Mister

Bromfeld wanted from Tex he got, no questions asked. He decided, though, he'd remember real good where he buried the pistol. Knowin' where to find it again might just come in real handy someday, especially if'n he was the only one who knowed where it was hid.

- - -

Half an hour had passed since Winfield and Mackie followed Tex Clugman out of Western National's east lot, and the big Buick ahead of them was still rolling out Santa Monica Boulevard toward the coast. They'd just passed the Los Angeles Golf Club and were coming up on Westwood when Mackie announced, "I'm afraid I've got some bad news, Laddie."

Winfield took his eyes off Clugman's automobile long enough to glance at Mackie. "What's wrong, C. K.?"

"Well, it's poor planning on my part, but I wasn't figuring on a cross-country journey when I came in this morning or I would have filled up the tank. We're just about running on fumes."

Turning his attention back to the Buick up ahead, Winfield said, "Too bad, but it can't be helped. We'll just have to look for Clugman in the morning."

"Maybe not. I have a hunch about where he's going. Remember Bromfeld's ranch up the coast? He might be headed there."

Winfield didn't put much stock in the sergeant's hunch because Bromfeld's ranch was only one of an endless list of possible destinations. Still, he decided, as long as they'd come this far, the ranch was worth a try. "I suppose that's a possibility. Let's make a gasoline stop and then we'll see if your hunch is right."

Mackie pulled into a Texaco Service at Sepulveda. While the attendant filled the Dodge's tank, Mackie checked his notebook for the directions to Rancho Bromfeld he'd gotten from Bromfeld's butler. After pocketing his receipt for the gasoline, Mackie pulled back into the westbound traffic on Santa Monica Boulevard.

By the time they reached the coast, the evening fog was blocking what little remained of the waning daylight. C. K. switched on his headlights and turned right onto the coast highway. There was a distinct chill in the air, and Winfield was grateful that the top on Mackie's Dodge was up to block some of the cold, damp breeze.

A few miles north of Malibu Winfield spotted the small sign identifying Decker Canyon Road and Mackie turned right. After another right turn onto Decker-Edison Road, the sergeant slowed and switched off his headlights, saying, "If Clugman is here, there's no sense in announcing our arrival. The butler said Bromfeld's property was the first drive on the left."

Winfield stared through the gloom for the Rancho Bromfeld gate sign, but the gate was set back from the road about fifty feet and he almost missed it. They were nearly past Bromfeld's drive when Winfield said, "There it is."

Mackie backed up and turned into the drive. They noted that the gate was open wide and a chain with a padlock dangled from the gatepost. Winfield said, "That's a promising sign. Unless they leave the gate open all the time, your hunch might be right."

"Not much sense in having a padlock on the gate if they leave it open."

Without headlights their progress along the dirt drive winding its way up a hillside was slow. At the crest of the hill a dark rectangular shape loomed out of the gloom. Mackie said, "That must be the ranch house, but it's dark and I don't see any signs of life around. I guess we came up here on a wild goose chase. I'm sorry about that, Laddie."

As Mackie started to turn the Dodge around, Winfield said, "Hold it! I just saw a light flash back there somewhere behind the house. I don't know of any wild geese that carry lanterns to see where they're going."

C. K. stopped the automobile and stared in the direction Winfield was pointing. "I don't see it, Bobby. You sure?"

"Positive."

"Then we'd best take a look around."

Winfield noted with some surprise that Mackie removed his service revolver from its clips behind the dashboard. The fact that the sergeant felt their circumstances called for carrying the revolver confirmed Winfield's own sense that they were venturing into harm's way.

Out of the car, the two detectives split up with Winfield edging along the side of the ranch house and Mackie about twenty feet away using a line of trees for cover. Revolver in hand, he peeked around the back corner of the building. The light he saw earlier became visible again. It glowed steadily, and Winfield fixed its position amongst a grove of trees roughly fifty feet ahead.

The dense fog muffled sounds, but the lieutenant was certain he heard faint noises coming from the direction of the light. It sounded as if someone was digging a hole. Looking over at Mackie, Winfield gestured to move forward toward the light.

The sergeant continued along the tree line, while Winfield stepped out from the cover of the ranch house and crouching low, moved quickly to cross the open area ahead of him. He'd covered about half the distance when his foot struck some unseen object in his path. It clattered like an old tin can against a pile of rocks, and the lieutenant froze. Up ahead the lantern light suddenly swing in an arc and went out. A second later the loud report of a large caliber pistol shattered the stillness.

Realizing too late that the white shirt showing through the opening of his suit coat made a perfect target, Winfield dove for the ground, but he felt the solid impact of a heavy slug slam into his left shoulder before he hit the damp earth. Surprisingly, he realized as he brought his revolver to bear on the spot where he'd last seen the light, there was little pain from the bullet wound. Mostly his left arm just felt numb.

He heard Mackie yell, "You in the trees, this is the Los Angeles Police Department. Drop your gun and come out into the open with your hands over your head."

Clugman's reply came almost instantly. "Well now, Mister Policeman, I'm right sorry, but I just can't do that."

Clugman fired again, and Sergeant Mackie immediately answered the shot with two quick rounds from his own pistol. The sounds of sergeant's shots were followed by a brief rustling, and then absolute silence returned to Rancho Bromfeld.

Winfield started to get up and made it as far as his knees before the wooziness set in. He shook his head in an attempt to clear it, and Mackie arrived at his side. "You okay, Laddie?"

"His first shot got me in the left shoulder. I'm just a little dizzy, but I think I'm okay. Did you get him?"

"I heard him go down, but I don't know how badly he's hurt. You stay put a minute while I find out. I'll be right back."

The lieutenant thought he ought to say something, but nothing came to mind, so he just knelt there feeling the world spin around him. Several minutes later he saw the light in the trees again. When it began moving toward him, Winfield raised his revolver. He heard Mackie say, "Relax, Laddie; it's me. Tex Clugman, if that's who he is, won't be doing anymore shooting. I couldn't find a pulse."

Winfield nodded, and Mackie held the light up to the lieutenant's shoulder. "You're losing a lot of blood, Bobby. Let's get you into the house and see if there's a telephone."

After the sergeant made short work of busting the backdoor lock out of its jamb, they discovered that Rancho Bromfeld was equipped with all the modern conveniences, including a working telephone. Half an hour later, the place was abuzz with activity which Winfield observed through a haze that cycled back and forth from barely conscious to reasonably alert. During one of the alert moments he became aware that he was stretched out on a couch in a large, wood-paneled room. Mackie was nearby, involved in an earnest conversation with two sheriff's deputies. Closer to hand, Winfield became aware of some fellow in a white coat wrapping gauze and tape around his upper left arm and shoulder that now hurt like the dickens.

Winfield asked the attendant how bad the wound was, but the haze cycled back to barely conscious and all of the answer he got was something about being lucky. For the life of him, the lieutenant couldn't think of anything lucky about being shot or for that matter, being a clumsy oaf and alerting the gunman to his presence. With that thought, Winfield decided it hurt less to be unconscious, and he stopped trying to stay alert.

When alertness gradually returned on its own, Winfield found the scene had changed. He was now in a hospital ward with lots of beds and very few people around. In fact, the only other person he could see was Sergeant Mackie, who was sitting by the bed making notes in his ever-present notebook.

Trying to sound chipper, Winfield said, "Hello, C. K. How are we doing?"

Mackie looked up from his notebook and said, "Quite well, Laddie. In fact, under the circumstances, you are doing exceptionally well."

"I am?"

"You are. Clugman's slug went clean through the fleshy part of your shoulder and even missed the bone, or so the doctor tells me. Of course, your arm is going to be sore for a while and you'll have to take it easy, but the doctor says there should be no permanent effects from the wound."

Winfield recalled his hazy recollection of a man in a white coat telling him he was lucky and figured that's what he'd been talking about. He asked, "Would you care to fill me in on what happened out there?"

"That's why I'm here, Laddie. Well, that and to take you home. The doctor wants to look at you again, but we should have you out of here shortly.

"As for what happened, after Clugman shot you, I yelled that we were cops and to come out with his hands up. He said he wasn't going to do that and took a shot in my direction.

"Of course, I couldn't see him back there in the trees, but I fired two rounds in the direction of his muzzle flash. I guess I got lucky with one of them. When I went to look at him, he was on the ground with no pulse that I could find. Then we busted in through Bromfeld's back door, and after getting you settled, I called in some reinforcements."

Winfield said, "I'm sorry about what happened out there, C. K. I . . . ."

"You've got no reason to apologize, Bobby. It was pitch black. It might just as easily been me that gave us away."

"Thanks, C. K. Did I see some sheriff's deputies wandering around Bromfeld's place?"

"They were some of the reinforcements I called. Rancho Bromfeld is outside the city limits, so I had to call the sheriff's office to report the shooting. I did that right after calling an ambulance for you. We also had a visit from the country coroner's boys for Tex."

Concerned, Winfield asked, "Are we okay on the shooting?"

"I don't anticipate any problems. It was clear to the deputies that I shot in self defense, so other than a lot of paperwork, I think we're okay."

"We did enter Bromfeld's property without a warrant."

"That's true, but we were in pursuit of a suspect who might have been an intruder on Bromfeld's property. Furthermore, we didn't enter Bromfeld's residence until it became a life or death emergency. Also, we removed no evidence from the property except that which we had good reason to believe the suspect brought with him. I don't foresee a problem with any of that."

"Did you find out what the hell Clugman was doing out there?"

From the floor beside his chair, Mackie picked up a package wrapped in brown paper and tied with string. The wrapping was pulled open at one end. Holding the package up, Mackie said, "It seems he was burying this—a twenty-two revolver and a box of twenty-two cartridges."

"You don't say."

"I do. And I convinced the deputies to let me take this package because it is a crucial piece of evidence in the Lillian Lawrence homicide. I'll drop the pistol and the cartridge box off at our Criminal Investigation Laboratory in the morning so they can lift whatever fingerprints might be on it and test it against the bullet the coroner removed from our victim to see if it's a match."

Winfield, still trying to clear his head, thought about what Mackie told him for a minute. "So, if the test proves that's the murder weapon, the fingerprints should tell us who killed our victim." Remembering the history of the pistol Tom Bell gave Lillian Lawrence, he added, "If that's Miss Lawrence's gun, quite a few people have handled it in the past few months . . . . Tom Bell, Miss Lawrence, Tex Clugman, possibly L. A. Bromfeld, and heaven only knows who else. We're going to need some prints for comparison."

"True. We already have some of them, or we will have. The lab has Miss Lawrence's prints, and by tomorrow they will have Clugman's. And while I was waiting for the doctor to put you back together, I telephoned Tom Bell to see if he would help us get his fingerprints. He was eager to do anything he could to help, and said he would make a trip into town tomorrow and have his prints taken at Central Division."

Winfield said, "We also need Bromfeld's fingerprints. That will be difficult without tipping him off that we're on his trail."

"Not so difficult as you might think. Clarence, the Bromfeld butler, was very cooperative when I saw him yesterday. I'll swing by Bromfeld's tomorrow morning before I go to the crime lab and see if he can loan us something his boss handled recently."

"That won't stand up in court, though, because we won't be able to prove the prints are Bromfeld's."

"That's right, Laddie, but if we get a preliminary match, we'll have grounds to arrest Bromfeld. Once we have him in custody, we can take his fingerprints officially, and that will stand up as evidence. But we mustn't get ahead of ourselves here. We have to take this one step at a time, and the first step is establishing whether or not we actually have the murder weapon."

"It would sure be a nice break if it is. Did you find anything else on Clugman?"

Looking at his notes, Mackie said, "He had a wallet with around fifty bucks in it but no identification. He also had a pocket watch that matches Mae White's description of the watch and chain Lillian Lawrence gave her father. The inscription on the back of the watch confirms that. It says, 'To Father with love, Lilly.' So with the watch as evidence to support the stories of Maria Skouris and Cubes Conway, there's a good possibility we've solved the Harry Lee murder case for the sheriff, even if Clugman is no longer amongst the living to pay for his crime."

Winfield said, "I sure wish we could tie Bromfeld to Harry Lee's murder, but without a statement from Clugman incriminating his boss, all we have is the hearsay statement from Cubes Conway, and that won't do the D.A. any good in court."

"No, it won't. Unless something else turns up, it looks as if Bromfeld gets a free ride on Lee's murder."

Winfield thought things over again and said, "What about Bromfeld? When he finds out we caught Clugman burying the Lawrence murder weapon—assuming we can prove it is the murder weapon—on his ranch, he'll know we're on to him. There's a good chance he could disappear on us."

"We've got twenty-four hours. I talked the deputies into keeping mum on everything that happened tonight for that long. If the crime laboratory gives us results that incriminate Bromfeld before tomorrow night, we can arrest him for Lillian Lawrence's murder before he knows anything about what happened tonight."

Winfield frowned. "That is if Captain Royce will let us do our job."

"I've already spoken with the captain, Laddie. He said if the laboratory boys prove the pistol is our murder weapon and they can match Bromfeld's fingerprints to those on the pistol, we can make our arrest."

The lieutenant shook his head. "We still have an awful lot of 'ifs' between us and an arrest." After a pause, he added, "Would you please see if you can round up that doctor so we can get the heck out of here?"

When Sergeant Mackie returned after several minutes, he had the emergency doctor in tow. The doctor poked and prodded Winfield for a few minutes and asked him some questions. Finally the doctor said, "Okay, Mister Winfield, I will release you, but only on the conditions that you promise to see your own doctor during the next few days to get the dressing changed and make sure the wound hasn't become infected and that you take it easy for a while. You lost quite a bit of blood and your system needs some time to recuperate."

Fifteen minutes later Mackie and Winfield were back in C. K.'s Dodge heading for Hollywood. Mackie said, "Tomorrow morning I'll take care of rounding up Bromfeld's prints and taking the whole kit and caboodle to the crime laboratory downtown. I'll call you at home as soon as we have some results."

"Like hell you will! I'll meet you at the station like usual and, we'll both take care of those things. I'm not going to be left out of the finish of this thing."

Mackie started to remind Winfield of the doctor's instructions but stopped because he knew damned well it wouldn't do any good. He simply said, "Okay, Lieutenant, as you wish."

THIRTY-TWO

Thursday - September 9, 1926

Thursday morning Detective Lieutenant Winfield found himself up with the chickens again but it was pain and anxiety rather than memories of a pleasant evening with Mae White, that were on his mind as the sun came up. The soreness in his arm was as bad as any pain he'd experienced, but then he'd never been shot before, either. His anxiety came from the knowledge that their entire case against L. A. Bromfeld hung on the Criminal Investigation Laboratory's inspection of the pistol Tex Clugman was burying at Rancho Bromfeld.

When C. K. walked into the detective room at the Sixth Precinct stationhouse, Winfield was already halfway through his second cup of coffee. The sergeant said, "How's the arm this morning, Bobby?"

Winfield looked up, and putting on the best smile he could muster, he said, "Tolerable. How are you this morning?"

"All things considered, not bad. After cleaning my revolver last night and writing up a statement for the sheriff's deputies, I got to bed kind of late, but I'll catch up on my sleep tonight."

The lieutenant looked at his wristwatch and said, "It's almost eight o'clock. Bromfeld has left for the studio by now. You ready to head over to his place and see what we can do about getting a fingerprint sample?"

"Sure. Give me just a minute to retrieve our evidence from last night. I stashed Clugman's package in our safe last night just to make sure nothing happened to it."

"That was wise. We've got a lot riding on that pistol. How long do you think it will take the crime lab to get us some results?"

Kneeling at the evidence safe in one corner of their office, Mackie worked the combination dial and said, "I imagine that depends on how busy they are. We've got Captain Royce's weight behind us on this one, though, so that ought to get things moving."

Their ride to Bromfeld's mansion took a little more than thirty minutes because they made a quick pass by Western National Film's east lot to be sure Bromfeld's Packard was in the administration building parking area. It was, so they drove to De Mille Drive with greater confidence that Bromfeld was still unaware of their interest in him.

As usual, Clarence answered their knock at Bromfeld's. Mackie said, "Good morning, Clarence. I apologize for the intrusion, but I'm afraid we need your assistance again."

The butler actually seemed pleased to see them when he said, "Certainly, Sergeant Mackie. I'm happy to help in any way I can."

Winfield was taken aback by the change in Clarence's attitude toward them, and he had to wonder what Mackie said to the man on his last visit to engender such a change. As Clarence showed them into Bromfeld's foyer, Mackie said, "What we need is some object your employer handled recently, something we can use to obtain a sample of his fingerprints."

After a moment's thought, the butler said, "I believe I have just what you need. I'll be right back."

Mackie and Winfield exchanged glances as the butler headed off down the hall. Winfield said, "Clarence is a lot more cooperative than I expected. What did you say to him when you were out here Tuesday?"

C. K. smiled and said, "I simply pointed out the importance of doing his civic duty."

When Clarence returned, he was carrying a drinking glass wrapped in a cloth napkin. He asked, "Will this do? It is the glass in which I served Mister Bromfeld's orange juice this morning. Mister Bromfeld and I are the only ones who have touched the glass since it was washed yesterday."

Mackie accepted the glass, noticing it still contained a few drops of juice. The sergeant said, "Thank you, Clarence. This will do nicely; however, we need to take a sample of your fingerprints so the laboratory can isolate Mister Bromfeld's prints. Is that okay with you?"

"Certainly, sir. It will be a new experience. I've never had occasion to be fingerprinted before."

After taking a set of the butler's prints with the fingerprint kit Mackie carried in his automobile, the detectives climbed back into the sergeant's Dodge and drove to Central Division headquarters on First Street in downtown Los Angeles. Once there, they went directly to the Criminal Investigation Laboratory on the second floor.

While Sergeant Mackie told the woman seated at a desk in the lab's reception area they were there to see Lieutenant Kennedy, Winfield stared with fascination at the laboratory through windows lining the back wall of the reception area. It was a brightly lit room with white walls and a collection of tables holding a variety of interesting looking gadgets. In 1923 the Los Angeles Police Department became the first major metropolitan police force to have such a facility, and even though Winfield had visited the lab several times, the place never failed to fascinate him because he firmly believed what he saw there represented the future of crime solving.

Mackie and Winfield were kept waiting only a few moments before a tall, gray-haired man in a white laboratory coat and wire-rimmed spectacles came out to meet them. Mackie said, "Hello, Jim. How are things?"

"Just fine, C. K. I understand you have some high priority items for us to examine."

The sergeant looked a little surprised. "We do, but how did you know?"

"I tend to remember things Captain Royce tells me when he calls in the middle of the night. He called last night around nine to say you would be in this morning and that I was to give the evidence you brought us our highest priority."

"Thank you, Jim. Have you met Detective Lieutenant Bobby Winfield? He heads our Homicide Division out in the Sixth Precinct."

Kennedy turned to Winfield, and offering his hand, he said, "I believe we've met a time or two. Nice to see you again, Lieutenant. Now, let's go inside and get down to business."

In the lab, Kennedy led them to an empty table covered with a spotless sheet of stainless steel. Winfield set his briefcase on the table and began removing the items it contained, beginning with the paper package Clugman attempted to bury the night before."

Mackie said, "We recovered this package last night. As you can see, it's been opened. That's the way we found it. Looking through the open end of the package, we were able to see that it contains a small caliber revolver and a box of cartridges. It appears to match the description of a firearm given to our victim for her protection by her fiancé—a man named Tom Bell."

Donning a pair of thin, black rubber gloves from his coat pocket, Kennedy carefully removed the revolver and the cartridge box from the package, setting them on the tabletop next to the paper in which they'd been wrapped. Leaning over the table to look more closely at the pistol, he said, "It is a Smith and Wesson Ladysmith, Third Model—a twenty-two caliber revolver with a seven-round chamber and a three-inch barrel."

Examining the pistol more closely with a magnifying glass he took from another coat pocket, Kennedy added, "The nickel finish is in like-new condition, as is the polished wooden grip. What would you like us to do with this revolver, Sergeant?"

"First, we want to know if this is the gun that killed Lillian Lawrence; and second, we want to know whose fingerprints are on it."

Returning the magnifying glass to his coat pocket, Kennedy said, "Alright. We have the slug the coroner removed from your victim, so we'll test fire this revolver and see if their markings match under the microscope. First, however, we'll lift all of the fingerprints we can from it. I could see several sets through my magnifying glass. Do you have prints for comparison?"

Mackie nodded. "Actually, there are several possibilities for comparison, beginning with the victim, whose prints you already have. Then we have a fellow by the name of Eugene Clugman. He's in the county morgue this morning, so they'll have his prints. Another possibility is the victim's fiancé, Tom Bell. I spoke with him last night, and he said he would come in this morning to have his prints taken."

Kennedy said, "Mister Bell was here when I arrived this morning. I have his print sheet on my desk. Any others?"

Removing the orange juice glass, still wrapped in its napkin, from his briefcase and setting it on the table, Winfield said, "Yes, one additional set. This glass was used this morning by our prime suspect. We believe it has two sets of prints on it." The lieutenant brought out the print samples they'd taken from Clarence and added, "This set comes from the second individual who handled the glass this morning, the suspect's butler."

Carefully holding the glass by its base, Kennedy used his magnifying glass to give it a once-over. "Yes, I can see several clear prints. We can lift those without difficulty. One point you must remember, however, is that humans come equipped with ten fingers. We have to hope that any prints your suspect may have left on the revolver are from the same fingers he used to hold the orange juice glass."

Winfield nodded. "We understand that, Jim. How soon do you think you can have some results for us?"

Kennedy stared at the items on his lab table for a moment and replied, "To some extent that will depend on how quickly we get the sample prints from the county morgue."

Mackie said, "Would it speed things up if we went to the morgue and hand-carried Clugman's prints back here?"

"That would certainly help, Sergeant." Looking at his wristwatch, Kennedy added, "It's only about nine-thirty, so if you get those sample prints back to me in short order, I should have the answers you need before lunch. Will that do?"

Winfield said, "We couldn't ask for better. We'll head over to the morgue now. And thanks for moving us to the top of your list this morning."

"You're welcome, but you have Captain Royce to thank for that. I'll get to work now. See you soon with those prints."

It took the detectives about half an hour to make the roundtrip between the coroner's office and Central Division. After dropping the sample prints off at the lab, Mackie said, "Well, Laddie, now we wait."

"Let's drop in on Captain Royce while we're waiting. I want to clarify our marching orders regarding Bromfeld in the event his fingerprints are on the murder weapon. It might save us some time if we did that now."

Captain Albert Royce oversaw the Los Angeles Police Department's Homicide Division from the top floor of Central Division Headquarters. The two walls of his office without windows overlooking downtown Los Angeles were paneled and decorated with photos of current and past police department dignitaries along with framed citations and commendations.

As the captain's receptionist showed them into his office, Royce stood behind a desk commensurate in size with his position and said, "Good morning, detectives. Lieutenant Winfield, it's good to see you up and around so soon after your unfortunate experience last night. How are you feeling?"

Shaking the hand Royce offered, Winfield said, "Thank you, sir. I'm feeling much better this morning."

"Very good, Lieutenant. Now, gentlemen, sit down and tell me to what I owe this unexpected visit. Surely the laboratory results aren't in yet."

Winfield said, "No, sir, we don't have the results yet, but we were told to expect them before noon. And by the way, sir, thank you for instructing Jim Kennedy to give our evidence top priority."

"No thanks are necessary, Lieutenant Winfield. Lillian Lawrence's murder is very much in the public eye, so it behooves the department to resolve her homicide with dispatch. And, I might add, I will be quite impressed with your efforts on this case if it turns out you have positively identified Miss Lawrence's killer. Solving a complex homicide in four days will be quite an accomplishment, assuming that's what you've done. Now, again, why are you here?"

The lieutenant said, "We thought it might save some time to come in while we're waiting for the lab report in order to clarify our instructions in the event the lab tells us L. A. Bromfeld's prints are on the gun that killed Lillian Lawrence."

Royce appeared to deliberate his answer for several moments before saying, "In that event we have no choice but to take Mister Bromfeld into custody and charge him with Miss Lawrence's murder. However, let me make one point very clear. There must be absolutely no doubt about Mister Bromfeld's guilt. The false arrest of a highly-placed citizen in a major case such as this one would be a great embarrassment to the department, and I want no such embarrassments occurring on my watch. Understood?"

"Understood, sir. Positive lab results, along with the other evidence we've compiled, would be conclusive."

"Just the same, Lieutenant, I want you to take your case to District Attorney Keyes before you make your arrest. I've already discussed this case with him in some detail, so he understands our concerns. He will be expecting your call."

A little disappointed that he and Mackie faced yet another bureaucratic hurdle to clear before making their arrest, Winfield said, "Yes, sir. I sincerely hope, however, that Mister Keyes is in his office today because it is imperative that we make our arrest before tonight. By tomorrow morning L. A. Bromfeld will have heard about the incident at his ranch last night, and he'll know we're on to him. If that happens, there's a good chance of him disappearing on us before we can make our arrest."

Speaking in stern tones, Captain Royce said, "That is a risk we may have to take. You will discuss the case with D.A. Keyes before making an arrest. Is that clear?"

"Yes, sir."

Softening his tone somewhat, Royce added, "I will place a telephone call to his office and inform Mister Keyes you may be calling him later this morning for a meeting. That might help insure his availability to you."

"Thank you, sir."

Winfield's frustration was evident to Mackie as the detectives rode the elevator to the ground floor. C. K. said, "Relax, Bobby. Asa Keyes is a no-nonsense sort of fellow. I'm certain he'll see us as soon as possible. He will be as anxious to resolve this case as we are."

"I know that, but . . . ." Realizing that the elevator operator—a disabled L.A.P.D. officer—was listening to their conversation, Winfield left his thought unsaid.

On the first floor, the detectives walked down a long hallway to the Central Division homicide office. It was only a few minutes past ten-thirty, and Winfield planned to kill some of the remaining time by making a couple of telephone calls.

While Mackie chatted with old acquaintances, Winfield placed a call to Maria Skouris at the exchange she gave them for her aunt in Long Beach. As expected, she was relieved that Tex Clugman was no longer a threat to her and that Clugman's accomplices in Harry Lee's murder were behind bars. So when Winfield asked her if she would like him to arrange a ride back to Hollywood for her, she accepted with little hesitation. The lieutenant told her to expect an officer within the hour and that a sheriff's deputy by the name of Blake would be calling her soon for a formal statement. He concluded their conversation by instructing Miss Skouris to call him without delay if she encountered any problems with Club Fiesta manager, Ricky Mendez, regarding her job.

Next Winfield called the Sixth Precinct stationhouse and gave instructions for a patrol officer to pick up Miss Skouris in Long Beach and return her to the Sunset Court Apartments. His last call was to Dick Blake at the sheriff's Hollywood substation. The sergeant wasn't in, so Winfield left a message informing Blake that the eyewitness to Harry Lee's murder was being returned to her home at the Sunset Court Apartments.

By the time he finished his telephone calls, it was eleven-fifteen. Winfield suggested to C. K. that they go back up to the Criminal Investigation Lab in case Kennedy finished examining their evidence sooner than expected.

THIRTY-THREE

At eleven-twenty Winfield and Mackie returned to the Criminal Investigation Lab where the receptionist greeted them with the news she was at that moment typing their evidence report. She offered them seats in the reception area while she finished her typing. Fifteen minutes later the receptionist applied paperclips to an original report and its carbon copy and then disappeared into the lab area.

When she returned a few minutes later, Jim Kennedy was with her. He said, "Come in, gentlemen. I'll go over our findings with you."

Seated in chairs hastily arranged around Kennedy's desk, Winfield and Mackie waited anxiously while Kennedy unclipped the original report and arranged the pages on his desk. Finally he said, "The first bit of good news I have for you is that the Smith and Wesson revolver you brought in is without a doubt the gun that killed Lillian Lawrence. A test bullet fired from it is a perfect match for the bullet the coroner removed from the victim."

Winfield relaxed a little. Regardless of whatever additional evidence the lab found or didn't find, at least they had the gun that killed Lillian Lawrence.

Continuing his report, Kennedy said, "Beyond that, I can tell you that the pistol has not been cleaned since it was last fired. The cylinder contained one spent cartridge.

"Now, the fingerprint situation is a little more complex. Unfortunately, all of the prints on the grip were smeared beyond recognition. We also checked the spent cartridge and found partial prints there, but they were also smeared. So the only useful prints we have are those from the metal surfaces of the pistol.

"We are somewhat fortunate that the pistol was thoroughly cleaned at some point in the not-too-distant past, but before it was last fired, which means what prints we found were clearer than they would have been had the pistol not been cleaned at that time. Also, some of the prints we found were layered one on top of the other, which confuses identification somewhat but does give us something of a chronology for when each person handled the gun."

Winfield stirred in his chair, wishing Kennedy would hurry up and get down to whose prints he actually found. Studying his report again for a moment, Kennedy finally came to the part the lieutenant was waiting for.

"All told, we were able to lift useable prints from four individuals. The oldest prints match those of the victim, Lillian Lawrence. Next we found what we believe are a thumb and forefinger print on the barrel that match the coroner's sample print set for Eugene Clugman. From their position and the way the package was wrapped, it appears those were made by Clugman pulling the pistol at least part of the way out of its packaging and then pushing it back in, as though he wanted to get a better look at it. Since those were the only two of Clugman's prints we found, it's doubtful he fired the pistol.

"Of the remaining prints, the most recent, judging by their position relative to the others, are three that match those on the drinking glass you brought in. While I can't say with any certainty that the owner of those prints actually fired the gun, he definitely was the last person other than Clugman to handle it."

Winfield grinned broadly at Mackie and said, "We have him!"

Looking somewhat less joyful, C. K. asked, "You said you found prints from four individuals. Who was the fourth, Tom Bell?"

Kennedy shook his head. "No. The fourth set of prints does not match any of the samples you provided. In my estimation, they likely belong to a woman or a man with small hands. In either instance, it is unlikely that the owner of the fourth prints fired the weapon.

"And that, gentlemen, is the gist of my report. I will retain the carbon copy along with my original notes to be kept in our files. Here is the original report for you to take. Do you have any questions?"

Accepting the report from Kennedy, Winfield looked at Mackie, who shook his head. Placing the report into his briefcase, the lieutenant said, "Jim, we owe you. Not only did you get the report finished when you said you would, you also gave us the evidence we need to bring a killer to justice. Thank you."

Shaking the hand Winfield offered, Kennedy said, "That's our job. I'm glad we were able to come up with the evidence you need. Often we aren't that successful. This is a new science, and we're still learning."

By Winfield's watch it was a few minutes before noon when they walked out of the lab. He said, "C. K., I'm going down to the homicide room to borrow a typewriter so I can type a summary investigation report for D.A. Keyes. Would you please call his office and see if you can get us on his schedule for this afternoon—maybe at one-thirty?"

"Will do. Then I'll run across the street to the sandwich shop and bring us back some lunch. Will you be able to type alright with your arm in that sling?"

Winfield nodded. "It will slow me down some, but I'll get it done."

It was precisely one-thirty by the wall clock in the district attorney's outer office at the Hall of Justice when Winfield and Mackie walked in and announced their presence to Asa Keyes's secretary. Five minutes later they were seated in D.A. Keyes' office.

Keyes was a somber-looking man with a receding hairline and piercing eyes that intimidated all but the most confident and truthful people he questioned on the witness stand. He stared at Sergeant Mackie for a long moment before turning to study Winfield. He said, "Alright, detectives, let's hear what you have."

Winfield removed his summary investigation report, the Criminal Investigation Lab's findings, and other documents, including Mackie's original crime scene notes, from his briefcase. "We've prepared detailed reports for you, so I'll just hit the highlights. We believe we have sufficient evidence to arrest a man named L. A. Bromfeld for the murder of Lillian Lawrence. That evidence is as follows:

"It was determined at the murder scene that the victim was most likely shot by a left-handed person, and L. A. Bromfeld is left-handed. Despite his denial, the fact that Bromfeld was in Miss Lawrence's hotel room is supported by an El Pantera cigar butt found at the crime scene. El Panteras are quite expensive and unique, and we have a statement from the sole importer of El Panteras west of the Rockies that L. A. Bromfeld is his only customer in southern California.

"Comparing L. A. Bromfeld's account of his time on the night of the murder with the statements of two other witnesses leaves a gap of at least twenty minutes for which he cannot account. That gap is within the coroner's time-of-death window. These facts indicate L. A. Bromfeld had the opportunity to murder Miss Lawrence.

"As for means, a pistol was taken into evidence last night as an employee of L. A. Bromfeld was attempting to bury it on property owned by Bromfeld. This pistol has been conclusively identified by the L.A.P.D. Criminal Investigation Laboratory as the gun that killed Lillian Lawrence. Furthermore, the lab found L. A. Bromfeld's fingerprints on that gun.

"That leaves motive as the last element necessary to establish guilt. We have statements from numerous witnesses that Lillian Lawrence intended to walk away from her contract to make motion pictures at Western National Films, the company managed by L. A. Bromfeld. Further evidence of this is found in Miss Lawrence's behavior. Prior to her murder she sold her home and accepted a marriage proposal with the understanding of her fiancé that she would no longer be making motion pictures.

"According to the suspect's own statements, this decision by Miss Lawrence would have resulted in a considerable loss of revenue to Western National Films unless the company was prepared to risk bad publicity by taking Miss Lawrence to court. According to an officer of the company, however, Western National carried a life insurance policy on the victim that pays the sum of one million dollars in the event of her death. While this amount is far short of Western National's potential earnings had she fulfilled her contract, it is significant compensation gained as the result of her death. So realizing Lillian Lawrence could not be persuaded to stay at Western National, Bromfeld knew the only way his company could recoup their investment in Miss Lawrence without risking the bad publicity of a lawsuit was through her death.

"Very briefly, those are the points of evidence we feel justify the arrest of L. A. Bromfeld."

Asa Keyes took notes on a yellow legal pad throughout Winfield's presentation of the evidence. When the lieutenant finished, Keyes studied his notes for a moment before responding. "You say the murder weapon was recovered last night while an employee of Mister Bromfeld was attempting to hide it. Who was this employee and what statements has he made regarding the pistol?"

Winfield said, "His name is Eugene Clugman, and we have no statements from him because he was killed during a gunfight resulting from his attempt to resist arrest."

Keyes looked up from his notes and glared at the lieutenant. "That is truly unfortunate, Detective. This Clugman might have given valuable testimony had you not been so quick to take his life."

Winfield felt anger rising. "Mister Keyes, we were not, as you put it, 'quick to take' Mister Clugman's life. The circumstances last night were that we came under fire from a man we already knew to be a murder suspect in two states—here and in Texas." Gesturing to his left arm, the lieutenant continued, "He fired on us, wounding me with his first shot. After identifying ourselves as police officers, Clugman gave us no choice but to defend our own lives by returning fire. The man's own actions brought about his death."

Keyes glared at Winfield for a long moment before saying, "Alright, Detective, we can save that discussion for another time. Let me see your reports."

Winfield handed the paperwork to Keyes. The D.A. scanned through the pages quickly and tossed the reports on his desk. Leaning back in his chair, Keyes said, "Assuming, as I must that your reports are accurate, I see adequate evidence here to place L. A. Bromfeld under arrest for the murder of Lillian Lawrence. I instruct you to do so as soon as possible and to deliver him to Central Division Headquarters for booking. I will call Captain Royce and inform him that I have directed you to arrest the suspect.

"Because I am at the moment personally handling another highly public case, I am going to turn the prosecution of Mister Bromfeld over to Assistant District Attorney Abraham Singer. I want you to meet with Mister Singer tomorrow morning at ten o'clock for the purpose of providing whatever additional information he may need to prepare for Bromfeld's arraignment tomorrow afternoon—assuming, of course, that you don't find it necessary to shoot Mister Bromfeld, too. I will inform Mister Singer of the appointment. That will be all until tomorrow morning."

With that, Asa Keyes neatly stacked their paperwork on a corner of his desk and turned his attention to another stack of paper. Winfield and Mackie exchanged glances and left the office.

After making a telephone call to the Sixth Precinct and instructing the desk sergeant to have two patrol officers and a department sedan standing by in thirty minutes, Winfield and Mackie returned to Mackie's Dodge. On the way back to Hollywood, Winfield said, "Well, that was more fun than should be allowed."

Mackie glanced at the lieutenant and said, "You handled Keyes in a very professional manner. I probably should have given you some warning about the D.A.'s manner, but I don't know that it would have helped. There is nothing I could have suggested that would have been an improvement over what you did."

"Thanks, C. K. Bringing a case to Keyes is not something I would want to do very often."

Upon arriving at the Sixth Precinct stationhouse the detectives found Patrol Officers Olmstead and Otis standing next to a department Ford sedan. Sergeant Mackie informed the men of their mission. Then with Mackie and Winfield in the lead, the two-car caravan of official L.A.P.D. vehicles departed for Western National Films.

Jake Blore was manning the east lot entrance, and he gave Mackie a raised-eyebrow look when Mackie gave him a wave and drove onto the lot without stopping. The studio gossip, Winfield thought, would surely be flying by quitting time.

Leaving Otis out in the administration hallway to watch the doors of Bromfeld's inner and outer offices, Winfield, Mackie, and Olmstead walked right past Bessie Shipman toward the door to Bromfeld's inner sanctum. Bromfeld's secretary jumped to her feet and moved to block their entrance to the inner office, saying, "Stop! You can't barge in here like this."

In the lead, Lieutenant Winfield said sternly, "Step out of the way, Miss Shipman, or I'll move you out of the way."

Something in Winfield's tone of voice convinced her he meant business. Glaring at him, she reluctantly stepped aside, saying, "Your superior will hear about this!"

Ignoring the woman's righteous indignation, Winfield opened the door and strode confidently into Bromfeld's inner office. The man rose from his chair, angered by the intrusion. "What is this you are doing here? You cannot be coming . . . ."

Lieutenant Winfield interrupted Bromfeld, saying, "L. A. Bromfeld, you are under arrest for the murder of Lillian Lawrence. Officer Olmstead, take Mister Bromfeld into custody."

As Allen Olmstead stepped forward to put a pair of handcuffs on Bromfeld, the man's face turned bright red and he began screaming at the top of his lungs. "Are you insane? I am not killing Lillian. I am having nothing to do with her death . . . ."

Winfield interrupted Bromfeld again. "Save it for the judge, Bromfeld. We've got you dead to rights. You killed Miss Lawrence and you are going to the gallows for it."

Bromfeld continued screaming and violently pushed Officer Olmstead away. Mackie stepped forward and helped the patrol officer cuff Bromfeld's wrists. They manhandled him out of his office and down the hall with Bromfeld screaming his rage like a mad man, even after Olmstead and Otis got him into the back seat of the Ford. Olmstead slid in after him and Otis climbed into the driver's seat.

Mackie told him, "Otis, take the prisoner to Central Division Headquarters and hold him until I get there. I'll be close behind you."

Otis saluted and said crisply, "Yes, sir."

As the black Ford headed back toward the main gate of Western National Films' east lot, Mackie turned to Winfield, who was leaning on the fender of the sergeant's Dodge. C. K. said, "You look a little worn around the edges, Laddie. Unless you object, I'm going to drop you off at the stationhouse so you can take it easy on that shoulder for a while. I'll take care of seeing that Bromfeld is properly booked."

Winfield did not object, and fifteen minutes later he flopped into the chair behind his desk, feeling as if he'd been through the ringer. It was nearly four-thirty when Winfield heard Mackie and the patrol officers return from Central Division Headquarters.

Mackie walked into the detective room and looked at Winfield. He said, "You feeling any better, son?"

"Much better, thank you. How did it go at Central? Did Bromfeld ever calm down?"

"No, he was still screaming his head off when they dragged him off to a cell. Then just as we were finishing the paperwork, a fellow showed up announcing that he was Bromfeld's lawyer and demanding to know the bail amount.

"Danny O'Brian, the duty booking sergeant, told him bail wouldn't be set until the arraignment tomorrow afternoon. Then the attorney demanded to see his client, and Danny told him he couldn't see Bromfeld until the booking procedure was finished. The guy was still sitting there cooling his heels in the lobby when I left."

"You think the judge will grant bail?"

Mackie shook his head. "It's not likely with a capital offense like murder. Laddie, I don't mean to meddle, but I think it might be a good idea for you to see a physician like the emergency doctor told you to last night."

Winfield managed a smile and said, "I'm a step ahead of you, C. K. I just made an appointment for first thing tomorrow morning. I told the woman on the phone I had to be done in time for a ten o'clock appointment downtown."

"Good. Just remember, though, your health comes first. You won't be much good to the department if you don't take care of yourself."

"I will, C. K. I promise."

Mackie grinned at him. "Sorry, Bobby. You about ready to head for the barn?"

"Pretty soon. I think I'll stick around a little while and make a telephone call or two. The telephone at Missus Haney's is kind of public."

"Alright, son. I'll leave you to your calls. I'm going to call it a day."

As Mackie walked out of the detective room, Winfield called after him, "Have a good evening, C. K."

"You, too, Laddie."

A few minutes after five, Winfield called Mae White's exchange. Her maid answered, "Miss White's residence."

Winfield cleared his throat and said, "Ah, this is Detective Lieutenant Winfield. May I speak with Miss White please?"

"One moment please."

To the lieutenant it seemed as if a good deal more than a moment passed before Mae finally came on the line. She said, "Bobby! I'm sorry to keep you waiting like that. How are you?"

"I'm good; how are you?"

"I'm very good now that I'm talking with you. You sound tired. Are you okay?"

"Well, I'm a little worse for wear today after a little set-to we had last night with Tex Clugman, but I'll survive."

"Tex? What happened?"

"Oh, we followed him out to Bromfeld's ranch intending to arrest him for Harry Lee's murder, but he didn't want to be arrested. Tex shot at us and . . . well, Sergeant Mackie had to shoot him. Tex is no longer with us."

"Oh my! Were you hurt?"

"Not badly. Tex's first round hit me in the shoulder, but the doctor says I'll be . . . ."

"Oh, Bobby! You were shot? That's awful! Are you sure you're okay? Is there anything I can do?"

"I'm okay, Mae. Really. I just need a little rest. We've had a couple of very long days."

"I should say you do need rest. What made today so long for you?"

Winfield paused a moment, thinking about how he should tell her about Bromfeld's arrest. Finally he decided he was too tired for diplomacy; he simply said, "Mae, we arrested L. A. Bromfeld today for Miss Lawrence's murder. Tex Clugman was up at Bromfeld's ranch trying to bury the gun Tom Bell gave Miss Lawrence. That's what he was doing when we showed up.

"Our crime lab confirmed that the pistol Clugman was burying is the same gun that killed Miss Lawrence. They also found L. A. Bromfeld's prints on it. Sergeant Mackie and I met with District Attorney Keyes this afternoon, and he ordered us to arrest Bromfeld."

There was silence on the line for a long moment before Mae said, "I'm truly sorry to hear L. A. killed Lilly, but I'm certainly relieved that you found her killer."

"Bromfeld didn't take it too well, but his lawyer was already at Central lock-up trying to spring him. I expect he'll get a fair trial."

Another long moment went by before Mae said, "Bobby, what can I do to make you feel better? Would you like to come over for a quiet dinner? Or can I bring you some dinner?"

As tempting as the offer was, Winfield declined, saying, "Thank you, Mae, but I think the thing I need most right now is some rest. If the offer is still good tomorrow night, I would love to take you up on it."

With a smile in her voice, Mae White said, "Bobby, the offer is good any time you want. How would six o'clock tomorrow night be?"

"That would be fine. I'll look forward to it."

"Okay, then. It's a date. Now you go get some rest."

"Thanks, Mae. Goodnight."

Stretched out on his bed at Missus Haney's boardinghouse, Winfield wanted to review the day's events in his mind, but his brain kept playing back the smile he'd heard in Mae White's voice. Actually, he finally decided, it was quite a pleasant way to drift off to sleep.

THIRTY-FOUR

Friday - September 10, 1926

Detective Lieutenant Winfield was early for his eight o'clock appointment with Doctor Thomas Brown. Taking a seat in the waiting room, Winfield opened the L.A. Times he picked up on the way to the doctor's office. He expected the Times to make a big to-do over L. A. Bromfeld's arrest, and they didn't disappoint him.

A banner headline across the top of the front page proclaimed, "Studio Boss Charged With Lillian Lawrence Murder." Below the banner, a line of slightly smaller type added, "Western National Films Chief L. A. Bromfeld Arrested In Actress Shooting."

The wording of the article below the headlines left little doubt in Winfield's mind as to where the Times got its information. Nearly every paragraph contained a reference to Homicide Captain Albert Royce, including one that said, "Captain Royce said detectives working under his direction at L.A.P.D.'s Hollywood Division cracked the case."

It didn't surprise Winfield in the least that neither his name nor Mackie's appeared anywhere in the article. Albert Royce was not one to share credit, especially in a headline case like this one. To most people who read the Times article, it would appear that the captain single-handedly brought the dastardly villain to justice.

A few minutes before nine Winfield left Doctor Brown's office with a fresh dressing on his arm and the news that his wound showed no signs of infection. The doctor instructed him to continue taking it easy for a while longer and to return on Monday for another fresh dressing.

When Winfield walked into the Sixth Precinct stationhouse fifteen minutes later, Patrol Officer Otis greeted him from the complaint desk and reported that the switchboard had been overflowing all morning with calls from reporters and news services requesting interviews. As instructed, Otis was referring all such calls to Captain Royce's office.

As Winfield entered the detective room, C. K. looked up from his desk and said, "Good morning, Bobby. How's the arm?"

"Doctor Brown said he didn't find any sign of infection, so I guess it's doing okay." Noticing a copy of the Times on Mackie's desk he added, "I guess you've already read the Times' account of Captain Royce's heroic capture of L. A. Bromfeld."

C. K. grinned at Winfield description of the article and said, "I have indeed, Laddie. The citizens of Los Angeles are fortunate to have such a fearless crime-fighter looking out for them."

Glancing at his wristwatch, Winfield said, "I guess we had best get started for the Hall of Justice so Asa Keyes can begin claiming his share of the limelight."

A few minutes before ten o'clock, Winfield and Mackie walked into the office of Assistant District Attorney Abraham Singer. Singer was tall and slender with a pencil-thin mustache below a rather prominent nose and quick brown eyes Winfield guessed didn't miss much.

Introductions completed, Singer offered the detectives seats opposite his desk and said, "Gentlemen, I probably should have called you this morning to save you the trip into town, but it seemed better to give you the news in person."

Puzzled, Winfield asked, "What news is that?"

"Well, the arraignment we are here to prepare for this morning isn't going to happen any time soon, if ever."

Now completely baffled, Winfield said, "What? Why not?"

"Because our prisoner, L. A. Bromfeld, has suffered a massive brain stroke. It seems Mister Bromfeld couldn't be roused by jailers at the Central Division lock-up this morning, so he was rushed to County Hospital by ambulance. This all happened around six-thirty a.m.

"Doctors at County diagnosed Bromfeld with having . . ." Singer referred to a piece of note paper on his desk and continued, "severe brain ischemia. In effect, he's turned into a vegetable, and as a result, he is in no condition to stand trial for his crimes."

Sergeant Mackie asked, "What are the chances of recovery?"

"Nonexistent. According to the brain doctor I spoke with at County, there is no likelihood that Mister Bromfeld will ever recover his faculties to any significant degree."

Winfield said, "Do the doctors know what caused this brain stroke?"

"The doctor I talked to said it was most likely brought on by severe stress, and that's where things get sticky. Bromfeld's attorney is already shooting his mouth off about how the shock of being falsely arrested for Lillian Lawrence's murder caused the stroke, and he's telling the press he plans to sue the L.A.P.D. and the county for damages."

Winfield said, "They never miss an opportunity, do they?"

Singer said, "No, they don't. As long as you're here, though, we might as well go over the case so I can answer the false arrest charges. Is that okay with you gentlemen?"

The lieutenant nodded, and the three men spent the next hour going over the evidence against L. A. Bromfeld detail by detail. When Singer was satisfied all his questions were answered, he said, "It seems clear that District Attorney Keyes was justified in ordering Bromfeld's arrest yesterday. In addition, fingerprints taken when Bromfeld was booked are identical to the sample on the drinking glass you officers obtained at his home, so there is no question that he handled the murder weapon. I see no reason we would not have gotten a conviction if the case had gone to trial."

"That's a big relief. I'm certainly glad you gentlemen have been thorough in your investigation. I need to speak with Mister Keyes first, but I'm pretty sure we can convince Bromfeld's attorney that he has no case for a lawsuit."

Singer thanked the detectives for their help, and forty-five minutes later Winfield and Mackie were back at their desks in the Sixth Precinct detective room. Winfield said, "Well isn't this a fine kettle of fish. It seems Bromfeld is getting away with at least one murder and perhaps two."

"I guess he is if you consider becoming a vegetable a satisfactory way of spending the rest of your life."

"It beats being hung by the neck until dead."

Mackie said thoughtfully, "I'm not too sure about that."

Looking across at his partner, Winfield put into words what he'd been thinking for quite a while. "C. K., it seems to me something's been bothering you for the past couple of days. What's on your mind?"

The sergeant seemed to think about how to answer the question before saying, "I'm not sure, Bobby. I just have this feeling that something's out of whack with all this."

"You mean with our investigation of Lillian Lawrence's murder?"

"Yes. I keep thinking we've overlooked something, but I've gone over everything several times, and I don't see what we could have missed." After a pause C. K. added, "I guess it really doesn't matter at this point. Don't let my crazy notions bother you, Bobby. This case is over and done with, and we have other fish to fry."

At six o'clock that evening, Winfield knocked on the door to number 412 at the Garden Court Apartments. When Mae White opened the door, she immediately noticed his arm sling. "Oh, Bobby, your arm! You didn't tell me it was in a sling. Does it hurt a lot?"

Stepping through the door she held open for him, Winfield said, "Not so much today. I saw my doctor this morning, and he said it's healing fine, so I should be able to get rid of this sling soon."

Mae closed the door and stepped close to Winfield, accepting a one-armed hug and giving him a brief kiss on the lips. That this greeting seemed perfectly natural was still new to him. They'd gone from cop and witness to lovers in a very short time. He didn't know whether or not that was proper, but it felt right, so he accepted their new relationship without question.

During a dinner of tasty lamb chops Mae proudly proclaimed she cooked herself, Winfield gave her what few details he had on L. A. Bromfeld's condition. When he finished, Mae said, "I don't like to wish anyone ill will, but after all the misery he's caused others for the sake of greed, I can't help but feel L. A. has gotten exactly what he deserves. What do you think will happen to him now?"

Winfield shrugged. "I guess if they turn him loose from the hospital, he'll end up in a nursing home of some sort. I have to wonder what Ruth Bromfeld will do now."

"I don't know her too well, but I imagine she will feel obligated to make sure her husband is properly cared for. After what he's put her through, she deserves better."

Leaving the subject of the Bromfelds' future there at the dining room table, Winfield and Mae moved to the living room where she served coffee from a silver tray. Then, for the first time since they met, Mae White and Bobby Winfield spent a long time just talking about subjects of absolutely no importance to anyone but themselves—subjects like their favorite foods, places they enjoyed, and things they were fond of.

After a while Mae slid closer to Winfield and leaned her head on his good shoulder. He put his right arm around her, and they just sat quietly like that for a long while. Winfield couldn't help feeling some amazement that he was sharing this intimate time with a beautiful woman who was desired by most of the men in America.

That train of thought was derailed when Mae said quietly, "You know, besides missing Lilly terribly, the more I think about her, the more I believe she had the right idea all along."

"What idea is that?"

"Oh, just her decision to stop making movies and marry Tom—to move to his ranch out in the country and raise kids. For her, it would have been the first time in her life she was truly happy and free."

"And for you?"

Without hesitation she said, "The same. I've thought about it a lot lately. I mean, I have this beautiful apartment and lovely clothes—everything most girls dream of, but it's all just . . . stuff. None of it means anything. For the first time in my life, I'm realizing that what I really want are the same things Lilly wanted—a real home to share with a man I love and respect, a place in the world that's bright and alive with the laughter of children, and . . . well, all the things that really matter in life. What about you, Bobby? Do you ever have such thoughts?"

"I do."

Mae suddenly leaned forward and turned to face him. "Really, Bobby?"

"Really, Mae."

She looked deep into his eyes and said, "That's wonderful! I somehow had the feeling you were . . . oh, I don't know . . . maybe a man dedicated to saving the world from bad guys or something."

"Are the two exclusive of one another?"

Mae thought for a moment. "No, I guess they really aren't."

She gave him a soft kiss on the lips and slid back down to rest her head on his shoulder again. A few minutes later she sat up and faced him once more, saying, "Bobby, will you do me an enormous favor?"

"Of course, Mae. What is it?"

"From now on, will you please call me Millie? That's my real name. Well, Mildred, but I prefer Millie and I hate the name Mae. It just isn't me."

"Consider it done, Millie."

They kissed again before she returned to her comfy position. No more words passed between them for a long time until Winfield realized how late it had gotten. Standing in her entryway, he said, "Thank you for a wonderful evening, Millie. I can't tell you how much I've enjoyed this time with you."

She looked into his eyes for a long time before saying, "Bobby, you are the most thoughtful, loving, and . . . well, just the most wonderful man I ever met. Thank you for being you and sharing you with me."

Winfield had no idea what to say, so he just held her close with his good arm while they shared a long, gentle kiss. It was a moment he would remember and cherish for the rest of his life.

EPILOGUE

Saturday – September 22, 1952

Homicide Division Captain Robert Winfield sat in his dining room overlooking the Pacific Ocean from Palos Verdes and contemplated two items on the table before him. One was a yellowing envelope on which the ghost of the word "Bobby" was barely visible in faded black ink. The other item was a scrapbook filled with news clippings, photographs, and other treasures—the physical reminders of memories made during the past twenty-six years.

Winfield gently opened the scrapbook's padded leather cover. Across the top of the first page the words, "In loving memory of a dear friend," were written in Millie's flowing script. Below the words were four tiny Kodak snapshots of Lillian Lawrence clowning for the camera with Millie and Tom Bell. An article from the Hollywood Daily Citizen was neatly pasted below the photos:

LILLIAN LAWRENCE LAST RITES
September 17, 1926—Last rites for popular motion picture actress Lillian Lawrence were held today at the First United Methodist Church of Hollywood. A crowd of several hundred mourners lined Franklin Boulevard outside the church to pay their respects to the beloved Miss Lawrence . . . .

The scrapbook's next page held another newspaper article, this one from the Los Angeles Times:

MAE WHITE ANNOUNCES RETIREMENT
FROM MOTION PICTURES

January 23, 1928—The popular screen actress, Mae White, today announced her plans to leave the motion picture business. In a statement issued by Western National Films, Miss White cited personal reasons for her decision to leave the silver screen . . . .

Winfield smiled at the memories he associated with the Times announcement. They had laughed about her "retirement" at the age of twenty-seven. For some, the article marked the end of an era. For Millie and Bobby it marked the beginning of a new and happier time.

After a few pages of snapshots made during what Millie laughingly referred to as their "eternal courtship," Winfield came to the wedding announcement, a six-inch by four-inch white card surrounded by pink roses. In embossed letters it said:

Miss Millie Glaum and Mister Robert Winfield
request the honour of your presence at their wedding ceremony
on Saturday, the ninth day of June, Nineteen-Twenty-Eight
at one-thirty in the afternoon.
La Venta Inn
796 Via Del Monte
Palos Verdes, California

The invitation was only sent to about three dozen sent to their closest friends. Winfield vividly remembered the ceremony held under a gazebo overlooking the Pacific Ocean. To his eyes, Millie looked like a dream as she walked toward him in a beautiful white wedding gown while Bobby waited nervously with his best man, C. K. Mackie. Fannie DeWitt, Millie's choice for maid of honor, stood next to them.

Following a few pages of snapshots taken on their three-day honeymoon in Carmel-by-the-Sea, Winfield came to a memory that wasn't as pleasant. Millie had questioned the need to include it in their book of memories, but he insisted that the article needed to be there because, to him, the L.A. Times obituary marked the end of a major event in both their lives.

FORMER MOTION PICTURE MAGNATE PASSES

October 17, 1928—Leonard Aaron Bromfeld died Sunday, October 14, at the Hollyridge Nursing Home in Hollywood, California. "L. A. Bromfeld," as he was better known, headed Western National Films between 1923 and 1926 and is credited with that studio's rise to success. Bromfeld died of complications resulting from a stroke suffered two years ago. He is survived by his wife, Ruth Hampton Bromfeld . . . .

Winfield associated much happier memories with the next entry in their scrapbook—the birth announcements of their children, Chester R. and Clarrisa Winfield, twins born on September 30, 1929. Chet, of course, was named for the kids' godfather, Chester K. Mackie.

The next dozen pages of the scrapbook were crowded with pictures of Claire and Chet growing up. Winfield recalled those days with special fondness because they were a fulfillment Millie's dream of having children who made their world bright and alive with laughter.

Claire, who was the spitting image of her mother, attended UCLA, where she earned her degree in journalism. Last year she moved to Winfield's hometown of San Francisco to become a reporter with the San Francisco Examiner.

Chet attended Winfield's alma mater, Cal Berkeley, receiving his degree in aeronautical engineering. After graduation, Chet married a delightful young woman named Sally and enlisted to do his service in the Army Air Corp. Just a week ago Winfield received a letter postmarked Dayton, Ohio, near where Second Lieutenant Chester Winfield was stationed at Wilber Wright Field. In the letter, Sally and Chet informed him that he would soon become a grandfather. Winfield shook his head at that thought. It was hard to believe his little tyke was about to have a child of his own.

The next several scrapbook pages were filled with clippings and photographs devoted to Millie's charity work. As the children began their own lives and needed less of their mother's attention, Millie turned her seemingly boundless energy toward helping others, beginning with behind-the-scenes work with the U.S.O. and the Red Cross during WWII. After the war Millie continued her efforts, mostly with disabled veterans. The crowning recognition of her contributions was found on a page which held a letter on official White House stationery. In the letter President Harry Truman thanked Millie Winfield personally for her tireless efforts on behalf of American soldiers.

Winfield's own war efforts were somewhat less spectacular. Deemed to be in a job necessary to home front security, Winfield was temporarily assigned to a counter-espionage task force established by the L.A.P.D. in 1942. It was in that role that he spent the next three years investigating and preventing crimes against the U.S. defense industry installations within the Los Angeles city limits. When the war ended, he was reassigned to homicide, working with C. K. out of Central Division.

The next newspaper clipping Winfield encountered flooded his mind with memories of the many years he and Sergeant Mackie worked together on the L.A.P.D. The L.A. Times reported:

DECORATED POLICE OFFICER RETIRES

December 6, 1946—The Los Angeles Police Department today announced the retirement of Detective Sergeant Chester "C. K." Mackie. Mackie, a veteran of 40 years service with the L.A.P.D., received many decorations and commendations throughout his career, including the Police Star and the department's highest award for bravery, the Medal of Valor. For the past twenty-five years Mackie has served with the L.A.P.D. Homicide Department out of the Sixth Precinct in Hollywood and Central Division headquarters.

Winfield clearly remembered the day C. K. told him of his decision to retire. In C. K.'s words, "Helen has put up with my long and odd hours for a very long time. Now she needs me to be home with her. Besides, Laddie, I've taught you everything I know."

He also remembered delivering an emotion-filled speech at C. K.'s retirement ceremony and leaving the podium at its conclusion with tears in his eyes. Over the years since, Winfield remained close to Mackie, visiting him often and even occasionally calling on his experience when faced with a particularly tough homicide.

On the next page in the scrapbook, he came face to face with the primary reason for C. K.'s decision to retire. It was a short obituary from the L.A. Times:

HELEN MACKIE PASSES

May 10, 1947—Longtime Hollywood resident, Helen McPherson Mackie, died at Hollywood Presbyterian Medical Center last Wednesday. Mrs. Mackie's passing was preceded by a long battle with heart disease. She is survived by her husband, Chester Mackie.

Winfield remembered Helen as a kind and caring woman who frequently went out of her way to do small kindnesses that meant a lot, like often including a little something extra in C. K.'s lunch pail to make sure the lieutenant had a proper lunch back in his bachelor days. Helen's death hit C. K. hard, leaving him feeling lost and alone for the first time in his life. During those days, Millie's love for her husband's partner of so many years became apparent as she saw to it C. K. was never alone unless he wanted to be. With almost daily visits and frequent dinner invitations, Millie and Bobby saw Mackie through what must have been the toughest time of his life.

A few pages later, Winfield found another news clipping carefully and proudly pasted into place by Millie. It was the Los Angeles Times announcement of his promotion to captain:

L.A.P.D. PROMOTES DETECTIVE TO HOMICIDE CAPTAIN

September 1, 1949—The Los Angeles Police Department today announced the promotion of Detective Robert Winfield to the position of Homicide Division Captain. Winfield, who has served the department for nearly 24 years, replaces James Winger as the man in charge of L.A.P.D.'s murder investigation division. Winfield, the recipient of numerous department commendations during his career, assumes his new responsibilities on this date.

On the final page of the scrapbook was an item Winfield added to the memory book only a few days earlier. It was a funeral program. On the cover Millie's photo appeared below the words "In Loving Memory." Under her picture were printed the dates of Millie's life, January 12, 1901 – September 7, 1952.

The end had come quickly for Millie. She'd gone to see their doctor about stomach pains, and less than six months later, the cancer doctor found that day took her life.

Winfield wanted to open the funeral program and read the beautiful verse it contained about the many lives Millie had touched with her love, but he couldn't. The pain of her loss was still too fresh. Besides, as the greatest beneficiary of Millie's love, he needed no verse to remind him of even one moment during the years they spent together making the dreams they dreamed one night in 1926 at the Garden Court Apartments come true.

He wiped the tears from his eyes, breathed a deep sigh, and closed the scrapbook. Standing up from the table at which he and Millie spent so many hours and sliding the yellowing envelope into his inside coat pocket, he walked out to the driveway and climbed into the unmarked Oldsmobile sedan the department provided for his use. During the forty-five minute drive to Hollywood he did his best to put his memories aside and focus on the task he now needed to perform.

Retired Detective Sergeant C. K. Mackie still lived in the same home on La Mirada Avenue in which he and Helen were living when Winfield first visited them nearly three decades earlier. As he pulled to the curb, it seemed to Winfield that the little wood-frame bungalow looked exactly as it had the day he first saw it. For that matter, so did Mackie. Oh, C. K. was mostly bald now and his posture was a little less erect, but he seemed just as robust as he'd been in the days when they prowled the streets of Hollywood together in the sergeant's Dodge roadster.

Winfield's knock on the door was answered almost immediately. Mackie opened the door and said, "Bobby! Good to see you. Come on in!"

"Hello, C. K. I hope you don't mind me barging in unannounced like this, but . . . ."

With the same smile and twinkle in his eyes Winfield had grown so accustomed to over the years, C. K. said, "Now, Laddie, since when have you ever needed an invitation to visit my home?"

Inside, Mackie ushered Winfield into the bungalow's tidy little kitchen—the room that had always been the center of activity in the Mackies' home—and said, "How about a cup of coffee? I just made some fresh."

"Sounds good, C. K."

After pouring a mug for his former boss, Mackie invited Winfield to join him at the kitchen table. C. K. took a swallow from his cup and said, "Now, to what do I owe the pleasure of your company on this fine day? And don't be tellin' me you just stopped by for a visit because you were here only a few days ago."

Winfield solemnly reached into his pocket and brought out the yellowed envelope. Placing it on the table in front of Mackie, he said quietly, "I brought something for you to read."

C. K. stared at the envelope for a long moment, and without touching it, he leaned back in his chair. Looking Winfield straight in the eye, he said, "You came here to tell me you just learned that L. A. Bromfeld didn't kill Lillian Lawrence. Is that about it?"

Unable to hide his surprise, Winfield stammered, "Yes, but . . . but how do you know that?"

Mackie took another swallow of coffee. "Bobby, in all the years you and I spent together on the force, we only left one case unresolved, and I've had twenty-six years to think about that case. I've looked at the evidence from every conceivable angle, and there is only one way in which all the puzzle pieces fit. Realizing that, I also realized there was only one person who knew what really happened that Saturday night back in 'twenty-six, and that person—may the Lord bless her soul—was Millie, or Mae White as we knew her then."

"Then you knew . . . ."

C. K. interrupted, "I knew only that one day Millie would have to tell you the true story. She was too kind-hearted and loved you too much to keep her secret from you forever. And when we learned the sad, sad news that Millie would be leaving us soon, I knew that day was not far away."

Winfield knew full well what Mackie was leaving unsaid. In a roundabout way his good friend and former partner was telling him they made a big mistake, largely because Winfield lost his objectivity and ignored those irritating little pieces of evidence that didn't fit quite right. He said, "Well, C. K., you might as well read Millie's letter and see if you got it right."

Mackie shook his head. "I don't believe I will do that, Bobby. I would rather be able to honestly say I never saw what's in that envelope." After a pause, he continued, "If it's important to you, just give me the gist of what Millie had to say."

Winfield nodded. "Okay, C. K. We'll do it your way." Gesturing toward the envelope, he said, "Millie wrote that letter way back before we were married and kept it in an old beaded handbag at the back of our closet shelf for all these years. Then while I was sitting with her at the hospital the night she died, Millie told me about the envelope and said I needed to read what was in it.

"Then she was gone, and with the service and everything else, I forgot what she told me about the envelope until a few days ago. What Millie wanted me—or us—to know is that she . . . well, she lied about what happened the night Lilly died. The truth is, she did talk to L. A. Bromfeld out in the hotel parking lot. He told her he'd convinced Lilly to continue making movies. Millie told him he was a liar and Bromfeld flew into a rage. He called her some names, threw the cigar he'd just lit on the ground, and drove off in his Packard.

"At Lilly's room, Millie knocked and got no answer. She tried the door and found it unlocked. Inside, Millie discovered Lilly on the floor just as we found her the next morning, except the little Smith and Wesson revolver was there next to the body. There was also a note addressed to Tom Bell on the nightstand. In the note Lilly told Tom she couldn't marry him, and that she would rather be dead than go on without him.

"That was when Millie put two and two together and realized Bromfeld must have threatened Lilly with something terrible he knew to keep her working at Western National. She thought Bromfeld probably threatened to tell Tom Bell about Lilly's father or something along those lines.

"Millie goes on to say she sat on the bed crying and cursing L. A. Bromfeld because she knew he killed Lilly just as surely as if he pulled the trigger himself. That thought was what gave Millie the idea of how she could make Bromfeld pay for what he did to Lilly and, before that, to her father.

"She picked up the revolver, the note to Tom Bell, and a box of cartridges that was on the dresser and put them in her handbag—the same handbag in which she would eventually hide that envelope addressed to me. Then she went around the room knocking things on the floor to make it look as if there'd been a fight or a struggle.

"Millie was standing there looking around the room when she thought of what else she could do to ensure that Bromfeld was charged for killing Lilly. She ran out to the parking lot and found the cigar Bromfeld threw away during their argument. She took it back to Lilly's room, and though she described it as the most disgusting thing she'd ever done, she put the cigar in her mouth and lit it. After getting the room smoky, she closed the windows so it would stay that way. Then she put the cigar out in the ashtray and threw the butt on the floor.

"After that, Millie left the hotel to complete the last part of her plan. She went to Bromfeld's mansion and parked down at the street end of his drive.

Millie walked up the drive, planning to put the pistol and cartridges somewhere on the property where they were sure to be found. When she got to the top of the drive, however, she saw Bromfeld's Packard sitting there. Remember the butler telling you he took his time about putting it in the garage that night?"

Mackie nodded.

"Millie decided Bromfeld's car was perfect place to leave the gun, figuring someone was bound to find it there. She slid the pistol and cartridge box under the front seat and was just closing the car door when the butler finally came out to put Bromfeld's car in the garage. Millie hid in some bushes until he drove away in the car. Then Millie went home and cried herself to sleep."

Winfield paused and took a deep breath. "That's essentially the story. The rest of the letter is an apology for deceiving us. Millie said that was the only time she ever lied to me, and she . . . she hoped I . . . wouldn't hate her for it. As if I could ever hate her for anything."

Winfield and Mackie sat quietly for a long while, both men occasionally glancing at the envelope on the table between them. Finally, C. K. said, "Bobby, thank you for telling me Millie's story. I know it wasn't an easy thing for you."

Winfield nodded. "Was Millie's story how you had the case figured?"

"Mostly. I didn't know how she came by Bromfeld's cigar, but I reasoned out the rest of the story. It was the only way to account for the bits and pieces of evidence that bothered me for so many years, like the gunpowder residue on the victim's hand and the fourth set of fingerprints on the pistol—the ones the crime lab never identified. They were Millie's.

"Her story also accounts for the hotel room windows being closed on a hot night and the fact there was just one cartridge in the pistol's chamber. The only reason anyone puts one cartridge in a gun is if they only intend to fire it once. And it also explains the condition of the cigar we found on the floor. Bromfeld chewed his cigars to pieces, but the cigar in the room was hardly chewed at all."

Winfield nodded again. "Now the big question is what do I do with that envelope? Lillian Lawrence's suicide note is in there, too. Millie couldn't bring herself to throw it away."

C. K. said, "Well, Bobby, let me ask you this: Besides you and me, who's left to care about what's in that envelope?"

Winfield thought about the question for a while. Finally he said, "I guess Tom Bell and the company that paid Western National's million dollar life insurance claim on Lillian Lawrence."

"That's right, but that insurance outfit—the Motion Picture and Theatrical Indemnity Company—was bought out by another company back before the war, and that company went out of business about four years ago. I checked.

"As for Tom Bell, is it worth digging up old and painful memories for him to know the woman he loved killed herself for reasons we will never fully know or understand? Lillian Lawrence is long gone, and by now he has surely put her to rest in his mind."

"I guess that's true, but there's the matter of the official record."

"What official record? Bromfeld was never even arraigned on the murder charge. The only public records of the case are an arrest report buried in the department files somewhere and a few old newspaper articles nobody cares about. In a way, you could say Bromfeld was taken from our hands and tried for his crimes by a higher court."

Winfield thought about his friend's words for a few moments and said, "I guess that's all true, but are you suggesting I do nothing with Millie's . . . confession?"

"I'm not suggesting anything. I'm just thinking out loud about what would be accomplished by revealing the contents of that envelope. About the only result of doing that would be to tarnish an exemplary reputation with the department."

Puzzled, Winfield said, "What do you mean?"

"Thank about it, Laddie. If you take that envelope to the brass, they will have to do something about it, and the only person left to do something to is you. In my opinion, you are worth a lot more to the people of our fair city as you are than as a disgraced former homicide captain."

"Thank you for that, C. K., but tell me, what would you do if you were me?"

"I can't do that, Bobby. You are the only one who can make that decision. I will say this, though; if I saw you take that old envelope out to my trash barrel and put a match to it, I would feel no obligation to stop you or even remember it ever existed."

A few minutes later Winfield and Mackie were standing next to C. K.'s backyard incinerator. Winfield struck a kitchen match on the charred old metal drum and stood there for a moment with the yellowed envelope in one hand and the burning match in the other. He glanced up at Mackie and C. K. gave him a slight nod of reassurance.

Winfield touched the match to the envelope and dropped it into the barrel. Then both men stood there watching the smoke carry silent memories from a long ago time into a cloudless sky.

THE END

ABOUT H. P. OLIVER

While new to the literary world, H. P. Oliver is no stranger to writing. After earning his journalism degree at San Jose State University, Oliver spent the next thirty-some years writing award-winning entertainment and educational media.

Now he's turning his creativity to the task of writing historical mysteries. About this endeavor, Oliver says, "To be truly engrossing a mystery needs a little meat on its bones--something beyond just figuring out who done the evil deed. Taking a good mystery back in time, or even basing it on actual historical events, is a great way to endow a yarn with color and depth. Historic locations give a writer the opportunity to take his/her reader where they've never been before."

H. P. Oliver lives in northern California near the Cosumnes River and spends much of his time working on projects throughout the western states. His interests center on vintage films, restoring classic cars, and of course, history.

MORE BOOKS BY H. P. OLIVER

SILENTS! is H. P. Oliver's third mystery in history and the first to be published in both print and electronic-book editions. If you enjoyed SILENTS! and you are among the millions of avid readers worldwide who appreciate the many benefits of electronic books, you will certainly enjoy the following e-books by H. P. Oliver:

THE TRUTH BE TOLD

The Truth Be Told takes us back to 1932 for an alternative version of a real-life tragedy. History tells us a talented young actress named Peg Entwistle committed suicide that year by jumping from the famous Hollywood sign, but what if history got it wrong? And after all these years, does it really matter? It does to Peg. This is her story and how she finally told it eight decades after her death.

PUZZLES FROM THE PAST

Puzzles From The Past is an anthology consisting of three action-packed mysteries heavily steeped in WWII intrigue and espionage. Crafted in ways that challenge readers to solve the mysteries right along with the stories' characters, Puzzles From The Past evokes a strong sense that you are actually part of history itself.

For more information about these mysteries in history, plus video trailers, visualizations, and purchase links for all of H. P. Oliver's novels visit the author's fan site at http://www.hpoliver.com.